MARROW

PRESTON NORTON

D1402398

MARROW

Future House Publishing

FHP

Cover design by Jonathan Diaz

Cover design © 2015 by Future House Publishing

Interior design by KristiRae Alldredge

ISBN-10: 0989125351
ISBN-13: 978-0-9891253-5-2

CHAPTER 1

Having super powers isn't always as super as it sounds.

Actually . . . that's a lie. It's pretty much awesome.

It was the last day of Finals at FIST (Fantom Institute for Superheroes-in-Training). There were exactly ten of us who had qualified for the Sidekick Internship Program. All fourteen years old. All dangerous in our own unique ways. Based on our scores and overall performance, we would be evaluated and paired up with Superheroes who would serve as our mentors for the summer. With top-notch scores, I could be teamed up with a hero like Nova. Or Apex. Or the most legendary hero of them all . . .

Fantom, himself.

Fantom wasn't just the founder of FIST. And he wasn't just a Superhero either. The guy was an icon. A symbol of hope. He was the fastest, strongest, smartest, insert-whatever-awesome-adjective-you-can-think-of-*est* hero of them all. And the guy had style. Oh man, did he have style.

Legend had it that Fantom was the first of the Supers—merely a kid out on a boat with his parents when the Gaia Comet struck. (It was the foreign radioactive energy of Gaia that gave birth to the Supers.) The comet made impact right where they were sailing, killing Fantom's parents instantly. However, fate or pure luck allowed Fantom to emerge unscathed, and he was reborn with power unparalleled by any other Super.

Fantom was going to be my mentor. I had already decided that.

I was going to kick this Final in the butt.

Sure, we all had to sign an insurance waiver in case of injury, psychological damage, dismemberment, death . . . blah blah blah. But basically, I already had a free ticket to spend my summer with a seasoned Superhero, fighting crime and basking in my awesomeness.

The ten of us students were lined up in the Battle Dome—a white, spherical room with half a dozen sliding doors leading into separate Challenge Chambers. We trained here on a regular basis. Contrasting the glaring white of our surroundings, each of us was suited in matching black bodysuits—unrestricting, muscle-stimulating, cold and heat resistant, and even flameproof. You'd never suspect it though. The material was so light, it almost felt like you were wearing nothing.

"Are you ready to eat my dust, Bonehead?" asked Nero, sneering to my left.

Nero was a punk. A tall, skinny punk with black hair and a smirk on his face that made me want to punch him every time I looked at him. He was also telekinetic—meaning he could move objects with his mind. This easily made him one of the top competitors.

But being *one* of the best was inconsequential since I *was* the best.

"You know, *Zero*, it's funny," I said under my breath. "I always thought it was necessary to actually have a brain in order to use mind powers. How do *you* do it?"

Despite my hushed tone, my comment had not gone unheard. A girl laughed—Sapphire.

"Marrow, if there was a superpower that made you good at comebacks, I'd swear that was your real power."

Sapphire was standing to my right. She was as cute as you could possibly be with blue hair. No, she didn't dye her hair that color so it'd go with her pretty blue eyes (although they matched perfectly, I'll have you know). It was somehow associated with her power—the ability to manipulate water and ice. It sounds like a wimpy power until you actually see what she can do with it. Even when there's no water nearby, she can freeze the moisture in the air, creating an icy blast. And good luck if you tick her off and there *is* water near. When I first met her and heard what her power was, I laughed and called her the Ice Queen. Unfortunately, I made the mistake of doing this while we were training by the courtyard fountain. She made the fountain erupt and hit me with it like a mini tsunami.

The nickname, Ice Queen, died the day it was conceived.

Nero was scowling on my other side. He may have had almost top scores at FIST, but the kid was about as witty as a box of rocks. He couldn't come up with a comeback to save his life.

And everybody knows that a Superhero needs to be good with comebacks.

There was a subtle *whoosh* as the sliding door directly in front of us opened. Out stepped a black man in a black leather vest and camo pants. He was our instructor at FIST. His name was Havoc, and he typically dressed like he had ransacked Mr. T's wardrobe. He was built like a barbarian with his facial hair trimmed and shaped like curving sharp-edged tribal tattoos. I had never seen Havoc smile. Not once.

"You finally made it," said Havoc, his thick arms pulled behind his back. "The Final Challenge."

I don't think any of us could fight the smiles on our faces. I know I couldn't. I could feel the adrenaline screaming through my veins.

"So here's how this is going to work," Havoc continued. "We're going to divide you into pairs."

Several students groaned. Others lit up with excitement. I felt myself stuck somewhere in between the mixed response. Working as a team had its perks, depending on who your teammate was. Sapphire, for example, was an *excellent* teammate. And not just because I liked to show off in front of her. Or because she looked hot in her bodysuit. Or because . . . well . . . you get what I mean.

Unfortunately, working as a team was a double-edged sword because there were also teammates like Nero. Or . . . Nero.

Yeah.

I mean, the guy had skill, don't get me wrong. Unfortunately, the kid deliberately tried to make things as difficult as possible. It was like a part of his twisted moral code or something.

"Come on," said Nero, groaning. "I didn't get this far to have someone else screw it up for me."

I rolled my eyes. "You're one to talk," I grumbled under my breath.

"You talkin' about me, Marrow?" asked Nero, snapping his head at me.

"Oh no, I was talking about your mom."

Nero went rigid, his face reddening as everyone laughed. I assumed he was scraping the back of his telekinetic brain for a comeback. Of course, he had nothing.

"Both of you, shut your pie holes!" Havoc barked.

Nero and I knew better than to push Havoc's buttons. Both of us bit our lips simultaneously.

Havoc's chest puffed out as he took a step forward, his eyes bouncing between the two of us. "That's the whole point of this, isn't it? To be *teamed* up with a *real* Superhero? If you ninnyhammers can't even work as a team with someone on your own level, then why should we waste our time placing you with an experienced hero?"

His piercing glare homed in on Nero who immediately cringed and stared at his feet. It took every ounce of will power for me not to grin.

"You have anything else to say, princess?" asked Havoc, still glaring at Nero.

"No," Nero murmured.

"No?" Havoc repeated, hovering even further over the student. "Just no? No what, Nero?"

"No sir," Nero hastily added. Because Nero and I were the same height, it was easy to tell that he was cowering.

"That's right! No, sir, you do not have anything else to say!" Havoc took a step back, sweeping his gaze past all of us in a row. "Does anyone else feel an urge to waste my time with their stupid comments?"

No one spoke. No one was that dumb.

"Good," said Havoc, snorting. "On that note, let's get you turds divvied up. These pairs come straight from Oracle, so I better not hear any whining from any of you about how unfair it is."

Again, he scoured us with his terrifying gaze as if daring us to challenge him. Personally, I would rather challenge a volcano.

I had only met Oracle once. Though hardly a Superhero, she did have a supernatural power. She was a Telepath. She could see inside your head. Read your thoughts. Her level of telepathy was so advanced, in fact, that she had the ability to see images from the future—signs, visions, premonitions . . . you know . . . weird stuff like that. Other than that, she was just your average wrinkly old cat lady. Seriously . . . like two dozen cats. It didn't help that she smelled like mothballs and boiled cabbage. Oh, and she was blind. That's only important in the sense that she creeps the bejeebies out of me every time she looks at me with those blank milky eyes. I know she can't see, but there's definitely a sense of awareness in there.

Havoc removed an envelope from the inside of his leather vest. Slowly, he opened it with his meaty fingers. "And the pairs are . . ."

Sapphire . . . Sapphire . . . Sapphire . . . I was going to be paired with Sapphire.

"Sapphire . . ." Havoc read aloud from the sheet of paper he held.

My breath stopped short.

". . . will be paired with . . . Whisp."

Have I mentioned how much I hate working in teams?

Whisp was a scrawny kid with big glasses. He was easily the worst when it came to hand-to-hand combat, but he made up for it with perfect scores in weapons knowledge, equipment handling, medical training, escape and evasion techniques, and *especially* computer hacking. Seriously, give that kid a computer to crack and he'll know that thing inside out in minutes. Even I can't do that. And his super power? Get this . . . he talks to animals. I'm not kidding. He's an animal whisperer, hence the nickname, Whisp. He'll talk to a squirrel and tell it to go gnaw your legs off. And it will. He's very persuasive in that department.

Unfortunately, his power is pretty useless unless you happen to have a city zoo handy.

Of course Oracle would put Dr. Dolittle and the Ice Queen together.

Havoc continued to rattle off partners' names, but I was only halfway paying attention. At this point, I didn't even care who I got paired with. Just so long as I didn't get stuck with . . .

"Nero and Marrow," Havoc bellowed—there was no hiding the slight smirk on his face. "You two are a team."

Oracle obviously hated me.

Neither Nero nor I spoke as Havoc finished off the names. I simply bit my lip, hoping that, somehow, Nero and I could simply ignore each other as we finished the Challenge. I suppose the *one* good thing was that I didn't have to worry about him not being able to keep up. Now if only I knew that he wouldn't *deliberately* be my biggest obstacle.

"That's everyone," said Havoc. "Once the timer starts, each team must pick a Challenge Chamber door. And yes, the Challenge inside each door differs. Each will be based on one of the Defeated. If you've studied your history, this will be to your advantage. If not, then may God have mercy on your pathetic little souls."

The Defeated were infamous Supervillains who had already been vanquished. Unfortunately, a disturbing number of these were Superheroes-gone-bad, several of them FIST graduates. These were the villains that Fantom specialized in defeating. Nothing infuriated Fantom more than a Superhero overcome by greed, using his or her power for vile purposes. Fantom was merciless in these circumstances.

These were the villains that he killed without blinking.

"Our virtual recreations of the Defeated are, of course, simplified," said Havoc. "But that's not to say that they aren't capable of killing you. If there is no danger, there is no challenge. But, of course, I, and several specialized teams, will be observing your every movement. If it's obvious that you or your teammate won't make it out of this alive, we will intervene. However, if we have to do so, you and your teammate will be disqualified from the Sidekick Internship Program. Any questions?"

If anyone did have a question, I doubted they had the guts to ask. Havoc liked explaining things as much as he liked smiling—which, I already mentioned, is never.

"Good," said Havoc. Without another word, he lifted his thick wrist and glanced at his watch. At least it *looked* like a watch. He scrolled his thick finger on the small round face and pressed a button. At that very instant, a digital number ten lit up over each chamber door.

Nine.

Eight.

The timer continued to count down as each team randomly began selecting their own door. Nero and I, without even looking at each other, began walking to the door straight ahead—the one Havoc had come from.

"Just stay out of my way, Bonehead," Nero muttered under his breath.

Now you're probably wondering why Nero always calls me Bonehead. Believe it or not, there's actually a reason for that particular nickname. It may be the only halfway clever thing that's ever come out of his mouth, even if he does milk it for all its worth.

It's associated with my power—the ability to alter my bone density. Yeah, it may sound like an awkward power, but people usually have a change of heart when they see me in action.

I am the highest scoring student at FIST, after all.

"No sweat, Zero," I said with a nonchalant shrug. "Hey, is it possible for you to telekinetically kiss my butt?"

Three.

Two.

One.

The sliding door opened. Nero and I stepped inside.

Though our surroundings were obscured in darkness, it was obvious we were in a sewer. Circular passageways of metal and concrete branched out in several directions. Pipes lined the ceilings and walls. An inch-deep layer of murky water splashed beneath our feet. However, down the distant passages, I could sense shadowy movement. We weren't alone.

I glanced back at the doorway, which strangely appeared to be a mere opening in thin air. As the sliding door then closed on its own, it was like a dimensional portal closing. All indication of an opening vanished entirely. There was no turning back now.

"Wading in poopy water with Zero," I said with a sigh. "It doesn't get much better than this."

For once, Nero didn't respond to my insult. His distracted gaze wandered. "I'm sensing an electric lighting system in here. I can feel it."

"Electric lighting in a sewer?" I said, raising an unconvinced eyebrow.

"It's not a real sewer, Bonehead. It's a Challenge Chamber."

Though we had to strain to see in the shadows, we pressed forward. Neither of us hesitated reaching and grabbing and feeling, searching the walls blindly. Maybe we just didn't want to look like wimps in front of each other. I know my pride refused to give Nero the pleasure. Even when I heard something—several somethings—crawling across the floor. The walls. Even the ceiling.

My hand grazed a lever, slanted downward. "I think I found it."

Gripping the handle with both hands, I forced the lever up.

The lights turned on. The entire sewer was moving. Swarming. Fat hairy bodies pulsed and squirmed, elongated legs twitching and clawing.

Spiders. Lots of 'em.

And they were nearly as big as us.

CHAPTER 2

The spiders rampaged forward in a synchronized wave. Their scratchy, stampeding legs resonated throughout the spacious tunnel. Hungry pincers flared open from their slimy mouths.

Nero was already on it. He levitated from the floor, telekinetically lifting five spiders with him. His black hair swayed over his pale face, his expression dominated by sick satisfaction. Without even moving a muscle, a hundred legs instantly dismembered themselves from their fat hairy abdomens, spewing a shower of goopy yellow blood.

I was only a second behind him.

I mentally tapped into my bone structure and immediately felt myself become lighter.

Have you ever wondered how small animals and insects can move so fast for their size? How a squirrel can be so balanced jumping from tree to tree without a second thought? How a bird can swoop from the sky and snatch a fish out of the water?

I'm like the human version of those creatures.

I leapt into the air, practically flying. Time seemed to fall into slow motion as I soared. As I came down on the front line of racing spiders, I channeled as much density into my fist as possible. I hit the floor like a meteor. The metal and concrete of the sewer floor shattered, sending up waves of spiders in the explosion.

Smoke billowed up as debris rained down. Spiders staggered through the rubble, disoriented.

I wasn't about to wait for them to regain their bearings.

I darted to the nearest spider—slightly smaller than the others—and snatched it by its rear leg. I shuddered slightly at the bristly texture beneath my fingers but didn't let that slow me down. Adding just enough density to my arm for added strength, I swung the spider up like a hairy ball and chain. Another spider had already reared back and lunged at me. I smacked it with its cousin, sending it sailing.

I've never been above a good game of whack-a-mole, and that certainly showed here. Lifting my spider bludgeon, I beat and smashed away at the force of arachnids scuttling towards me. Spinning a full three hundred and sixty degrees, I managed to gracefully bash away half a dozen spiders at once.

The bodies—some still twitching—were beginning to stack up around me. I forced myself to step up on their bulbous corpses for a better swinging range.

Then, rather abruptly, the spider I was using as my weapon detached from its leg. It took a little longer than it should have for me to realize I only had a hairy appendage as a weapon now. Yellow mucus spurted out the end.

One particularly fat spider took advantage of my sudden disarmament, lunging at me with pincers flailing.

I shoved the dismembered limb into the back of its throat. Stunned and convulsing, the spider toppled down the hill of corpses.

Nero, meanwhile, hovered past me, a spider levitating in his telekinetic grasp. He squeezed his raised fist, and the spider contorted and crumpled in midair. And then he tossed it aside, like a kid bored with a toy.

Mildly distracted, I barely noticed the new spider dropping from the ceiling, suspended by a thick, slimy cord. It screeched as eight dangling legs reached down for my head.

I responded with a left uppercut. With only the bare minimum bone density to slow my arm, it shot up like a missile. It wasn't until momentum was already on my side that I tapped specifically into the bone density of my hand, channeling as much weight as I could into the blow. The spider might as well have been a piñata. My fist launched with the force of a cannonball, blasting right through the spider in a slimy, yellow explosion.

Making my fist light once more, I ripped my gooey arm free. I then grabbed the spider at the base of its pincers. Distributing just enough weight in my arms, I ripped the pincers out and apart like a wishbone. The spider dropped with a thud. I repositioned my grip on these new weapons, grabbing them by their hairy husks. The fanged pincers gleamed in the overhead light like twin daggers.

I leapt down from the mound of yellow-stained corpses as more spiders ascended. I added to my gravity as I magnified my entire bone density tenfold. I dropped like an anchor. Two unfortunate spiders happened to be beneath me as I plummeted. I crushed them into the floor.

Retracting my bone density on impact, I refastened my grip on the pincers and plunged into an onslaught of oncoming spiders. I practically glided across the floor. I slashed and sliced and stabbed, weaving through the throng of hairy bodies and appendages like a ghost. Limbs dropped. Wounds oozed. Bodies fell.

And then the ground rumbled beneath me. I redirected my gaze as the biggest spider yet lumbered out of the shadows like a gangly, eight-legged bear. Lifeless bodies were shoved aside as it plowed through, roaring rather than screeching. I flipped the pincers in my hands, grabbing them by their fanged tips. Pulling both of my arms back, I flung them like throwing knives. With my enhanced speed and reflexes, they whizzed like bullets.

One pincer sunk deep into the massive spider's face, between several sets of eyes. The other shot through the back of its snarling throat. Yellow blood spurted out the back of its head. With a resounding thud, it collapsed heavily amid its fallen kind.

I whipped around, fully prepared to punch the next spider's head clean off.

However, the only spiders in sight were dead and dismembered with occasional parts still twitching. My head kept jerking from side to side as I continued to turn.

"They're dead," said Nero in a flat tone. I glanced over to find him standing in the corpses rather than levitating. "We got all of them."

Despite the good news, he hardly looked pleased.

As I stopped to catch my breath, I normalized my bone density. Even though there was no external change, it was amazing how fat I always felt after returning to normal.

"You took out forty-two of them," Nero grumbled.

"Forty-two?" I said. I was caught off guard by the randomness of the comment. Though Nero was only a Telekinetic, hardly a Telepath, he still had a gift for keeping track of such things without even trying. "How many did you get?"

Nero snorted and redirected his attention elsewhere.

Ah. So that explained the sour look. I'd taken down more spiders than him. Nero was the sorest loser of them all.

"Arachnis," said Nero.

"Huh?"

"Arachnis," he repeated. "She's the Defeated we're facing in this Challenge."

Arachnis. I knew that name. "She was one of the traitors that Fantom killed, right?"

"Yeah," said Nero, nodding. "She was one of the first. A real nasty one from what I've heard."

"Good," I said. "Let's beat the tar out of her. Can you sense her?"

Nero paused a moment, his gaze wandering, and his lips pursed. There was something in his eyes that I couldn't put my finger on.

Apprehension?

"I think she's that way," said Nero, pointing down a particularly dank tunnel. "East."

Only Nero would know which way was east in an underground sewer hideout. We both started in that direction. Trudging through the inch-deep water, I was immediately glad that our bodysuits were waterproof. Even if it was just to keep our feet dry. And poop-free.

I couldn't believe Nero was actually being this cooperative. Out of the corner of my eye, I noted that his eyes were still lowered, and his mouth was pulled into a straight line.

"What's up?" I asked, trying not to sound concerned. Which I wasn't. Honestly, the only thing I was concerned about was finishing the Challenge.

Nero looked over at me, silent. As if mulling over whether he would actually respond or not. I was finding it increasingly difficult to maintain eye contact.

"Back in 1995 . . . a hero named Cortex fought Arachnis," Nero said finally. "Before Fantom killed Arachnis. He was an Omnipotent."

I blinked. An Omnipotent? I'd never heard Nero mention Omnipotents before. Omnipotents were Supers with both telekinetic *and* telepathic power. Though Omnipotents were termed to be practically invincible, they were also, ironically, extinct.

"So . . . I'm assuming Arachnis beat him?" I asked.

"She killed him," said Nero.

"Oh," I said. I had no clue what else to say.

"There's a chance that Arachnis might have a defense against mind powers," said Nero. "If that's the case . . . just be ready."

I couldn't believe what I was hearing. Was Nero seriously admitting that he might be useless in this fight? As much as the prospect boosted my ego, I didn't like the idea of fighting a freaky spider lady on my own.

"It's just a virtual recreation of Arachnis," I said, attempting to sound like I didn't care. "A dumbed down version. Besides, if Arachnis had any sort of defense against an Omnipotent, it would probably be a block against telepathic power, not telekinesis. Cortex probably walked in cocky, thinking he could read Arachnis's mind, and he couldn't."

Whether or not I actually believed my words, they sounded convincing enough coming out of my mouth.

"Yeah," said Nero, forcing an uncertain smirk. "You're probably right."

The tunnel grew murkier as we progressed, our shadows blending against dark walls. The hope of light glimmered distantly ahead like a single star in a black sky. Despite the sloshing water beneath our feet, a new sound permeated the atmosphere. Soft and shrill, echoing indiscernibly.

"Do you hear that?" asked Nero.

I didn't respond right away, still straining to discern what it was. Suddenly, random, high-pitched sounds began to correlate with each other. It was then that I noticed the melodious nature of the sound. It was a female voice . . .

Singing.

Whether we were drawing nearer or the voice was growing louder, the words became clear.

"The itsssy bitsssy ssspider walked up the water ssspout . . . Down came the rain and washed the ssspider out . . ."

I shuddered at the eerie, hissing voice. From what I could gather, she seemed to be singing the same song over and over. It was Arachnis, no doubt. If she was trying to scare us . . . well . . . she wasn't doing a bad job.

The narrow expanse of the tunnel finally expanded into a vast chamber. The sheer size of it was obscured by veils of draped webbing. These were all connected amid an infrastructure of thick strands intertwining the floor, walls, and ceiling. The end result was a sticky, white labyrinth.

A nest.

As I stepped out into the open, the floor crunched beneath my feet. I glanced down. The floor was blanketed in small skeletons—rats, fish, and several other animals that I did not care to identify. Pulling my gaze up, Nero and I cautiously proceeded into the labyrinth.

Through the transparent sheets of webbing, a hulking silhouette was finally visible—even bigger than the last spider I had taken down, although strangely human in shape. Whatever the nature of Arachnis's power, it had obviously come with physical side-effects.

Arachnis finally ceased her singing, only to be replaced with the rhythmic chant of another nursery rhyme.

"Little Missss Muffet sssat on a tuffet, eat her curdsss and whey . . . Along came a ssspider, who sssat down bessside her . . . and had a Little-Missss-Muffet-filet."

Even with layers of web between us, Arachnis turned a very human head our direction. The details of her face were obscured, but it was obvious she was looking directly at us. Nero and I both froze.

"Hello, my delectable little guests," she said in a voice as melodious as her singing. She gestured with a thin, elongated arm. "Come. Come so that I may see you clearly."

Nero and I exchanged anxious glances. The element of surprise was clearly out of the question.

"We should communicate to each other with Morse code or something," Nero whispered.

"Morse code?" I repeated. "Seriously? Are you a Boy Scout?"

Nero flushed red.

"Havoc," I breathed, looking away. "If one of us says 'Havoc', we both attack."

Nero simply nodded, avoiding eye contact as well. Without another word, we followed the last sheet of webbing as it curved inward. At last, we stepped into the open core of the nest.

Arachnis appeared both beautiful and horrifying. She seemed human from the waist up, but even that was pushing the definition of human. She was covered by a black, gown-like top with a swooping neckline. Two pairs of abnormally long arms met with twenty spindly fingers interlocked. Her face was statuesque, a flawless complexion complemented by full lips and lush eyelashes. Her eyes, however, were big and black . . . accompanied by several smaller pairs of eyes clustered together. Sharp, black hair sliced down to her bare shoulders. Four gargantuan legs jutted out like angled tree trunks. Her most notable feature, however, was an abdomen the size of a hot-air balloon, pulsing gently behind her. Though not as hairy as her spider minions, her legs and abdomen were dominated by a splotchy but very distinct brown and black striped pattern.

It was almost impossible to believe that this *thing* was artificial.

"You killed my babies," said Arachnis in a surprisingly calm tone.

I blinked myself back to the reality of the situation. Even if she wasn't real, the Challenge certainly was. We had one goal: kill her.

"Your babies tried eating us," I said with a casual shrug.

"They are ever so hungry," said Arachnis, sighing.

She scraped a long, gangly arm across the floor, brushing the small animal skeletons. My stomach churned.

"Then again, so am I," said Arachnis, glancing back at her enormous, pulsating abdomen. "Eating for two hundred makes you especially hungry."

Nero eyed her with obvious disgust but held his ground.

As she turned back to us, her gaze suddenly became fierce. "Have you come to kill me too?"

"We came to tell you something," I said. I allowed a long pause, hoping that Nero would know where I was going with this.

"Oh? And what would that be?" asked Arachnis.

Mentally tapping into my skeletal structure, I minimized my bone density. Just standing there, I felt like I could fly at any second.

"Havoc," I said.

Arachnis raised a confused eyebrow. "Wh—?"

Nero and I simultaneously sprang into action before a word could escape her mouth. Nero summoned several large, sharp rib bones from the floor, causing them to hover at his side like missiles. Meanwhile, I leapt into the air, careful not to hit the sticky, white canopy above me.

I started channeling as much density into my fist as possible, but before gravity could bring me down I was slapped against the sticky surface of the ceiling. Arachnis's lanky arms had shot out, grazing the webbed walls with her fingers. As a result, the ceiling had caved slightly.

I was left there, dangling, my heavy fist weighing me down. I was like a fly on flypaper.

From that perspective, I was left to watch as Nero's bone projectiles shot forward but then halted in midair. Not only that, but they wavered, as if they had struck some rubbery invisible force.

No. It was another web. She had somehow pulled it in front of her as a shield.

Arachnis's lips twisted into a sick smile. As she raised both pairs of hands, I noticed something glistening from each of her fingertips: strands of webbing. Like strings.

The realization hit me like a fist. Everything was connected. She had this entire nest on strings. Arachnis was controlling the entire web like a puppeteer.

And we had walked right into her trap.

"Nero!" I screamed. "Stay away from the walls! She's controlling—!"

It was too late. Arachnis twisted a hand with her index finger curled in. A practically invisible strand gleamed as it was triggered. A section of webbing dropped like a net.

Nero sensed it coming. His hands flew up—a natural reflex when he was channeling his telekinesis. The sticky net halted midair, levitating only inches from his head. His usual cockiness was lost in wide-eyed shock.

That was all the distraction Arachnis needed. With an impressive heave of strength, she twisted the enormous tail-end of her abdomen. The bulbous blob pulsed and then launched a powerful string of web at Nero, who was already preoccupied; it hit him directly in the face. Nero toppled backward and the net fell over him. His face was swallowed in thick, suffocating webbing. As he squirmed and fought, the sticky net bound him tighter.

"You'll find that it's rather difficult to concentrate on your telekinesis when you can't breathe," said Arachnis, sneering. "And now . . . it's lunchtime."

I watched in horror as Arachnis crawled toward Nero. And here I was, a helpless observer.

Of course, Havoc and his team of onlookers wouldn't let this artificial Defeated suck Nero dry. But the moment she reached him, it would be game over. Nero and I would both be eliminated from the Sidekick Internship Program.

Over my dead body.

CHAPTER 3

I glanced from Arachnis, dragging her massive abdomen across the skeleton-laden floor, to my heavy fist, still hanging lower than the rest of my body. I had yet to normalize my bone density after my failed super punch. And then the most obvious idea came to me.

I tapped into my skeletal structure, building as much density as possible into every last bone in my body. The sticky, webbed canopy drooped with my sudden explosion in weight. I could feel the sticky fibers straining to hold me.

Arachnis was only a yard away from being directly below me. My body dipped lower as the web tore slightly. She took another long, dragging step.

Bull's-eye.

The web snapped. I dropped like a bomb.

I missed her head. What I hit instead was her bulbous spider-abdomen, and that exploded on impact. Literally. Exploded.

I was momentarily blinded, submerged in bug guts. Fake bug guts, I had to remind myself. Arachnis wasn't real. Nevertheless, she screamed in an inhuman screech.

The smell was awful, like roadkill and vomit and Brussels sprouts, blended together into a smoothie. When I finally managed to open my eyes, the entire nest was sprayed in yellow.

"You!" said Arachnis, howling. Though she staggered around with a slight limp, she appeared much more agile without having to drag her big, fat spider-butt around. Her four arms were tense, all twenty long fingers curled into fists. As she turned, however, I couldn't help but notice the slight gleam of a metal frame where Arachnis's abdomen had been.

She's just an artificial recreation, I reminded myself, straining to calm my nerves. A robot. She's not real.

Arachnis brought a massive leg up over me and then thrust it down, fully intending to crush me.

Sucking the density from my leg, I kicked out with inhuman speed. I didn't pump the weight back in until the very last second.

With a sickening crunch, the spider leg snapped back. Arachnis screamed, and her entire body toppled towards me. This was it. My arm went light as I readied myself for a final punch. One swift move, and then my fist would become a wrecking ball, right through her robotic face.

I prepared to deliver the punch, but my entire body went rigid. Every muscle had suddenly seized.

The force of Arachnis's falling body hit me hard. I was defenseless. I cried out as one of her heavy legs smashed into my shin like a baseball bat. Fiery pain exploded and seared every nerve.

Arachnis pushed herself up off of me with her four pairs of arms, her horrifying scowl only inches from my face.

"You disgusting little insect!" she snarled. "I will eat the skin off your face!"

As she reared her head back, rows of needle-like teeth erupted from her gums.

Why couldn't I move? I was officially panicking now. It was as if some invisible force was gripping me. As if . . .

Nero exploded from the sticky net that had seemed to permanently bind him. He levitated there for only a brief moment as Arachnis whipped around in surprise.

"Wha—!" she started to say, her black eyes wide.

Nero shot forward like a human bullet. Arachnis released me, her arms lashing out in defense, but it was too late. Headfirst, Nero blasted right through her. Sparks exploded.

The next thing I knew, Arachnis's lifeless body was rolling off of me. At least half of it. The broken robotic inner-workings were still sparking from the severed midsection. The other half was partway across the room. Even from that distance, lying on the floor, I could see her blank eyes staring back at me. Smoke smoldered from both halves.

Nero was facing away from me, his daunting silhouette slowly drifting to the ground like something from a nightmare.

Nero . . . Did he use his telekinesis to stop me from delivering the final blow?

Did he just stab me in the back?

A doorway appeared in midair, and out stepped Havoc. He was clapping. And smiling! Remember that part when I said that Havoc never smiles? Well this was going against all the laws of nature.

"Great job, Nero," said Havoc, clapping the skinny little traitor on the shoulder. "I'm not gonna lie. That was possibly the most impressive takedown I've ever seen in my entire career. I know you had a rough start in there, but believe me . . . you can expect a near-perfect score."

Several other members of the FIST training team appeared on the other side of the two-dimensional doorway, clapping as well. All eyes were on Nero. I was as invisible as Arachnis's obliterated robotic corpse.

Nero seemed to be deliberately avoiding my gaze.

I staggered to my feet, shaking with rage. My hands clenched into white-knuckled fists. I couldn't even form words, I was so furious. At last, the only hint of coherence exploded out of me in two words:

"He cheated!" I screamed.

The clapping stopped. I was no longer invisible. Every pair of eyes turned to me. Nero included—wide-eyed and slack-jawed. Was he really shocked that I would actually call him out? What the heck did he take me for?

Havoc, meanwhile, was scathing me with a look one would give a fly before swatting it.

"I beg your pardon?" said Havoc. There was less question in his tone and more accusation.

I didn't like that nobody was giving Nero a disbelieving stare.

"I was about to take Arachnis out!" I erupted in my own defense. "And then Nero stopped me! I couldn't move!"

Havoc continued to stare at me for several long seconds, his thick arms folded and his shaved head lowered slightly. "You're saying that Nero used his telekinesis on you," said Havoc. "After it very clearly appears that he saved your butt from getting disqualified. Is that what you're telling me?"

He didn't sound convinced. Not even a little bit.

"Yes," I said, struggling desperately to maintain my cool. "That's exactly what I'm saying."

"That's a very serious accusation you're making, Marrow," said Havoc.

I took a deep breath, biting my tongue. "I realize that," I said through gritted teeth.

It was several long seconds before Havoc tore his gaze away from me. At last, he turned to Nero. "What do you have to say about all of this?"

Nero was still wide-eyed and appeared much more confused than guilty. This only irritated me further.

"I didn't do anything to Marrow," he said in the most disgustingly earnest tone I had ever heard.

Nero's words grated against every last nerve in my body. I couldn't take it anymore. Something snapped—as if the white-hot rage boiling inside of me had disintegrated any hint of rationality left in me.

With Havoc's back turned to me, I marched right up to Nero. Of course everyone in the room noticed, but before anyone could react, it was too late.

I punched Nero in the face. He hit the floor louder and faster than you could say, 'Marrow, get yo' lily-white butt to my office right now!'

And Havoc can say that pretty loud and fast.

CHAPTER 4

Havoc's office was about as warm and inviting as an interrogation room. Although such a comparison probably gives interrogation rooms a bad name. My seat was cold and metal, opposite a magnificent mahogany desk with a plush, red velvet, throne-like chair. Behind this chair was an elaborate painting of Havoc posing in a skin-tight costume—back when he was a full-time Superhero. Not a pretty sight. The side walls were adorned with past portraits of leading FIST faculty in their Superhero days—the Flaming Phlegm, Gertrude the Great, the Black Blob, etc . . .

Ask me if any of these people should have ever been allowed to wear spandex. Go on. Ask me.

The answer is HECK NO! For the love of all that is holy!

The worst part, however, were the three caged parrots in the corner of the room. Their names were Socrates, Plato, and Aristotle. Of course, in a school of supernaturally-gifted students, Havoc had to have an obsession with supernaturally-gifted birds. Unlike parrots who simply repeated words and phrases, these three pets were every bit as communicative as human beings.

And every bit as obnoxious as Nero.

"I wonder when Havoc will be here," said Aristotle, ruffling his red feathers. He flexed the colorful tips of his wings and yawned. "It's taking an awful long time, isn't it?"

Plato—covered in blue feathers with a yellow belly—shrugged his wings. "Deliberating on a suitable punishment, no doubt."

"What punishment is there to deliberate?" asked the snowy gray-feathered Socrates. "The lad is going to get his bum kicked out of school."

I bit my lip, resisting the ever-growing urge to smash the birds into the wall. My academic career was already on a thread.

"Or perhaps they'll hold a formal execution," said Plato.

"Ooh," said Aristotle. "I like executions. Perhaps they'll make him walk the plank?"

"You idiot," said Socrates, rolling his eyes. "They'd need a pirate ship in order for him to walk the plank. If any sort of execution is in order, they'll probably have his body disintegrated with laser beams and ship his remains into outer space."

Being communicative obviously didn't make the birds intelligent.

The door creaked open behind me. All three parrots perked up simultaneously. I reluctantly glanced back as Havoc entered. Good news and bad news. The good news was that the birds always shut up when Havoc was in the room. The bad news was that Havoc didn't look happy. And I had generally come to associate Havoc's "happy face" as a very stern expression.

Havoc's not-so-happy face was one you would expect Satan to have while experiencing a violent bowel movement.

Havoc seated himself and slapped a folder on his desk. The veins in his forearms pulsed and his thick fingers interlocked as he glared at me. No words. Just your average, soul-penetrating glare.

"So . . . did you find anything?" I asked, perhaps a bit too casually.

Havoc's clenched jaw shifted from one side to the other. "Oh, we found stuff alright," he said. "Where would you like me to start?"

I responded with a blank stare. "Uh . . ."

"How about we start with the lie detector?" Havoc suggested. "We hooked Nero up to it and asked him if he used his power against you in any way."

"And . . . ?"

"He passed, Marrow," said Havoc. "He passed with flying colors."

I blinked. How was that possible? There was no way. No stinkin' way! Unless . . .

"What if he used his telekinesis?" I asked. "That could've tweaked the machine, couldn't it?"

"We were monitoring his telekinesis," said Havoc in a flat tone.

"But aren't there people who are trained to pass lie detectors?" I asked. "I mean . . . If he has mind powers, wouldn't that make it so he—?"

"He's a Telekinetic, not a Telepath," said Havoc, cutting me off sharply. "Besides, we monitored his brain at all times. He didn't *tweak* the test. Don't insult my intelligence."

I shook my head slowly. This didn't make any sense at all. But if they monitored his brain at all times . . .

"Did you monitor his power during the Final Challenge?" I asked.

"Of course we did."

I hated that Havoc was making me ask the questions he already knew I would ask. "And . . . ?"

"To be quite honest, the telekinetic power in that Challenge Chamber was off the charts at the end," said Havoc. "Our computers couldn't process it all."

I perked up. "That's it!" I exclaimed. "That's—!"

"However . . . !" said Havoc, interrupting me once more, "we *could* monitor where Nero was directing his telekinetic energy. And his focus was solely on escaping that spider web and attacking Arachnis. Not you, Marrow. He didn't direct a single telekinetic thought at you."

"Then how come I couldn't move?" I asked. "Why would I make this up?"

Havoc shrugged. "Sometimes, in the heat of battle, people just freeze. It's nothing to be ashamed of, Marrow. It just happens. Some of us just aren't cut out for this line of work."

I bolted up from my seat in a sudden rage. My arms were rigid at my sides and my fists were clenched.

"I did not freeze!" I snapped. My breath was ragged. I had never felt so insulted in my entire life.

Havoc responded just as rashly, flying up and towering over me from the other side of his desk. "I don't care what you *think* happened or didn't happen. I'll tell you what *did* happen. You punched a fellow student in the face *after* the Final Challenge! Do you realize that those Challenges are filmed and broadcast live to all the top Superheroes? Even Fantom himself! You've made a complete and utter mockery of this entire institution! I have every right and reason to expel you, right here, right now."

My breath stopped short in my throat. I had trained my entire life for this. To be expelled from FIST would be to throw away my entire life. Everything that I had worked for.

This had suddenly become a much bigger issue. This wasn't about Nero cheating anymore. It was about me. About my entire future getting flushed down the toilet.

"You know, it blows my mind," said Havoc. "You have the highest IQ of all the students here—even Whisp. You're a prodigy by every definition of the term. So why do you go so far out of your miserable way to be a cocky, little, juvenile, delinquent punk?"

My normal response to this question would have been, 'Do you know what happens to "smart" superheroes like Whisp? Superjerks give them superwedgies.' But something told me that wouldn't be the smartest answer to give at the moment.

"I know you are your father's son," said Havoc, "but that doesn't mean you have to *be* your father."

My entire body went rigid. If there was one thing I hated—even more than I hated Nero, if that's even possible—it was being compared to my father. If you could even *consider* him a father, that is. Which I didn't.

As much as I wanted to explode, however, I couldn't. I dropped back into my seat. Nausea swept over me.

Whether or not he noticed my sudden dread, Havoc's expression softened. With a sigh, he sat down as well.

"Fortunately for you, Marrow . . ." said Havoc, "you received the second highest scores out of all your fellow classmates."

I glanced up as a sudden glimmer of hope ignited.

"Nero received a 9.6," said Havoc. "You were right behind him with a 9.4. The only student to even come close was Whisp with an 8.9. And I'll remind you that these scores come straight from the Heroes Guild. Every Superhero with a name, basically."

Whisp got third place? Huh. Who'd a thunk?

"So here's the deal," said Havoc. "The good news is that the Guild recognizes your talent. However, none of them feel comfortable taking you on as a sidekick themselves."

I blinked. How was this good news?

"However . . . there is one hero that several of the Guild members had in mind. A relatively new hero. I'm sure you've never heard of him. He's not a Guild member himself. He actually lost his membership a year ago after an . . . er . . . incident." Havoc cleared his throat as he continued. "He's somewhat of a wild card. I don't really know the details. But anyway, he's shown a lot of promise in the past, and the Guild is willing to give him a second chance—both of you a second chance—working with each other."

I was speechless. If I had been told this yesterday, I would have freaked out. The top of my class, and I was being teamed up with some no-name rogue rookie.

But what other choice did I have?

"Okay," I said, maintaining a calm, cool tone. "Who is he?"

Havoc placed his thick fingers on the folder and slid it to my side of the desk. Taking a deep, nerve-wracking breath, I opened it.

Front and center was a professional photo of him. At least . . . it was supposed to be professional. The scraggly, unshaven man appeared to be in his late twenties. His long hair was knotted in unkempt dreadlocks, and he was wearing a Bob Marley t-shirt with cutoff sleeves. He also had his fingers pulling the insides of his cheeks, stretching his mouth impossibly wide. I'm not kidding. His face was like elastic as he stretched his mouth open two or three feet. And, of course, he was sticking his tongue out.

Below the photo, his name was labeled in bold letters: Flex.

Who was I kidding? My future was already down the toilet.

CHAPTER 5

Nero was teamed up with Fantom.

When I found out, I felt sick. Like, really sick. I was reminded of the last time I ate a chili cheese dog right before riding a roller coaster. My stomach was churning like a volcano ready to erupt. I ran to the bathroom, fell to my knees, and puked my guts out.

The Teaming Ceremony was disgusting. Crystal chandeliers, five-star food catering, and even a celebrity M.C. I had no idea who the guy was, but Sapphire and a bunch of other girls in the room screamed. I'd never seen so many moms freak out like that either.

My mom wasn't there. Parents were always invited to the Teaming Ceremony, but it's kind of hard to do that when you're dead. I barely knew her, but that didn't make me miss her any less. I could hardly even remember her face, but those that knew her said I had her smile.

My dad, on the other hand . . . I just tried to pretend he didn't exist. FIST took me in before he had the chance to ruin my life.

Which was ironic since I was already doing a good job of that on my own.

I heard the bathroom door open and close behind me. I didn't care. I continued retching even after I was certain that my stomach had been completely wrung out.

"You okay?" an anxious voice asked.

Wiping my mouth with my sleeve, I turned to find skinny little Whisp standing behind me. Behind his thick glasses and mousy hair, his eyes were filled with genuine concern.

"Wonderful," I said. "Now leave me alone."

I immediately cringed at the harshness of my tone. Apparently I wasn't completely numb to feeling. Not yet, at least.

Whisp didn't budge.

He had been next in line after Nero. Meaning I stormed out right as he had been called onstage. Because I was sitting in the far back, he was probably the only one that had noticed my abrupt exit.

With a sigh, I turned around and sat cross-legged in the stall. "So who'd you get teamed up with?"

"Nova," said Whisp.

My jaw dropped. Nova was an A-list Superhero. This shouldn't have surprised me, however, since Whisp *did* score the third highest score. And unlike me, he wasn't condemned by academic probation. It was just shocking, comparing a devastating force of nature like Nova to a scrawny kid like Whisp. I mean, the kid used an inhaler, for crying out loud.

Surprisingly, I wasn't so much jealous as I was impressed.

"Wow . . . that's awesome," I said, still dumbstruck. "Did I miss any other good ones?"

Whisp responded with a very calm and composed shrug. If he was excited about being Nova's sidekick, he was doing an excellent job of hiding it. "Sapphire was teamed with Specter."

Specter. Another A-lister. Her power was simple enough—when concentrating, she could walk through walls or other objects. She could even pass through living things if she wanted to. Specter always pushed her power to the limit, using techniques that stretched the imagination. This made her a formidable opponent in any fight.

Somehow, it didn't surprise me that Sapphire would be teamed with her. They seemed equal as far as feminine tenacity was concerned.

"I heard you were teamed up with Flex," said Whisp.

My head perked up. He already knew? Were the rumors seriously spreading that fast? I couldn't believe it. Overnight, I had singlehandedly become the laughing stock of FIST.

Except Whisp wasn't laughing.

"Flex and I grew up in the same orphanage," he said.

I blinked. Orphanage? I had no idea Whisp was even an orphan. And he knew this guy?

"You're lucky to be teamed up with him," said Whisp. "If I could . . . I'd trade places with you."

Whisp's calm expression remained unchanged. I hardly considered myself a people reader, but somehow, it was very obvious to me that he was telling the truth. And yet I couldn't help but ask:

"What's so special about him?"

"He always believed in me," said Whisp. "He was adopted way before me, but even then, he always visited me. He believed in me when no one else did."

I rolled my eyes. Okay, so Flex was a nice guy. Big deal. That still didn't make him a good Superhero.

"His power is being stretchy," I grumbled. "He's not even in the Heroes Guild anymore. Some hero."

"Being in the Guild doesn't make you a hero!" Whisp snapped. "Being a hero doesn't even have anything to do with superpowers. Supervillains have some of the greatest powers, don't they? Does that make them heroes? What the heck do you think a real hero is, Marrow?"

I was speechless. I'd never seen Whisp so riled up about anything before. Not like this.

"What it really comes down to is what you do with whatever power you have," he said, not bothering to wait for a response. "Sometimes, all a hero needs is someone to believe in him."

Whisp stood there, staring at me for several long seconds. Then he reached into his pocket, pulled out his inhaler, and took a big huff of it. Quietly pocketing it, he marched out of the bathroom.

CHAPTER 6

If I had to rank the things I hated most in the world, they would go in the following order:

1. A certain psychotic parental figure who I refuse to acknowledge by his technical title. We'll refer to him as Scumbag Number One.

2. A certain no-good, cheating classmate who I refuse to acknowledge by his real name. We'll refer to him as Scumbag Number Two.

3. Packing.

Yep . . . packing.

And then the honorable mention would probably be Brussels sprouts. Now if you've ever had the misfortune of trying Brussels sprouts, you should have a pretty good idea of how much I hated packing. If I had to put my level of hatred into words, I would describe it as complete and utter loathing from the darkest depths of my soul.

Pulling out entire dresser drawers, I dumped the contents into my suitcase like most people would throw garbage into a trash can. I then placed my luggage at the foot of my desk and simply pushed everything off and let it fall inside. In all of five minutes, I had a mountain of unfolded clothes, textbooks, and electronics towering inside my suitcase and no idea how to close it.

In a desperate attempt against all the laws of physics, I struggled to push my ridiculous mound of belongings down. I finally squashed the pile down to about half the size, but doing so required both of my hands. If I lifted even one, my crap started bulging back up. With both hands preoccupied, I eyed the suitcase lid with growing frustration.

For the first time in my life, I found myself wishing I had Nero's stupid telekinesis.

Biting my lip, I stuck my leg out, trying to use my foot to pop the lid over the top. Unfortunately, the pile was still too high, and I looked like a moron trying to kick it down repeatedly, only to have it bounce back up.

Change of plans.

Bending at an awkward angle, I sat down on my hands. With my bodyweight in place, I pulled my hands free. I craned my neck backwards, glancing at the suitcase lid.

Okay . . . now what? Hadn't exactly thought that one through.

"Need some help?"

I glanced up from my luggage to find Sapphire standing in the doorway of my dorm. Her slender arms were folded, and she tilted her head sideways, allowing her rich blue hair to drape at a slight angle. An amused smirk crept across her face.

I glanced from her to the overly-stuffed suitcase beneath me. "You wouldn't happen to have a garbage compactor handy, would you?"

"Hmm . . ." Sapphire shook her head with a smile. "Sorry. Fresh out." Without even waiting for my consent, she walked right into my dorm and pulled the suitcase lid up. "Move your butt, fatty."

I chuckled and followed along, shoving my hands under my butt and flipping back around. We both pulled and pushed the lid down while the luggage threatened to burst. I increased my bone density as Sapphire worked furiously on the zipper. Finally, we had it zipped all the way.

Everything I owned, all in one miserable, little suitcase. Both of us plopped down on top of it, claiming our small victory in exhausted silence.

"You should invest in another suitcase," said Sapphire.

"Why?" I asked, scrunching my eyebrows in a deliberately clueless look. "It all fits, doesn't it?"

Sapphire punched me playfully in the arm—it was less painful than getting smacked by mutant spider lady, but more painful than a playful punch should be. I bit my tongue and forced a smile.

"So . . . this is it," she said. There was a strange hesitation in her tone. Her hand—distinct with painted blue nails—was resting right in between us. Just chilling there like a hitchhiker waiting to get picked up.

If I'd earned the perfect score that I was supposed to, I would have held her hand in a heartbeat. No joke. I would have snatched that sucker like a fish out of the water and wouldn't have given it a second thought. Heck, I'd just start making out with her right now. Why? Because I'd be a hotshot. Sapphire wouldn't be able to say no to me.

But no . . . I got screwed over. Suddenly, I was the problem student that nobody knew what to do with. And I was getting teamed with some weirdo Superhero that nobody knew about.

"Yep," I said, abruptly standing up. "Well . . . thanks for the help."

Sapphire bit her glossy lip and nodded awkwardly, "Yeah. No problem."

If that wasn't awkward enough, I then reached out and shook her hand. Yep. A big, fat, loser handshake.

With that, we parted ways.

Dragging my luggage through the shiny, white corridors of FIST, I tried to force Sapphire out of my mind. The last thing I needed was for that awkward exchange to replay over and over in my mind. When did God or Karma or the Universe decide to hate me all of a sudden?

All I could see was Sapphire's hand in between us. I really wished I had grabbed it.

No! Stupid hand. Get out of my head!

Karma actually listened this time. Unfortunately, Karma had a twisted sense of humor. Lost in my own thoughts, I hardly noticed as Nero rounded the corner.

We nearly collided into each other. Stopping just a split-second short, we stared at each other eye-to-eye. Of course, one of Nero's eyes was purple and swollen.

My lack of satisfaction in his injury was unsettling.

Nero stared at me wide-eyed. Well . . . at least one eye was wide. The look on his face wasn't difficult to read. It had "oh crap" written all over it.

After a few of the longest seconds of my life, Nero averted his gaze elsewhere and continued past me. I turned and watched him as he hurried off.

I wanted to yell at him. To insult him. I racked my brain for some cutting remark that would pierce whatever little part of him still had a soul.

Nothing came. I watched, speechless, as Nero disappeared down the corridor.

If the human brain had an on/off switch, I would definitely be flipping it off right about now. Some thoughts just didn't deserve to exist—like this great ocean of emptiness inside of me, whirlpooling, spiraling, careening into an endless abyss. I was drowning inside of myself. And it is a fact of nature that when your life is threatened, you'll do anything—ANYTHING!—to survive.

These were the sorts of thoughts I imagined one would have before getting thrown in a padded room with a straitjacket. Or in jail.

I met Havoc in the lobby. White marble floors and ivory decorations gave it a classic Victorian look, contrasted by sleek, white computers at the front desk and a giant hologram recording of Fantom playing on a loop.

Fantom's barrel-chested frame was accentuated in a sleek red and black bodysuit, made vibrant through subtle but intricate textures and stark, muscular curves. A crimson cape draped over his broad shoulders. A black mask blended with his dark, slicked-back hair, obscuring all but the lower half of his clean-shaven face, emphasizing his strong cleft chin.

"When the Gaia Comet first hit Earth, we thought it was the end," said the projected image. Fantom's articulation was both eloquent and dangerous, resonating through the entire lobby. "Instead, it was merely the beginning. Gaia narrowly missed the sun, which acted as a fusion reactor. When the Gaia Comet made impact with the ocean, this alien nuclear fallout caused a radioactive mutation in nearly five percent of humankind. These so-called mutants became known as Supers. The age-old mythology of Superheroes became a reality. At the Fantom Institute for Superheroes-in-Training, we seek the most gifted young Supers and train them to the very brink of their supernatural capabilities. We train them to be beacons of hope. Symbols of justice. Weapons of light. In a world where every evil has its own agenda, we, at FIST, have only one objective—to fight for a better world."

His words didn't have their usual stimulating effect on me. All I could think about was Nero and how much I wanted to punch his face inside out.

"You ready to fight for a better world?" Havoc asked, snapping me out of my trance. Though he spoke in a soft tone, there was no hiding the inherent edge in his voice. The end result was not so much inspirational but rather resembled a drill sergeant in a good mood.

"I'd rather jump in front of a train right now," I muttered under my breath.

"What was that, Marrow?" Havoc snapped.

"I said . . . I'm ready to bump up the pain . . . right now," I fumbled for a more appropriate answer. "The pain against . . . evil, I mean . . . you know . . . when Flex and I kick their butts . . . and stuff."

Havoc snorted. "Are you ready to go or what?"

Honestly, I was more ready for the train idea. Unfortunately, that probably wasn't one of the options Havoc was offering. Still, leaving FIST didn't seem like such a bad option.

I nodded.

Havoc extended his brawny open palm with fingers the size of fat sausages. "Take my hand."

I glanced awkwardly between Havoc and his extended hand.

"Oh, for Pete's sake!" Havoc rolled his eyes. "I'm not asking you to the prom, Bonehead!"

You know you have a good student/teacher relationship when your teacher calls you the same stupid nickname that your jerk classmate does.

Havoc grabbed my hand, or rather, swallowed it whole within his massive grasp. That was only weird for a second. Suddenly, the ground disappeared beneath us, and our surroundings erupted into a haze of wispy smoke. My insides lurched as my body felt like it was being blasted out of a cannon.

Suddenly, solid ground slammed against the bottom of my feet. My legs buckled on impact. If it hadn't been for Havoc's solid grasp, I would have lost my balance for sure.

Have I mentioned that Havoc's power is teleportation? If not . . . well, there you go. It's way cool to watch him in action.

Actually doing it is enough to make you poop your pants.

The hazy mist took shape, forming two towering walls. Their distorted surfaces soon became brick, tainted by graffiti. It was a long, narrow passage with no ceiling.

An alley—the sort of sketchy alley you would generally stay away from if you weren't keen on the idea of being jumped and mugged or having other horrible things done to you.

Unless, of course, you were being accompanied by a big guy who made your average street thug look like a ballerina.

As I glanced over at Havoc, there was not even a hint of concern on his rigid face. In fact, he looked a little bored.

We moved out of the alley and into the open street. Traffic flowed and choked down a nearby intersection. More than a couple people wailed on their horns in the process, the sounds blending together into a noisy, incoherent blur. The sidewalk was just as occupied with people moving in droves—dressed for work in shiny suits, prim and proper skirts, as well as grubby, unkempt uniforms. And then you had plenty of gangster wannabes with their pants sagging to their knees, punks with their tattoos and body-piercings, and hipsters with their hemp styles and thick-rimmed glasses. It was like a zoo. A strange people zoo that had decided to let all of its specimens out of their cages to roam around in the open.

Cosmo City.

Havoc guided me into the flowing throng. Skyscrapers loomed over us in all directions, sunlight gleaming white against their glassy surfaces. At least I was in the heart of city life. If any Superhero hoped to make a name for himself, he couldn't hope for a better hub than the Cosmo. With all the scum on the streets, the place was just begging to be cleaned up.

That one little glimmer of excitement died when we arrived at our destination.

A crooked, weathered sign out front read: *Slumhole Apartments*. Yep, you heard right. Slumhole. And let me just say, the place lived up to its unfortunate title. The building was three floors of ugly. Cracked windowpanes, chipped and broken brick walls, and enough obnoxious neon graffiti to make the Fresh Prince of Bel-Air gag.

"He lives here?" I asked, hoping against all hope that Havoc was just lost and confused, staring at this abomination of an apartment building for no apparent reason.

Havoc responded with a subtle nod, although his face was distorted in silent repulsion.

We started up a dirty, cobwebbed stairwell to the third floor to apartment number 303. The mail slot was stuffed with letters and junk mail, complemented by a growing heap on the floor below it. Havoc eyed the pile of mail like a hawk, hunched over, and plucked a single letter from the bunch. Though his big hand covered most of it, I couldn't help but notice the FIST logo stamped in the corner.

Havoc raised his fist and pounded the door with such force that it rattled on its hinges, and mail rained down from the overstuffed slot. A part of me was afraid he might smash the whole door down.

No one answered.

Havoc pounded on the door again, more furiously than ever. Cursing under his breath, he roared, "Flex, you in there?"

There was no response.

Havoc didn't ask for my hand this time. He grabbed it, and after a split-second of distorted gravity, we teleported three feet forward, on the other side of the door.

I should have saved my judgments until I was inside the apartment. To put a lack of cleanliness in the ranking order, this apartment fell somewhere between filthy stinkin' disgusting and sweet-mother-of-Moses-what-poor-creature-died-in-here? Cans were strewn everywhere—soda cans, energy drink cans, beer cans . . . enough aluminum to make a spaceship. Plates of half-eaten food were scattered on every flat surface, gathering mold. And that was just the living room. I took one step towards the kitchen, and the stench hit me like a brick. I was now convinced that someone had died here. A small part of me hoped it was Flex.

No such luck. Once the shock factor of the mess had worn off, I realized there was music playing in the back room—a chill, reggae beat. There was also a voice singing, separate from the music recording, and completely off-tune. Havoc took a brave step forward, immersing himself in the unsanitary obstacle course. I took a deep breath and followed.

The little details of this disaster area seemed to say a lot about Flex. The television was on, and Stewie was attempting to assassinate Lois Griffin. An outdated video game console was sitting in front of it, but apparently a game hadn't gone so well since both controllers had been smashed into the nearest wall, still attached by their cords. Havoc and I stepped through food wrappers, mostly belonging to Twinkies and Ding Dongs. The hallway was littered in piles of crusty, wrinkled clothes shoved in the corners.

Havoc opened the bedroom door, and the source of the music (and the off-key karaoke) was revealed. A man was sprawled sideways across a queen-sized bed wearing nothing but his boxers. Nappy dreadlocks fanned out around his head. In one hand, he held an alcohol bottle wrapped in a paper bag. The other hand was waving through the air like a conductor leading an orchestra. The orchestra just happened to be Bob Marley playing from a beat up CD player.

"Because every little thinnnnng . . . gonna be alrighhhhht . . ." Flex sang in a slur.

Havoc seemed to be running on his last thread of patience. Marching forward, he unplugged the CD player and ripped the bottle out of Flex's limp grasp.

"Hey, what's the big . . . ?" Flex protested, struggling to get up. "Who do you think you . . . ?" His train of thought seemed to falter before he could finish either sentence. At least he managed to sit upright. Cocking his head sideways, he blinked and scratched the scruff on his face as he slowly absorbed the large black man towering over him. "Havoc?"

"No, it's the tooth fairy," said Havoc. "Flex, are you seriously drunk at one in the afternoon?"

"Drunk?" said Flex, struggling to process a response. "Psh. Naaaah." He proceeded to laugh hysterically. "This is just a little something to wash down breakfast, that's all."

"You're drunk," said Havoc.

"No, no, no, no, no," said Flex, shaking his head unsteadily. He attempted to become serious, although his unnaturally huge eyes bugged out of his face. He raised his hand and pointed his index and middle fingers to his eyeballs. "See these eyes? These are the eyes of a hawk. I see everything that's going on around here."

"No you don't," said Havoc. "You're plastered out of your mind."

Flex opened his mouth to respond, but seemed to change his mind halfway and plopped backward on his bed. "You're right. I'm drunk."

Havoc hardly seemed satisfied with this small victory. Raising the letter he had retrieved from the mail slot, he dropped it on Flex's vacant face. "Checked your mail lately?"

Sputtering as he shook the letter off his face, Flex sat up. "Yeah. I like checked it last week or something." Pinching the letter with two fingers, he lifted it away from his body like some dead thing. "What the heck is this?"

"Several months ago, you accepted an invitation from FIST," said Havoc. "You agreed to be a potential trainer for the Sidekick Internship Program, if you were so chosen."

"Yeah? So what?"

"You were chosen."

A hint of realization suddenly flickered through Flex's eyes. His gaze slowly shifted to me and then jolted back to Havoc, wider than ever.

"Whoa, whoa, whoa! Wait a sec. I only agreed to that for the money. I didn't think they'd actually be stupid enough to pick me!"

Well this just kept getting better and better. I had been pawned off to some hippie alcoholic mooching off the system.

"Well, apparently they *are* stupid enough," said Havoc. Stepping to the side, he gestured to me. "Flex, this is Marrow. Marrow, Flex. You'll be spending the next three months with each other. Any questions?"

"Yeah," said Flex. "Do I look qualified to train a freaking sidekick?"

"Nope." Havoc shook his thick bald head. "But that's not my problem."

With that he turned and exited the bedroom.

"Wait!" said Flex. He bolted out of bed but flopped onto the floor just as fast. Tangled in his own bed sheets, he eventually managed to free his legs and stagger upright. He cast one frenzied glance at me before chasing after Havoc. "You can't leave this kid here with me!"

"Watch me," Havoc called from the hallway.

I abandoned my suitcase and slowly followed the two of them as a hopeless spectator. It wasn't bad enough that I was being dumped with a hero reject. Oh no. I was officially being rejected by the reject as well.

As Havoc started across the living room, Flex flung his arm forward. Against every law of physics, his arm stretched thirty feet like a bungee jumping cord. His hand latched onto the doorknob. If that wasn't weird enough, he pulled back and then flung himself across the room like a slingshot. He hit the door with a weird *splat* and then puffed out into his normal human shape—which was still quite eccentric as, wild eyed, he blocked the doorway with his gangly limbs.

"I'm not letting you through here without that kid," said Flex.

Havoc chuckled to himself. "I didn't use the front door."

In a subtle *poof* of wispy smoke, he vanished.

Flex continued to stand at the front door in a blank daze. His gaze slowly drifted across the living room to me. Our eyes remained interlocked for several long seconds, and we were like two wild animals staring each other down. At least Flex seemed like a wild animal. I felt more like a rat in a cage. Finally, Flex let out a long sigh and staggered off into the kitchen, rummaging through the pantry. He came away with another liquor bottle in hand.

"I'm not nearly drunk enough for this," he said.

Taking a long swig, he shuffled back to his bedroom and shut the door.

CHAPTER 7

Flex's nasty apartment was my arch nemesis. I was dead set on defeating it.

After a fast trip to the quickie mart on the corner, I was armed with scouring pads, sponges, a box of garbage bags, and a monstrous bottle of Greased Lightning all-purpose cleaner. Heck, I even bought a carton of plug-in air fresheners. And before you go calling me a clean freak, believe me, I wouldn't have bothered if the place didn't smell like Flex's dead grandmother was hiding under the floor boards.

Honestly, I'd never taken the initiative to clean in my entire life. But this . . . this wasn't just about cleaning. It was about survival. If I was going to *live* in this hole for the next three months, it at least needed to be *livable*. Currently, it was a biohazard.

Most of the battle involved filling garbage bags. The worst part was scraping half-eaten moldy food off of a gazillion mismatched plates before stacking them by the sink. Some of them were completely engulfed in moldy fuzz, practically unidentifiable. These particular dishes triggered my gag reflex more often than not. Four trash bags later, Flex's apartment looked practically empty.

After filling the sink with water, I dumped the toxic dishes inside. I was almost shocked to find that Flex actually owned dish soap. The bottle was practically full and looked like it had only been used once. I squirted a hefty amount into the sink and watched the foam rise before wielding my dish scrubber like a battle axe.

As for Flex's crusty, nasty clothes lying around, I simply tossed them in a pile in front of the bedroom door. The pile became a small mountain reaching up to the doorknob. By the time I finished, I was only slightly disappointed to not find the slightest hint of a Superhero jumpsuit. Then again, maybe that just meant that it was hung up in his closet or folded up nice in his dresser.

Bam. Smack. Thunk. My cleaning spree was interrupted as a series of sharp sounds from a neighboring apartment pierced through the thin walls. This was accompanied almost simultaneously by a harsh male voice shouting indiscernibly.

Shortly after, a girl screamed.

I rushed to the door and peered through the peephole just as the door across the hall burst open and slammed shut. A cute blonde—probably fifteen years old—with a midriff top and a belly button ring had stormed out. Not a second later, some punk kid in a white tank top and sleeve tattoos—maybe a year or two older than her—burst out as well. His hair was buzzed short, with a scraggly attempt to grow a goatee hanging from his chin. He grabbed the girl by the arm, jerking her towards him.

My hand tensed on the doorknob.

"Mia, don't you dare walk away from me when I'm talking to you," he said.

"Let me go!" she said, struggling to break free. "Tad, you're hurting me!"

Tad. With a name like that, the guy was officially the king of douche bags. This was confirmed as he proceeded to twist her wrist.

"Teach you to talk back to me!"

Mia screamed. Her free hand flew out to slap him, but he caught this hand as well. Tad then released it only to backhand her in the face.

I threw the front door open.

"Get your hands off her!" I shouted.

The hallway went silent. Both Tad and Mia turned to face me with looks of bewilderment. The moment was enough for Mia to break free of Tad's grasp, but he was too preoccupied with me to care now. His wide eyes narrowed and his slack jaw clenched shut with gritted teeth.

"You say something, kid?" he asked, chest puffed out.

"Uh, yeah, duh," I said. "Did you not understand me? Do I have to use smaller words? Maybe I could spell it out for you?"

"What'd you say?" Tad took a step closer. "You have a death wish or something?"

"Ha! Death wish . . . that's funny," I said, pretending to chuckle. "Says the loser who picks on girls half his size to make himself feel tough. Seriously, dude. It's pathetic. Why don't you go be a juvenile delinquent somewhere else?"

Tad's nostrils flared. Cracking his knuckles, he started towards me. "I hope you're hungry, 'cause I'm gonna give you a knuckle sandwich in that fat mouth of yours."

Knuckle sandwich? Wow. This guy was as bad at comebacks as Nero.

I tapped into my bone structure and felt the pressure beneath my feet disappear. I was a feather on the ground. Tad reared his elbow back and launched a wide and extremely sloppy punch. I doubted he'd ever hit anyone but girls his entire life.

My hand lashed out, and I increased the density in my arm, tripling my normal strength. I caught his fist in my palm like a baseball. Actually, it was more like a flimsy softball tossed underhand.

Then I twisted it.

"Ow, ow, ow, ow, ow owwy! OWWY!" Tad wailed in a shrill voice.

Yep. He really said "owwy." Twice.

Increasing the remainder of my bone structure to match my heavy arm, I became an unbreakable anchor. "Does that feel good?" I asked in a calm voice.

Tad whimpered and shook his head vigorously. "What are you? Are you . . . ? You're . . . you're one of those Super freaks, aren't you?"

The moment I noticed, it was too late. Tad's free hand came out of his pocket with the metallic glint of a switchblade.

The blade stopped short. Something *whooshed* past my right ear, hitting Tad's face with a *smack*. He flew out of my grasp, across the hall, and into the opposite door with a hinge-rattling *thud*.

It took a moment to register what had just intervened. Tad had been punched. I was staring at the fist that did it. But this fist was attached to an arm stretching across the hall and over my shoulder like a skinny, flesh-toned anaconda. I whipped around, and sure enough, Flex was there, standing in the middle of the living room in his boxers. From where he stood, I realized he had thrown the punch an impressive thirty feet or more. As his arm swiftly snapped back, regaining its normal length and shape instantly, he pointed his index finger like the barrel of a gun.

"You."

He was pointing at Tad. He met Flex's fierce gaze with his mouth ajar. A line of red connected his bloody nose and cut lip.

"Get out of here before I throw you down the stairs," said Flex.

Tad was shaking as he staggered hastily to his feet. "Freaks!" he said. "All of you! You'll be sorry. Just wait. You'll be sorry!"

With that, he took off down the stairs.

Rather than lowering his hand, Flex's pointed finger shifted to me. "You. Get in here. Now."

Flex may have looked like a drunk hippie with his clumpy dreadlocks, scraggly face, and gangly build, but right now, he was a pissed off drunk hippie. I bit my lip and reluctantly stepped inside.

"Hey," said Mia. She shifted from one foot to the other as I turned around and met her gaze, tucking a lock of blonde hair behind her ear. "Thank you." Her timid gaze shifted to Flex. "Both of you."

"Stop dating douche bags, Mia," said Flex. With that, his arm shot across the living room and slammed the door shut behind me.

I watched his elastic arm as it snapped back into place. He then proceeded to fold his arms with a stern gaze.

Hey, at least he wasn't passed out in his room, right? And he actually looked halfway sober now.

"What was that?" asked Flex.

"That jerk hit her," I said. "I was just trying to help."

"Trying to help," said Flex. "That's interesting. Because to me, it looked like a twelve-year-old brat nearly getting shanked outside my apartment."

"I'm fourteen," I grumbled.

"I don't care if you're a hundred and fifty-two," said Flex. "What you did was stupid."

I bit my lip, struggling to keep a calm face. I could feel the irritation boiling hot. "I had everything under control."

"Starting a fight outside *my* apartment is not keeping things under control," said Flex. "What happens when that punk brings all his punk friends over to start a fight?"

"What, are you afraid?" I asked. "I could take that punk and all his friends by myself. I don't need you."

"Oh yeah?" he said, raising an amused eyebrow. "And was getting stabbed part of your plan?"

"I had it under control," I repeated.

"You haven't even hit puberty yet," said Flex. "You don't have anything under control."

"At least I'm not some drunk wasting away my power," I said.

Flex rolled his eyes. His casual reaction just made me even angrier. He didn't appear insulted at all.

"And you're just an annoying little brat that I have to babysit," he said in a bored tone. "Now if you don't mind, I'm going to go back to bed. I'd like to wake up to my hangover in peace and quiet."

"That's it?" I said. A hint of despair crept into my tone. "You're just going to go back to your room and pass out again? Don't you care about anything?"

"Yeah," said Flex. "I care about sleeping. Now if you don't mind . . ."

Flex shuffled back to his bedroom. I found his lack of anger alarming. It was like he wasn't really alive. Like he was a zombie or something.

Just an empty thing without a soul.

CHAPTER 8

Worst night's sleep of my life. Ever.

I crashed on the couch, which I discovered had a spring sticking up somewhere underneath the middle cushion. I tried to sleep around it, but that only resulted in me shifting my position a million and a half times. When I finally awoke to daylight, I had a crick in my neck and an ache in my shoulder. I felt like I was a hundred and fifty-two years old.

It took several long seconds for my senses to register the dramatic music in the background. The grunts and smacks of fake punches and kicks. Buttons being mashed repeatedly.

I rolled over to find Flex playing a video game.

Not just playing. Like . . . he was seriously into it. His eyes were fixated, and his thumbs were moving faster than an army of texting teenage girls. He sat cross-legged, hunched over, with his face way too close to the TV screen, like a little kid on Saturday morning. But at least he had clothes on—sweat pants, a ratty old cutoff t-shirt, and a beanie pulled tight over his dreadlocks.

Okay, so video games were hardly the pinnacle of ambition, but at least this was a step up from yesterday. And it was nice to actually see him passionate about something.

"Whatcha playing?" I asked, forcing perhaps a tad too much enthusiasm in my tone in an attempt to compensate for yesterday. It was then that I glanced past the back of his head and noticed a certain caped crusader stringing punches through a group of thugs. "Batman?"

"Arkham Origins," said Flex in a half-trance.

He removed one hand from the controller only to reach for his can of Mountain Dew Code Red. He took a quick sip and returned to the fight.

I blinked incredulously and glanced back and forth between Flex and the TV screen. I didn't know if he could see the horrible irony here, but it was almost too much for me to take.

"You're a Superhero . . . and you're playing a Superhero video game?" I said

"Uh . . . yeah. It's Batman," he said.

"But you're a *Superhero*," I said, putting extra emphasis on the "super" part. "I mean . . . Batman doesn't even have a superpower!"

"Batman doesn't need a superpower," said Flex. "He's Batman."

Someone desperately needed to inform Flex that Batman's name alone was not the ultimate justification of the universe. I sighed. But maybe I could use this to my advantage.

"What's so great about Batman?" I asked.

Flex stumbled with the controls. Batman fell as two clowns simultaneously pummeled him into the ground. Flex seemed to take the defeat reasonably well as his attention shifted to me.

"Are you kidding me?" asked Flex. "He's Batman. Everything's great about him."

I officially felt like I was having a conversation with a seven-year-old.

"I mean . . . Batman is like a symbol of justice," he said. "He always sacrifices for the greater good. It doesn't matter that he doesn't have a superpower. If he sees something that needs to be done, he does it. If that's not a hero, I don't know what is."

Okay, now we were getting somewhere.

"So . . . does Batman inspire you to be a better Superhero?" I asked. It was a stupid question, I'll admit. But right now, it seemed like the only way of getting through Flex's rubber skull.

Flex had already started navigating through the menu to start a new game. He halted the moment the word "Superhero" came out of my mouth. Setting his controller down, he scooted around on his butt to face me.

"Let me tell you something about Superheroes," he said. His tone was dead serious. "They don't believe in fighting for justice. They believe in getting famous. Once they make it big and score a big advertising deal, it's just a job to them. They're celebrities. They save the world so they can maintain their popularity so they can make more money."

"Well . . . I mean . . . they have to support themselves somehow," I said.

"It's not about supporting themselves," said Flex. "They're greedy. And they're corruptible. Did you know that forty-two percent of every Superhero ever recorded has gone bad? Forty-two percent! That's almost half of us! And thirty-nine percent of those are FIST graduates. Why do you think that is, Minnow?"

My expression went flat. "It's Marrow."

"Yeah, whatever."

I pushed my pride aside, wanting desperately to respond back with something smart. I had nothing. Forty-two percent? I didn't realize the percentage was that high. Especially the thirty-nine percent that were FIST graduates. I mean . . . FIST *drilled* justice into our heads. It wasn't just about fighting. It was about morals. And if we ever joked about it, then Havoc would, in the immortal words of Dwayne "The Rock" Johnson, "layeth the smacketh down."

"You know what it is?" asked Flex. "It's power. Power makes people go bad. You give someone a little bit of it, and all they want is more."

I opened my mouth to respond, but I had nothing. Every word pierced like a needle. Not because this was suddenly some big epiphany. Not because I suddenly believed every word he said.

It was because I personally knew a Superhero-gone-bad. One that many referred to as the most infamous Supervillain of all time.

My father.

His name was Spine. He was the only Supervillain ever to have eluded Fantom. For this reason, many considered him Fantom's arch nemesis. Even though he had disappeared, it was likely that he was still out there. Somewhere.

"What about Fantom?" I asked. The confidence in my argument had become notably hollow.

"Fantom doesn't believe in justice," said Flex. "What's the point of a judicial system if he kills every villain he fights?"

"But . . . but they're evil, aren't they?" I said.

Flex didn't respond. Instead, he stood up and chugged the remainder of his Mountain Dew and then crushed the aluminum can against his head. It looked like he was about to toss it on the floor when his wandering gaze suddenly scoured the living area.

"You cleaned up?" asked Flex.

I sincerely hoped that he wasn't just now noticing it. "Yeah," I said.

"Why'd you do that? I had everything where I wanted it."

He threw the crushed can at the waste bin; instead of going in the bin, it bounced off the side and hit the floor. Flex sighed and started for his bedroom. I perked up at this familiar sight.

"What are you doing?" I asked.

Flex stretched out his lanky arms, tilted his head back, and yawned. "Going to bed."

"Again?" I said. "How much do you sleep?"

"Not nearly enough," said Flex. I couldn't tell if he was joking or serious.

"What am I supposed to do?" I asked.

"I don't care. Go knit a sweater or something."

"You should care," I said. "I'm your sidekick. You're supposed to be my mentor."

"Go play Batman."

"I'm not playing freaking Batman."

"Your loss," said Flex with a shrug. He stepped into his bedroom and shut the door.

I wasn't about to let a door stop me this time. I burst through, slamming the door against the wall in the process.

Flex whipped around, daggers in his glare. "The heck do you think you're doing?"

"You know, Whisp had all these good things to say about you," I said "And for a second, I almost believed him. I thought, 'You know, maybe—just maybe—I have some super cool mentor that nobody knew about.' But no . . . you're just a washed up nobody who doesn't want to be anybody. I don't know what the heck he sees in you."

"Well Whisp always has nice things to say about everybody," said Flex, rolling his eyes. "I'm sure he'd say something nice about you even though you're a self-inflated, annoying little buttmonkey. Now get lost."

"I'm not leaving here until you start training me," I said.

"If you don't get out of my room, I'll kick your butt inside out!" Flex snapped.

"Good!" I said. "Fighting you is better training than sitting around your crappy apartment."

Flex's nostrils flared. After standing rigid for several long seconds, he marched around his bed and retrieved a letter from the nightstand—the same letter that Havoc had given him. He then threw it at me like a Chinese throwing star. I managed to catch it before it could veer off course and flutter to the floor. I was surprised to find that the envelope had already been torn open.

"There," said Flex. He tossed himself on the bed in exasperation. "Go knock yourself out."

I raised the envelope from the corner like some dead creature. "What am I supposed to do with this?"

"Our first mission assignment is in there," Flex grumbled. "Go without me. It's a one-man job anyway."

I stared absently at the envelope in my hands. Blinking myself back to reality, I fumbled to remove the letter inside. "They already assigned us a mission?"

"Uh . . . yeah. Duh. Every newly-teamed Superhero and sidekick get assigned their first mission in advance. Didn't you go to the Teaming Ceremony?"

Ah. That explained it. I was probably puking my guts out during that important tidbit of information.

"And we're responding to this mission a day late?" I don't know why I even bothered pointing this out. It was obvious Flex didn't care either way.

"Yeah, well on a scale of one to ten, I'd say the urgency of this mission ranks a negative eleven. You know Oracle?"

"Yeah, who doesn't?"

"Well apparently she *thinks* someone is snooping outside her place," said Flex. His assurance was underwhelming. "She reported it to the Guild, and now they want us to check it out."

I removed two folded up sheets of paper from the envelope. The first was a corny congratulatory letter informing Flex that he would be training a sidekick. This included a list of qualities expected in a Superhero trainer. (Basically a list of everything Flex wasn't. I refrained from pointing this out.) The second page outlined a mission that was labeled as "Top Secret." It then proceeded to retell the mission exactly as Flex had explained, but managed to stretch it into four long paragraphs, ending with Oracle's address and basic directions to her house.

"You happy?" said Flex. "Will you leave me alone now?"

I could definitely see why Flex didn't want to go. It was a belittling excuse for a mission. Like asking the Crocodile Hunter to help get a cat out of a tree because he's good with animals. But what else was there to do?

Still, it felt weird going by myself.

"You sure you don't want to go?" I asked, hopeful.

"I would rather glue acorns to my naked body and be eaten alive by an army of rabid squirrels." With that said, he rolled over face-first into his pillow, emphasizing that the conversation was over.

"Okay," I said, nodding. "I'll take that as a no."

CHAPTER 9

Oracle's house was only a twenty-minute walk from Flex's place. And I use the term "house" loosely. It was wedged awkwardly between two apartment buildings, standing slightly crooked, as if it had been transported mysteriously off the set of a Tim Burton film. It looked like it might collapse without the support of the neighboring structures. However, it did surprisingly have a front lawn, encompassed by a rickety picket fence. The fence had once been white, but the paint was now cracked and peeling like dead skin after a sunburn. It might have seemed like a peaceful place were it not for the construction site across the street. Bulldozers groaned and rumbled across the dirt clearing while jackhammers rattled against shattered concrete. As equally troublesome were the picketing signs surrounding Oracle's house that had been left after months of protesting. Signs like "Stay out of my brain," or "Only God should read minds," or my personal favorite, "I already have enough voices inside my head."

For the most part, Supers have been extremely welcomed by society. However, Telepaths (as well as Omnipotents before they went extinct) were the glaring exception. Though the Guild pushed for equality among all Supers, people in general didn't like the idea of someone who could go inside your head. They claimed it was "unconstitutional." The Anti-Telepathy Movement had been going on for ages, and Oracle—being the most powerful living Telepath—was the centerpiece of their protesting. Unfortunately for the protesters, Oracle had been nothing but helpful whenever the government requested her assistance. Her services had been requested during multiple national security threats. For that reason alone, I seriously doubted that Telepaths were going anywhere.

I unhooked the rusty gate latch and pushed it open. The hinges groaned in protest. The floorboards of the porch were no less disagreeable, squealing under my weight. I barely had time to knock as the door was swiftly opened. There stood Oracle, hunched ever so slightly, wearing a knitted purple shawl and an ugly gray dress that looked more like a parachute than a piece of clothing. Her frizzy gray hair billowed out, outlining her wrinkled features. And then there were those eyes—pure white like milky marbles. Those eyes seemed to see nowhere and everywhere all at once.

"I knew you would be coming," said Oracle in her warm, grand-motherly tone. "Come in, Marrow. I've just made tea."

What did I expect paying a surprise visit to a Telepath?

I followed Oracle into her cramped cottage. Just as I remembered, she smelled like mothballs and boiled cabbage. This time, however, I detected a hint of garlic as well.

It had been five years since my last (and only) visit to Oracle. I was eight years old when she summoned me to her home, spoke to me of my surfacing power, and helped me understand my potential. This was a typical ritual for most Super children. Oracle's matriarchal one-on-one meeting with each child had become a staple of Super culture.

The inside of her home was exactly as I had remembered it. To one side, the wall was lined with bookshelves and a vast library of dusty hardbacks. On the opposite side, newspaper articles were pinned to a wall-encompassing map of Cosmo City with connecting lines drawn and notes written in red ink. It was the sort of conspiracy theory décor I would expect to see in the home of a paranoid schizophrenic. It appeared especially out of place with the flowery throw blankets draped over the nearby armchair and sofa and the lacy doilies on the coffee table and nightstand.

Eight-year-old, not-so-prodigious Marrow had once asked why she decorated the place—and *how* she decorated it!—if she was blind.

Oracle had merely smiled and replied, "You don't always need eyes to see. Some of the blindest people I know have both eyes and can see just perfectly." From that point on, I decided to take the precious opportunity to shut my food hole. The conspiracy diagram still didn't make sense for a blind person, but I could only assume that her telepathic power somehow gave her a sixth sense in that regard.

I approached the eerie wall. Upon closer inspection, I realized it was outlining several Supervillains still on the loose and their recent crime scenes.

Spine was the oldest villain on the map, and his face was plastered all over it. I hastily redirected my attention.

Of course, scattered all over the place, Oracle's two dozen cats were lounging on nearly every flat surface. One particular gray tabby arched its back and hissed at me from the carpet.

"Maximus, you know better than to hiss at our guests," said Oracle, waving a scolding finger.

Maximus slouched his shoulders and seemed to shrug indifferently as he wandered off.

"Have a seat, Marrow."

I sank into the couch. Oracle disappeared into the kitchen and, sure enough, returned with a tray of tea cups. I generally didn't drink tea, and she didn't bother asking me what I liked. She already knew. Handing me my cup, I sipped a rich, icy tang of peppermint. Meanwhile, she set the tray down, leaned back in her plush armchair, and sipped from her own cup with a look of utter euphoria.

"Ah, honey vanilla chamomile," she sighed her satisfaction.

I took another sip from my cup, unsure of how to proceed. How do you ask a question to someone who most likely already knows what you're going to ask?

"I know what you're thinking," said Oracle. "You're wondering why a renowned telepath such as myself would need help dealing with someone snooping around my place. Why I can't just report the person directly to the police."

See? Didn't even need to ask. Not only was it exactly what I was wondering, but in a lot less words. I nodded and only afterward realized how pointless this acknowledgment was.

"The answer is really quite simple," she said, "and yet perplexing at the same time. This person that's snooping around my place is invisible to me."

"But . . . you're blind," I said. "I mean . . . I thought you sensed this person telepathically. What does it matter if they can go invisible?"

"I don't mean physically invisible," said Oracle, shaking her frizzy head. "I mean invisible to the mind's eye."

I blinked, confused more than ever now.

"I heard someone walking outside the house," she said in response to my silence. "Whoever it was didn't feel the need to be especially quiet about it. Not that they needed to. This person, as far as I can tell, is completely immune to my telepathy."

I raised a disconcerted eyebrow. "Immune? Is that even possible?"

"In very few instances, yes. A Telepath more powerful than myself would have the ability to block me. However, I have my doubts that a Telepath could have accumulated so much power and gone unnoticed until now."

"How else can someone be immune to telepathy?" I asked.

Oracle shrugged beneath her shawl. "It depends. Certain powers have unexpected side-effects when it comes to mind powers. For example, I think you'd be interested to know that your trainer is immune to my power."

"My trainer?" I repeated questioningly. "Flex?"

Oracle simply smiled and nodded.

"But . . . how?" I asked. "He's rubber. How does that make him immune?"

"Well, saying he's rubber is not quite accurate," she said. "Flex's body is composed of purely-biological particles that have a natural elasticity. Not just his flesh and bones, but his organs as well. That includes his brain. Somehow, because his brain is made of a different material than ours, my telepathic senses literally bounce right off it. I couldn't read his mind any more than I could read an animal's. And heaven knows I would pay big money to read Maximus's mind."

Oracle chuckled to herself. I was having a difficult time sharing her sense of humor.

"What if it's Flex?" I asked.

"Flex?" Oracle repeated. "Snooping around my place? Oh, I highly doubt that."

"But he fits the description, right? And he only lives like ten blocks away."

"He fits the qualifications, I suppose. But heaven help that boy if he had a single motivation left in the world. He has no reason to spy on me. He may be a bit of a bum, but he has a good heart."

I snorted my irritation at this response. "Well he sure seems to have a thing against Superheroes."

"Flex wasn't always like that," said Oracle. "Once upon a time, he was one of the best. His grades at FIST were some of the highest the school had ever seen. He achieved top scores in the Sidekick Internship Program as well. And when he became a full-fledged Superhero, he was one of the best."

I rolled my eyes. "Right."

"Oh, you don't believe me?" asked Oracle. "I'll have you know that Flex single-handedly intercepted twenty-nine armed robberies. He defeated seven powerful Supervillains. He even saved one hundred and thirty-one passengers from a train on an elevated railway that nearly derailed, stretching across the front like a bungee cord. In all my days, I've never ever heard of anything like that."

I couldn't tell if Oracle was telling the truth, or if she was just senile. The Flex she was describing certainly wasn't the sorry excuse for a hero that I was teamed up with.

"So what happened?" I asked, almost challengingly.

Oracle's expression became solemn. "Someone he cared for turned on him."

"Turned on him?"

"Went evil," said Oracle. "Became a full-fledged villain."

I was speechless. "Oh," was the only word that escaped my mouth. Suddenly, Flex's Superheroes-gone-bad rant made a lot more sense. He had seen it happen firsthand. I didn't want to know who it was. I knew too much already.

Flex was not so different from me.

"So if it's not Flex, do you have any other idea who the snoop might be?" I asked.

I detected the slightest hint of fear in her wavering milky eyes. "There's only one other living being I know who had a natural immunity to my telepathy."

"Who?"

Oracle pursed her lips in a straight line. "Your father. Spine."

CHAPTER 10

Oracle's words pierced my gut and twisted my insides like a fork in spaghetti.

"My father?" I said, breathless.

Leaning forward, the withered old woman set her cup on the coffee table. She interlocked her knobby fingers, contemplating her next words.

"You haven't seen him," said Oracle. This was not a question. Then again, she didn't need to ask questions. She could see straight into my brain.

"Of course I haven't seen him," I said. "He's a sadistic psychopath. Why would I have seen him?"

Oracle did not respond right away. She continued to stare at me for several long seconds before leaning back in her armchair. Whatever was going on inside her head, she clearly wasn't satisfied. I was swallowed in a realization that singed my nerves.

"Is that the reason I'm here?" I asked. "So you could look inside my brain and see if I was in cahoots with my old man?"

"I never assumed you were in *cahoots* with anyone," said Oracle. "But I couldn't leave any possibility unchecked. If Spine really has returned, there was a possibility that he might have shown himself to you. I had to make sure."

Suddenly, I felt violated, knowing that Oracle had probed my brain. Sure she had done it once before, but that was to determine the nature of my power. I didn't like being interrogated, even if I was oblivious to it.

"So that's it," I said. "That was my mission. Come over here so you could poke around inside my head." I could barely contain my irritation. Even when I was trying to make the most of my crappy situation, I was being manipulated.

"I know how you feel, Marrow," said Oracle. "But that's not the only reason you're here. I need your help with something else."

I bit my lip, fighting back a surge of cynicism. "Oh yeah?" I grumbled. "What's that?"

"I need you to bring Flex here. I need to speak with him."

Great. The most menial task in the world, which also happened to be the most impossible. Something snapped inside of me. I wanted to throw my hands in the air in exasperation. I wanted to pull my hair out. I wanted to scream. I had worked so hard to be the best at FIST, only to get shafted by that cheating scumbag, Nero. Yeah, I was cocky, but I deserved to train with Fantom! I earned it! And now here I was, nothing but a messenger boy, and apparently the untrustworthy son of a Supervillain who needed to have his thoughts examined by a brain-hacking Telepath.

But instead of saying any of those things out loud, I laughed.

This wasn't a normal laugh. There was nothing funny about it. In fact, a part of me wanted to break down and cry like a big, fat baby. The result was the sort of maniacal laugh you'd expect from some sort of whack job in a straitjacket.

"Is something funny?" Oracle asked. Her expression was neither shocked nor irritated by my bizarre reaction. I was reminded again that she could still see directly inside my head. I could only imagine what a mess it looked like inside there.

"Oh, no, no, no, no, no," I said, shaking my head overzealously. "Why would something be funny? You're only asking me to fetch the one lazy bum who doesn't listen to a single freaking thing I say!"

My voice amplified with every word until I was practically shouting.

Again, Oracle seemed unfazed. In fact, her tight-pressed mouth loosened with the slightest hint of sympathy.

"Marrow, can I show you something?"

Breathing in through my nose, I attempted to calm myself. My wild-eyed hysterics lowered a notch. "Show me what?"

"I'm not just a Telepath," said Oracle. "Sometimes I see things. Dreams. Prophetic images. Glimpses of the future."

Standing upright—as far as her back would allow—Oracle stepped around the coffee table and approached me. She then sat down beside me on the couch.

"Would you like to see my most recent premonition?"

I didn't know what to say. I'd never heard of Oracle showing anyone anything of the sort. In theory, this sounded like the opportunity of a lifetime. But how exactly did she intend to show it to me? Better yet, did I even *want* to see what she had to show me? I was starting to feel genuinely weirded out.

So naturally, I said, "Okay."

Oracle reached forward and placed a clammy, withered hand on my forehead. "Now don't wig out," she said. "This is going to feel a little—"

Her sentence never finished. But it *felt* like I was being folded inside out as Oracle's bookshelves and conspiracy theory décor suddenly swirled together in a raging vortex of color. It was like a Skittle volcano exploding through the eye of a tornado, and I was right in the middle of it. My body felt like Jell-O being sucked through a vacuum cleaner, but as far as my uncontrolled vision could see, I didn't seem to have a body anymore.

All at once, the color flashed into a solid image—a shocking, surreal image, just as epic as it was horrific.

I was back inside Oracle's house—at least what used to be her house. The place was ravaged to ruins. Furniture was thrashed and broken, and fragile decorations were shattered. An entire wall had been blown wide open, leaving a gaping, jagged hole of broken planks and splinters. A hazy, smoldering view of the blood-streaked evening sky glowed from the other side, accompanied by the red and blue flash of police lights.

Bodies were littered all over the floor, contorted in awkward, limp angles. Motionless.

Two dark figures stood opposite each other like shadows in a mirror. One I recognized instantly. Every muscle was accentuated in a red and black bodysuit. A simple, black mask obscured the top half of his sculpted, masculine face. A crimson cape trailed behind him like fire.

Fantom.

The other figure was even bigger, but lacked the sleekness. Thick, dark hair erupted from his scalp, long and knotted, meeting his beard like the mane of a lion. He wore a heavy, black coat over his hairy bare chest. His ripped and tattered pants were tucked into army boots that seemed capable of crushing a human skull. His gloves were ripped off at the fingers, exposing dirty, chipped fingernails like claws. The most terrifying feature, however, was his eyes. They were crisp and blue, like a tropic ocean bleached by the noonday sun.

They were my eyes.

My father's eyes.

Spine.

His power was like mine, but with an addition that had scary possibilities. This was made manifest as he raised both fists and sharp bones spiked out of his knuckles. This was just *one* of the nearly limitless ways in which Spine was notorious for manipulating his bone structure.

I barely remembered my father, but this dark stranger seemed nothing like that distant memory. My father was merely a dream. This monster was reality.

My bizarre, fixed perspective zoomed out as the two men charged each other, fists pulled back. The image was bending . . . distorting . . . rounding. The scene was soon captured within a sphere, discoloring to a sharp tint of blue. The center was dotted black, and white encompassed the blue.

It was an eye. My eye.

I zoomed out on my face, bruised heavily on the right side, with deep cuts over my right eyebrow and lip. I was sprawled belly-first on the floor. Flex was lying behind the cut and bruised version of me. His battered form observed the scene in wide-eyed horror.

A white light flashed and then dimmed to a dark, cluttered living room. I was staring at Oracle's empty eyes now. Her hand was still on my forehead.

I blinked. I was back.

Oracle pulled her hand away and rested it in her lap. She didn't speak or even smile. Apparently I wasn't the only one disturbed by what I had just seen.

"What was that?" I finally managed to ask.

"Exactly what it looks like," said Oracle. Her face was grim. "A battle that looms over our future. And apparently it happens in my house and both you and Flex are there to witness it."

There were so many questions racing around my skull, I could barely focus. But one managed to escape my mouth, as the image was the most fresh in my mind.

"All those people . . ." I said, breathless. "Were they . . . ?" I couldn't bring myself to say it. The word was like acid, burning my thoughts.

Oracle's face remained expressionless. "I don't know."

So many people . . . What were they all doing in Oracle's house? The lingering image sent shards of ice into my skin.

Oracle cleared her throat after I failed to say anything. "Your father . . ."

"Don't call him that," I snapped. I couldn't fight the defensive edge to my tone. "He's not my father. Not anymore."

"I'm sorry," said Oracle with an understanding nod. "Spine, like you, has the ability to alter his bone matter. After much practice, he has mastered a very particular type of bone matter in his skull that prevents my telepathy from reaching his brain. It's not so different than the way Flex's elasticity deflects my power. And after my recent premonition, I cannot ignore the possibility that Spine was the one outside my home."

"Why?" I asked. "Why snoop around your place and not do anything? It doesn't make any sense."

"There's much of this whole situation that doesn't make sense," said Oracle. "But Flex was a part of this premonition also. That is why I need you to bring him here."

"But you can't even read his mind," I said.

"I don't need to read his mind," said Oracle. There was solid assurance in her grandmotherly voice. "Flex will tell me everything that I need to know."

I wasn't in the mood to challenge her. My mental capacity for arguing was maxed out. But that didn't change one slightly significant question.

How the heck was I going to get him here?

Even with everything I had seen and heard, it didn't change the fact that Flex was still the most stubborn bum in the universe. I stood a better chance of convincing him to wear a bear costume and hibernate for the winter. Actually, he might accept that challenge willingly.

Oracle stood up from the couch and shuffled over to the long line of bookshelves. It wasn't until she reached the end that I realized that a small section in the corner was a solid shelf of black. They were VHS tapes. Though her eyes couldn't see, she ran a knobby finger across the tapes before stopping at a particular cassette. She removed it and cradled it gently in her veiny hands. For a brief moment, she appeared lost in thought. After a few long seconds, her head perked back up and she wandered into the kitchen. She was gone for only a moment. When she returned, she held a manila envelope in the other hand. Slipping the videotape inside, Oracle licked it shut and handed it to me.

"You give this to Flex," said Oracle, "and he will come."

CHAPTER 11

I didn't realize how long I'd been gone. As I left Oracle's crooked house, the sun was already sinking behind the sharp-edged horizon. Skyscrapers stabbed into the painted orange sky like razorblades. My eyes drifted down to the package in my hands.

There was no message or even a name on the manila envelope. What the heck was this thing? How was a stupid videotape supposed to get Flex to leave his apartment?

I wondered if the cassette had any sort of label on it. If Oracle hadn't licked the envelope and sealed it shut, I would have looked already. Would Flex notice or even care if I ripped it open? It wasn't like he was expecting a package from Oracle. I could just hand him the tape without the envelope, right? He'd never know better.

As much as I justified it in my mind, something outweighed my curiosity. I didn't even know what it was. Unusual, since my curiosity almost always prevailed.

I tucked the package into my jacket, out of sight. Hopefully out of mind.

My eyes grazed a man in a business suit removing a paper from a clunky metal newspaper dispenser. As he vanished into the crowds, I immediately recognized the two faces on the front page of the newspaper in his hand—each glaringly recognizable.

Fantom and Nero.

I nearly tripped on my own feet. After stumbling, flinging my arms out desperately for balance, and nearly running into half a dozen people at once, I regained my balance. Weaving frantically against the current of people, I broke free of the crowds. Then I hunched down for an eye-level view of the newspaper dispenser.

Sure enough, it was Fantom and Nero. Fantom looked as epic and daring as he always did, fists at his sides, chest puffed out, and sporting a toothpaste-ad smile. Surprisingly, Nero wasn't sporting the cocky smirk I would have expected. His mouth was a straight line, and his eyes stared off into some invisible point in space. Maybe Nero wasn't happy being Fantom's sidekick after all.

As much as I wanted to relish his unexcited expression, the newspaper headline had to go and ruin it for me:

FANTOM AND NEW SIDEKICK, NERO, CAPTURE FLAME-WIELDING VILLAIN, TORCHER, AND UNVEIL THE CRONUS

Cosmo City – Fantom has done it again and in true hero fashion. Notorious Supervillain, Torcher, created a stir Thursday morning when he literally "opened fire" on a gas tanker truck. The tanker exploded, injuring the driver and seven other motorists and passengers on the highway. Torcher proceeded to set fire to multiple vehicles, but was intercepted in record time by Fantom who happened to be training his new sidekick, Nero, nearby.

Literally flying onto the scene, Fantom used his super speed and strength to immobilize Torcher in minutes while Nero—via telekinesis—twisted a nearby guardrail around him in order to secure him. For the first time in Fantom's crime-fighting history, the world-renowned Superhero delivered a Supervillain to the CCPD rather than killing him in action. Despite his fame, Fantom has been under scrutiny for years for his violent tactics. When asked if this sudden change was

due to his training a new sidekick, Fantom responded that it was much bigger than that. He restated his distrust that Cosmo City's correctional facilities are equipped to handle an able-powered Super, let alone the dozens that he has faced over the past year alone. However, his capture of Torcher became a springboard for the unveiling of a revolution in radioactive technology—the Cronus Cannon.

Ever since the impact of the Gaia Comet and the birth of the Supers, Fantom has demonstrated immense interest in the science behind Gaia's alien radioactivity. Thus was born the Tartarus—a unique underwater research facility designed to further study the properties of Gaia's point of impact. At the heart of the Tartarus and the scientists' experimentation is the Cronus. Fantom announced that the Cronus Cannon is a machine that utilizes Gaia's energy to remove a Super's power. In essence, it acts as a reversal of the comet's radioactive mutation. The Cronus, says Fantom, is the solution to Supervillainy. Although the government has yet to approve such a correctional method, Fantom feels confident that it is only a matter of time until it is approved.

"The power of a Super is a gift," said Fantom in a recent interview. "If that power is abused, then it needs to be taken away. I believe the day will come when the title 'Super' will actually live up to its meaning."

Indeed, that day may soon come. Until then, Torcher's uncertain fate hangs in the balance. Torcher is yet another Superhero-gone-bad. It is presumed that his moral spiral began when his brother was mugged and killed last fall. Over the ensuing months, Torcher has been responsible for numerous arson-based crimes. He certainly seems the perfect candidate for the Cronus.

When newcomer, Nero, was asked what he thought of working with Fantom as well as this revolutionary new development from the Tartarus, he said, "Fantom is great, and the Cronus is what we need. I know a fellow FIST classmate that could use a good zap from it."

Nero is training with Fantom for the summer as one of the most promising young . . . (Continued on page 7.)

I wanted to throw up.

I couldn't process what I had just read. Tartarus? Cronus Cannon? What did it matter?

All I cared about was pushing Nero off a very steep cliff. Preferably into a chasm with jagged rocks below. Shark-infested waters were a plus.

I pulled my gaze away from the front page story. I had to walk away before I ripped the newspaper dispenser out of the concrete. The crowds were still thick on the sidewalk. My excitement for being in Cosmo City was dying. I was hardly claustrophobic, but being around this many people was making me nauseous.

I decided on a shortcut through an adjacent alley. At least, I hoped it was a shortcut. If it continued through, it could very well cut my trip in half. Veering out of the herd of people, I merged into the open alleyway. I stretched my elbows with a renewed sense of freedom.

Despite the shadows, the neon graffiti seemed to glow on the brick walls. Most of the graffiti spelled words, but the outlandish designs made them about as simple to read as Chinese. These bright messages were instantly contrasted by grimy litter strewn on the floor, murky puddles, and an occasional cockroach scurrying from my presence. The only dumpster in sight was already filled to the brim.

What a lovely detour. If this turned out *not* to be a shortcut, I might punch a wall and smash my way through.

I rounded the corner and was thankful to see an end to the alley and moving traffic beyond. Thank freaking goodness. I pulled my jacket tight, securing the package, and walked faster.

A silhouetted figure stepped into the alley, blocking my way.

I halted. Not that size had ever bothered me before. If some thug wanted to pick a fight with me, so be it. I hoped he had good health insurance.

My train of thought shattered as several footsteps echoed behind me, splashing carelessly through the puddles. I whipped around. There were almost a dozen of them—punk kids that looked like they were in their late teens or even early twenties, some with Mohawks, others wearing spikes. One even had so many piercings in his face he resembled a pincushion. All of them were armed with crowbars, chains, or aluminum baseball bats. At their lead was a familiar face with a shaved head, sad excuse for a goatee, tank top, and sleeve tattoos. His lip was puffed out and shiny where Flex had decked him in the face.

"I told you you'd be sorry," said Tad, sneering. He flipped out his switchblade.

My stance tensed, but I refused to let any intimidation show. If these punks were half as stupid as Tad, this would be an easy fight.

"Bring it, turdbucket," I said.

"Oh, no, we're just here to enjoy the show," said Tad. He pointed his switchblade past me. "We have a freak of our own. *He's* the one who's gonna hurt you."

My stomach sank. I turned to find that the large man on the opposite end of the alley was approaching. Light spilled across his gargantuan frame. His face was uglier than my butt—this huge, disproportioned thing with beady eyes, a bulbous nose, and teeth like a horse. Mutton-chop sideburns extend well past his large ears, engulfing his cheeks. Though his legs were thick and sturdy, his hairy arms were just as large, weighing his upper half down like a gorilla, barely contained in a trench coat.

I could hear Tad's grin grow wider behind me. "Meet Nightmare. He's going to hurt you."

I wasn't about to be caught off guard. I tapped into my bone structure, and my feet became clouds, barely touching the ground. When Nightmare made his move, I would be ready to strike back.

Nightmare didn't move. In fact, he didn't even seem to be looking at me. His beady eyes shifted past me, gazing further down the alley.

"Hey, Nightmare what the freak are you waiting for?" said Tad. "We aren't paying you to stand there and look stupid."

Nightmare's ugly-as-butt face didn't flinch. "I didn't come here for your money."

At that moment, one of the gang members screamed—Pincushion Face. He backed away from the others, wide-eyed and swinging his baseball bat frantically.

"What the . . . ?"

"Hey, man, what are you—?"

Another gang member cried out. And then another. In a matter of seconds, the entire gang had suddenly become a psyche ward, shrieking and swinging weapons at invisible forces. Tad was practically sobbing as he dropped his switch blade and took off down the alley.

A shadow fell over the alleyway, accompanied by a screech that reverberated throughout the skies. My shocked gaze darted heavenward. The clear sky had become a churning pool of billowing darkness. However, no storm could have been nearly as frightening as the flock of winged creatures circling above. One particular creature swooped low, bug-eyed, open-jawed, and baring a crowded mouthful of razor teeth. The winged monster might have been a flying monkey if it had a single hair on its body. These creatures were more reptilian, their scaly skin glazed in a slimy residue.

A second shadow loomed over me from behind. No sooner had I spun around, than Nightmare grabbed the back of my head and brought a cloth to my mouth. My senses hardly had a moment to process the fumes before my world became a blur, and I slipped into nothingness.

CHAPTER 12

I woke up to blackness—cold, disorienting blackness. My head throbbed. A ticking sound resonated within my skull like the sound of a clock, but without any sense of rhythm.

Tick . . . tick tooock tick tick . . . tick tooock tooock tick . . .

The only thing that really assured me that I was awake was the itch from a bristly rope securing me to a cold, metal chair. The rope was tied so tight that my arms and legs had that prickly feeling you get when your blood stops circulating. I didn't even bother trying to break free. My power was useless without momentum. I tried shaking my chair. It didn't budge. It was clearly bolted to the floor.

The chair . . .

I had an idea. Tapping into my bone structure, I accumulated as much density as I could. The pressure of my butt on the seat intensified. My feet were cement blocks. My head felt like a boulder and was becoming nearly impossible to hold upright.

The chair didn't break like I'd hoped. It didn't even squeak under the pressure. It must have been made of solid steel.

I normalized my bone density with a gasping breath.

This was bad. This was really bad. Suddenly, being a prisoner in Flex's apartment didn't seem like such a terrible thing anymore.

Nightmare—that was the guy's name. It made sense. The darkness . . . all of those flying creatures . . . Tad and his trolls were freaking out at nothing before I saw what they were seeing. The creatures weren't real. It was just a nightmarish hallucination. At least I knew that Nightmare couldn't hurt me with his power.

Of course there were always the good, old fashioned methods of torture.

What did he want me for, anyway?

The answer was almost too obvious. It had to do with my father. I was sure of it. What else was I worth to anyone?

A pillar of light blinded me from above, buzzing loudly. Even as I squeezed my eyes shut, I could see flashing lights on the inside of my eyelids. I gradually squinted, peering through my eyelashes. The overhead stream of light was extremely concentrated, shining down on me in a perfect circle. I still couldn't see anything else in the room.

A door opened and closed behind me. Slow footsteps paced closer.

"Good morning, Marrow," said a deep, resonating voice. "Did you sleep well?"

Part of me wanted to spit out a witty insult. The other part of me was scared of what he'd do to me if I did. Not that I was in the right state of mind to come up with anything clever. I was too terrified out of my mind to even think.

"What do you want?" I asked. My voice was already trembling. Wanting to end this as soon as possible, I added, "I don't know where my father is, if that's what this is about. I haven't seen him in years."

Nightmare chuckled as he paced around my chair, stopping in front of me. His gorilla arms were clasped behind his back. His big teeth caused the lower half of his face to stick out. Accompanied by his thick, mutton-chop sideburns, he looked like a cast reject from *Planet of the Apes*.

"I already know where your father is," said Nightmare. "He's the one who arranged this little rendezvous."

I choked. I literally couldn't breathe. This guy was working with my dad? What the heck did my old man want with me? Somehow, I didn't think it was for a friendly father/son reunion. The chloroform and ropes didn't exactly hint at such a possibility.

When my lungs finally remembered how to inhale again, I could only manage a one-word response.

"Why?"

Nightmare smiled. And no, not in the friendly way. This was the sort of smile that would give little children psychological damage and years of therapy. No hallucinations necessary. He was just that ugly.

"I understand you met with Oracle," said Nightmare. "Mind telling me what you two were chatting about? That old bat doesn't invite just anyone to have tea with her."

I had absolutely no resolve to hold back information. Maybe it was because I didn't think it was all that valuable. Or maybe it was because I didn't want to experience the interrogative techniques of a modern-day Neanderthal.

"She told me someone was snooping around her house," I said. "Someone that she couldn't sense with her telepathy. And then she showed me a vision she had of Fantom and my dad. They were fighting."

"A vision of Fantom and Spine fighting," said Nightmare. "Interesting. Who won the fight?"

"Uh . . . I don't know," I said. "They actually hadn't started fighting yet. They were about to fight, I guess."

"And that's everything she told you?" Nightmare asked.

I racked my brain frantically. "Yeah. That's everything."

Nightmare licked his giant horse teeth behind his fat monkey lips. "Hmm. I don't believe you."

"W-w-w-what?" I said, sputtering. "No! No, I swear, I'm telling the truth. That's everything."

The cold, concrete floor suddenly became water—a dark, murky surface with no apparent bottom. Nightmare disappeared as I plunged downward. Water filled my mouth faster than I had a chance to realize what was happening. I tried to cough but gagged instead, staring in wide-eyed horror at the interrogation light rippling on the surface above. I was sinking fast, still strapped to my steel chair. Ten feet. Twenty feet. The water was becoming darker. Colder.

I was going to die.

Just when I thought my lungs couldn't take any more, I was back in the shadowy interrogation room. Nightmare was standing in the exact same spot he had been in only moments before. He wasn't smiling anymore.

"It's amazing how real pain can be in your mind, isn't it?" said Nightmare.

I found myself gasping for air, barely able to process what had just happened. A hallucination? *That* was a hallucination?

"Now are you ready to tell me everything?" asked Nightmare. "Or would you like to see what else I can do with my powers?"

My mind was spinning. Tell him everything? What else could I tell him? I'd already told him—

Wait. No, I hadn't. There was something else. I could've kicked myself. It was the main reason Oracle invited me over to begin with.

"I'll take your silence as a 'no,'" said Nightmare.

"No, wait, wait, wait, wait, wait!" I said. "There is something! I forgot something!"

Nightmare shifted his arms in front of him, grabbing his right wrist with his left hand. Waiting.

"Uh . . . I was there," I said, struggling to process my thoughts. "I mean . . . I was there in the vision. Flex was there too. We were both beat up pretty bad. That's why Oracle wanted to talk to us. She thinks we might be connected to this somehow. I dunno."

"That's everything?" said Nightmare. He raised a thick eyebrow, unconvinced.

"Um . . . no, there's something else," I said. "Oracle wanted me to give something to Flex. A videotape. She said if I showed it to him, Flex would come visit her."

As soon as I said this, I wondered if I was telling him something he already knew.

"Did you watch it already?" I asked. "The videotape?"

Nightmare responded with a glare that said, 'none of your stinkin' business.'

I responded with an apologetic, cowering look that said, 'Sorry I even asked.'

Nightmare continued to stare at me for several long seconds. I felt like I was waiting for a bomb to explode. Would it blow up? Maybe it wouldn't. Who knew!

"I don't believe you," said Nightmare.

"What?" I said. "You don't believe what?"

Nightmare didn't answer. Instead, I heard the grinding of machinery as the back of the room opened up behind me. I could tell because of the light pouring in and especially the sudden, violent gust of wind. The ground beneath me slanted at an increasing downward angle. My chair slid backwards down a long, metal ramp.

"Whoa, whoa, whoa, wait!" I cried.

Too late.

The ramp ended and I was suddenly freefalling through the sky. I was staring at the tail of a giant, gray airplane. It continued to soar into the billowing clouds as I plunged, falling at over a hundred miles per hour. I looked up at the plane until it was lost from sight. It was only then that I realized I was screaming my throat raw.

Calm down. Calm down. This was just another hallucination. This wasn't real.

I took a deep breath, which was actually kind of difficult with the whipping wind current around me. The toppling and spinning was making me dizzy. However, once my chair found a steady, aerodynamic position to descend, it actually wasn't that bad. Not nearly as bad as drowning. The splotchy green and brown landscape below me was really kind of beautiful . . . in a sick and twisted falling-to-your-death sort of way.

If this was just a hallucination, could I still communicate with Nightmare?

"Okay, you can bring me back now!" I shouted into the rushing sky. "Just tell me what you don't believe!"

No response. Only the howl of the wind. The ground below was growing considerably closer.

"Can you hear me?" I asked. Desperation was creeping into my voice. "C'mon! I know you can hear me!"

I could now see tiny details—individual trees, roads, power lines . . .

I closed my eyes. It was just a hallucination. I wouldn't hit the bottom. As long as I kept my eyes shut, everything would be just fine.

I kept falling. The anticipation of the *splat* was clawing beneath my skin.

Out of some sick reflex, my eyes opened.

Grassy green death rushed at me so fast, I barely had time to scream. By the time any sort of sound could escape my throat, I jerked violently and futilely against my restraining ropes, still tied to my bolted down steel chair.

Nightmare hadn't moved an inch.

Even though I could barely move my body, I could feel myself shaking. I had never trembled so hard in my entire life. I couldn't take another hallucination like that. It was too real.

I waited for Nightmare to speak. He said nothing. I wondered if he was even breathing. The guy was like a wax sculpture.

"Just tell me what you want to know," I said. "I'll tell you whatever you want."

Nightmare was silent for several long seconds. His expression didn't budge.

Finally, he shrugged his gorilla-sized shoulders. "You tell me what I want to know."

My mouth drifted ajar. Was this some sick kind of joke? This guy was certifiably insane.

"I don't know what you want," I said. "I'd tell you if I knew. I've told you everything that happened. Help me out here. Please!"

"You know," said Nightmare. "I know you know."

I shook my head frantically. "No! I don't know!"

"I don't believe you."

"What?" I said. I was ready to hyperventilate. "NO! No, no, no, no, no—!"

The overhead light shut off. But even without the light, I could tell the texture of the floor had changed. It was moving—a squirming, writhing mass. Hissing.

Something long and scaly flicked my ankle with its tongue and proceeded to slither up my leg.

Indiana Jones and I have three things in common. Good looks? Check. Unquenchable sense of adventure? Double check.

Snakes?

Triple check. Yeah. We're both terrified of snakes.

Giant rolling boulders, Nazis, and human-sacrificing cults I can handle. But so help me if there's a snake in the equation. Let alone a slimy, slithering room full of them.

CHAPTER 13

My brain had no concept of time anymore. Hours? Days? It was all a horrific blur. Twice, the hallucinations had been so much that I simply blacked out. (The snakes may or may not have been one of them.) I had no idea how long my blackouts lasted, but every time I woke up, a TV dinner tray was set up in front of me with a meal—a bowl of some sort of rice and bean slop and a glass of water with a straw. The water was easy enough to sip, but I literally had to shove my face in the bowl to eat. I didn't care that it was all over my face. Impressing Nightmare with my table manners was the least of my concerns.

It didn't help that I couldn't stop shaking. Every muscle ached even though I physically hadn't done anything in who knew how long. It felt like my body was falling apart.

It was during these quiet moments, however, that I could think most clearly. The more Nightmare interrogated me, the more it seemed like he wasn't even looking for information. Could it be that he simply wanted to torture me? Maybe this was just a test. An experiment, to see how long it would take to literally kill me using his hallucinations. Or, if not kill me, turn me into a human vegetable. It would explain why Nightmare wasn't explaining what he wanted to know.

No. I refused to accept that possibility. There had to be something he was looking for. Some detail of my meeting with Oracle that I had overlooked.

It's amazing the details you can remember when they're being tortured out of you.

"She was wearing a purple shawl and an ugly, gray dress, and she smelled like garlic," I said, knowing full well how unimportant this information probably was. "She had a big map of Cosmo City on the walls, with connecting lines and a bunch of notes written in red. It was pinpointing the crime scenes of different Supervillains with a bunch of newspaper clippings. She had a gray cat named Maximus who hated my guts. She made tea—mine was peppermint and hers was . . . uh . . . honey vanilla chamomile. And . . . she said there were only two people immune to her psychic powers: Flex and Spine."

I made a conscious effort to omit the family connection between me and Spine. This was his fault. I was being tortured because of him.

"Your father?" said Nightmare as if to rub in the fact.

"Spine," I repeated.

"How is your father immune to her power?"

This wasn't the first time Nightmare had shown interest in a topic. He had done it at least seven other times, and as soon as I rattled off every useless piece of information I knew on the subject, he never brought it up again. He actually seemed bored with any such topic if I tried mentioning it again. A part of me felt like he was doing this just to give me false hope that the interrogation was actually going somewhere. I mean . . . why would he even ask me a question like this? If he was working with my father, shouldn't he know the answer to that question?

"He's able to change the bone matter in his skull so it deflects Oracle's telepathy," I said. "She can't get inside his head when he does."

"What sort of bone matter is it?" asked Nightmare.

Was he kidding? What sort of bone matter? Did he think I was a freaking bone doctor or something?

"I don't know," I said. "I don't think Oracle even knows."

Nightmare pursed his lips. Somehow this made him look even more like a monkey.

"I don't believe you," he said.

I didn't have the energy to protest. It was pointless. I had already rehearsed this routine so many times I had lost count.

I was suddenly outside in the sunlight. Even though I knew the sun was fake, I couldn't help but cherish the warm rays. I was still tied to my chair, although I was tipped over on my back rather than sitting upright. My confusion was cleared up instantly as I turned my head to the right.

Train tracks. I was laying on train tracks. Great.

A horn blared from the opposite direction. I turned to my left. Sure enough, a bulky, gray silhouette dotted the horizon, distorted in the afternoon heat waves.

I attempted to squirm in my chair, but naturally, the chair was tied to the tracks. I was just like the damsel in distress in those cheesy westerns. Except for the part where someone actually comes to rescue me.

Closing my eyes, I attempted to relax in my chair. Nothing was going to hit me.

"Happy thoughts, happy thoughts, happy thoughts . . ." I said to myself.

Oh geez. I sounded like Peter Pan.

I couldn't think of anything happy. In fact, the only thing my brain could seem to process at the moment, other than my impending death by train, was my meeting with Oracle. A meeting that I had recounted to Nightmare a hundred times now. This was less like searching for a needle in a haystack and more like searching for a particular needle in a needle stack. The details . . . All these useless details . . . They were ricocheting around the inside of my skull like a pinball machine.

He's able to change the bone matter in his skull so it deflects Oracle's telepathy.

She can't get inside his head when he does.

. . . the bone matter in his skull . . . she can't get inside his head . . .

I opened my eyes.

That was it.

Not the information Nightmare was looking for, supposing that such information even existed. But it was a solution of sorts. It was something that could at least salvage my sanity. Nightmare wasn't a Telepath per se . . . but his power involved getting inside my head.

What if I could shut him out?

My power *was* a simpler version of my father's, after all. How hard could it be?

The train's horn blared louder. I didn't even bother looking at it. I needed to concentrate. Tapping into my skeletal structure, I concentrated on my skull. That was the easy part. I wasn't exactly sure what to do next. Altering my bone density was like flipping a switch; there were only two ways it could go. But this was more than just making my skull heavier or lighter. I had to somehow change the substance of it entirely.

I decided that increasing the density was probably part of it. A bone with higher density seemed less likely to be penetrable. At least that was the logic in my head.

I felt my head become a bowling ball on the gravel. This was particularly uncomfortable since my neck was craned back slightly. I could survive discomfort, however. This was the first glimmer of hope I had felt in what seemed like ages.

Okay. Now what?

Concentration became impossible as the distant vibrations became violent rumblings. My brain rattled inside my bowling ball skull. Before I could even cast the train a second glance, the sun became an interrogation light and blue skies were swallowed in a shadowy room.

Nightmare eyed me with a heavy eyebrow lifted ever so slightly, throwing off the symmetry of his already misshapen face. Did he suspect something?

He didn't say anything. I didn't say anything. Our silence was an awkward standoff. After nearly a solid minute of this, I couldn't take it anymore. So I did the unthinkable.

"Well what are you waiting for?" I asked.

His eyebrow elevated a notch higher. Again, he said nothing. Did nothing. He was definitely suspicious. I didn't know if this was good or bad.

"Is awkward staring your other superpower?" I asked. "Nightmare by day, Creeperman by night?"

Again. Nothing. Time to bust out the heavy artillery.

"So I was talking to your mom the other day," I said. "Well . . . at least I tried to. I don't speak monkey though."

Apparently Nightmare's mom was the breaking point. He hit me with his next hallucination instantly.

Snakes again.

* * *

I wasn't human anymore. I didn't fear death.

I had endured every sick death ever conceived by man or nature. I was caught in a mudslide, eaten by a lion, got run over by a crappy purple Scion . . .

Okay, okay, those are the lyrics to a Train song. But the first two really did happen. I was sure the Scion would be only a matter of time.

It had been hours since my last hallucination. Maybe longer. I couldn't tell. Nightmare would leave more frequently now. Sometimes he would come back with food or water. Most of the time he would come back with just his ugly face. But he didn't speak anymore. Not a word. He would just hit me with hallucination after hallucination.

Tapping into the structure of my skull, I would concentrate on the density. Not increasing it or decreasing it. Just concentrating. Applying mental pressure. Hoping that—someway, somehow—the substance of my skull would magically transform.

And then I would get sucked into a tornado. Or hit by an apocalyptic meteor. Or . . .

Snakes.

Apparently Nightmare thought he had a sense of humor. Despite the darkness, I could tell that the floor was squirming and wriggling like before. I could feel them rubbing against my ankles. This time, however, there was something bigger lurking in the writhing masses. I could see its elongated body, thicker than mine, shimmering in the shadows. It slithered closer. Though its head was invisible to me in the shadows, two yellow eyes were locked onto me, weaving back and forth as the creature closed the distance.

My throat felt tight. My mouth was dry.

It's not real. It's not real. It's not real.

A bulky head the size of a watermelon reared back, preparing to strike.

I felt an itch in my skull—like something was crawling inside it.

My vision flashed and distorted like a bad television signal. The monstrous snake suddenly became very jerky and awkward. Some of the snakes started slithering backwards.

My world folded inside out.

The hallucination collapsed. The snakes were gone, replaced by Nightmare and a glaring interrogation light.

I did it. I didn't know how, but I did it. I shut out the hallucination.

Something was wrong.

I knew simply from the look on Nightmare's face. He was smiling. Except with an ugly face like that, it was more like the devious look a chimpanzee had before he flung his own poo at some poor, unsuspecting tourist.

"I see you've found the answer," said Nightmare.

"The answer?" I said. His smile was seriously unnerving me. "What answer?"

Nightmare's image spazzed out. I say "image" because he looked less like a real person now and more like a hologram. Just like the hallucination I had just freed myself from, his every movement was twitching and his image was warping.

"All that we see or seem . . ." said Nightmare.

The walls around me seemed to be closing in. The room was imploding. My reality began to erode before my eyes, peeling like old paint.

". . . is but a dream within a dream."

I blinked. When I opened my eyes, my entire world had changed.

I was lying in bed, staring at an off-white ceiling. I lowered my gaze only slightly to find that this was connected to off-white walls, accompanied by equally boring curtains. A machine to my left emitted a gentle, electronic chirp that synchronized to my heart rate.

I was in a hospital.

CHAPTER 14

Absolutely no time had passed between my interrogation with Nightmare and the hospital. I had simply blinked and I was here. Was this another one of his hallucinations? If so, this had to be the most elaborate and subtle buildup for a death yet. Whatever the case, my head was throbbing again and the ticking sound had returned, reverberating inside my brain.

Tick tooock tooock tick . . . tooock tooock . . . tick . . .

I groaned as I sat upright, only now noticing the IV in my arm and the white, spotted hospital gown I was wearing. I felt stiff—as if I had been lying here for ages.

"Marrow . . . ?"

My gaze darted to where a pair of chairs that matched the bland, off-white decor had been arranged in the corner. Scrawny, mousy-haired Whisp stood up from one of them. A glimmer of blue hair shifted beside him. Sapphire pulled herself upright, blinking the sleep out of her eyes.

Her gaze met mine.

"Marrow!"

She bolted from her seat, attacking me in hug. I grunted on impact as she hit me with the unintentional force of a football lineman. Even though it hurt more than I cared to admit, I was absolutely positive now that this wasn't another death hallucination, although I could barely breathe in Sapphire's death hug. Whisp stood up as well but with slightly more consideration for personal boundaries.

They were both wearing bodysuits that I realized correlated with their hero trainers—Sapphire's was ironically blue, trimmed in white, and Whisp's was purple and black.

"What happened to you?" Sapphire asked, finally pulling herself together.

Honestly, I was just as excited to see her, but I could barely move after being tied to a chair for so long. Which brought up an entirely new question . . .

"How'd I get here?" I asked, unintentionally ignoring her question. I realized this after the fact, but Sapphire didn't seem to mind.

"Flex found you unconscious in an alley yesterday," she said. "You've been out for almost forty-eight hours since he brought you here. Whisp and I came as soon as we found out."

The idea of Flex actually leaving his apartment to find me was unbelievable. More than unbelievable. It was just flat out impossible. But there was something much more disconcerting that drew my attention.

"Alley?" I said.

There was no way. It couldn't be.

"Yeah," said Sapphire. "Apparently it happened after you visited Oracle. Flex said he interrogated some punk who he thought was responsible. The guy said he and his friends saw some Super named Nightmare knock you out. Apparently he just left you there.

I couldn't believe it. This whole time . . .

The interrogation itself had been a hallucination.

All that we see or seem is but a dream within a dream.

Nightmare's bizarre last words suddenly made sense. But why? Why would he stage a fake interrogation like that? What was the point?

"Are you okay?" asked Whisp. I blinked, redirecting my gaze to the scrawny animal whisperer. I almost forgot he was there.

Okay? Well I wasn't being psychologically tortured anymore, so that was a plus. However, something about Nightmare's mysterious mind game left me more than uneasy.

"Does anyone know who Nightmare is?" I asked. Again, I didn't realize I had ignored someone's question until after the fact. But like

Sapphire, Whisp didn't seem to mind. I was the one in the hospital bed, so I guess that gave me some leniency.

"Well . . . Flex seemed to recognize the name," said Whisp. "But he seems to be the only one, and he won't talk about it. Nova and Specter said they don't know anyone named Nightmare." He paused, biting his lip, before adding, "Flex doesn't seem too happy about any of this."

Well that was a shocker—Flex not being happy about something. I wondered if that goon was even capable of being happy if he wasn't drunk or playing video games.

"Where *is* Flex?" I asked.

"Downstairs," said Sapphire. "In the lobby with Specter and Nova. They're . . . talking."

She seemed to be using the word "talking" very loosely.

Without a word, I ripped the tape and IV from my arm and started for the exit. Whisp watched me, wide-eyed behind his thick glasses like I'd just gone crazy or something. I probably looked crazy enough rushing off in a hospital gown.

"Where do you think you're going?" said Sapphire.

"I need to talk to Flex," I said.

"You're a hospital patient!" she said. "You can't just go wandering around."

"Oh yeah? Watch me."

I felt bad just up and ditching Sapphire and Whisp like that. I was flattered that they even came to visit me. But something was going on here, and I was determined to get to the bottom of it.

The hallways were practically empty. Passing by the nearest window, I noticed that it was dark outside. I then glanced at a digital clock on the wall and was shocked to find that it was 3:17 a.m. That explained why it was so dead. Although I received a few awkward glances from the occasional passing nurse, I ignored their looks and entered the nearest elevator. I pushed the level one button a couple of times and the door started to close.

A hand with bright blue nail polish forced its way in, stopping the doors, and they reopened. An irritated Sapphire and a reluctant Whisp filed into the elevator with me. Sapphire practically stabbed the level one button with her index finger and the doors closed again. There was a subtle shift of gravity and a gentle hum as the elevator descended.

"You're a real butthead, you know that?" said Sapphire. The friendliness was gone. She stared straight ahead, not even bothering to look at me.

Whisp bit his lip and tried to blend into the elevator wall.

"Sorry," I said in a half-mumble. Which was true. I was sorry. Sort of.

The silence was thick and suffocating. But I had already suffocated quite a bit lately thanks to Nightmare, so I was used to it.

"What's going on?" Sapphire asked. She was looking at me now and there was even a hint of concern in her voice. "Talk to me. Please. You owe me that much."

I made the mistake of making eye contact with her—big, blue pleading eyes that put every homeless puppy to shame.

I sighed.

"I've been interrogated by Nightmare for the past who knows how long," I said. "He wanted to know about my visit with Oracle. At least that's what he said."

"Interrogated?" said Sapphire. "You mean before he knocked you out?"

"No, I mean while I was knocked out. Apparently the entire interrogation was a dream. That's his power—hallucinations."

Sapphire was silent for a long moment. "Okay. That's weird. What did he want to know about your visit with Oracle?"

The elevator halted with a *ding* and the doors slid open.

"No idea," I said. "That's what I'm hoping to find out."

The lobby was easy to find—a long, curving room with sleek light fixtures and maroon leather furniture. It was empty except for three obvious figures.

Specter's already curvaceous body was accentuated in a blue and white bodysuit matching Sapphire's. Specter was a tall, statuesque blonde with full lips and eyelashes that belonged on a camel. Okay, maybe that's not the best comparison in the world since she was a drop dead gorgeous cold hard ten, and camels are . . . camels. But seriously. Her eyelashes were huge.

Nova was a stocky man with a beard and a shaved head, dressed in a durable purple and black plated uniform well-adjusted to his power—exploding.

And then there was Flex, wearing baggy shorts, flip-flops, and a t-shirt with cutoff sleeves that read, "Jamaican Me Crazy."

His voice carried above all the others.

"HE'S WHAT?"

"Flex, calm down," said Specter.

"Don't tell me to calm down!" said Flex, shaking his head with dreadlocks flailing wildly. "I have no reason to calm down!"

"I told you telling him was a bad idea," Nova grumbled beneath his beard.

"Hey," said Flex, pointing his finger. "You can shut your donut hole, you ugly old warlock. How long were you planning on hiding this from me anyway?"

"No one was hiding anything from you, mop-head," said Nova. "All of this information was in your packet. Too bad you don't know how to read anything that isn't an alcohol label."

"Really, Flex, it's not that bad," said Specter. She attempted to place a soothing hand on his shoulder, but he shrugged it away.

"That kid is Spine's son!" said Flex. "The Guild must think they're a bunch of comedians. There's no way I'm training him. I would rather train a freaking honey badger."

Sapphire and Whisp exchanged hesitant glances beside me.

"Good!" I shouted, marching out into the lobby. "I don't want you training me anyway!"

Specter and Nova both shot me startled glances. Flex didn't even look at me, rolling his eyes instead.

"What could I possibly learn from you anyway?" I asked, throwing my hands in the air. "You don't know anything about me."

"I don't need to know about you," said Flex. "I know enough about your dad."

"Oh, right," I said. "Because you and the rest of the world are all experts on everything there is to know about my father. I'm sure the news told you everything you need to know."

Flex sighed. "Marrow—"

"No!" I said. "You know what? He's as much my father as you are my trainer. Forget FIST. Forget this stupid Sidekick Internship Program. I'm done with it. All of it. I don't need anybody."

I started for the exit.

I had no idea where I was going. I didn't even know where I *could* go. Never mind the fact that I was still in my hospital gown. All I knew was that I had to get out of here. I couldn't take it anymore.

"Marrow!" said Sapphire.

I walked faster.

"Marrow, it's not like that," said Flex.

I whipped around, every muscle in my body tense. "Oh, it's not? Well please, tell me what it's like then!"

Flex's mouth opened, but no words came out. He looked about as ready to talk as he was ready to train a sidekick.

I started for the exit again.

"Your father trained me," said Flex.

His words seared into every nerve ending in my body. My next step faltered. Turning slowly, I met Flex's gaze, solemn and regretful.

"I was Spine's sidekick," he said.

CHAPTER 15

There comes a time when someone says something so astronomically, catastrophically, mind-blowingly WHATTHECRAPTASTIC that the fabric of the universe is ripped wide open and the space-time continuum comes to a complete halt. It was like those movies when an explosion goes off, and all the character can hear is this shrill ringing sound that doesn't technically exist because it's actually coming from ear drums that have momentarily forgotten how to be ear drums. Things are happening, and people's mouths are moving, but the world is disconnected.

That's where I was.

I proceeded to walk outside.

But I didn't leave like I said I would. Neither did Flex ditch me like he said he would. Instead, I found a nice, cold, mildly uncomfortable place on the curb and waited for the universe to realign itself until it made sense again.

But the fact of the matter was that it *did* make sense. It made so much sense that it hurt. The Guild had two problems—Spine's son and Spine's sidekick. Why not combine the problems into a nice, little package and let the problems sort themselves out?

That's what we were—two problems that the Guild was just trying to get out of the way. No wonder Flex wanted nothing to do with me.

Flex sat down on the curb beside me. He was holding my clothes in his lap.

"I told everyone they could go," said Flex.

I nodded. Sort of. It was really more of a wobbly bobble-head thing, but Flex seemed to recognize it as a nod regardless.

"Do you wanna get dressed and go home?" he said.

I repeated my bobble-head response. I didn't *really* want to go. But then again, this curb sucked, and it was cold outside, and I was basically wearing a dress made out of a bed sheet, and I was beginning to lose feeling in my butt.

I went back inside to change and we left in his crappy old Volvo. Most of the ride was silent. The tension was gone, but the silence was thick and suffocating.

"You were there?" I finally asked. "You were there when he—?"

I couldn't finish the question. It made me sick just thinking about it.

Why? Why did I suddenly care? Spine wasn't my father. He was a monster. Heck, he even sent Nightmare to interrogate me or torture me or whatever the heck that whole thing was supposed to be.

"Yeah," said Flex, his mouth pulled in a bitter, straight line. "I was there."

I wanted to just leave it there. Nothing good would come from knowing the details. But the question was itching on my tongue.

"Why?" I asked. "What happened?"

I realized it was a vague question only after I asked it, but Flex seemed to understand. A soft patter of rain swept over the car in a sudden gentle wave. Flex flipped the windshield wiper on, staring contemplatively into the storm.

"I ask myself that every day," said Flex.

Of course Flex wouldn't know the answer. That's because there wasn't an answer. It wasn't healthy for me to pry into this. What sort of answer was I expecting anyway?

"Oh . . . okay," I said. I hated how disappointed I sounded. "Not that it matters or anything. My father was just a sadistic psychopath who only cared about himself anyway."

"That's not true," said Flex.

His instant response shocked me. In fact, even he seemed surprised by his quick and bold reply.

"Your father was one of the best men I ever knew," said Flex slowly, choosing his words carefully. "He was everything that a hero should be. And for the record, I've never seen a father care for his son as much as Spine cared about you."

I was breathless. Why? How could that be true? It didn't make any sense.

"If I had to guess, I'd say it was your mother's death that started it," said Flex. "A car accident—something so simple. Spine had saved so many people, but he couldn't save her. He didn't go from good to evil overnight, but he did stop feeling. He just stopped caring. I think a tragedy like that could make anyone spiral out of control if they let it. It's the only possibility that makes sense. All I know is that he loved your mother more than life itself. Living without her just wasn't an option."

I hadn't noticed until now the moisture trickling down my cheek. I hastily wiped it away. I couldn't take this conversation anymore.

"So who's Nightmare?" I asked, vying desperately for a subject change.

Flex was caught off guard by the change of topic but didn't seem to mind it. "A friend of your father," he said. "The two have been friends since before he trained me."

"And Nova and Specter didn't know who he was?" I asked.

"Nightmare was a Super, but he never even tried to be a hero," said Flex. "Or a villain, for that matter. He was a recluse. He lived out in the woods and didn't want anything to do with people. The two of them would occasionally go fishing and ramble about politics and philosophy, but I've never even talked to him. Just seen his face a couple times. One ugly dude."

"Yeah he is," I said with a weak laugh. "A mother couldn't love that face."

"Not even a little bit," said Flex, chuckling.

Our laughter faded awkwardly. As much as I wanted to make light of the situation, it was obvious neither of us was in quite the laughing mood.

"So . . . what happened with Nightmare anyway?" Flex asked.

It would have been really easy to give him the extremely condensed version of the story that I'd given Sapphire. After surviving *at least* forty-eight hours of torture, the last thing I wanted to do was talk about it. But I wanted answers even more. My experience with Nightmare wasn't exactly something I could just shrug aside. And as far as I knew, Flex was one of the only people who actually knew who this guy was.

So I told him everything.

Flex listened quietly. Once I started, it was impossible to stop. The words became a landslide coming out of my mouth. Flex's facial expression didn't budge the entire time. After I finished, I had to take a deep breath. I already felt queasy.

It was another long moment before Flex finally spoke.

"Spine . . . ?" he said. The name came out with all the subtlety of a gag reflex. "He told you Spine sent him?"

"Yep," I said, grimacing.

"And the whole thing was just an elaborate illusion?"

"Yep."

"And Oracle thinks Spine has been spying on her?"

"Yep."

Flex stared at the road ahead for a moment longer before he unexpectedly pulled one hand away, glancing behind him as he groped the back seat. This sudden diversion did not last long. He returned with a familiar package in a manila envelope.

"So this is for me?"

The videotape.

"You have it?" I exclaimed questioningly. "I thought Nightmare took it!"

Flex shook his head. "It was tucked in your jacket when I found you."

I couldn't believe it. Nightmare hadn't bothered to search me? He was interrogating me about my visit with Oracle! I even told him I was carrying a package from her!

And he didn't bother going back to get it?

Flex crinkled the manila package beneath his fingertips. "It's a VHS tape, isn't it."

It didn't sound like he was asking.

"Uh . . . yeah," I said.

"And it's supposed to motivate me to go visit Oracle?"

I nodded, but my mind was preoccupied with something else.

"You haven't watched it yet?" I asked.

Flex tossed it back in the back seat. "Don't need to. I already know what it is."

My mouth hung slightly ajar as I glanced back and forth between Flex and the package in the backseat. "Well? What is it?"

"A home movie," said Flex.

"A what?"

"I was an orphan," Flex explained. "Oracle adopted me before I was admitted into FIST. It didn't matter that she was blind; that crazy old lady had a moral code to videotape everything. I don't know which home movie it is, but I'm sure it's one of them. Worst home movies ever, by the way. Everything's way off center. My head is cut off half the time."

I nodded slowly as I processed everything. It suddenly made perfect sense why she trusted Flex so much. Also why she had his entire hero track record memorized.

I couldn't imagine the two of them living under the same roof.

"So . . . do you want to visit her then?" I asked.

"No," said Flex in a flat tone. Then he sighed. "But we're going to anyway."

"When?"

"Right now."

"What? Now? It's like four in the morning."

"Good," said Flex. "That means we'll catch her at home."

I didn't have the energy to protest. Instead, I simply slumped back in my seat.

Suddenly my head pounded. The familiar ticking sound that I kept waking up to was echoing through my skull louder than ever now.

TICK TICK TICK TICK . . . TICK . . . TICK TOOOCK TICK TICK . . .

That's when I noticed two headlights from my side window. I wouldn't have given the car a second glance, but the headlights didn't seem to be angled straight. They faced the ground and then moved, flashing me directly in the face before streaming up and cutting through the storm clouds.

None of the car's wheels were touching the ground.

"What the—?" said Flex.

Out of sheer instinct, I tapped into my skeletal structure, fortifying myself. Not a second later, the flying car smashed into us. My head whipped so fast, the next few seconds became a blur. Our surroundings spun and toppled. Gravity reversed as we rolled. Our dangerous momentum came to an abrupt halt as we hit something else from Flex's side.

I was numb. I didn't know if that was a good thing or a bad thing. I couldn't think right. I blinked several times, trying to register my surroundings. We had hit the solid concrete base of a street lamp. The car practically folded around it. Flex was hanging limp from the shoulder strap of his seat belt. There was a gash across his forehead, accompanied by a bloody nose and a cut lip.

I tried to say his name. I couldn't. Either that or I couldn't hear myself speak. All I could make out was a high pitched ringing sound that pierced my skull.

"Flex . . ."

I heard my voice that time, although it was strained and barely audible. Fortunately, I could hear the sounds of city life as well—a barking dog, a distant siren, the sound of the freeway like gentle ocean waves . . .

Metal screeched beside me. My door was ripped off, landing on the ground with a heavy *clank*.

An invisible force gripped every inch of my body and wrenched me from the car. It didn't seem to matter that my bone structure was still at its densest. My insides defied gravity as I soared across the street—four whole empty lanes. I hit a solid surface behind me—literally smashed into it. My body was still numb to the impact, but I felt brick crumble around my super-enhanced frame.

If my skeletal structure had been at its normal density, I would have been out cold for sure. Maybe even worse. This invisible force felt like the concentrated power of a hurricane.

Telekinesis?

A tall, skinny silhouette levitated out of the shadows. As the figure drifted past a nearby street lamp, his face was illuminated.

It was Nero.

CHAPTER 16

"Hello, Marrow," said Nero. His usual cocky smirk was gone. There was something far more threatening in his eyes.

"Nero?" I gasped. "What are you doing?"

Nero levitated closer, gliding across the shadows like a ghost. It wasn't until now that I noticed he was wearing a sleek red and black bodysuit designed to match Fantom's. He stopped only an arm's length away from me, as if taunting my inability to move.

"They were supposed to kick you out of FIST," said Nero. "You were supposed to be just another orphan on the street. You weren't supposed to get a second chance. Especially not with Flex."

"What the heck are you talking about?" I asked. As soon as I did, I felt stupid. I knew exactly what he was talking about. "This is about you cheating, isn't it?"

Nero rolled his eyes. "Cheating is such a subjective term. There is no cheating when it comes to survival of the fittest. I *am* the fittest. So I did what I had to in order to survive."

I already knew Nero had cheated. It was the only explanation for what happened at the Final Challenge. But somehow, having him flaunt it in front of me and then tell me it wasn't technically cheating renewed every ounce of anger and hatred I had ever had towards him.

"How?" I said through gritted teeth. "I called you out in front of Havoc. He said there was no way you could have cheated."

"A magician never reveals his secrets," said Nero with a tantalizing smile. "But I will tell you that I am much more powerful than you think I am."

"So what are you doing here now?"

"Isn't it obvious? I'm here to kill you, Marrow."

The casual way he said this made it difficult to take him seriously. I mean, this was Nero. Brooding, awkward, pain-in-the-butt Nero. He was a lot of things, but he wasn't a killer.

But then my gaze shifted to Flex's battered Volvo folded around the street lamp. As far as I could tell, Flex hadn't budged.

Was he . . . ?

No. I shook the thought from my head.

"Why would you want to kill me?" I asked. "Didn't you already get what you wanted?"

I was surprised at my own boldness. I didn't sound even a little afraid. Heck, I didn't *feel* afraid. My tone was more skeptical than anything else. Somehow, the threat of death didn't seem to register in my brain anymore. Maybe it was because I had already died at least a hundred different deaths in the past couple days.

"Yes, I did," said Nero, nodding unconvincingly. "Being trained by Fantom is all I ever wanted. Once I finish the Sidekick Internship Program and graduate FIST, I'll have a reputation to last me a lifetime. I'll already be a celebrity."

"Peachy," I said. "So what's the problem?"

"You are, Marrow. As long as you're in the picture, my credibility stands threatened. The more credibility *you* have, the less *I* have."

"Credibility?" I repeated. "Are you nuts? How do I have any credibility?"

"Because they teamed you with Flex!" said Nero, throwing his hands in the air. His eyes were wide and hysterical. "Don't you get it?"

"Uh . . . I don't know about you, but I've actually met Flex," I said. "So, no. I don't get it."

Despite my nonchalant tone, I couldn't help glancing at the totaled car once more. Flex still hadn't moved. Why wasn't he moving? My stomach clenched as I considered the worst.

"Flex and your dad were a team!" said Nero. "Not just a hero and a sidekick. They were an unstoppable force. If it wasn't for your stupid mom getting herself killed and your psycho dad losing it, they probably would have been the greatest Superhero duo of all time. I know. I've done my research. Flex and Spine weren't together long, but they set some records. Although records are easily forgotten when a hero goes bad. And your dad was the worst."

My arms started shaking. Despite Nero's control over my body, my hands balled into fists. I could put up with a lot of Nero's crap, but he was pushing every bit of patience I had.

"You are your father's son," said Nero. "Your power is just an underdeveloped version of his. You together with Flex . . . your powers mesh. It wouldn't take much for you two to recreate their success."

I tapped into my skeletal structure, commanding my fortified bones to fight the power restraining them. My veins bulged from the effort. The air around me felt as solid as concrete.

My knees budged.

It wasn't much, but it was enough for me to brace the soles of my feet against the wall. I flattened my palms against the wall as well, pushing as hard as I could.

I'm stronger than Nero. I'm stronger than Nero. I'm stronger than Nero.

"And that's why I have to kill you," said Nero. "And it'll be all too easy to frame Flex. Splash a little beer on him and voilà! A tragic car accident. Just like your mom. Poetic, isn't it?"

I screamed. The wall groaned and cracked behind me, my hands and feet crushing into the brick.

Nero's telekinetic grip snapped.

I flew forward faster than he could blink. Rearing my arm back, my fist flew forward like a fleshy bullet, connecting with his face. Nero hurtled backwards, a human skipping stone across the four-lane road. His momentum was only broken as he hit a wooden apartment sign that read, "Welcome to Sunnyside," accompanied by a smiling sun wearing sunglasses. The sign splintered on impact.

I didn't stop. Reversing my density, my feet glided me across the street. The wind sliced past me. I leapt up, defying every natural law of gravity. My insides lifted with me. I pulled my fist back, preparing to come down on him like a comet.

Nero blinked, mouth ajar, as he registered the world of pain he was about to be in. His arms flew up, guiding his telekinesis no doubt. I mentally dared him to even try and stop me in the air. Go on. Try.

I didn't see the dislodged stop sign flying through the air until it hit me in the face.

I tapped into my bone density only a split second later. With my delayed density tapped, I hit the ground like a bomb, breaking the street around me. I laid there, numb, for several seconds, swallowed in a cloud of dust. It wasn't until I registered the two-foot crater of shattered asphalt around me that I saw a silhouette hovering over the dust cloud. The silhouette was red.

Too much red. This thing was way too big to be Nero.

The dust dispersed, revealing a floating, crimson Volkswagen Beetle. Nero was barely visible, levitating behind it.

"Red punch buggy," said Nero.

The Beetle dropped.

I sucked the density from my bones and practically bounced off the ground. There wasn't enough time to jump out of the way though.

I jumped up instead.

My bones became solid steel as I rocketed skyward with my new-found momentum, fist in the air, Superman-style. I sliced through the framework like butter—not-so-smooth butter with layers of greasy metal and leather upholstery. I exploded out the other end like a missile to where Nero was hovering.

I didn't even have to move my fist. Nero's demented smirk barely had a chance to become wide-eyed shock. I pummeled him in the stomach.

Nero crumpled as we both fell. My skeleton became light and I landed like a cat. Nero hit the asphalt like a limp fish.

"You didn't say 'no punch backs,'" I said.

Again, I wasted no time for retaliation. I rushed forward, fist raised. Time to finish this.

Nero rolled over, his eyes barely focused on me. Apparently that was all the concentration he needed. He lifted a wobbly arm, fingers outstretched.

My windpipe closed.

I stumbled and fell to my knees. I couldn't breathe. Grabbing my throat with both hands, I fumbled desperately to remove whatever it was that seemed to be strangling me. There was nothing.

Nero casually crawled to his feet and dusted his jumpsuit off. A smile slithered across his thin face as he shook his head, eyeing me like a pathetic piece of roadkill.

"I'm sorry I have to go Darth Vader on you like this," said Nero. "I know it's not very sportsmanlike. But I *really* want you to die. I'm sure I'll get over it."

CHAPTER 17

I gagged and wheezed, gasping for breath. My lungs felt like they were caving in. My surroundings became a blur. Black spots danced in front of me, and I crumpled to the floor. I stared at Nero's feet as he drew near.

This was it. I was going to die. Just like that.

Something long and fleshy shot out like a whip and nailed Nero in the face.

My windpipe opened. Oxygen flooded into my lungs. I gasped, barely able to contain the sudden airflow.

As my orientation slowly returned, I crawled onto my hands and knees. I craned my head up to witness my hero.

Flex.

I couldn't believe it. He waltzed up, cocky as ever, as his arm whipped back into place. He wiped his bloody lip with it. His dreadlocks bounced as he cracked his neck from side to side.

"Nobody picks on my sidekick except for me," said Flex. "You got that, you brain-warped little gremlin?"

Nero and I both staggered upright at the same time. His eyes darted hesitantly between the two of us. Fighting two Supers obviously wasn't in his plans.

"You okay, Flex?" I asked, not daring to take my eyes off Nero.

"Dandy," said Flex. "You?"

"Never better," I said unenthusiastically. "Don't go easy on this kid, okay?"

"You kidding? He totaled my car. I'm going to kick his butt inside out."

"I guess that means I have to stop going easy too, huh?" said Nero.

Nero clapped his hands together. This was followed by a lurching metallic groan. I noticed movement out of both sides of my peripheral vision. Two cars catapulted from opposite sides of the street, aimed to smash Flex and me together. I lunged forward while Flex dove out the opposite side. I landed in a roll and scrambled to my feet. My disoriented gaze shifted from side to side. Where was Nero?

Out of pure instinct, I glanced up. Sure enough, Nero was soaring high into the twilight atmosphere. It was obvious that this wasn't some elaborate retaliation.

Stop going easy? The punk was running away!

Sure I could jump high with my power, but this was far beyond my range. I frantically scanned the vicinity for any tall jumping point. Nothing came close.

"He's getting away!" I screamed at no one in particular.

Flex shuffled beside me, his eyes fixed skyward. His face seemed way calmer than I'm sure mine was at the moment.

"Says who?" asked Flex.

"Says who?" I repeated hysterically. I pointed at the sky as if there was a giant sign hanging there that said, 'DUH!'

Flex's gaze was still fixed up, too preoccupied with who knew what to notice my panic.

"Uh . . . you don't have a concussion, do you?" I asked.

Stupid question to ask someone with a concussion.

Flex finally met my gaze with the hint of a grin. "How do you feel about slingshots?"

"Huh?"

Flex whipped his right hand out like he was chucking a football—except his hand *was* the ball. His arm shot out, stretching thin like a rubber band before latching onto a nearby streetlamp. He repeated the movement with his left arm, grabbing the pole of a hanging traffic light. Gritting his teeth, he dug his heels into the ground to keep from sliding.

"How do you feel about flying?" he asked, grinning wider.

I decided to take back every mean thing I had ever said about Flex. The guy was a genius. An infuriating, psychotic genius, but a genius nonetheless.

I rushed to Flex, pumping density into my bones as I pressed my back against his chest. I took a heavy step back, stretching Flex's arms more. And another step. And another. I was starting to feel more and more resistance.

"How far can you stretch?" I asked.

"As far . . . as you think . . . you need," said Flex through his teeth. His voice didn't sound too convincing.

I increased my lead-footed pace, pulling back five yards. Ten yards. At twenty yards, Flex's arms looked like thin bungee cords ready to burst. At this point, Nero was barely a red speck in the sky.

Flex's face was much redder.

"Please . . . take your time . . ." said Flex. Beads of sweat trickled down his forehead.

I tapped into my skeletal structure and zeroed out my bone density.

My feet were ripped off the ground. My insides flattened against the back of my rib cage as I blasted skyward. The wind shrieked in my ears and whipped my skin and clothes. My lips flared out as I whizzed face-first. I couldn't breathe. My surroundings were a disorienting blur.

And then I saw it—a flare of red growing larger and more defined.

I was hurtling right on target.

"NEEEEERRRRROOOOO!!!!!" I shouted into the wind.

Nero glanced back just in time for my density-packed fist to nail him in the face. The sickening smack of knuckles against flesh resonated through the atmosphere.

My momentum ceased. Nero and I plunged downward, side-by-side. Flailing my hand out, I grabbed his limp arm. He was out cold. I pulled him close, back against my chest. Sliding my arms under his armpits, I interlocked my hands around his chest. We were tumbling down to the grassy field of a park. Swinging my body in the air, we plummeted with my back to the ground.

Grass or no grass . . . this was going to hurt.

I waited until the last moment to increase my bone density. I hit the grassy surface like a meteor. Dirt exploded around me. The ground might as well have been made of Jell-O. By the time our bodies finally stopped, we were wedged several feet deep in earth. Chunks of soil rained down on us. I had Nero as a human umbrella, but I would have rather taken my chances with the falling debris. Bits of grass were the last to fall, fluttering like confetti. As the dust cleared, I could see Flex just barely past Nero's fat head.

"Comfy down there?" Flex asked.

"Please get me out of here," I said. My voice was muffled with Nero's hair in my mouth. "I can't wait to turn this jerk in to the police."

"Police?" said Flex. "This is bigger than the police. We need to call the Guild."

CHAPTER 18

Flex and I made headline news.

TV, newspapers, radio . . . You name it, they were buzzing about it. Some no-name Superhero and his sidekick intern had defeated some other rampaging, telekinetic sidekick intern, sending him to the hospital comatose and in handcuffs. I'm sure it helped that the culprit was the sidekick of none other than Fantom, himself. I'm sure it helped even more that the no-name Superhero and his sidekick also happened to be the former sidekick and son of the infamous Supervillain, Spine. The next morning, Flex's apartment complex was bombarded by news reporters. A barrage of microphones was shoved in our faces as we attempted to leave.

"Why did Nero want to kill you, Marrow?"

"What have you been doing all these years, Flex?"

"Do you two feel connected by your relationship to Spine?"

Flex groaned, shaking his head. "Come back when I'm drunk," he said. "I'll tell you all about it."

"Nero cheated on the FIST Final Challenge," I added into the dozen microphones as an afterthought. "FYI."

We walked to the nearest convenience store and Flex bought a six-pack of energy drinks.

"Aneuryzm Energy," said Flex, holding up the six-pack proudly. "Nectar of the gods. This stuff is magic."

The letter "z" on the misspelled label was designed as a lightning bolt. It was electrifying a cartoon man's head, causing his brain to explode.

"Aneurysm?" I said. "Uh . . . is this stuff safe?"

"Safe?" said Flex. "You're a Superhero. Don't ever ask me if something is safe again."

A thousand milligrams of caffeine later . . .

"Gaaaaaaaaaaahhhhhhhhhh!" I screamed, eyes bulging. I mashed the buttons on the controller without really knowing what I was doing. That seemed to be my best strategy so far.

"Die, infernal insect!" Flex howled, raising his controller while still pushing buttons at an impractical angle.

The bright, flashing colors of Marvel vs. Capcom 4 were almost too much for me to handle. Wolverine was moving in for the kill, steel claws extended, while Spider-Man looked like he was doing the hokey-pokey. I grabbed the controller with one hand and proceeded to slap all of the buttons with the palm of my hand.

"My . . . Spidey . . . senses . . . are . . . tingling!" I said, shouting each word as I smashed the controller.

"My Wolvey senses are going nuts!" said Flex.

Spider-Man sprayed a glob of web in Wolverine's face and then roundhouse kicked him over the ledge of a building.

"K.O." said the voice in the television. "Spider-Man wins."

"Did I just do that?" I asked. I dropped the controller on the floor, as if holding it might reverse my K.O.

"No!" Flex shouted at his controller. "That's the fifth time in a row you've beaten me!"

"Sixth," I said. "If you include the time you sneezed and accidently walked off the ledge yourself."

"I'm not counting that," said Flex.

"Okay. Five."

Flex fell back on the floor, arms outstretched and dreadlocks fanned out. "I want to go run a marathon," he said.

"I want to run two marathons," I said. "But I want to run the second marathon backwards."

"I want to run a marathon on my hands," said Flex. "You know . . . like a walking handstand marathon. Except running."

"That would be cool."

"I know. Like . . . why hasn't anyone done that before?"

"They'd have to invent running shoes for your hands," I pointed out.

"Yeah," said Flex. "That'd be weird. How would you even tie shoes on your hands?"

"Velcro?" I suggested. "You could use your teeth."

Flex shrugged. "That could work."

He began waving his hand in front of his face for no discernible reason. Then he began lifting it up and down, touching his nose as if testing his depth perception. After practicing this exercise for fifteen whole seconds, he rolled his head to face me.

"Nero really said he thought Spine and I could have been the greatest Superhero team of all time?" he asked.

"Uh . . . yeah, I guess," I said.

"And that's why he was worried about you and me?"

"I s'pose."

Flex rolled his head back to where he could stare at the ceiling. "Huh."

"Huh" was right. It was mind-boggling to think that Nero could get so worked up over something that seemed so unspectacular.

But could he be right?

"You were there though," I said.

Flex rotated his head back to me and raised an inquisitive eyebrow. "Huh?"

"I mean . . . you were there fighting side-by-side with Spine," I said. "You should know. Were you two really that good?"

Flex's eyes drifted as he thought. He was silent for a long moment. It was weird that he had to think about it so long.

"We were good," he finally said. "Really good. It's just . . . I dunno. It was such a long time ago. It doesn't feel real anymore."

"Was that slingshot move something you used to do with him?" I asked.

Flex chuckled. "We learned that move on the fly. We were fighting this Super named Vulture-Tron. Shot him clean out of the air."

"Did you two have any other special moves?"

"Psh! Heck yeah we did. The whip . . . the ball and chain . . . We had loads of moves."

"What was the whip?" I asked.

"Well . . . basically your dad would grab me and swing me around like a whip. Real classy stuff."

"What was the ball and chain?"

"I would swing your dad around like a ball and chain," he said. "Even classier."

"Sounds like it."

"The man was crazy," said Flex. "Every time we were on the job, he would do the most insane things to save someone's life. Nearly got himself killed in the process almost every single time. And then, after I'd tell him how stupid he was, he'd get this cocky look in his eyes, and he'd say, 'Hey, if you aren't willing to lose your life, how can you save anyone?' Every single time, he'd say that. He said it so much that . . . I dunno. I started believing it. That was the sort of Superhero I wanted to become. Until . . . well . . . you know."

"Yeah . . ." I said. My voice faded to silence. What was I doing? Asking questions about my dad? The same dad that abandoned me? That had a reputation as the most infamous Supervillain of all time? He had killed people. Lots of people. And then there was the whole ordeal with Nightmare . . .

So why did Flex have to make him sound so cool?

"Do you miss him?" I asked.

Flex hesitated. Then he nodded. "Yeah," he said. "More than I care to admit."

I bit my lip. I hated this emotional hole I was digging myself into. I couldn't help it because I felt empty . . . but it only left me feeling emptier.

"I'm tired," I said. "I need another brain aneurysm."

"It's just Aneuryzm," said Flex. "And I drank the last one."

I grumbled, rolling onto my stomach and planting my face in the floor.

"I agree," he said.

There was a sudden pounding that seemed to shake the very fabric of space and time. I thought my brain was going to explode like the cartoon guy on the Aneuryzm can. The pounding started again—only this time I realized it was just someone knocking on the door.

Only one person in the universe knocked like that.

Flex staggered to his feet, tripping over his own lanky legs before shuffling to the door. He didn't get there in time. Instead, the air seemed to ripple, and suddenly Havoc was standing in front of the doorway. He looked as big and bad as ever with shirt sleeves that might as well have been painted onto his massive arms.

Havoc's gaze shifted from Flex to where I lay on the floor. I forced a weak smile.

"Hey, you," I said.

"What's the matter with him?" Havoc asked, turning to Flex. "You didn't give him alcohol, did you?"

"Whoa, relax," said Flex. "He just had an Aneuryzm."

"WHAT?"

"No," said Flex, squeezing his eyes shut and rubbing his temples. "Not like that. It's . . . ah, never mind. What do you want anyway, 50 Cent?"

"What'd you call me?" said Havoc, raising a threatening eyebrow.

Flex blinked several times. "Did I say that out loud? Wow. Awkward. I really need to go to bed."

Havoc rolled his eyes and dug his beefy hand into his pocket. When he removed it, he was holding an envelope.

"This is an invitation to the Tartarus," he said. "Fantom is living in the research facility for the time being. He wants to personally speak to you two. He wants to . . . *thank* you . . . for your service."

Havoc had to force out these last words, like a dog barfing up grass.

"Are you going to apologize to me?" I asked.

"Apologize?" said Havoc. "For what?"

"For Nero cheating on the Final Challenge and me getting in trouble for it," I said. "Duh."

Havoc snorted. "Nero is in handcuffs because he made an attempt on both of your lives. Not because of the Final Challenge. We still don't have any *conclusive* evidence on that. And since he's in a coma in the hospital, we can't exactly interrogate him."

"Conclusive evidence my big, fat hairy left toe," I said. "Why else would he try to kill me? 'Cause I'm good looking?"

"Maybe I'll *think* about apologizing if you can pick your raggedy white butt off the floor," said Havoc.

Standing up sounded exhausting. "Humph," I said as I rolled back onto my face.

"So wait," said Flex. "You're just going to teleport us over to the Tartarus right now?"

Havoc eyed us both like something slightly less evolved than earthworms. "Not dressed like a couple of bums, I'm not. If I'm gonna take you two to see Fantom, you're gonna suit up."

CHAPTER 19

Flex and I stared at ourselves in tri-panel mirrors. His bodysuit was a vivid array of green, yellow, and red. He was pretty insistent on those colors, even when Havoc told him he looked like a puke stain. Flex said they were Bob Marley's colors, and that was pretty much the end of the dispute. At least his mask was the conventional black design, wrapping narrowly around his eyes.

My bodysuit was actually glaringly different—black with a white skeletal design. But not like the hokey skeleton Halloween costumes. This jumpsuit looked like a literal x-ray of my skeleton. The texture of the suit had a holographic effect that made the bones shift wherever you were looking at it from. My mask covered a slightly larger portion of my face and resembled a skull.

In short, I looked kick-butt awesome.

"Whoever decided that all Superheroes should wear spandex needs to die in a hole," said Flex.

"It's not spandex," said Havoc. "These suits are made from an unstable molecular fabric. They adapt to your body as you're wearing them and acclimate to your respective powers."

"I've got a wedgie," said Flex, picking the fabric from his butt.

"Way more than I needed to know," said Havoc.

"Aren't we supposed to have matching suits?" I asked.

Havoc shook his head. "That's a popular myth. Every sidekick thinks they're supposed to look like their hero trainer. The public doesn't want a Superhero Mini-Me. The best sidekicks are the ones that stand out."

"Oh," I said.

"You're welcome."

"These seriously feel like Kim Kardashian's pants," said Flex.

"You wear Kim Kardashian's pants?" asked Havoc.

"You know what I meant."

"Sure I do, Kim."

"Go die, 2Pac."

* * *

I wondered how the unstable molecular fabric would react if I peed my pants.

The moment Havoc teleported Flex and me aboard the Tartarus research facility, I felt like I was on a different planet. We stood inside a beehive-like, glass-plated dome filled with more tubes, pumps, gears, and blinking computer lights than I could begin to define. Through the transparent walls, I could see that the Tartarus consisted of a series of similar glass domes. Together they formed a vast circle connected by narrow glass passageways, bathed in a rippling blue glow. Most of the domes had their own submarine boarding docks, including ours. These were no ordinary submarines though; these vessels were whale-shaped with a metal, insect-like exoskeleton. Several yellow-tinted bubble windows bulged from the framework.

In the center of the Tartarus was the true gem, however—a gargantuan rock formation, twisting and contorting into gnarled, jagged points. Its entire surface emitted a neon green, misty aura. A scaffolding infrastructure was built around it.

The Gaia Comet.

The comet's surrounding infrastructure had one particularly grabbing feature—a hulking metal machine built onto the side of it. It looked suspiciously like a gigantic gun, the barrel of which led directly into the largest of the interconnecting domes. One word was inscribed on its surface.

Cronus

Our sudden appearance in the Tartarus did not go unnoticed. A man in a white lab coat with big glasses and an even bigger comb-over approached us. (I'm not kidding about this comb-over. His hair was parted practically at his ear, scraped thin like butter over his shiny head.)

"Ah, Marrow and Flex," he said, grinning. "What a pleasure. We've been expecting you. My name is Dr. Jarvis. I'm the lead researcher here at the Tartarus."

"Cool place you got here," said Flex, his gaze still wandering. "Does it have a pool?"

"Fantom does in fact have a pool in his private living area," said Dr. Jarvis.

"What? Seriously? I was just being sarcastic."

"Fantom is funding the Tartarus," said Dr. Jarvis, "so when he's on site, which is quite often, we see to it that he's comfortable."

"Man, what a rough life," said Flex.

Havoc rolled his eyes. "I'll leave these two with you, then, Dr. Jarvis."

"Thank you so much, Havoc. Your service is greatly appreciated."

Havoc nodded and then shared a warning glance between Flex and me. "Don't break anything."

He vanished, causing a slight ripple in the air.

"I'll break your face, Busta Rhymes," Flex muttered under his breath.

"Alright then," said Dr. Jarvis, clapping his hands together. He looked way more excited than any scientist should ever be. "Let's not leave Fantom waiting."

Dr. Jarvis led us onto a glass tube elevator on the inner circle of the Tartarus. As we descended, we were given an unobstructed view of Gaia and its elaborate surrounding infrastructure. Dozens of men in white contamination suits scurried back and forth within the metal and glass labyrinth of passageways built into the comet's surface.

I stared past them, however. My gaze was pulled into the comet itself. The jagged edges like grasping claws . . . The green mist that seemed to take on a life of itself . . .

Marrow . . .

A voice entered my head like a haunting choir of voices conglomerated together.

Can you hear me, Marrow?

My vision distorted, crackling like radio interference.

What are you hiding inside your head, Marrow?

Something flashed before my eyes for a fraction of a second—a pair of glowing green eyes belonging to a face hidden in shadow.

Brother is going to kill you, Marrow . . .

CHAPTER 20

"Marrow?"

I blinked, snapping my head upright. Flex and Dr. Jarvis were both shooting me looks of concern.

"You okay, Marrow?" Flex asked when I didn't respond. "You look like you just saw a ghost."

I had no idea what I saw, but a ghost didn't seem too far-fetched.

"Er . . . yeah," I mumbled in the most unconvincing way possible. "Hey, did . . . did you guys hear that?"

Dr. Jarvis adjusted his glasses, eyeing me like I was an interesting science experiment.

"Hear what?" Flex asked.

"Uh . . . nothing," I murmured. I didn't feel comfortable recounting such a bizarre episode with some scientist here to analyze me. I would just tell Flex about it later.

Maybe.

Was I really so sleepy that I was hallucinating? This was definitely the last time I pulled an all-nighter with Flex.

Those eyes . . . I couldn't shake those eerie green eyes from my head.

My gaze was inevitably drawn back to the gargantuan Cronus Cannon in a conscious effort to forget my awkward episode.

"So how does the Cronus work, anyway?" I asked.

"It's quite simple really," said Dr. Jarvis. He seemed eager to move past my awkward moment. "Do you see that chamber that the Cronus

Cannon is pointing into? When we place our subject inside that chamber, the Cronus basically extracts their power using Gaia's own energy to draw it back into the comet."

"That whole big chamber is for one person?"

"Well, there is also a sealed observation room built into the back of the chamber. But yes, you're correct. It is a large chamber. We actually designed it to contain more than one subject if the need ever arose."

"How do you even know if this thing works?" I asked.

"We have test subjects," said Dr. Jarvis. "Kosher ones, of course. The government is fully aware of all our experimentation here."

"Who the heck would volunteer to be a test subject?" Flex asked.

The elevator reached the lowest level with a sharp *ding*. The glass doors slid open to a sleek, white-paneled hallway. Muffled screeches, howls, and snarls resounded from the far end of the corridor.

"Animals?" I asked.

"Sort of," said Dr. Jarvis, smiling knowingly. "Let me show you."

As he led us down the white hallway, the creature sounds grew louder. The hallway appeared to reach a dead end, but the wall was, in fact, a door, zipping open at our approach.

The noise erupted to a deafening level. There were no windows in this chamber—only cages. Hundreds of them. Some had bars, others were sheets of durable glass or plastic, depending on the shape or size of the creature inside it.

I had never seen creatures like these before.

They all shared a similar aquatic appearance, but the similarities seemed to end there. Some were scaly, some were slimy, and some were shielded inside crustacean-like shells. But all of them were shockingly big. One looked like a hairless amphibian sub-species of grizzly bear, glazed in mucus. Another creature was a pile of squirming tentacles, at the center of which was a snapping, rotten-toothed maw. The creepiest one, however, was a gaunt, transparent-skinned creature with a hunched, human-like body, underdeveloped fins in weird places, webbed claws, saucer-sized eyes, and a jaw full of needle teeth that had no skin to restrain its enormous mouth.

My stomach roiled at the sight of this last creature. "What are these?"

"Mutants," said Dr. Jarvis. "Gaia's nuclear fallout may have only affected humans on land, but in the ocean, the nearby sea life experienced drastic mutations. A large portion of our Gaia research has focused on the radioactive effects on these sea creatures."

"Sea creatures?" said Flex. "But . . . none of them are even in water."

"Yes, that would be because they all have lungs now."

"Lungs? How?"

"Well, it's rather simple if you believe in evolution," said Dr. Jarvis. "If you believe that man came from apes which came from amphibians which came from fish which came from single-cell organisms, then it only makes sense. The radioactivity is speeding up their evolutionary processes. Warping them, yes, but speeding them up nonetheless. Using these creatures as Cronus test subjects, our purpose has been to reverse this evolution. If we can do that with these creatures, then we should be able to extract a Super's power."

My gaze continued to wander throughout the lined cages of mutated creatures. It looked less like a science lab and more like a horror freak show.

"Do you really need this many of them?" I asked.

"Well, it's always better to have too many than not enough," said Dr. Jarvis. "Although . . . Fantom has found another use for them. In fact . . ."

Dr. Jarvis didn't finish his sentence. Instead, he excitedly proceeded through the chamber of sea mutants. The tail of his lab coat fluttered at his quickened pace. He gestured for us to follow. Flex and I shared confused glances before trailing close behind.

Amidst the noise of the creatures, a new sound emerged: a heavy thumping sound. There was no rhythm to it—merely a sporadic, resounding series of thuds.

Boom. Boom, boom, boom. BOOM!

Dr. Jarvis reached the end of the room, and the white door whizzed open. This new chamber was bigger than anything we'd entered thus far.

It was more of an arena than anything else. We stood on an elevated walkway circling around a vast, cylindrical pit. The top was sealed shut by a slightly-domed glass ceiling, separating us from a long, deadly drop.

Boom, BOOM!

The sound was coming from below us, although this time it was followed by a roar that resonated with the force of a screaming train. Flex and I followed alongside Dr. Jarvis, approaching the glass.

A monster lurched below us, sleek and gray. There was no neck connecting its broad head with the rest of its thick body. Its bulky face ended in a sharp, pointed snout. Serrated, razor teeth protruded from exposed gums. A curving dorsal fin sliced through the air. Its shark-like features ended there, however. Muscular arms and legs bulged out from its body, ending in webbed claws. Though the creature's tail was much stumpier, it provided the balance needed for it to stand upright, exposing its white underbelly.

"The creatures are excellent for combat training," said Dr. Jarvis. "This is Specimen 751. Although we like to call him Thresher. Not the most scientifically accurate name considering that he's a mutated great white. Not even a hint of thresher shark in him. We just thought it sounded cool."

The monster's small black eyes were trained on another figure in the cage.

Fantom.

Though he was still clad in his red and black jumpsuit, he wasn't wearing his mask. It made him look that much more human and vulnerable. Nevertheless, he held his ground as Thresher lumbered forward. The chamber echoed with heavy, thundering footsteps. The creature's dorsal fin swayed between its shoulder blades. Releasing another deafening roar, it lunged forward with gnashing teeth.

Fantom did not react until the last second. Thrusting both hands out, he caught the mutant shark by the top and bottom halves of its jaws. Though he was a mere fraction of its size, his super strength brought the monster to a jarring halt. Fantom's boots slid backwards on the stainless steel floor, but only a little bit. The creature struggled to snap its jaws, flinging saliva. Fantom slid his fingers between its jagged teeth for a better grip.

I hadn't noticed until now, but Dr. Jarvis stood beside a small control panel built along the glass. He ran his finger along the touchpad and pressed a digital button. A microphone buzzed softly from inside the glass.

"Fantom," said Dr. Jarvis, his voice reverberating, "I don't mean to disturb you, but our guests have arrived."

Fantom nodded. Then he let go of Thresher.

The mutant shark retaliated instantly, lunging forward and snapping. As before, Fantom held his ground.

Then he swung his fist.

It happened so fast, I barely saw it connect. Suddenly, the creature was spinning a full three hundred and sixty degrees, crashing to the ground. Even from our elevated vantage point, the floor jolted beneath my feet.

"Holy crap," I said, barely maintaining my balance. "That was cool."

"Wow," said Flex, wide-eyed. "He made that look a little too easy."

It shouldn't have been that surprising. We all knew the truth. Fantom made everything look easy. It was just crazy seeing him in action. The guy was pretty much Superman. Minus a weakness to Kryptonite or anything else out there. Oh, and he wasn't a fictional character.

Fantom leapt into the air, defying every law of physics as he soared toward us. His red cape rippled behind him. As he reached the glass, two vertical lines appeared, and a curving glass pane slid open. Fantom let gravity take over as he stepped onto the elevated circular walkway. The glass pane slid shut behind him.

He looked even bigger in real life. His bodysuit hugged every bulging muscle on his body. His cleft chin was as defined as a baby's butt, and I mean that in the coolest and most un-awkward way possible.

"Marrow," said Fantom, a smile spread across his square jaw. "Flex. So glad you two could make it. I hope I'm not interfering with your schedule."

He shook both of our hands. Mine was almost swallowed in his firm grip.

"N-n-no, not at all," I stammered before Flex could point out that this was usually the time of afternoon when he finally crawled out of bed and started playing video games.

"Fantastic," said Fantom. "Here, follow me. I'll show you to my quarters. It's a little more warm and inviting than all these mutants and gizmos."

Holy crap. Fantom was taking us to where he lived. This was infinitely cooler than any backstage pass I had ever heard of. Ever. Period.

Fantom led the way around the curving elevated pathway to another elevator. This one was also a long glass cylinder ascending the outer Tartarus wall, but I was too preoccupied with our new guest to take notice of the exotic seascape. I wanted to touch Fantom's face just to make sure he was real. Would that be weird? Yeah. Just a little bit. Bad idea.

The glass elevator stopped, and the door slid open.

"Welcome to my digs," said Fantom, arms outstretched.

The moment I stepped inside, I decided that this was the ultimate bachelor's pad—a humongous studio-style living area decked out with sleek, curving, postmodern furniture, abstract paintings and sculptures that looked like they had wandered out of Picasso's head, a piano, an electric fireplace, and a high-tech kitchen that belonged on Star Trek or something. And then, if that wasn't cool enough, two of the connecting walls were glass, providing a stunning view of the ocean depths. A school of blue- and yellow-streaked fish drifted by and then scattered as a shark approached.

Basically it was the coolest fish tank ever.

Flex's gaze wandered to several classic framed movie posters like *Gone with the Wind*, *Casablanca*, and *Vertigo*.

"Movie buff, I take it?" said Flex.

"Oh, I the classics," said Fantom. "Sometimes I wish I was Clark Gable or Humphrey Bogart, living inside their beautifully scripted fictional worlds. Living every day as part of an epic masterpiece . . ."

"Right," I said. "Too bad you have to settle with being a Superhero celebrity living in a gazillion dollar underwater bachelor pad."

Fantom chuckled and gestured to the nearby sofa. "Make yourselves comfortable. Can I get you two anything to drink?"

"I'll have a bee—" Flex started to say, and then seemed to think better of it. "Coffee," he said less excitedly. "I'll have a coffee."

"Do you have any energy drinks?" I asked.

Fantom chuckled as he strolled into the kitchen. "Sure do. Two caffeine rushes coming up. Rough night's sleep, I take it?"

"You could say that," said Flex. "I wasn't expecting so much publicity for beating the tar out of your sidekick. Er . . . no offense or anything."

"None taken," said Fantom. His back was turned while he was fast at work on the drinks. "You know, I suspected something was wrong with Nero. He seemed distracted. Paranoid. Like something was hanging over his head. I figured he was just fidgety. I never would have expected he was capable of something like this."

"Yeah," I murmured. "Me either."

It surprised me how bothered I was by Nero's sudden turn. I hated his cheating guts, and now he'd finally gotten what he deserved. Right? Shouldn't I be happy?

"I invited you two here so I could thank you personally," said Fantom. "Especially you, Marrow. From what I understand, this whole escapade started because of a certain Final Challenge."

"You heard about that?" I asked.

"Oh, I know *all* about it," said Fantom. He returned from the kitchen with a coffee mug in one hand and a clear glass filled with a fizzling yellow beverage and ice cubes in the other. "I've already had some experts look into it. Nero not only hindered your performance during the Challenge, but he telekinetically tampered with the machines monitoring his brain. Extremely advanced telekinesis. I can see why no one would have thought to look into it. So on behalf of everyone at FIST, I want to apologize."

I could barely hold onto my glass as Fantom handed it to me.

"And since I no longer have a sidekick, I want to make you an offer," he said.

I knew where this was going. I couldn't breathe.

He was going to ask me to be his new sidekick.

"Actually, it's an offer for both of you," said Fantom, glancing at Flex. "I was wondering if you two wouldn't mind doing an interview with me tomorrow on the Morning Show with Donnie Danson and a photo shoot with *Cosmo Talk* magazine afterward. I've already talked to them and they'd love to have you on board."

Okay, maybe not an offer to be his new sidekick. But an interview with Fantom was easily the next best thing.

Flex pretended to nod casually. "Yeah, I think we can squeeze that into our schedule."

"Great," said Fantom, clapping his hands together. "I'll let my publicity manager know."

He seated himself across from us and crossed his legs. His cheerful countenance took on a subtle seriousness.

"Now with that out of the way . . . I've been meaning to ask you some questions, Marrow."

"About what?" I asked. As if I didn't know.

"Well, for starters, I understand that Oracle showed you her most recent premonition—a battle between your father and me. And then you were kidnapped and interrogated by some unknown Super named Nightmare who seemed to express great interest in this visit."

"Yep," I said, perhaps a little too nonchalantly. "Pretty much."

"Interesting," said Fantom. He leaned forward, interlocking his fingers. "I know this may be hard for you to hear, but I think it's obvious your father is planning something big. Maybe something that could destroy this whole city. I need you, Marrow. I need you to help me stop your father. I need you to tell me everything."

CHAPTER 21

Something didn't feel right.

I told Fantom everything I knew. None of which made any sense. In fact, it seemed to make even less sense as I repeated it to Fantom— Nightmare's dream interrogation, his supposed interest in my visit with Oracle, and his association with my father. Nero's sudden attack was the cherry to top it all off. It hurt my head just thinking about how none of the pieces seemed to fit.

I couldn't think. And every time I tried, my mind drifted to Nero. His words still haunted me.

I'm here to kill you, Marrow.

I'd already beat the skinny little punk. Why did his stupid threat still bother me? I couldn't figure it out. Something wasn't right.

And then there was the ticking sound. Before it had only been in brief, infrequent spurts. But now it never seemed to stop.

Tick tooock tick tick . . . tick tooock tooock tick . . . tooock tooock . . .

Top that off with my episode on the Tartarus—that otherworldly voice, those glowing green eyes—and it was official. I was going insane.

I hoped that our interview on The Cosmo Show with Donnie Danson would make me feel better. The sheer spectacle of it was definitely a distraction. The CTN (Cosmo Television Network) tower was the tallest tower in all of Cosmo City, slicing through clouds and pollution like a knife. The inside was just as stunning—a sleek composition of hard edges with slanting and curving walls. As we moved past the lobby, every room and hallway seemed to share an artistic asymmetry.

I had caught glimpses of The Cosmo Show on TV, but it hardly compared to what the studio looked like in person. It was like a planetarium on steroids. The domed studio ceiling was adorned with holographic images of swirling galaxies and sprawling nebula clouds. The longer I stared at it the more I felt like gravity was going to reverse, and I would topple aimlessly into outer space.

Frantic men in CTN shirts and electronic headsets interrupted my moment of mind-bending euphoria as they rushed us backstage. A man with a clipboard and a nametag labeled "Bob" reviewed The Cosmo Show proceedings with us. I found myself paying more attention to the hairy wart in between his eyes.

Honestly, I'm not even sure why Fantom wanted us to join him. During the show he ended up doing the vast majority of the talking. Not that I minded. As popular a TV personality as Donnie Danson was, the guy creeped me out. I was choking on the chemicals in his swooping, gravity-defying hair from ten feet away, and his unflinching grin was big enough to give small children nightmares. Seriously, the guy was like a smiley mutant hybrid between the Joker and the Cheshire Cat.

The banter between Fantom and Donnie was seamless, although the occasional question was directed specifically to Flex or me. Flex handled his questions well, milking a few laughs from the audience. Every question that Donnie threw my was like a deliberate kick to the face.

"So, Marrow . . ." said Donnie, leaning forward on his desk and interlocking his fingers. His lips were peeled back, revealing all twenty-eight of his teeth. "What does it feel like to be the son of the most dangerous and deadly Supervillain of all time?"

"Uh . . ." I said. "It . . . sucks?"

The photo shoot was way worse.

The studio itself was an impressive, white-walled room strewn with white background canvases. It hurt my eyes trying to distinguish between all the white. And then there were spotlights hanging from the ceiling, lights on stands, and a number of strange lights that looked like umbrellas. All of them appeared to be arranged very specifically.

People were running around everywhere, some with papers in hand, others fumbling with equipment. My fifteen seconds of star-struck glee vanished when I met our photographer, Pierre, and the shooting commenced.

"No slouching, Marrow. You have ze posture of a monkey."

"What is zat face, Marrow? You look constipated."

"Chin up. Shoulders back. Eyes on me."

"Give me a smile, Marrow. Zis is a photo shoot, not an execution. What kind of smile is zat? You look like a homicidal sociopath."

"Ah, la vache! Je ne peux pas travailler avec cet imbécile!"

Pierre threw his hands in the air and stormed away from the camera after this last exclamation.

By the time the photo shoot was over, my head was ready to explode. Or implode. Or maybe just decompose. I followed Flex back to the rental car and closed my eyes as he drove. The ticking sound . . . Nero's words . . . They swirled together inside my skull like a mental Frappuccino.

Tick tooock tooock tick . . . tooock tooock . . . tick . . .

I'm here to kill you, Marrow.

Tick . . . tick tooock tick tick . . .

I'm here to kill you . . .

Tick tick tick tick . . .

Marrow . . .

Tick . . .

"I want to go visit Nero," I said. I blurted the words out faster than I could realize what I was saying. Something about visiting Nero just felt right.

I sounded like a crazy person.

"What?" said Flex. He looked as if I had just asked him to the royal ball in Chinese.

I decided breathing was probably important and made sure to enunciate. "I want to go visit Nero."

"That's what I thought you said."

I waited expectantly for a response. "Well?"

"You are aware that he's in the hospital?" asked Flex.

"Yeah, I know."

"In a coma."

"Uh-huh."

"Because he tried to kill you, and you punched him in the face while flying through the air at a hundred miles an hour."

"Yep."

Flex went silent.

"Okay," he said.

I blinked. "Really?"

"Yeah," said Flex. "The hospital is close. And . . . I was actually wanting to do something myself. So I'll just drop you off. Pick you up in an hour?"

"Wait—what are *you* doing?" I asked.

"Nothing. Just stuff."

"Uh-huh. Right. And I'm the Queen of France."

"Oracle," said Flex. His scraggly face flushed. "I'm going to visit Oracle."

Not the answer I expected. My suspicions were more along the lines of "the liquor store" or "I'll tell you when you're older."

"Oracle?" I repeated.

"I just wanted to visit her . . . by myself," said Flex. "Not that I don't appreciate your company or anything. It's just . . . you know . . ."

I didn't know. But frankly, as long as he was visiting Oracle, I didn't care. I was too keen on visiting Nero anyway. However, I still needed one more thing. And since Flex wanted to get rid of me . . .

I eyed Flex's cell phone sitting on the center console.

"Do you have Specter's number?" I asked.

"Huh? Specter? What do you need her number fo—?"

He paused before he finished his sentence and rolled his eyes. Grabbing his phone, he unlocked it with his thumb and handed it to me.

"Tell your girlfriend I said hi."

I didn't realize how insane this was until I was standing over Nero's hospital bed. His face seemed so calm. Peaceful. For the first time in my life, I didn't want to punch him in the face. Of course he was only in this situation because I *had* punched him in the face, but that was beside the point.

Not only was he in handcuffs, but the entire room had been telekinetic-proofed. Minus his IV and the machines monitoring his vitals, every loose object had been removed. Every other object, including his bed, were bolted to the floor. Sure, if Nero could fling a car, he could easily break the bolts. However, there was a motion sensor set up in the room, and a police officer stood outside, armed with a tranquilizer gun and ready to act the moment Nero woke up.

If he woke up. The doctors had no idea when he would regain consciousness.

I doubted the police officer would have even let me in if he hadn't seen my face all over TV. It helped that I was probably the only person in all of Cosmo City wearing a skin-tight skeleton bodysuit. I would have to try really hard to stand out more than I already did.

TICK TICK TICK TICK . . . TICK . . . TICK TOOOCK TICK TICK . . .

The ticking was louder than ever. I pressed my index and middle fingers to my temples as if I could squeeze the ticking out of my skull. I was only slightly aware of the door as it opened and closed behind me.

"Marrow?"

It was Sapphire. I slowly turned to meet her gaze. Her blue hair seemed to frame the concern in her eyes.

"Marrow, what are we doing here?" she asked.

I'm here to kill you, Marrow.

"It doesn't make any sense," I said, shaking my head. I wasn't exactly sure if I was talking to Sapphire or Nero's voice in my head.

Sapphire folded her slender arms and bit her lip. "What doesn't make sense?"

Everything. Nothing made sense. But that wasn't my response. There was something else. Something that had been bothering me for a while.

Something I hadn't really realized until now.

"Marrow," I said.

Sapphire shot me the sort of look one would usually reserve for someone dancing in the middle of the street in their underwear or throwing their own poop around like a monkey.

"Huh?" she said.

"Marrow," I repeated. "Nero never called me Marrow."

"What are you talking about?"

"Nero has always called me Bonehead," I said. "He's never called me Marrow. Not even once."

"Okay . . ." said Sapphire, clearly missing the point.

"Do *you* remember him ever actually calling me by my name?"

"Well, no, but what does that have to do with anything?"

"He called me Marrow when he tried to kill me," I said.

Sapphire was silent for a moment, her face unreadable. "So what are you saying?"

"I don't know. I don't know what I'm saying. It just doesn't make any sense."

"So you called me here because Nero actually said your name?"

"It's weird though, isn't it?"

Sapphire was unimpressed. "I think you're reading way too much into this. Just because he called you Marrow doesn't mean—"

"But he kept calling me Marrow," I protested. "Over and over again. And he didn't call me Bonehead once. That goes against everything I know about Nero. If you're Nero, you call me Bonehead because that's as far as your cleverness goes. And that's that."

"So . . . what? You think this isn't Nero then?" Sapphire gave a humorless nod to the hospital bed.

I opened my mouth to respond, but the door opened. Whisp timidly poked his head inside. "Hey, guys."

"Whisp?" said Sapphire. Her head whipped back to me. "You told Whisp to come too?"

I ignored her. "Whisp, do you ever remember Nero calling me by my name?"

Whisp blinked behind his thick glasses. "Uh . . ."

"Marrow, stop it," said Sapphire.

"He always called me Bonehead, right?" I pressed. "Do you remember him calling me Marrow? Even once?"

"Well . . . I don't think so," said Whisp.

"He was trying to kill you!" Sapphire snapped. She stepped directly between Whisp and me, meeting my gaze with a fierce glare. "He's never tried to kill you before, has he? People aren't exactly going to be themselves when they're trying to kill you, are they?"

I didn't have a response for that.

"I know this has been hard on you," she said. "It's been hard on all of us. We all went to school with Nero. But that doesn't change what happened. Nero made a mistake. A big mistake. And nothing can change that. So you need to stop whatever it is you're trying to prove, because you sound like a crazy person. You're seriously scaring me, Marrow."

That shut me up. I was crazy. I was literally losing my mind, and I was dragging Sapphire and Whisp into it.

"Is this a bad time?" Whisp asked, fidgeting awkwardly. "Because I can leave if it is."

"No, it's . . . I'm sorry," I said, lowering my head. "Both of you. I don't know what's gotten into me. I haven't been myself lately."

Sapphire stepped forward and wrapped her arms around me. "It's okay, Marrow. We're here for you."

"I think you're right," I said. "I think I really am going crazy."

"Don't talk like that."

"I'm being serious," I said. "I keep hearing this sound. This . . . ticking. Like a clock, except it has no rhythm. The ticking is all over the place. And ever since Nero attacked me, it's gotten worse."

Sapphire's arms went limp around me. She stepped away, eyes widened and mouth slightly ajar. "You've heard it too?"

Her reaction made every hair on my body rigid. "Wait—*you* can hear it?"

"Well . . . not right now," she said. "But I've heard it. I thought it was just part of a really bad migraine or something."

Whisp's nervous gaze darted between the two of us. He shifted uncomfortably where he stood. Sapphire and I both simultaneously turned to face him.

"Yeah," he murmured, nodding his head slowly. "Me too."

Okay. This was too weird. It was one thing if I was hearing a ticking sound inside my head. I was crazy. Big deal. But if all of us had been hearing the same ticking sound inside our own heads . . .

"You can hear it right now?" Sapphire asked me.

"Yeah," I said. "You can't?"

Sapphire shook her head.

"Whisp?" I asked.

"Not since yesterday," he said.

TICK TICK TICK TICK . . . TICK . . . TICK TOOOCK TICK TICK . . .

The ticking continued to pound my skull. It was so relentless I could barely think.

"When did you start hearing the ticking today?" Whisp asked.

"When?" I squeezed my eyes shut in a futile attempt to clear my mind. "Uh . . . I dunno. I woke up to it."

"Has anything made it worse?"

I opened my eyes. My gaze drifted to Nero lying peacefully in his bed.

"Yeah. It got worse when I came here."

Now that I thought about it, there was only one other time when the ticking sound was this bad. It was on the drive back from the hospital two nights ago.

Right before Nero attacked us.

"Nero," I said, breathless. "It's always worse when I'm around Nero."

Sapphire's eyes grew even wider, bouncing back and forth between Whisp and me. Meanwhile, Whisp had his lips pursed in a straight line, his gaze concentrated on some invisible point in space.

"What does it sound like?" Whisp asked.

"Huh? You just said you've heard it."

"Yes, I know I've heard it," he said. "But I can't hear it right now. What does it sound like?"

"Um . . ." I said. I actually struggled to concentrate *on* the sound now that I had spent so long trying to concentrate in *spite* of it.

TICK TOOOCK TOOOCK TICK . . . TOOOCK TOOOCK . . . TICK

"I dunno," I said. "It's a ticking sound. Like a clock. Except some of the ticks are longer than the others. Deeper. Like they're scratching on my skull or something."

"And there are spaces between some of them, right?" said Whisp. "Like some of the ticks are grouped together?"

"Er . . . Yeah, I guess so," I said.

"Like . . . Morse code."

Morse code? I didn't really know anything about Morse code. But I had heard someone else mention it recently.

We should communicate to each other with Morse code or something.

"Nero knows Morse code," I said. "He wanted to use it when we were about to fight Arachnis in the Final Chall—"

My breath fell short as I realized where Whisp was getting at with this.

Was Nero trying to communicate with us?

Whisp dashed out of the room. This earned a baffled look from the police officer standing outside. Sapphire and I exchanged puzzled glances, but Whisp was only gone for a few short seconds. He brushed past the police officer and came into the room with a custom St. Luke's Hospital pen and notepad in hand. He shoved both of them into my chest.

"Write it down," said Whisp.

"What? How am I supposed to write down ticking?"

"Use dots for the short ticks and dashes for the long ones. And be sure to leaves spaces when the ticks pause."

"You know Morse code too?" I asked.

"Yeah. Don't you?"

"Um . . ." I chose not to answer the question, focusing instead on the ticks. Holding the paper against the wall, I immediately started drawing dots and dashes.

TICK TOOOCK TICK TICK . . . TICK TOOOCK TOOOCK TICK . . . TOOOCK TOOOCK . . . TICK . . . TICK TICK TICK TICK . . . TICK . . .

I scratched my pen on the paper furiously. I didn't go far past this point when Whisp stopped my hand.

"The pattern is repeating," he said. "Let me translate it."

I surrendered the pen and paper to him as he took my place at the wall. Whisp stuck his tongue out of the side of his mouth as he scribbled down letter after letter with hardly a pause in between. He dropped his writing hand and held the paper up for us all to see.

L P M E H E

"Lipmeehee," I said, pronouncing the letters together as one word. "Well that's helpful. Morse code can kiss my butt."

"No, wait," said Sapphire, snatching the paper and pen out of Whisp's hands. She proceeded to jot down new letters. At first I thought they were random, but I quickly realized she was starting from a different point in the loop.

It took her only seconds to finish. When she did, she seemed to falter. She held the paper away from her like it was diseased, and her hand began to tremble. Whisp and I crowded around her.

H E L P M E

Help me.

CHAPTER 22

The brief silence felt like an eternity. None of us spoke. None of us moved. The two words seemed to scream from the paper.

"What is this?" Sapphire finally said. Her voice seemed to waver in sync with her trembling hand.

She knew. We all knew. All three of our gazes shifted in synchronization to Nero lying on his bed.

"It's Nero," said Whisp. "Somehow he's using his telekinesis to cause the ticking." His voice choked slightly as he added, "H-h-he . . . he wants us to help him."

"Because he's in a coma?" asked Sapphire.

"No," I said, shaking my head. "I heard the ticking a couple days before then. I mean . . . I even heard it right before he attacked me."

"So what are you saying? Nero's being mind-controlled by someone?"

There was clearly a mocking edge to her tone. She obviously intended the comment as pure sarcasm. However, Whisp and I exchanged uncomfortable glances.

"Oh nuh-uh," said Sapphire, shaking her head in a blue flurry. "That's ridiculous. Mind control isn't real. I mean . . . it just isn't! Right?"

Whisp shrugged. "Superheroes weren't real until the Gaia Comet hit. Who's to say there isn't a Super out there who has the power to control minds?"

"I think we're jumping to conclusions here," said Sapphire. "Just because we *think* the ticking sound is louder around Nero and he just *happens* to know Morse code doesn't mean some Super is mind-controlling Nero to make him assassinate you, Marrow."

She had a point. The message was real, but we had no solid proof that it was, in fact, Nero.

Unless . . .

I approached Nero's bed. Now that I was familiar with the rhythm of the ticking, it was obvious that this Morse code message was ticking on a loop. There was very little conscious effort going into it. But it was a conscious effort nonetheless. I leaned into Nero's ear.

"Nero . . . do you need help?" I whispered.

Sapphire rolled her blue eyes. "Oh my gosh, Marrow. Are you kidding me? He's in a coma. He's not going to—"

The ticking stopped

"SHHHHHHHHHH!" I said, shushing Sapphire with a fierce pointed finger. Sapphire stared at my fingertip, appalled, as if I had just pointed a bazooka at her.

I waited. Whisp leaned in closer, adjusting his glasses as if that would make some profound difference. Sapphire continued to glare at my finger and looked like she might break it.

Tooock tick tooock tooock . . . tick . . . tick tick tick . . .

I bolted up, ripping the pen and paper from Sapphire's hands. This new ticking pattern didn't continue on a loop, but I had already slashed the paper in a violent line of dots and dashes. As I stabbed the last dot, I pushed the paper into Whisp's face.

"What does it say?" I asked.

Whisp's eyes zipped across the dots and dashes, but he didn't bother writing it out this time.

"Yes!" he exclaimed. "It says 'yes'!"

My heart pummeled inside my chest. I leaned into Nero's ear again.

"What do you need help from?" I asked. "What's happening to you?"

A series of ticks erupted into my brain faster than ever. I attacked the paper with my pen, struggling to keep up. When I had two lines of dots and dashes, the ticking ceased. I gave the notepad to Whisp.

He took one glance at it and took my pen. He scribbled letters down and then lowered it for us to read.

INSIDEMYHEAD

Inside my head.

The hair on my arms and neck pricked.

"Who?" I asked into Nero's ear. "Who's inside your head?"

Tick—

Then it stopped. Everything stopped. I waited for several long seconds, expecting it to continue at any moment.

Nothing.

Sapphire and Whisp glanced between me and the single dot I had drawn on my notepad.

"What's going on?" Sapphire whispered.

"E?" said Whisp, reading the single dot on the notepad. "Nero is being mind-controlled by someone named E?"

TOOOCK TOOOCK TOOOCK—!

The ticking erupted with greater force and urgency than I had ever heard before. I scrambled to readjust my pen, copying the dots and dashes which looked more like chicken scratch than anything that was ever meant to be read.

. . . TICK TOOOCK . . . TICK TOOOCK TICK TICK . . . TI—

The ticking stopped abruptly. As if something had smothered it. I hesitated before ending the message with one last dot.

Nero's eyes and mouth opened wide beside me.

He gasped, but that soon became a croaking sound. Thrusting his back off the bed, his body formed a contorted arch. His heart monitor buzzed with activity.

Nero dropped to the bed, motionless. His heart monitor flatlined.

The police officer ambled into the room but hesitated the moment he entered. A nurse burst in past him, followed by several more people in medical scrubs and white coats. In mere seconds, the room was swarming.

"Oh my gosh oh my gosh oh my gosh," said Sapphire in wide-eyed panic.

"Get these kids out of here," a doctor ordered amidst the chaos.

A nurse stepped forward, shepherding us out the door with extended arms. "I'm sorry. You three have to go."

"Is he okay?" I asked. "Is he alive?"

The door closed in front of us.

I was so stunned that I hardly noticed Whisp as he ripped the pen and paper from my hands. He scribbled hastily while Sapphire observed over his shoulder.

His handwriting slowed. Sapphire's jaw dropped.

When Whisp finally finished, he dropped the paper. He stared past me as if he might pass out.

"Whisp?" I said, finally snapping out of my own daze. "What's the—?"

My gaze shifted to the floor for only a second. That was all I needed to see it—a single name that impaled me.

ORACLE

CHAPTER 23

Oracle? The weird old cat lady who smelled like mothballs and boiled cabbage? *She* was controlling Nero?

She tried to have him kill me?

"This has to be some kind of sick joke," said Sapphire, shaking her head. "There's no way."

I wanted to agree. I really did. I mean, what motive could she possibly have for killing me? But one glaring detail kept me from agreeing.

She was a Telepath. And not just any Telepath. *THE* Telepath. Her power was all about getting inside people's brains, and she was the best at it. Motivations aside, she was easily the best equipped for the job.

Could she really be so powerful? Could she really go this far?

Whisp took a deep huff from his inhaler as if it might be his last breath. "We need to do something," he said. "We have to tell our partners."

Sapphire attempted to nod, but her unsteady attempt more resembled a dashboard bobblehead doll. "Specter's at the gym right now. It's only a couple of blocks away."

"Nova isn't far either."

The realization didn't hit me until then.

Flex.

My voice became lodged in my throat. Both Sapphire and Whisp turned my way when I didn't speak.

"Marrow?" said Sapphire. "Are you okay?" Her gaze penetrated me for a few long seconds before her eyebrows shifted ever so slightly. "Where's Flex?"

I didn't reply.

I ran instead.

"Marrow?" asked Whisp.

"MARROW!" Sapphire yelled. I might have been a little terrified by her tone if I wasn't in such a panic already.

Oracle *wanted* Flex to visit her. But if she was the one behind Nero's attack, who knew what her true intentions were. Was he in danger? He *was* the laziest, most unmotivated Superhero of all time, after all. One detail set him apart however—a detail Oracle had shared with me herself.

His brain was immune to her power.

I ran faster.

Out of the corner of my eye, I noticed a plastic barrel water dispenser vibrate beside me. Then it exploded. The plastic shrapnel missed me, but the water erupted in a very concentrated horizontal stream, blasting me in the side. I barely tapped into my skeletal structure, bracing myself for the impact. I hit the wall and then slumped to the floor, sopping wet.

"W-wh-wha . . . what the . . . ?" I sputtered.

As I staggered upright, slipping on the wet tile floor, Sapphire stormed up to me.

"Sapphire? Was that y—?"

Sapphire slapped me in the face. If you remember me telling you how much her playful punches hurt, multiply that by eight hundred and fifty-seven, and that's how much this hurt. It hurt even more than being blasted into the wall with water, but maybe that's because I had a split second to brace myself. This, however, caught me completely off guard. I opened my mouth to adjust my jaw which felt like it had been knocked out of place.

"Ow!" I said. "What was that for?"

"Don't you dare run off like that again!" said Sapphire. "What do you think you're doing, anyway?"

"Flex is in danger!" I protested. "He's visiting Oracle right now. I need to help him!"

"Are you stupid?" asked Sapphire. "Oracle tried to kill you with Nero! She *wants* you dead!"

"What are you, my mom?" I asked. "Get out of my way!"

"You are NOT going over there!"

"I'm not going to let Flex die!" I snapped. I stepped forward, shoving my way past Sapphire.

Sapphire shoved me even harder back into the wall. And then she slapped me in the face. Again. I blinked in stunned shock. The good news was that the left side of my face was pretty much numb at this point.

"And I'm not going to let you die!" said Sapphire. "I will not let you be that selfish. There's nothing heroic about getting yourself killed and hurting the people who care about you. I know you *think* nobody cares about you, but they do."

A mascara-stained tear trickled down Sapphire's cheek.

"I do."

After two slaps in the face, I was surprised when she leaned forward and hugged me, her face in my shoulder. After several seconds of stunned silence, I awkwardly wrapped my arms around her as well. I mean, what else was I supposed to do with them? Stand there and look like a tree?

Whisp shifted uncomfortably where he stood. I attempted to shrug and gave him a look that said, 'Girls. Go figure.'

He shrugged also and gave me a look that said, 'This is why I play computer games instead.'

Sapphire finally let go and wiped away at her eyes. "Sorry. I don't know what came over me."

"No, it's . . . uh . . . fine," I said. I raised my fist and coughed into it.

Whisp's gaze was once again bouncing back and forth between our embarrassing exchange. "So . . . should we maybe be getting help right about now?"

Sapphire turned from Whisp to me with a quiet, pleading look.

"Yeah," I said, nodding slowly. "Let's get help."

The three of us raced for the elevator. Fortunately, the door opened right as I pushed the button. Burnished wood panel walls surrounded us. The sleek metal doors slid shut and the elevator descended. I stood closest to the doors, ready to bolt out the moment they opened.

"We'll probably need more than just Nova and Specter," said Whisp. "If Oracle is half as powerful as I think she is, we'll need all the help we can get."

There were a lot of Supers out there to choose from. But I'm pretty sure all three of us were thinking of the exact same person.

We were nearly to the ground level when the elevator lights began to flicker above us. Our smooth descent jerked and shuddered.

The elevator then came to a complete halt.

"You've got to be kidding me," said Sapphire. "This seriously cannot get any worse."

The lights went out entirely.

"Well this is awesome," I said. "Remind me never to take the elevator again."

Neither Sapphire nor Whisp said anything.

"Hello? You guys?"

The lights flickered back on. I released a very audible sigh.

"Oh, thank goodness," I said, turning around. "For a second I thought—"

Whisp and Sapphire both stood side by side with their eyes rolled back, exposing nothing but the whites.

"Sapphire!" I said, gasping. "Whisp! What happened to your eyes?"

Whisp and Sapphire opened their mouths and spoke simultaneously.

"Hello, Marrow," said their combined voices. Together, they had a very demonic quality that stripped any sort of humanity out of them. "Your friends aren't home right now."

CHAPTER 24

"Oracle . . ." I breathed. My eyes shifted between my possessed friends. "Is that . . . you?"

"The one and only," said Whisp and Sapphire together. "Do you like my new outfit?"

Both Sapphire and Whisp gestured to themselves in synchronized motions.

"It takes a couple years off, doesn't it?"

If Oracle was trying to be funny, it wasn't working. "What happened to their eyes?" I asked.

"It's a normal effect of my true power," said Whisp and Sapphire's voices. "It takes a great deal more concentration on my part to normalize their eyes, and my mind is in a hundred places at the moment. Thanks to you and your meddling friends, secrecy isn't as high of a priority anymore. I've been planning this all along, but we're going to have to move ahead of schedule now."

The elevator lights continued to flicker. I glanced around at the stationary elevator.

"How'd you stop the elevator?" I asked. "You're a Telepath, not a Telekinetic."

"I'm controlling the electrician downstairs as well. You will find that when you can control any*one*, you can control any*thing*. But enough talk. There's been a change of plans. You are going to come to me."

The elevator hummed to life as it lurched downward. The lights ceased flickering.

"I don't get it," I said. "Why not just mind-control me too?"

"A very valid question. The truth is that I *can't* mind-control you. Not anymore, at least. For some reason I can't enter your brain anymore. I can't even read your thoughts."

"What? Really? But . . . why?"

Even as I asked, a thought occurred. During Nightmare's interrogation, I had consciously attempted to mimic my father's immunity to telepathy. Sure, I was only trying to build a barrier against the hallucinations, but still . . . Is that what was happening now? I had a permanent, unconscious barrier against all forms of telepathy?

"I have my suspicions," Sapphire and Whisp said.

The elevator door chimed as it reached the ground level. A shadow slipped over me. I turned to find a massive, muscular silhouette filling the opening.

It was Havoc. Or at least it used to be. His eyes were white like Sapphire's and Whisp's.

"Havoc?" I gasped. "You have Havoc?"

"Honey, I can *have* anyone that I want," said Oracle through her human puppets. Havoc's deep voice had now joined the chorus, making it that much eerier. "Don't underestimate me, Marrow. The truly unique thing about my power is that I can access the powers of those I control. If I control their brains, I literally have access to everything. I don't even need to learn how to use it. All of that knowledge is right here at my disposal. Now, I've arranged a ride for you. How about we discuss this in person?"

"And if I refuse?" I said.

Havoc, Sapphire, and Whisp laughed in haunting harmony. "Supposing that you *could* fight off three Supers under my control . . . I think you're fully aware of my visitor this morning."

I cringed. Flex.

"Sticks and stones may not be able to break his bones . . . but there is more than one way to skin a cat, so to speak. The easy way or the hard way. Take your pick."

My hardened gaze stared into Havoc's blank white eyes. Finally, I sighed. "Where are you?"

Havoc, Sapphire, and Whisp all curved their mouths into unnerving smiles. "The same place I always am. I never leave Maximus home alone."

Whisp and Sapphire stepped forward, each of them taking me by the hand. Forming a circle with Havoc, he swallowed their hands in his grip.

Our surroundings exploded into a smoky haze. Gravity became a suctioning vacuum, and I felt like I was being folded inside out, exploding through a black hole.

Only a second later, my feet were on solid ground again. My disoriented gaze shifted up from the carpet.

Oracle's house didn't look anything like I remembered.

All of the furniture had been pushed aside, replaced by spotlights, television cameras, and cameramen. Several people were tinkering with cords or electrical equipment as Oracle's armada of cats slunk between their feet. But this was not just any one television news crew. I stood by a window and noticed at least a dozen news vans and crew members skittering around like ants. I spotted several different channel logos on vehicles, equipment, and uniforms. It looked like every big news crew in Cosmo City was crammed into or around Oracle's house. And beyond them, red and blue lights flashed. A perimeter of police cars surrounded the scene.

All of their eyes were white. Every one.

I pulled my gaze away from the window. Inside, the crews' mind-controlled efforts had a very obvious focus. Every light, every camera, was pointed at a single figure tied to a chair and gagged. Flex's eyes were red and swollen. It was obvious he had been crying, but I don't think it was so much *what* was happening to him as *who* was doing it to him—Oracle, the woman who took him in from the orphanage. Probably the only mother he ever knew.

I had cried like that before.

"You probably think I'm insane."

Oracle's voice was unmistakable. Cameramen and technicians stepped aside as she emerged from the crowd. She was hunched slightly, resting on a cane, wearing an ugly black dress and an uglier knitted shawl. Her milky white eyes stared past me.

"Oh, I don't *think* you're insane," I said. "That would imply that I had any doubt about it."

"How little you know," said Oracle. "I'm not the villain, Marrow. I'm the hero. I'm simply a breed of hero who's willing to do whatever it takes to accomplish what needs to be done."

"And what would that be?"

"Isn't it obvious?" she said, gesturing to everything surrounding us. "Your father, Marrow! This is all for your father! There are several hackers under my control who will tap us into the CTN Tower and get us on every television screen in Cosmo City. I'm going to kill Spine once and for all—the one thing that Fantom could never do. And I'm going to use you and Flex as bait."

CHAPTER 25

This had to be the worst idea in the history of bad ideas. Right up there with underwear. Seriously. It's like a prison for your butt. Who decided we have to wear those anyway?

"Bait?" I repeated. I raised an incredulous eyebrow. "If we're bait, isn't he actually supposed to *care* about us?"

"Such naivety," said Oracle. "You really don't get it. He's your father. Of course he cares about you."

"No, I don't think *you* get it," I said. "He *abandoned* me. He's as much my father as Larry the Cable Guy is. I might as well be dead. That's how much he cares about me."

Oracle shook her head of frizzy gray hair. "There was once a day when I could see inside Spine's head. And he loved you infinitely more than his own life."

"Yeah, before my mom died and he went out of his freaking skull, maybe," I said. I attempted to say this without emotion, but the words cracked slightly coming out. It was even more uncomfortable having this conversation with the crowd of mind-controlled news crews bustling around.

"I would think the same thing too," said Oracle. "But there is one piece of evidence that proves otherwise."

I rolled my eyes, unconvinced. "What's that?"

"I can't read your mind anymore," said Oracle.

"What does that have to do with anything?"

"Everything," said Oracle. "I could read your mind when you came to visit me, and now, only a few days later, I can't. What does that tell you?"

"Uh . . ." I said.

"It tells you that something in that very short window of time made you immune to telepathy," she said. Her head cocked slightly as she stared past me. "But you already know what that is, don't you? You know the what . . . but you don't know the *who*."

"I officially have no idea what you're talking about," I said. Which was partly true. The last thing she said made about as much sense as . . . well . . . underwear.

"You probably already know that you developed a telepathic barrier during your interrogation with Nightmare," said Oracle. "But you probably also think that this was your own doing. What you don't realize is that that's what Nightmare wanted all along. That's what Spine wanted."

I blinked. There was no way I had heard correctly.

"Your father used Nightmare to make you immune to my power," Oracle continued, filling in the silence.

"Ha," I said in a flat tone. "That's funny. Because I thought he was interrogating and torturing me. My bad."

"The interrogation and mind torture were a cover," she said. "Nightmare's hallucinatory power is telepathic in nature. It's all based in the brain. His goal was to use it over and over again until your power altered the bone matter in your skull, creating a psychic barrier. This was your father's unconventional attempt to protect you from me. I'm sure your father experimented with the very same method to develop his own immunity to my power. I must say, it's a clever trick."

I couldn't believe it. All those hours of psychological torture, being killed over and over again . . .

They were to protect me?

I didn't know if I wanted to hug my father or punch him in the face.

What was I thinking? Of course I still wanted to punch him in the face. Over and over and over again. But still . . .

"If my father cares about me, that means there might still be some good inside him, right?" I asked. "Why go to all this length to lure him in and kill him? I mean, he's pretty much disappeared, hasn't he? He hasn't hurt anyone in ages."

"Love for a child does not make one a good person," said Oracle. "Shortly before he developed an immunity to my power, I had the misfortune of peering inside his head. He's evil. *Pure* evil. I've never felt so much anger and hatred in one person. And he's coming back. I've seen it. You've seen it. And when he does, Marrow, people are going to die."

"Yeah, but Fantom—" I protested.

"Fantom will fight him, but we don't know who will win," said Oracle. "I'm not willing to take that risk. So I'm taking matters into my own hands. Any casualty in the process will be for a worthy cause. I'm sorry, Marrow."

A massive hand clasped onto my shoulder. I didn't even have to glance at it to realize it was Havoc. A smoky mist exploded around me. I teleported twenty feet forward, right beside Flex, only now there was another chair right beside him. Havoc shoved me into it. Another white-eyed cameraman was approaching with rope.

Like heck I was going to go along with this. I always wanted an excuse to punch Havoc in the face.

I tapped into my skeletal structure, making my arm light for a swift, last second, weight-intensified blow. I barely had a chance to move my arm, however, before a freezing mist engulfed me. Every limb and muscle went rigid. Sapphire emerged as the mist cleared. I glanced down to find that my entire body was coated in a thick sheet of ice from the shoulders down. It pricked my skin like tiny needles everywhere.

"There's no need to get so worked up over this," said Oracle as she walked towards me from across the room. "Whether you realize it or not, this is the greatest heroic purpose you could ever serve—to help defeat the most horrific Supervillain of our day. This is what you've lived your whole life for, right? To be a hero? Embrace it, Marrow. This is your destiny."

Havoc retrieved the rope from the cameraman and was fast at work tying my ice-coated body to the chair. This might have been a mildly impossible task if I hadn't been conveniently frozen in an awkwardly bent position with my butt sticking out. Geez, did I always look this idiotic when I fought?

"W-w-w-w-what are you going to do with us?" I asked, trembling inside my icy shell. I couldn't stop my teeth from chattering.

Oracle opened her mouth to respond but paused, raising her head to some invisible distraction.

"Everything's ready," she said, every wrinkle accentuated by a sick smile. "Are you boys ready to be TV stars again?"

Dozens of empty white eyes were all trained on us. Several faces were halfway hidden behind cameras directed our way. A particular display screen was facing us so we had a clear view of what we looked like on camera. Flex and I looked horrible—he, red-eyed and gagged, and me, shivering in a sheet of ice. Oracle was beaming like a psychopath.

A portable sign with the words "On Air" lit up in green.

"Good evening, Cosmo City," said Oracle. Several cameras zoomed in on her face. "Allow me first to apologize for interrupting your normal programming. My message is actually only for one individual—one whom you all know well. One whom you all once feared."

"Spine."

Oracle's smile vanished and her brow hardened over her milky eyes.

"I know you're out there, Spine," she said. "I'd like you to come pay me a visit. Now, before you question whether this is worth your while, let me show you what is at stake here."

Oracle reached a knobby hand to Flex's gag and pulled it down to his neck. She then hobbled aside, and the cameras zoomed out. The display screen honed in on us in all our pathetic glory.

"Do you two have anything to say to the camera?" she asked.

Flex glared fire at Oracle but didn't open his mouth. I had about as much to say.

"Very well," said Oracle. She turned back to the cameras. "Here's how this will work, Spine. I will give you until 7:00 p.m. That is in roughly one hour. If you are a minute late, I will execute one of our lucky guests here tonight on live television. Please don't make me resort to that. I just had new carpets put in."

The "On Air" sign blacked out.

CHAPTER 26

"She's lost it," Flex whispered.

Now that the broadcast was over, all of the mind-controlled television crews were standing in random places around the house, staring into space. Sapphire, Whisp, and Havoc were interspersed among the crowd. Meanwhile, Oracle was sitting in an armchair on the other end of the living room, sipping honey chamomile tea.

"Tell me about it," I muttered under my breath. The ice was finally melting off me, but Havoc had used up the entire length of rope tying me to the chair. I wasn't going anywhere.

At least if I died peeing my pants, I'd be too wet from the melted ice for anyone to ever know.

"No, I mean she has literally gone insane," said Flex. "I know Oracle. I lived with her, for crying out loud. There is no way she would ever rationalize something this extreme. I think all that telepathic power has backfired on her—like it's just too much for her brain. When you think about all the minds that she goes inside . . . I mean, it's the only explanation!"

"Okay . . ." I said. "So what are you saying?"

"I'm saying that when we break free and fight our way out of here, we can't kill her."

"You have a plan to escape?" I said with raised eyebrows.

"No," said Flex. "But when we figure one out, we can't kill her."

I rolled my eyes. "Well I don't think that'll be a problem if we don't have an escape plan."

"We'll get out," said Flex a little too casually.

"Right," I said, snorting. "And supposing we *do* somehow manage to break out, how exactly is any mental hospital supposed to treat a Telepath with this much power?"

"We're *not* killing her," Flex growled.

"Fine, whatever, we're not killing her," I said. "You just wake me up as soon as you figure out your escape plan, 'kay, Houdini?"

I rolled my head back at an uncomfortable angle and closed my eyes, ending the conversation.

This was bad. This was really bad. Dying was obviously the worst thing that could happen, but, for some reason, being saved by Spine didn't seem like a much better option. What exactly was he going to do with me and Flex if he did bother to "rescue" us? Spine: the most horrific Supervillain of our day, as Oracle so eloquently put it.

My stomach squirmed at the thought.

But who was I kidding? If Oracle was as delusional as Flex seemed to think she was, then Spine probably had no intention of even spitting in our direction. If Spine really had used Nightmare to make me immune to telepathy, it was probably to keep Oracle from digging up information on him.

He wasn't going to save us. We were both dead. But I guess I had him and Nightmare to thank for psychologically preparing me to die in a million different ways.

Thanks, Dad. You're a real pal.

Heck, I was even tied down to a stupid chair. This wouldn't be any different from those hours I had spent with Nightmare. Well . . . except for the part where I actually die.

I slumped my head in defeat. My downward gaze followed the rope securing my thighs to the seat of the chair. As my gaze drifted off the rope and onto the floor, I noticed the leg of the chair.

The flimsy leg of a cheap metal folding chair.

"I've got an idea!" Flex and I said simultaneously.

We exchanged disbelieving glances.

"Well, you tell me your idea first," said Flex. "Mine isn't that good."

"Uh . . . okay," I said. "I can increase my bone density to the point that I can break the legs of my chair. I should be able to squirm out of my ropes from there."

"Okay, never mind," said Flex. "My idea was better than that."

"Hey!" I protested. "What's wrong with my idea?"

"Do you see all these people? You may be able to wiggle out of your ropes in a minute or two, but if you break your chair, Oracle will have these guys swarm you faster than Republicans to a gun rally."

"Wow, you're not a biased liberal, are you?" I asked.

"Wha—okay . . . faster than Democrats to . . . I dunno . . . a tree-hugging convention or something. That's not the point. The point is that we need a way to break out of here fast."

"Okay, so what's your big idea?"

"It's simple," said Flex. "Your dad has the ability to grow his bone structure outside of his body. We just need you to grow a sharp bone that can cut through your ropes. Then you can cut me free too and we can fight our way out of here.

I responded with a humorless stare. "Is there a name for what's wrong with your brain?"

"What? I've seen your dad do it like a billion times. It's easy."

"Yeah. That's because it's my *dad's* power, not mine, fartbrain."

"Have you ever tried it?"

"Back when I was being tested to enter FIST," I said. "And I couldn't do it. Because it's my dad's—!"

"Because it's your dad's power, I got it," said Flex, rolling his head from side to side. "But apparently being telepathy-proof was your dad's power just a couple days ago. Now you can do it. But hey, what do I know? I'm just a fartbrain."

I didn't have an argument for that.

"Your old man tried to explain it to me once," said Flex. "He said it's like creating an imbalance in the bone density—lighter on the inside, heavier on the outside. Somehow, distributing the density like that pushes out new bone growth."

I wanted to argue. I wanted to tell Flex just how stupid his plan was. But I didn't for one reason.

I knew that he was right about my plan.

Even if I broke the chair, I wouldn't be able to get out of my ropes in time. It was either this or die or . . . yeah, dying was really the only other option. There was no way Spine would come.

"Fine," I said. "I'll try it."

I forced my focus into the bone in my wrist. That seemed like the most practical point to cut myself free. Tapping into the bones in my wrist, I could feel the density wavering slightly under my concentration. Separating the density was easier said than done. My power only went two ways—heavy and light. I couldn't just flip that mental switch sideways. I bit my lip and could feel my face growing red.

With a sigh, I released my connection.

"I can't do it," I said, breathless. "It's impossible."

"Where are you putting your focus?" asked Flex.

"Into my wrist."

"Hmm . . . Try your fingertip."

"Huh?"

"Your fingertip," he repeated. "It's a more defined point. It should be much easier to concentrate on it."

"What part of 'it's impossible' do you not understand?" I asked.

"The part where I'm supposed to believe whatever comes out of your underdeveloped twelve-year-old brain."

"I'm fourteen," I grumbled.

"Yeah, and I'm the Queen of England," said Flex. "Now shut up and focus on your finger."

I exhaled through flaring nostrils, but I didn't argue. I redirected my attention to my right index finger. As I did, I realized Flex was right. Concentrating at the end of a bone was much easier. All I had to do was push the density into the very tip, and the rest seemed to take care of itself. I could feel the density imbalance growing in my finger.

"Just be careful though," said Flex. "Spine said when he first learned to control his spikes, it hurt like—"

"OW!" I yelped.

Something sharp pricked my fingertip. My sudden outburst caused Oracle to lift her head. Her milky eyes stared past me from across the living room.

"Is there something I can help you with, Marrow?" she asked.

A simple "no" seemed like it might draw more suspicion. So instead I said, "Er . . . yeah, a burger and fries would be great. No pickles though. I hate pickles."

Oracle shook her head and returned to her tea.

My heart was hammering. Meanwhile, Flex leaned his head back, observing the back of my chair. His eyes widened as he jerked back upright.

"There's an *ike-spay* sticking out of your *inger-fay*," he whispered out of the corner of his mouth.

"Huh?" I said, shooting him a look of the utmost confusion.

"There's a spike sticking out of your finger!" he hissed. "Don't you know Pig-Latin?"

"Um . . . no, I don't speak Latin or pig," I said.

"Okay, whatever, that's not important," said Flex, shaking his head. "Can you do that with all of your fingers? You should be able to cut out of there in no time."

"Wha—? You want me to poke holes in all of my fingers?"

"The holes will close up when you retract the spikes," said Flex. "If you're anything like your father—which we've proven multiple times now that you *are*—your cells naturally heal at an accelerated rate to counterbalance your unstable skeletal structure."

"Yeah, but . . . do you have any idea how much it hurts?"

"I'm sorry, princess. Would you like me to fetch you a goblet to cry all your tears into? Oh wait. I can't because we're both tied up, and we're going to die!"

"Okay, okay, calm down," I said. "I'll do it."

Pushing a bone spike out of each finger one by one sounded like an excruciating process. If I was going to do this, I'd do it all at once. Doing it to the one finger was easy enough. Doing nine fingers simultaneously should be manageable.

I swallowed hard. This was going to hurt a lot.

Leaning my chin into my chest, I bit into the rope binding me.

"What are you doing?" asked Flex.

I tapped into the bones in my hands and exploded the density into my fingertips. My fingers reacted with stabbing fire. A subtle *sheeenk* sounded from behind me. It was a good thing I had the rope in my mouth. My jaw clenched so hard I thought I might bite right through it. When I spit it out, I could still see my teeth indentations.

Oracle's head snapped up again. This time she stood up and there wasn't an ounce of humor in her expression.

"What are you doing, Marrow?"

"Nothing," I said, shaking my head and blinking the tears out of my eyes.

Wow, that wasn't suspicious at all.

"Why were you biting the rope?"

Crap. I thought this woman was supposed to be blind.

"You didn't bring me my burger and fries," I said, struggling to blink away the moisture in my eyes. "I'm hungry."

"Are you crying?"

I quickly decided the psychic blind people were my least favorite type of blind people. Why even bother mentioning that they can't see?

"I just . . . I really love burgers and fries," I said, sniffling.

Oracle shifted her empty eyes to Flex.

"The kid loves burgers and fries," said Flex with a shrug.

Oracle's face contorted into a shriveled mass of wrinkles. "You two are up to something."

Great. Time was up. Showtime or no time.

I sank my new claws into the rope behind me.

I expected to have to scratch and dig frantically to slice my way through. Much to my surprise, my claws sank clean through. The ropes sank low around my chest.

There was a moment of awkward silence as Oracle and I glanced down to my loose ropes. And then our gazes met again.

Seriously, why she bothered looking down or up was beyond me. Blind Telepaths, geez.

I snapped out of my stupid daze and sliced through the ropes binding my legs. Too easy. I jumped to my feet and rope fragments fell to the floor. In two swipes, Flex was free too.

It wasn't until now that I noticed my claws—twelve-inch ivory blades protruding from each finger. They were about three times the size I expected.

"Nice delay there," said Flex.

"Oh, I'm sorry," I said. "Did you prefer being tied up?"

When Flex didn't follow up with a sarcastic response, I knew there was something wrong.

Oracle hadn't budged. I had assumed she'd simply frozen. Then I noticed that every white-eyed news reporter, cameraman, technician, and computer hacker in her house had formed a tight circle around us. There had to be nearly a hundred of them, and several more were funneling in from outside.

"Where do you think you're going?" asked Oracle.

"Disneyland?" Flex suggested with a shrug.

Oracle shook her wiry gray head. "Get them."

The crowd closed in around us like zombies with gaping mouths and reaching hands.

"Marrow," said Flex. "Do you remember me telling you about the Whip?"

My brain was in such a panic at this point, I had to remember to breathe just to register what he was saying.

"Uh . . . yeah?" I said uncertainly.

"Let's go Indiana Jones on these stiffs."

"Indiana Jones?" I repeated. The name alone seemed to empower me. Renewed confidence flooded my veins. "I can do Indiana Jones."

Reversing the density in my fingertips, I retracted my claws into my fingers. And yes, it hurt just as much as it did pushing them out. I shoved the pain aside as Flex and I clasped hands. Increasing my bone density and fortifying my arm, I became an anchor.

And then I swung.

Flex was surprisingly light as I whipped him out. His body stretched ten feet, nailing one man in the face with his feet.

My arms didn't stop. Flex flew in a circle. The first wave of people collapsed simultaneously. I kept swinging and Flex's elongated elastic body smacked the army of white-eyed faces seamlessly, mowing them down in droves.

Whackawhackawhackawhackawhackawhack!

Wave after wave fell. Flex's body swirled, stretching fifteen feet. Twenty feet. His body was almost unrecognizable—a colorful blur with flailing dreadlocks. Despite the friction of constant pummeling, his swift form hummed as he sliced through the air. The rise of piling bodies became an obstacle course that our attackers were forced to climb over. They were practically sitting targets.

"Yee-haw!" I hollered.

"G-g-g-e-e-e-t-t-t-t-t-t-i-i-i-n-n-n-g-g-g d-d-d-i-i-i-z-z-z-z-z-z-y-y-y," Flex wailed in a vibrating slur.

One moment we were an unstoppable force of nature, even though Flex looked like he was going to barf three hundred and sixty degrees. The next, Havoc appeared directly in front of me in a burst of swirling mist.

His sledgehammer fist nailed me in the face.

Fortunately, my increased bone density could easily withstand a blow from Havoc that would otherwise be crippling. Unfortunately, I was so heavy that I hit the floor like a boulder, smashing into the floor.

Flex, meanwhile, catapulted in the opposite direction, hitting the ceiling fan. His elastic body wrapped around it several times before the entire thing crashed to the floor.

Before I could normalize my density, Havoc grabbed me by the collar of my jumpsuit and hoisted me off the ground. Though I probably weighed more than he did at the moment, his biceps rippled in defiance. It would have seemed really cool if I wasn't scared for my life.

Come on, Marrow, use your head. Use your . . .

I grabbed Havoc by the forearms and pulled myself up to his eye-level. My skull was a bowling ball as I head-butted him in the face.

Havoc dropped. Making myself light, I barely managed to land on my feet.

I had hardly regained my bearings when a burst of bluish-white flashed in my peripheral vision. The blast hit the wall, encrusting the entire surface in ice. Flex stumbled out of the way, nearly backing into me as Sapphire stalked toward him.

"Your girlfriend is a real peach," he said.

"She's not my—"

A feline growl cut me short, followed by a hiss. Several more growls and hisses followed in a terrifying feline choir.

Cornering us from our other side, Whisp approached, flanked by an army of cats. Each feline crouched low as it prowled forward, preparing to pounce.

"You've got to be kidding me," I said.

A familiar gray tabby led the army of cats, arching his back and baring his claws.

"Maximus!" Flex exclaimed. "Bad kitty!"

Behind Whisp and the legion of felines, the scattered and beaten news crews rallied together. Even Havoc crawled up from the floor and joined the mismatched ranks, proving that his skull was every bit as thick as I had always assumed.

The Whip was great for knocking people over, but these creeps kept getting back up. We needed to hit them with something heavier. As much as I hated it, I already knew the weapon we needed.

Me.

"Ball and Chain?" I suggested.

Flex's open jaw curved into a smile. "Now we're talkin'."

Flex and I clasped hands again. I took a deep breath like it might be my last and retracted my bone density.

"When I squeeze your hand, let's get things heavy," said Flex.

I nodded, trying hard not to acknowledge how completely awkward that sounded.

I was immediately glad for my last breath. Flex whipped me back and slung his rubber arm forward, pitching me like a baseball. You know . . . except for the part where you actually let go of the ball. Everything became a disorienting blur. It felt like the last time I was freefalling out of an airplane without a parachute.

Thank you, Nightmare.

Flex squeezed my hand. I tapped into my bone structure, exploding in a brief burst of density. My timing was flawless, smashing into some poor sap who flew into the wall while I bounced back.

Flex's hand-squeeze was all I could focus on. He squeezed, and I went from a flying squirrel to a human wrecking ball. Impacting at such high speed over and over again in every direction made me feel like I was a slab of meat being tenderized. But I could hear bodies soaring and crashing through Oracle's living room—some as big as Havoc, some as small as—

"Meeeeeeeeeeooooooooooowwwwww—!"

WHACK!

"Sorry, Maximus!" Flex exclaimed rather distraughtly.

How Flex was able to talk while he was swinging me around I'll never know. I could barely breathe. Take the worst roller coaster in the universe and times that by infinity and you might have a smidgen of an idea of how nauseating this was. I definitely wasn't tall enough for this ride.

Naturally, the Ball and Chain had to end as smoothly as the Whip. Flex had just slung me for another blow when he simultaneously screamed and, instead of squeezing my hand, he let go.

I tapped into my bone density, hoping to slow my insane momentum and preparing to hit just about anything. *SMACK! BAM! POW!* I plowed through an obstacle course of indistinguishable people and furniture. When I finally came to a crash-and-burn stop, I was lying face down in a tangled pile of people. My human cushion was soft and smelled like cool mint.

I opened my eyes to find that I was lying on top of Sapphire, face to face. It was a lot less romantic than I would have hoped for, considering her bloody nose, her blank expression, and her pure white eyes which were infinitely creepier when they were inches from my face.

Of all the people to land on—seriously. The universe clearly hated me.

Normalizing my density, I squirmed off of the tangle of human limbs and scrambled to my feet. I soon realized I had made a mistake. The moment my body wasn't there to pin Sapphire's arms down, her palms came up with icy mist crackling at her fingertips. I lunged sideways, barely dodging a concentrated burst of blizzardy energy.

My redirected gaze skimmed past Flex who was now enveloped in hissing and clawing cats. The Ball and Chain clearly wasn't as effective fending off the smaller targets.

"Bad kitties!" Flex screamed. "Bad, bad—GAAAAAHHHHH!"

My brief moment of distraction was shattered as the carpet underneath me exploded in freezing mist and hardened to ice beneath my feet. I barely managed to scamper to my feet on the slippery floor.

Too late.

The zombie news crews came down on me in a fleshy tsunami. I felt like that dude who catches the football at the very last second before getting crushed into the ground by every single player on the opposite team. I didn't have a chance to tap into my bone structure and brace myself. I hit the carpet hard, completely immobilized under a wriggling human mass.

My power was useless without the ability to move. And apparently Flex's power was useless against an army of evil mind-controlled cats. So much for going Indiana Jones.

Defeat, however, took an unexpected turn for the strange.

The human dog pile writhing on top of me suddenly became still. Not a bump or a nudge. Not even a twitch. It was as if they had all suddenly died—minus the part where they were actually dead. I could still feel heartbeats and soft breaths.

The smothering weight of a dozen bodies lifted, toppling off me. I heard their limp forms tumbling a few feet away.

My brain faltered at my sudden freedom. As I rolled over onto my back, I gazed up at a man towering over me—bigger than Havoc and more frightening than Nightmare. The guy was built like something beyond human.

Dark, knotted hair erupted from his scalp, blending with his grisly beard. He wore a long leather jacket which seemed to be substituting for the shirt that he *wasn't* wearing. Nope. Nada in the shirt department. Nothing but a vastly hairy, bare chest beneath his unbuttoned jacket. But beneath all the grit and scruff, his crisp blue eyes were eerily familiar.

This man was my father—Spine.

CHAPTER 27

For several long moments, neither of us moved. We didn't even open our mouths. We just interlocked gazes, each carrying unspoken weight. I couldn't read anything in his eyes. That alone made him ultimately terrifying.

Finally Spine extended a calloused hand so big it could palm my entire face. Dirty, chipped fingernails protruded from fingerless, leather biker gloves.

"Marrow . . ." he said. His voice was a deep, resonating growl with a peculiar calmness to it.

Instead of the harshness I'd expected, I detected concern.

"You have to come with me," he said. "Now."

My gaze shifted across the room. Every person and cat in the vicinity was lying unconscious. Except for Flex. Still sitting on the living room floor, surrounded by motionless balls of fur, he stared at Spine just as slack-jawed as I was.

Despite the countless bodies littering the room, I somehow singled out a lone figure lying in the wreckage—Oracle. Her withered eyes were closed and a drop of blood trickled from her wiry gray hairline.

Was she . . . ?

I couldn't finish the thought. I couldn't even move. Every muscle in my body was concrete.

"We have to get you somewhere safe," he said. Urgency became evident as his hardened blue eyes wavered. "You're in danger."

"Stay away from him!"

Flex had snapped out of his stupor. Standing upright, he pointed an accusing finger like the barrel of a gun. His eyes were wild and furious.

"Stand down, Flex," said Spine. Considering his rough appearance, his calm composure was baffling. "There's no time for this. Marrow is coming with me."

"Oh, so you can train him to be like you?" said Flex. "Another bloodthirsty monster?"

"You don't know anything," Spine growled. "I don't care what you *think* you know about me. Marrow is my son and nothing can change that."

"Is that what this 'good guy' spiel is? Think you're going to win some twisted father of the year award?"

Flex paced slowly until he was standing between Spine and the door.

"You're not leaving here with Marrow," said Flex. "I'm not going to let you."

In the short time I'd known Flex, I'd never seen him so livid. His arms were rigid with balled fists.

"I'm warning you, Flex," said Spine, narrowing his gaze. "I'm taking Marrow, and that's final."

Flex shook his head slowly. "Over my dead body."

Spine's nostrils flared behind his beard. "Your choice."

No sooner did he speak than he was gliding across the floor like a skipping stone across water. Rearing his arm back, his fist became coated in a bone-plated glove. Flex didn't even have a chance to blink.

I had tapped into my skeletal structure before I even realized what I was doing. Flying across the room, my bones became lead at the last second and I pummeled myself into Spine. It was like running into a mountain, but I didn't hold anything back. We hit the floor so hard it rattled beneath us.

Flex froze as his wide-eyed gaze shifted between Spine and me. I ignored him as I staggered to my feet.

Spine shifted on the floor and slowly crawled to his hands and knees. His blue eyes met mine. There was no anger or even shock in his gaze.

Instead, he looked hurt . . . but not in a physical sense.

Why did I feel bad? I didn't know this guy. How could I even pretend that he was really my father? He was just a phony who happened to share my DNA.

"Son . . ." he said. He stopped there. He seemed to be out of words, which was fine by me.

"Son?" I said. "What? You think you can suddenly show up and decide to be my dad? Where were you when Mom died? Where were you when I actually needed you?"

"Marrow . . . you don't understand . . ." He staggered to his feet, but yet again, there was no threat in his stance. In fact, he appeared defeated already.

"No, *you* don't understand," I said. "You think you can just waltz up and decide to be my dad because you saved us from Oracle? Let's get one fact straight, okay? I. *HATE*. YOU!"

Flex no longer had the raging fury award—it now belonged to me. I was fuming so heavily I could barely control myself. I wanted to scream and punch and run and cry all at once. But all I could do was stand there and breathe like a wild animal, fists shaking at my sides.

I didn't know how far Spine could fake this caring father routine. But the single tear trickling down his cheek shattered any and all expectations I had. This act was suddenly way too real for comfort.

No. This was no act. It *was* real.

"I'm sorry I haven't been there for you," said Spine. He maintained a firm tone despite his glistening eyes. "But I've always loved you . . ."

A distant whistle sliced through the atmosphere, intensifying to a scream in seconds.

Then the wall exploded.

CHAPTER 28

A rippling shockwave threw me back. I hit the floor hard, feeling numb as I rolled and smacked into the far wall. Wood chips and splinters rained down with an assortment of shattered and tattered household debris. Everything was smothered in a choking veil of smoke. As the smoke dissipated, two figures emerged from the haze, staring each other down in a psychological standoff. On one side, Spine raised both fists and bone spikes sliced out of his knuckles.

On the other side, a red cape flared in the haze.

Fantom.

It wasn't until now that I realized it. This was it—the scene from Oracle's premonition. The smoldering hole in Oracle's wall. The police lights flashing around her home. The bodies on the floor. It all made sense.

"Going somewhere?" Fantom asked through gritted teeth.

Spine's face was an impenetrable mask. No emotion. Nothing. Although his raised bone spikes seemed to speak for themselves.

Spine charged.

He had obviously tapped into his bone structure because, despite his size, his movement was a blur. I barely noticed the bone-like scales that sprung from his face. They formed a solid mask over his entire head, engulfing all but his eyes and nostrils. He lunged headfirst, smashing into Fantom's face. Fantom's head snapped back. Before he could even fall, Spine caught him—only to head-butt him in the face again. And again. Over and over and over again. On his final blow the bony scales shattered, sending fragments everywhere.

Fantom's head was draped back, prominent chin up and jaw open. I couldn't see his eyes, but he didn't seem to be moving.

Flex had been sprawled across the floor, but he struggled now to push himself upright. "No way . . ." he gasped.

Then it started—a flat, eerie sound. As it quickened, I realized it was mock laughter. "Ha . . . ha . . . ha . . ." Fantom lifted his head slowly, adjusting his jaw and tilting his head from left to right to crack his neck. The slightest trace of a smile hadn't left his face.

"My turn," he said.

Fantom head-butted Spine so hard he flew across the room, tumbling and smashing into the adjacent wall. Fantom streaked after him. No sooner did Spine hit the wall than Fantom's fist connected with his face, smashing it into the drywall. Then, gripping Spine by his coat collar, Fantom ripped him out of the wall and chucked him at the ceiling like a doll.

A shockwave of air burst beneath Fantom's feet, sweeping the floor clean of debris as he launched into the air after him. Fantom zipped past Spine's soaring form, directly into his path. Spine's momentum caused him to collide with Fantom's fist once more. As Spine fell, Fantom plunged down with him, driving him faster to the ground.

Flex and I exchanged knowing glances. We hastily scrambled away until our backs were to the wall. I curled into a ball, bracing myself for the worst.

Fantom smashed Spine into the floor in an explosion of shattered floorboards, shredded carpet chunks, and all of the unconscious bodies that were still strewn about the room. Even crouched low, I was jolted off my feet, sprinkled in splinters and specks of obliterated debris.

As the haze cleared, a small but very distinct crater became visible through the house's foundation infrastructure. In the center of it, Fantom was straddling Spine, decking him in the face over and over again, shattering the few scales that remained of his skeletal mask. Spine's face whipped from left to right as he interchanged fists with each blow. Even though his black mask obscured the top half of his face, sweat was visible on Fantom's exposed cheeks. His smile was gone, replaced with clenched teeth.

His eyes shifted to me.

His left fist was raised for another blow, but it halted. He lowered it. Standing up from Spine's unconscious body, he dusted his bodysuit off. His gaze shifted from me to Flex.

"Flex, could I trouble you to call the police for me?" he asked. "Before I kill this man?"

* * *

As soon as the police arrived, the perimeter of unconscious cops surrounding Oracle's house began to wake up, along with the hundred or so news crew members scattered everywhere, inside and out. The way people were moaning and crawling off the ground, it felt like *Night of the Living Dead*. Everyone was coming back to life.

Everyone except for Oracle and Spine. Both of them were still unconscious, and Fantom was seeing personally to their incarceration. It was weird seeing Fantom interact with the police. Every order he gave, they did. Even the higher ranking officers didn't object to his unauthorized control of the crime scene. Then again, Fantom had single-handedly captured the most notorious Supervillain of all time *and* the most powerful Telepath in the world gone rogue. If the police resented him for it, they didn't show it. I sensed nothing but respect.

Oracle's head was padlocked inside a strange metal helmet adorned with several meters and gauges—a mind cuff. They weren't used very often, but in the rare instance that Telekinetics and Telepaths went bad, it was the only way to keep them under control. The mind cuff absorbed any sort of psychic energy emitted inside.

Oracle and Spine were towed away in separate armed vehicles guarded by nearly half a dozen officers each.

When police started questioning the waking police officers and news crews, they were oblivious to anything that had happened. The time was a mere blackout in their memory. Even Sapphire and Whisp had no idea what had happened since the hospital elevator.

Everyone wasn't so oblivious to the beating Flex and I had given them.

Ambulances started arriving several at a time, paramedics towing people off the crime scene in stretchers. Flex and I both sat on the tailgate of one ambulance, wrapped in red, cotton blankets that had been placed over our shoulders. When officers started interrogating us, Flex did the talking. I attempted to fill in the blanks, but when the conversation drifted to Spine, my voice fell, dead in my throat. I'd never felt so numb—so lifeless—in my entire life.

That single tear.

I've always loved you.

One particular officer, Jenkins, didn't like my speechlessness. He started pressing me specifically for details.

"So did your old man tell you anything, kid? Let you in on his plans?"

"Marrow hasn't talked to his dad in years," Flex cut in. "He—"

"Hey, Jack Sparrow, I wasn't talking to you," Jenkins snapped. His eyes narrowed on me. "Well, kid? You keeping any secrets with your pops?"

"Relax, officer," a familiar voice intervened. Fantom approached from the crowds, entering our small circle. "Marrow isn't an accessory to a crime. He's a hero. Cut the kid a break."

Jenkin's scowled and licked his teeth behind his lips. "Yeah, whatever," he grumbled and skulked off.

Instead of looking Fantom in the face, I found myself staring at his hands. The same hands that had beat my father in the face. Over and over again.

His knuckles didn't even have a scratch.

"You doing okay, Marrow?" Fantom asked.

I nodded. My head felt like it weighed a million pounds.

Fantom glanced at Flex, unconvinced. Flex simply shrugged.

I could feel Fantom's penetrating gaze return to me. I clearly wasn't star-struck anymore; I wanted to tell him to bug off and save the day somewhere else.

"Flex, could you give us a moment?" he asked.

Flex bit his lip, peering into my lowered gaze. He nodded hesitantly. "Yeah, okay."

Hoisting himself off the tailgate, he wandered into the chaos of blue and red flashing lights.

Fantom stared down on me for a long moment. I continued to stare holes into the ground. Finally he slouched down on the tailgate beside me.

"Sorry for beating your dad up," he said.

Not quite the comment I was expecting. Well, maybe it was, but I think I'd imagined it just a little more eloquently.

"What's there to be sorry about?" I asked. "He's a Supervillain. That's what you do. You beat up Supervillains."

"Yeah, but he's still your dad," said Fantom. "Supervillain or not. I know that wasn't an easy thing for you to see."

"It's whatever," I said, shrugging. "I don't care."

It only felt like a half lie since I felt so numb to any sort of emotion. I *wanted* to cry. I felt like I should. But instead, I felt completely detached. Disconnected from my body, from my brain, from reality—everything. Part of me wished Oracle had just killed me. Then I wouldn't be replaying that teary-eyed image of my father on an endless loop.

"You should care," said Fantom.

"Why?"

"Because that just means you're human."

I snorted. "Well being human sucks."

Fantom leaned back and chuckled. "Yeah, I guess it does. But then again, I suppose we're not your average human beings, now are we?"

I didn't respond. At the moment, I would kill to be normal. My power was just a painful reminder that I was my father's son.

Remember what I said before? That having super powers isn't always as super as it sounds?

Yeah. True story.

"What do you suppose it is that truly makes a hero?" Fantom asked.

I rolled my eyes. Fantom or not, I really wasn't in the mood for this conversation. FIST had shoved enough bull crap hero pep talks down my throat to last a lifetime and a half. My gag reflex couldn't take another one.

"Hey, hear me out," he said. "Is it about how many people you save? Is it about how many criminals you put behind bars or how many Supervillains you defeat? Seriously. Do you know what it is?"

"No, but I have a feeling you're going to tell me," I said.

"Dang straight I am," said Fantom. "In the end, being a hero isn't just about doing heroic things. It's about being a symbol. It's about what you stand for. And sometimes being a symbol means making the toughest decisions. Every society needs a symbol. It's been that way since the beginning of time. Every great civilization has had its gods and its heroes. Marrow, *we* are those heroes. When times are hard and evil is rampant, *we* are the symbols that people can look up to. *We* can inspire good in mankind. That is what being a hero really is."

Fantom leaned towards me, demanding eye contact.

"So tell me, Marrow . . . what do *you* stand for?"

"I don't stand for anything," I muttered.

"I don't believe you."

"I don't care what you believe."

"Ah, I see," said Fantom. "Is that why you stopped your father before he could hurt Flex?"

I had no response for that.

"You sure have a way of not standing for anything," he said.

"It was nothing," I said.

"It didn't look like nothing. Aside from me, you're the only person I've ever seen throw Spine down like that."

I raised an eyebrow in confusion. I'd been here the entire time Flex had recounted our story, and he was deliberately vague on the details of how I had intervened between him and Spine.

"How . . . ? How did you know . . . ?" I asked.

Fantom shrugged with a knowing smile. "Well, this entire thing did go down in a room full of cameras."

"You mean the cameras were still recording?" I asked in disbelief.

"Well, it's hardly Academy Award material," said Fantom. "Just a bunch of fragmented shots. But, with some careful video editing, I have a feeling we're all going to be internet sensations by morning."

I blinked as his words slowly sank in. I had barely recovered from my last moment of fame. The thought of experiencing that again was exhausting. At least Flex and I had Fantom to share the glory with this time. I was sure he'd absorb the majority of it like a sponge.

"You don't look so excited," said Fantom.

I didn't feel so excited.

"Does Flex know about this?" I asked.

Fantom turned his head, and I followed his gaze. Remarkably, I spotted Flex in an instant. He was immersed in a small crowd that had gathered around the back of the Channel 13 news van. The bright glare of a television screen held them all captivated.

"I think he does now," said Fantom.

I didn't respond. My gaze remained fixed on Flex's face. His eyes were big and then his mouth opened wide. Almost simultaneously, the crowd erupted into wild cheers and clapping. Several people patted Flex on the back. He let loose a wide smile.

I'd never seen him so happy.

"You two make a good team," said Fantom.

Slowly, I nodded. "Yeah. I guess we do."

Fantom was silent for a moment. "Marrow, I want to make you an offer."

Oh, great. This again. I rolled my eyes.

"I'm really not in the mood for another photo shoot or anything," I said.

Fantom chuckled. "That's not exactly what I had in mind."

"Oh. Well, please do elaborate," I said with a notable lack of enthusiasm.

"It's really quite simple," said Fantom. "I was hoping you would be my new sidekick."

CHAPTER 29

Verbal shellshock—that's what my brain was experiencing at the moment. Fantom's offer came like a flash grenade. I didn't know what to think. I *couldn't* think. And breathing had suddenly become as confusing as rocket science.

Everything I had ever wanted was suddenly being handed to me—right here, right now.

So why wasn't I excited?

Fantom's grin began to slip slightly as he waited for a response. So I responded with the first intelligent thought I could muster.

"Why?"

Most people would argue that that wasn't an intelligent thought at all.

Fantom leaned back and chuckled. "I admire your modesty, Marrow. We already know that you were the real top scorer in the Final Challenge, not Nero. And you've proven your courage twice in one week. You are true hero material. Honestly, there would be no justice in this world if I didn't take you on as a sidekick. And hey, we both know that I'm all about justice, right?"

Fantom said this last part with a smirk. I think he was trying to be funny, but I couldn't even fake a laugh.

I didn't feel like a hero at all. My gaze wandered back to Flex. His smile. The happiness was practically radiating from him.

"What about Flex?" I asked.

"Well, if you accepted, Flex would no longer be your mentor," said Fantom.

My countenance sank. "Oh . . ."

My disappointment was mind-boggling. What the heck was I sulking about?

"You two make a phenomenal team," said Fantom. "There's no doubt about it. But . . . there's a reason you two mesh so well."

I knew why. As much as I loathed it, I knew it all too well.

"Because Flex and my father were a good team," I mumbled.

Fantom nodded solemnly. "And there's nothing wrong with that, mind you. But, given the circumstances, it might be healthier for you to take a break from Flex. And I mean no disrespect to either of you. However, the more time you two spend together perfecting your teamwork, the more you'll be reminded of your father. And . . . well . . . I'm only trying to look out for your mental well-being."

My head was swimming. On one hand I saw a perfect future: Train with Fantom. Become the next big hero. It was an inevitable pathway to success. On the other hand I saw something that I couldn't quite put into words. Flex and I had made something out of nothing. We weren't just overnight heroes. I don't think I realized what Flex was to me until now—a big brother, a father, and a best friend all rolled into one. Was he obnoxious? Yes. Sarcastic? Of course. Rude? Booger-picking pirates had better social etiquette.

But I wouldn't have him any other way.

"And if you're worried about offending Flex, don't be," said Fantom. "He's a loner. Always has been, always will be. As great a team as you two make, he'll be happy for you. And he'll be happy to go his own way."

"Yeah . . . I guess," I murmured unconvincingly.

"I'm not asking you to make a decision right away," said Fantom, noting my hesitation. "Think it over. Sleep on it. I know you'll make the right decision."

People always say that. You know I'll make the right decision? How do you know what I'll decide? Are you a Telepath or something? How do you even know what the right decision is? How can you say that?

So, naturally, I said, "I accept. I'll do it."

"Really?" said Fantom. "You sure you don't need time to think it over?"

"It's the opportunity of a lifetime," I said. "What's there to think about?"

"That's the spirit. I'll have my driver pick you up from Flex's place. Say . . . tomorrow night at seven?"

"Sounds great," I said, forcing a bleak smile.

* * *

Marrow . . .

I was standing on the glass elevator of the Tartarus. It descended further than any elevator should ever be capable of.

Can you hear me, Marrow?

I felt like I was being pulled into the center of the earth. But even as I descended to treacherous depths, the Gaia Comet never strayed far from my view. Its jagged surface reached out to me with stone claws, pulling my gaze in with its alluring green mist.

What are you hiding inside your head, Marrow?

Neon green eyes glowed from the shadows—eyes without a body.

Brother is going to kill you, Marrow . . .

I woke up drenched in my own sweat, lying on Flex's piece-o'-crap couch. I tilted my head to the window. The sky was an off-black canvas, painted in the glow of city light and pollution.

A dream. It was only a dream.

Except that I remembered my experience on the Tartarus all too clearly. *That* wasn't a dream. I had no idea what it was, but certainly it was more real than I cared to admit.

Being awake only reminded me that I still needed to talk to Flex. Too much had happened that night. I resolved to tell Flex about my conversation with Fantom in the morning.

The thought of it twisted my insides.

Unlike me, Flex woke up a new person. Seriously. Nothing could bring him down. The insurance company finally called and told him that his Volvo was totaled—big surprise there—and he laughed it off. When we walked to the auto shop to pick up the belongings from his car, he winced slightly at the sight of the videotape from Oracle, still sealed inside a manila envelope.

He then threw the videotape in the trash on the way out and seemed to lighten up instantly.

I paused at the trashcan as he kept walking. "What are you doing?" I asked.

"What do you mean, what am I doing?" Flex asked. "What are you doing?"

"Don't you at least want to watch it?" I asked.

"Hmm," Flex thought aloud. "The video was a way of getting me to come visit her. When I finally did visit her, she used both of us as bait for Spine. Um . . . I'm going to say no. No, I do not want to watch it. Not even a little bit."

Flex turned back around and kept walking. I glanced back into the trashcan and cringed at what I was about to do.

I shoved my hand inside. Something slimy grazed my wrist. I shuddered as I fished the manila envelope out. Wiping my hand off on my pants, I hastily scrambled to catch up with Flex. His gaze shifted from me to the object in my hands.

"Really?" he said.

"I want to see what you looked like as a kid," I said, which was actually true. I was pretty sure he wasn't born with dreadlocks, but trying to picture him without them seemed impossible.

"You're weird." Flex's critical stare morphed into an amused smirk. "I like it."

* * *

My first concern as we arrived home was that Flex didn't have a VCR, and I wasn't exactly sure where I was supposed to find one. A museum, maybe?

I shoved this concern aside as Flex turned on the TV. I sprawled on the couch, facing the opposite direction. The last thing I needed was to see my father's face on national news.

". . . the Anti-Telepathy Movement has just become World War III," a female news reporter announced.

Not what I was expecting. I shot back upright on the couch and faced the TV.

"Senator Statman has been the leading advocate in the Anti-Telepathy Movement," the blonde news reporter continued. "Since Oracle's rampage last night, manipulating one hundred and sixty-two people as well as twenty-one cats, Statman has seized the opportunity to make a final, crippling blow on the community of telepathic Supers."

The screen shifted to an older, heavyset man with three chins and no neck. An army of microphones were shoved at his face.

"Telepaths are a danger to our nation," said Statman. "Not only is the right to have private thoughts violated but so is the right to control our own bodies and minds, as we have seen last night. Oracle is a Telepath whom we have trusted with matters of national security. Who is to say how many security breaches have been made and how many minds have been tampered with as the government has carelessly worked with her? Whether or not she was integral in the capture of Spine is a completely invalid point. Telepaths need to be more than just regulated. They need to have their powers taken from them."

The screen flashed back to the news reporter. "The President of the United States spoke in a public address earlier this morning, stating that every measure is being taken to assure that no such breaches have been made," she said. "The White House has also issued what has rapidly become known on the internet as the Cronus Order—a mandate to gather into custody all Telepaths and to have their powers removed via the Cronus."

Flex dropped the remote control onto the floor.

The screen shifted to a camera looking at the Cronus from inside Tartarus. The camera panned slightly, demonstrating the sheer scope of the cannon built onto the side of the Gaia Comet.

"Fantom recently revealed the Cronus Cannon," the reporter continued, "a machine built with the capability of utilizing and reversing the Gaia Comet's radioactive energy to extract a Super's power. The project was funded by Fantom himself and was developed by a team of scientists living on board the Tartarus research facility."

The camera switched to a man in a white lab coat. His big glasses and frightening comb-over made him easily recognizable as Dr. Jarvis.

"This is the sort of epidemic that the Cronus was created for," said Jarvis. "Taking a Super of Oracle's caliber into consideration, the Cronus needs to be used. And considering that there is technically no way of measuring the true level of a Telepath's power, the Cronus must be used on all registered Telepaths. If we care about our public's safety then there is simply no other way around it."

The reporter continued, "The Cronus Order commenced immediately following the President's address. Due to the high-risk nature of the Cronus Order, SWAT teams are being utilized to gather the Telepaths in a military-style tactical approach."

The screen became a shaky handheld camera view of an armor-clad police team breaking down a door and funneling into a house. A mother with a young child in her arms screamed. A father stepped forward to intervene but was shoved out of the way. Police barged through the house, shining flashlights down the hall and into bedrooms. Towards the back of the house, the camera and several lights honed in on a young boy in dinosaur pajamas standing in the middle of the bedroom.

"That's the target," said a voice from off screen. "Get him."

The boy cried as they approached. They had only taken a few steps when the sound and picture on the camera became distorted, pierced by a high-pitched noise. Several of the officers crumpled to the floor, screaming as they clutched their heads.

"Get him, get him, get him!"

One of the officers managed to stagger forward with a familiar metal helmet in his grasp. He practically threw himself at the kid, managing to wrestle the helmet onto his head and latch it shut.

The boy was screaming and squirming as the police carried him out of the house. The mother was screaming even louder, thrashing and crying as one of the officers held her back.

"Even renowned hero, Fantom, is assisting in the Cronus Order," said the reporter.

The scene transitioned to Fantom standing in front of a suburban backdrop. Several police officers rushed back and forth in the background, bathed in blue and red flashing lights.

"It's a matter of justice," said Fantom. "The Cronus Order came from the President of the United States himself. If I can't uphold justice in this capacity, then what good am I as a hero?"

"You've got to be kidding me!" Flex exclaimed. "Justice? This is supposed to be justice?"

Flex yelled and swiped the TV remote from the floor, only to chuck it at the wall. The plastic bottom panel and two batteries burst out on impact. Storming over to the TV, he kicked the button panel, miraculously managing to turn it off. Clutching handfuls of his dreadlocks, he staggered to the couch and collapsed beside me.

Dramatic much? Yeah, but I was used to it by now.

"This is sick," he said. "It's unconstitutional! Herding people up like cattle so we can use some experimental machine on them that hasn't even been tested on humans yet? They didn't even mention that tiny little fact, did they? And even if it does work, we're taking away something *incredible* from these people! A gift that's being treated like a curse. All because one Telepath went crazy. They haven't even looked into why she did what she did. She's obviously mentally unstable. But no, let's just assume that all Telepaths are evil and do away with the lot of them."

So much for nothing bringing Flex down today.

"And then here comes Fantom," he continued, hardly done with his rant. "'It's a matter of justice.'" He mockingly mimicked Fantom's voice, puffing his chest out with his hands on his waist. His poor imitation sounded more like Barney the dinosaur. "That chucklehead wouldn't know justice if it bit him in the—"

"But the order *did* come from the President," I intervened. "I mean . . . that kinda legitimizes it, doesn't it?"

"The President only gave the order because the government used Oracle to help them find terrorists," said Flex. "Her doing something like this immediately taints everything they've accomplished. So, obviously, they have to disassociate themselves from her in every way possible. But that's no excuse for a Super like Fantom getting sucked into their twisted charade. It's like he's *letting* himself be used as their puppet."

I was torn. As much as I disagreed with what was happening, I hardly thought that made Fantom a bad guy. My mind drifted to what Fantom had told me last night.

"Maybe he's trying to stand for something . . . more," I said, hesitating. "You know, more than just being a Superhero"

Flex cocked a skeptical eyebrow. "What are you talking about?"

"I just think you're only looking at the situation from one side. I think Fantom is trying to be a symbol that stands for more than all that."

"Why are you defending him?"

"I'm not defending him."

"You are *so* defending him," said Flex. "What'd he tell you last night that's suddenly made you his biggest fan? Did he ask you to be his new sidekick or something?"

Flex had the biggest smirk on his face when he said this last part. It made it that much more awkward when I didn't respond to his sarcastic question. The words became a hairball lodged in my throat.

Fantom was having me picked up tonight, and I still hadn't told Flex that I wasn't his sidekick anymore. At this point, though, I couldn't just dance around it. I had to tell him.

My delayed response and awkward expression seemed to speak for itself.

"What?" said Flex. He suspiciously analyzed my gaze for several long seconds, then shook his head. "No . . . he didn't."

I had no idea what to say at this point. So I said nothing. My continued silence waved like a giant red flag.

Flex's eyebrows lifted. "He did?"

After another brief hesitation, I slowly nodded. "He asked me last night."

"He asked you to be his sidekick," said Flex.

"Yeah."

Flex's mouth grew small as he absorbed my one-word response. "What'd you say?"

Did he seriously need to ask that? Would it be this awkward if I had simply turned down Fantom's offer?

"Well of course I said yes," I said. "What else would I say?"

"Oh, I dunno," said Flex, staring at the floor and kicking it with his foot. "Maybe 'No way, Fantom! Flex and I are the coolest team since Batman and Robin. Thanks, but no thanks.' Something like that?"

I didn't have a response for that.

"But I guess we're not," said Flex, filling in the silence. "So I guess it's good you didn't say that."

"C'mon, Flex," I protested. "You didn't even want a sidekick to begin with. Heck, you only signed up as a possible trainer for the money. But hey, we're both famous now, so money isn't a problem anymore! This is good for both of us. You get what you want, and I get what I want. I mean, you're a loner, aren't you?"

Flex looked like a dog that had just been kicked by his owner.

"I'm a loner because my hero turned his back on me," said Flex. He opened his mouth as if to say more but hesitated and then closed it again. With that, he turned and started for the door.

"Hey, where are you going?"

"Out," said Flex.

"Where?"

"OUT," he said even louder.

"WHERE?" I shouted back.

"I don't know," said Flex, rolling his eyes. "Probably to the bar where I'm going to consume copious amounts of alcohol. And when I can't possibly drink anymore, I'll probably keep drinking. Anything else you're dying to know?"

I sputtered as he reached the door. "Wait! When are you going to be back?"

"I don't know. Tomorrow?"

"Tomorrow?" I repeated. "But . . . Fantom's going to have someone pick me up tonight."

"Well that's great," Flex muttered. "Guess I'll see you . . . never."

Flex exited and started to slam the door behind him.

I tapped into my skeletal structure, and flew across the floor. Pounding the density into my arm, I shoved my hand in the door before it could close. I winced as the door slammed on my hand and bounced back open. I bit back the pain and met his glare.

"What are you doing?" asked Flex.

"Wait," I stammered. "Just . . . wait a sec, okay?"

"What do you want from me, Marrow?" he demanded, throwing his arms in the air. "You want me to congratulate you? Tell you how happy I am that all your wildest dreams are coming true? Fine. Congratulations. Now get lost before I throw you out the window."

My arm sank.

Flex slammed the door again.

Yep. So much for nothing bringing Flex down today. I slowly shuffled to the three-story window overlooking the filthy, graffiti-stricken street below. Only a short moment later, Flex stormed outside. He attacked the first thing he saw which happened to be a trashcan, kicking it out into the street. It happened to roll in front of a moving car which screeched to a halt. The driver exited the vehicle and started yelling and shaking his fist at Flex.

Flex yelled back even louder as he started towards the vehicle.

The man hastily jumped back inside his car, squealed around the trashcan, and sped off.

Flex only got halfway across the street before he dropped his head in his hands. His shoulders heaved and then his entire body started shaking.

A part of me wanted to go outside and talk to him. Say something—anything—that would end things on a better note than they currently were.

But what?

There was nothing I could say. The damage was already done.

Flex finally composed himself, shaking his head. Even from a distance, I could tell that he was blinking back tears. He shuffled around the corner and disappeared.

For all of my wildest dreams coming true, today didn't feel like it could get any worse.

CHAPTER 30

The long-anticipated knock practically rattled Flex's front door off its hinges. I leapt off the couch to answer it. As if I wasn't anxious enough already.

"Hallo," said a burly man with beady eyes and a handlebar moustache. "My name is Gustav. I am Fantom's butler. He asked that I pick you up."

His accent was thick with clipped vowels. The guy looked less like a butler or a chauffeur and more like a foreign spy or even an ex-con. I could see the tips of tattoos creeping across his wrists beneath the sleeves of his suit jacket.

"Oh," I said.

If I felt just a little disappointed that Fantom hadn't bothered to pick me up himself, it all vanished when Gustav led me outside to the limousine parked in the street.

"A limo?" I said, wide-eyed. "You came here in a limo?"

"No, I rode my magic unicorn across a rainbow to get here," said Gustav. He snorted his amusement into his immense moustache. "Of course I came here in the limo."

Sarcasm sounds a lot more deadly and serious in a Russian accent.

"Don't poop your pants, kid," said Gustav. "Just vait until we get to the submarine."

I nearly pooped my pants.

Gustav opened my door, gesturing for me to enter. If the limo looked big on the outside, the inside was practically its own club. Sleek

TV screens adorned every corner, edges were lined with neon lights, and there was even a bar with shelved glasses of varying shapes and sizes.

I hated that the limo bar immediately reminded me of Flex.

"Fantom also asked that I give this to you," said Gustav.

He extended his beefy hand. Clutched in his thick palm was something that resembled a wristwatch, but bigger and shinier.

"It's a vrist communicator," said Gustav. "He left a message for you on it."

I hesitantly took the wrist device. The head was an empty reflective surface that didn't respond to my touch. The band was a soft synthetic material that somehow maintained a firm, circular shape. When I inserted my hand, it instantly closed around my wrist, forming comfortably around it. I jumped. It was all I could do just to keep myself from screaming like a little girl. The screen immediately lit up with the words *One new message.* The words then vanished, replaced by Fantom's face.

"Hello, Marrow," he greeted, a smile stretched across his square jaw. "I'm sorry I couldn't pick you up personally. If all this Cronus Order business isn't enough to keep me busy, we've had an . . . er . . . issue . . . come up. I hope you'll understand. You can trust Gustav, though. He's the best there is at what he does."

The best there is at what he does? What could that be? Sticking people's feet in concrete blocks and dropping them to the bottom of the ocean?

"I'm looking forward to us working together," Fantom continued. "We're on the verge of something huge with the Cronus Cannon. I have a feeling that fighting crime is never going to be the same. We've got a lot of work to do, but I have every confidence that you'll be up to the task. Fighting today for a perfect tomorrow, Marrow. That's what we're doing."

Fantom winked. With a *bleep* and a brief flash, the message ended.

The limo ride was a thirty-minute trip to the coast. As the ocean sparkled into view, we found ourselves winding across slanted cliffsides which gleamed white in the sun. As we swerved around yet another curve, a monolithic structure appeared on the other side, built into the mountain. It was all rigid slabs of concrete bleakness, towering over a tunnel illuminated by eerie underwater lighting. Not that I know anything about submarines, but this thing looked like it belonged on the set of a Bond movie.

"Velcome to the Tartarus Submarine Base," said Gustav. "The technology is state of the art, but the architecture is modeled after the old nuclear submarine base in Balaklava."

"Lava what?" I said.

"It's in Ukraine."

"Oh."

The road descended until we were skimming beside the water. The tunnel gaped open like a hungry, toothless mouth devouring the road ahead of us. Gustav turned, and we were swallowed in shadow.

It took several seconds before my eyes adjusted to this new lighting. The interior was a ghostly concrete tunnel with thick arches and pipes running across the ceiling. A wide channel of water rippled and swayed down the long, gritty corridor, slapping gently at the ledge. A distant light emerged up ahead—multiple lights, all attached to some ominous form lurking out of the water, still and massive.

The submarine.

Actually, this thing was simply a submarine about as much as a Lamborghini is simply a car. Like the other submarines I had seen on the Tartarus, this one was whale-shaped with an insect-like exoskeleton structure. Glowing, yellow-tinted windows bubbled outward. A ramp was extended from the hull to the ledge. Men crossed it back and forth with dollies, hauling massive crates aboard. Gustav parked the limousine by the ramp, and we exited.

"That?" I said. "We're riding *that* to the Tartarus?"

Talking was basically the only way I could keep my mouth from gawking wide open.

"No, this is vhere the unicorn lives," said Gustav. "Ve're going to frolic across the rainbow to the Tartarus."

Again with the rainbows and unicorns?

"It was a rhetorical question," I muttered.

Gustav laughed at my response. Or maybe he was just laughing at my sour expression. Either way, he was laughing and I was scowling as we merged into the lane of cargo traffic boarding the sub.

* * *

Submarines are cool for about the first fifteen minutes. Then it's all groaning metal, creaky pipes, and staring through thick, tinted windows into murky blue nothingness.

As exciting as it was on the outside, the inside was claustrophobic and boring. The cargo overload certainly wasn't helping the situation. We might as well have been in a high-tech underwater U-Haul. The vessel was so jam-packed with crates and junk that Gustav recommended I stay in my room for the duration of the trip. If you could even call this box a room. It was more like a metal closet with a poorly cushioned rectangle that was theoretically supposed to be a bed. The so-called bed reached from wall to wall, and the room was just as wide in the opposite direction. No decorations. Just a bare light bulb with a dangling switch and a single round porthole window about the size of my head.

I left the heavy steel door open just so I didn't feel like I was in a prison cell. Heck, prison cells were better than this. At least they had bars so you could breathe. The floor outside my room was made of metal panels that clanked and clamored under the lightest step. Even a ninja couldn't sneak around this tin can.

I had switched the light off long ago, allowing a pillar of blue light to spill from the window across the opposite wall while red light flooded in from the outside corridor. If I had hoped to fall asleep, I was sadly mistaken. Even with the lights out, I was haunted by Flex's face. That hurt, empty face.

Was this a bad idea? Being Fantom's sidekick?

I mean . . . career-wise it obviously wasn't a bad move. With my name next to his, I would be remembered. And with me fighting alongside him, we would always win. Always. I would have the jumpstart I needed to make my Superhero legacy last forever.

So why did this feel so wrong?

Rolling onto my stomach, I screamed into my pillow.

Why why why why why why why why why why? I didn't even know what I was asking "why" about anymore. It seemed to embody a million different questions buzzing inside my skull. Why was Flex so upset? Why couldn't I be happy about this? Why did my chest feel like it was caving in, and I could barely breathe?

Lying face-first into my pillow wasn't really helping the situation, so I rolled onto my side. This was going to be a long ride.

CHAPTER 31

I didn't realize that I'd fallen asleep until I woke up to an annoying computer voice saying, "Please be ready to board the Tartarus in fifteen minutes." Crawling to my knees, I peered through the porthole window over my bed. The research facility was a vast accumulation of glassy spherical chambers bathed in the green glow of the Gaia Comet. The comet itself emerged from the midst of them like a ghostly monolith. The Cronus Cannon gleamed like a great fallen tower.

Okay, I could understand Fantom's fascination with this project. I could even understand the millions of dollars he had personally tied into it. However, I suddenly had the hardest time understanding why anyone would want to live down here. It was cool the first time, but now the Tartarus seemed less like a technological utopia and more like a tomb. How was it even practical for a Superhero like Fantom to live down here anyway? I mean, it wasn't exactly ideal for a fast response time if the world happened to need saving, you know?

Mechanical arms reached out from the Tartarus loading dock as we approached. The submarine drifted smoothly in between them, lurching slightly as it was clamped into place. My stomach lurched along with it.

"So how vas your first submarine ride?" Gustav asked as we filed toward the exit.

"I think I would've rather taken the unicorn," I said.

"Ha! Unicorn! That's a good one."

As we descended the boarding ramp, scientists scuttled hurriedly like ants, glancing at computer screens or clipboards and tampering with machinery. There was only one figure who wasn't in a white lab coat—Fantom. He was still wearing his Super suit which now appeared slightly scuffed and dirty, his slick hair disheveled, but still smiling his literal million dollar advertisement smile.

How the heck did he beat us here?

"Marrow," he greeted, brawny arms extended. "Glad to have you back. I trust Gustav kept you entertained?"

"But of course," said Gustav before I could respond. "I juggled for him and everything."

Fantom glanced down to my wrist. "Ah, good, I see you're already situated with your communicator." He raised his own wrist, revealing an identical wrist band. "If we happen to get separated during a fight, we have a way to keep in contact. And these are how we're notified of emergencies. Usually the calls will go through Gustav and he'll inform us via the communicator, but occasionally the Guild or the chief of police or other select individuals will alert us if the need ever rises. So be sure to keep your communicator with you at all times."

"Select individuals?" I said.

"Oh, you know . . . the mayor, the governor, the President of the United States. They like to keep a line of communication open. You know. Just in case."

"Ah . . ." I said, trying not to look too surprised.

"They're expensive little buggers too. I tend to update these things with every sidekick I get. I've even added a revision or two since Nero. This current edition has a tracking device. That way I can find you if you're ever lost. Sure would've come in handy when Nero went AWOL."

Fantom and Gustav both laughed. I made a weak attempt to chuckle along.

"At least we don't have to worry about my father kidnapping me, right?" I said.

This was my bleak attempt at humor. About as funny as the IRS, but I at least expected a pity laugh. Instead, Fantom and Gustav's laughter both faded on cue. Fantom forced a fake smile and nodded unconvincingly. "Yeah. Of course."

I didn't like where this was going.

"What?" I said, glancing between the two of them. "Did something happen?"

Gustav cleared his throat and readjusted his grip on my luggage. "Vell, I'd better get these to your room."

My gaze followed him as he started towards the nearest glass passageway. The door zipped open and then shut behind him.

"Walk with me," said Fantom.

This wasn't good.

Fantom was already walking, heading for the same exit as Gustav. I took several quick steps to catch up.

"There was an incident at Cosmo General Hospital a few hours ago," said Fantom. "The hospital where they're keeping your father."

This definitely wasn't good.

"Spine healed faster than we anticipated. He somehow managed to escape his restraints and got past the guards."

"HE WHAT?"

"He didn't escape though," Fantom inserted hastily. "I managed to incapacitate him before he got out of the hospital. But we still don't know how he got out. None of the guards' stories seem to be matching up, and even the security cameras glitched out. He didn't even break his restraints. We've doubled security, though. I would tell you that it won't happen again, but . . . well . . . it shouldn't have happened to begin with. The sooner we transport him out of that hospital and into a special containment facility, the better. Although I'm not going to be content until the Supreme Court legalizes the use of the Cronus on all Super-enhanced criminals."

My mouth was dry and my throat felt tight. I didn't know what to say. And even if I did, I didn't know how to say it.

Fantom cleared his throat, noting my discomfort. "Anyway . . . you're probably wondering how I beat you and Gustav here. Am I right?"

I blinked at the jarring change of topic. It took me a second to remember that I had been wondering exactly that when I stepped out of the sub. "Yeah. How did you?"

Fantom's familiar grin returned. "Follow me."

I followed him through several round, glass passageways interconnecting each sphere chamber to the next. They all looked pretty much the same to me from their beehive-like glass-plated infrastructure to the endless tubes, pumps, gears, and blinking computer lights. Until we reached our destination. Right when I thought Fantom couldn't possibly be any more filthy, stinkin' rich.

The chamber we ended up in didn't look much different from the others except for the sudden shadow cast over us and a narrow glass elevator tube in the center of the chamber leading upward. My gaze followed it up, landing on something that looked like a cross between a submarine, a jet, and a spaceship all rolled into one. Its core was a massive torpedo shape, though it gradually flattened and branched out into dual pairs of sharp, curving wings, bending out and meeting back together at the tips with sleek, bullet-shaped engines.

My mouth hung open and I craned my neck back until it hurt. "What . . . is . . . that?"

Fantom clapped his hand on my shoulder. "That, my friend, is the Fantom Wing."

"Yeah, but . . . what is it?"

"It's a submersible exojet. It's a durable, light-weight multicraft. It can fly, ascend as far up as the exosphere while withstanding intense levels of ultraviolet radiation, and, of course, submerge underwater with the same water pressure resilience as most submarines."

"What's an exosphere?"

"It's about as far as you can get into space while still remaining in the Earth's gravitational pull."

I blinked. "Oh."

"Oh is right," said Fantom, chuckling. "Its exterior is a resilient synthetic material crafted from rock samples of the Gaia Comet. Basically, this puppy is indestructible. It's still in the prototype stages, but I've taken it out for a spin a couple times. It's the only way I can justify living down here. From the moment I start her, I can make it out of the water in forty-seven seconds, and I can get to the coast in three minutes flat. Also, the cockpit only reacts to my DNA, so only I can pilot it. Don't have to worry about thieves that way."

The pain stabbing through my neck reminded me that I hadn't budged. When I finally met Fantom's gaze, he was grinning wildly.

"Pretty, isn't she?"

"Yeah, I'll say," I said, breathless. "I'd die to take a ride in that thing."

"Well you're in luck. Any emergency calls we get while we're in the Tartarus, that's our ticket out of here. No dying necessary."

I didn't respond with words. I couldn't. So instead I made this weird gasping/croaking sound that I'm sure was really impressive for a Superhero-in-training.

I am, of course, being sarcastic. Don't ever make a sound like that in front of someone you're trying to impress.

Fantom chuckled. "Well, how about I show you to your room now? Let you get situated?"

I nodded with my mouth still hanging slightly open.

If I was expected to memorize my way through the Tartarus, I was in big trouble. The place was a labyrinth. A big, fat, science-fictiony, fishbowl labyrinth. I was suddenly much more appreciative of the tracking device in my wrist communicator.

After completing what I swear was a complete circle, we reached a door that branched off from the glass corridor, separating it from the sphere chambers. Unlike the many automatic doors, this one didn't whiz open as we approached. Instead, Fantom reached into his pocket and removed a keycard.

Yes. He had pockets. Inside his skintight bodysuit. Was there anything this dude didn't have?

Fantom swiped the keycard through the door's control panel, which blinked green. He then grabbed my wrist and slapped the card into my limp palm.

"Don't lose it," he said with a wink.

The door slid open. I dropped the keycard.

I was dead. I mean, I had to be. Because I was suddenly in heaven.

Like Fantom's flat, my room had a single glass wall with a mesmerizing view of the reef. But hey, who cares about beautiful views when your room also happens to be an arcade?

Pinball machines? Check. Air hockey table? Check. Basketball hoop, big screen TV, and enough video games to choke a level 80 dark elf? Check, check, check. And then, if all of that wasn't enough, it even had a Mountain Dew vending machine.

MOUNTAIN. DEW. VENDING. MACHINE.

It was enough to make a grown man cry. At least, if I was a grown man, I would have felt completely justified in doing so.

It wasn't until I was already wandering inside that I even noticed my luggage. Gustav had set it in the middle of the room, and I nearly tripped on it.

"Well, I'll let you get situated in here," said Fantom. "If you need anything, your communicator has an option that'll reach Gustav. He'll take care of you."

I nodded vacantly while my gaze struggled to absorb everything at once. "Okay," I finally managed to say.

Fantom left, and the sliding door zipped shut behind him.

In the midst of all the glory and glamour that any kid could ever hope for in a bedroom, it was a wonder I even noticed what I saw next. On the nightstand next to my bed, there was a small, leather-bound book. As I stepped closer, I noticed the faded silver words emblazoned on the cover:

The Morse Code Handbook.

Of course, it came as no surprise when I opened it and read the name scribbled on the inside cover:

Nero.

It's amazing how a stupid little notebook can suddenly ruin the coolest bedroom in the world.

No. Heck no. Heck *freaking* no! I wasn't about to let that stupid jerk ruin this for me. I fumbled with the communicator on my wrist, *bleeping* and *blooping* my way through the interface. I finally found Gustav's name under my list of contacts and pressed "Call."

Gustav's face popped up, looking overwhelmingly unimpressed. "*Vow*, that didn't take long. Vhat do you vant, little man?"

Ladies and gentleman, I present to you the most condescending butler of all time.

"Can I call my friend Sapphire?" I asked.

"Do I look like your mommy?"

"Um. Okay, I want to call my friend Sapphire."

"Okay, thanks for letting me know. Do you have any other status updates you vould like to share?"

"Um. Yeah, like, how do I do that? Because I don't have a cell phone or anything, and even if I did, like, I don't even know if Verizon has service twenty thousand leagues under the sea."

"Your friend Sapphire—she is Specter's sidekick, yes?"

"Uh-huh."

"Okay. Scroll through the contacts on your communicator to Specter's name. Are you scrolling?"

"Uh-huh," I said. I minimized the image of Gustav's face, scrolled, and found Specter's name.

"And then press 'Call.'"

"Uh-huh."

"And then tell Specter that Gustav thinks she has a nice *popa*. That is Russian for butt."

"Uh . . ."

Gustav proceeded to promptly hang up on me.

Well, okay then.

I selected Specter from my contacts and pressed call. I obviously had no intention of relaying Gustav's heartfelt message, but that did not make this any less awkward.

Specter's face appeared—looking just as drop-dead-gorgeous and cold-hard-tenish as I remembered, and overall, way hotter than a camel despite her exceptionally camel-esque eyelashes. Naturally, she was wearing her blue and white bodysuit which surely emphasized her nice *popa* that was unfortunately off screen at the moment. The top half of her face was obscured by a white mask, but that only gave her this mysterious appeal that, like, oh my freaking gosh, what was I even calling for again?

Sapphire. Right. I was calling for Sapphire.

"Marrow?" said Specter.

"Sapphire," I said rather loudly. "Is she . . . uh . . . Hey, I need to talk to Sapphire. Well, I mean, I don't *need* to talk to her—like save-the-world *need*—but I was hoping to talk to her, and . . . um . . . Hi, Specter. How are you doing today? Fine weather we're having."

If this communicator had a function that could stop me from talking right now, that would be the greatest technological achievement of our era.

Specter smiled. "I'll go get Sapphire."

A moment later, Sapphire's face appeared. "Hey, Marrow. What the . . . ? Why's your face so red?"

"Um. Pushups," I said. "I was doing pushups."

"Oh. So . . . what's up?"

"This is up." I pulled the communicator away from my face and directed my wrist at my bedroom wall. I slowly rotated three hundred and sixty degrees so she could absorb my new bedroom in all its awesometacular glory.

"No way," said Sapphire. "Is that a Mountain Dew vending machine?"

"That is, indeed, a Mountain Dew vending machine."

"I thought those only existed in my dreams!"

"Now they exist in your dreams *and* my bedroom."

"Profound. Man, I still can't wrap my brain around the fact that you're Fantom's sidekick now. When Specter told me the news this morning, I practically spewed my orange juice. I mean, it's what you've always wanted. And now here you are, living the dream. With a Mountain Dew vending machine, no less."

"So when are you coming over?"

"To your bedroom? That exists at the bottom of the ocean?"

"Yeah. That."

"I can't."

"Oh," I said. I tried not to sound bummed, but that single "Oh" contained in its two-letter, one-syllable existence all the disappointment in the universe. Of course, the Flex situation may or may not have had something to do with my current state of unstable moodiness. I just . . . like, was it too much to ask to hang out with a friend? Here I was, having what was supposed to be the best day of my life, and a deep, dark part of me just wanted to cry. Was there a delayed side-effect of puberty that made you feel like you were turning into a girl?

"It's just that Specter has me on a really tight training program," said Sapphire. "I have almost a dozen different routines she has me doing throughout the day. She has a timer that goes off, not only in my bedroom, but throughout the whole house. And then it's off to mixed martial arts, or off to target practice, or off to torture interrogation resistance training or whatever."

"What? Wow. That's . . . uh . . . intense."

"I was just joking about torture interrogation resistance training. But seriously, it is intense. Specter always says that women have to be twice as good as men in order to get half the acknowledgement they get. So in order to be considered equal, we have to be four times better than any guy Superhero. Anyway, that's that, so I'm not really allowed to leave the compound. Er . . . house. Whatever. But if *you* want to come over *here* tomorrow afternoon, you totally can."

"Seriously? You don't have to ask Specter's permission first?"

"SPECTER!" Sapphire shouted. "CAN I HAVE A FRIEND OVER TOMORROW?"

"DO I LOOK LIKE YOUR MOM?" Specter's voice echoed back. "DO WHAT YOU WANT. JUST DON'T SKIP THE OBSTACLE COURSE OF DEATH AT TWO O' CLOCK OR YOU ARE DEAD MEAT."

Sapphire shuddered. "I hate the obstacle course of death."

"I can't imagine why," I said.

"I have stealth tactics at noon, but that usually only takes a half hour. Can you come at twelve-thirty? That gives us an hour and a half to hang. Longer if you want to watch me get pulverized in a million different ways for your entertainment pleasure."

"This already sounds like the best day of my life."

"I'm glad my pain and suffering brings someone happiness."

"You bet it does. Oh, random question: does Specter have a VCR?"

"Wow, that is random."

"You were warned."

"Um, I *think* she does. Wait, scratch that. I *know* she does. I saw one in her surveillance room."

"Specter has a surveillance room?"

"Specter has an *everything* room. Heck, she even has a scrapbooking room. But I'm allegedly not supposed to tell anyone that under the threat that I'll be murdered in my sleep. So tomorrow at twelve-thirty?"

"Tomorrow at twelve-thirty!"

It was only after Sapphire hung up that I realized I was still technically trapped in a luxurious underwater prison. I scrolled through the contacts on my communicator, selected Gustav, and pressed "Call." Gustav's face appeared, and contorted into a magnificent scowl.

"Unless you're bleeding to death," said Gustav, "I vould seriously reconsider vhatever it is you are calling me for."

"How would you like to check out Specter's *papo* tomorrow at twelve-thirty?" I asked.

Gustav was silent for a long moment. Finally, he said, "You have my attention."

* * *

Marrow . . .

My name echoed down the empty corridor. There was no mouth to the voice—just a ghostly whisper emanating with a character of its own.

The corridor was an infinite shadow. There was no glass or windows. Just a never-ending stretch of dark, dank metal, running pipes, and the occasional meager light bulb to tease the senses. Aside from the lingering echo of my name, all of the facility was asleep, lost in a deathly rest. The silence was tangible and suffocating. I could feel it in my throat.

Marrow . . .

A lone figure wandered into my view, his wiry build and dark hair unmistakable—Nero. The only thing missing was his stupid trademark smirk. The lack of it almost transformed him into an entirely different person.

His jaw was tense, and his eyes darted like hummingbirds.

Marrow . . .

A single door appeared from the shadows, painted in yellow caution stripes. Bold black letters were painted on the plated steel surface:

L-00/NE-00
Restricted Area
Authorized Personnel Only

In the place of a doorknob or handle was a numbered security pad. Nero seemed to ignore this, however. Instead he touched the door, his thin fingers grazing the metal. As he did, numbers flashed by faster than I could comprehend them. And yet, even as they vanished, they were engrained in my mind.

2-3-5-8-13-21.

Nero's head snapped up. His eyes shifted to the security pad and he punched the numbers exactly as they had appeared.

Marrow . . .

The door opened.

Something screamed—sharp and desperate.

No, not a scream. It was a siren, blaring ferociously and accompanied by flashing red lights. For a split second the corridor vanished, and I was falling. I landed on my bed. It took a second or two to register that I had been in my bed all along.

A dream . . . It was just a dream.

I fumbled to an upright position and glanced stupidly around the room. It took way longer than it should have for me to realize that the siren and the lights were both coming from the wrist communicator that I had set on my nightstand. Fighting my disorientation, I managed to grab the screaming wristband. The words, Red Alert, flashed repeatedly across the face.

I tapped the screen, not really knowing what I was doing, and immediately, Gustav's face appeared. His expression, however, was not tense with urgency so much as it was scrunched with awkward uncertainty.

The screen split a half-second later, filled with a cranky, groggy-eyed Fantom with his hair pushed up on the left side of his head.

"What's going on?" Fantom mumbled irritably. "It's not Spine again, is it?"

"No, no, nothing like that," said Gustav. He seemed reluctant to mention what it actually was at all. "There vas a police report. Apparently there's a . . . bar fight."

Fantom blinked. "A bar fight? You woke me up at two in the morning for a bar fight?"

"It's pretty bad," said Gustav. "There's a . . . er . . . Super involved."

No. There was no way. If my heart wasn't already on the fritz, this conversation was thoroughly doing the trick.

"A Super?" said Fantom. "Do we have him on record?"

"Yes . . . vell . . . that's vhy the police asked for us specifically," Gustav murmured. "It's Flex."

CHAPTER 32

We broke the surface of the water in forty-seven seconds and hit the coast in three minutes flat. I was too sick with worry to enjoy a second of it.

The cityscape whizzed below us as Fantom followed the coordinates he was given. Neither of us spoke, but Fantom's disgruntled scowl seemed to say it all. Though Gustav never said it, it was obvious the only reason the police called us was because of me. They thought I could calm him down. Just how worked up was he? I didn't know how out of control Flex could get, but I *did* have an idea of how drunk he could get.

The Fantom Wing's GPS announced that we had nearly reached our destination. Fantom pushed forward on the control rod. The exojet swooped into a deep spiral, slicing parallel to the nearest skyscraper. I managed to catch a glimpse of the Wing's blurred reflection across the sweeping glass surface before Fantom pulled back up. The force of the lower thrusters rattled us in our seats, causing me to clench my armrests tighter. I leaned into my window and watched a patch of green expand below us. We were descending on the city park. At last we landed with a metallic *clank*. The engines died, releasing a heavy mechanical sigh.

Fantom didn't waste a second bolting out of the pilot's seat. He marched to the exit ramp with clenched fists, grumbling profanities that'd I'd never even heard before.

"Wait," I said, "So what are we . . . ?"

"Stay here," said Fantom. "I'll take care of this."

"But I thought . . ." I mumbled. "I mean . . . er . . . maybe if I just talked to him for a second . . ."

"I said I'll take care of it!" he snapped.

I pinched my mouth shut and nodded timidly. Fantom's nostrils splayed, breathing death. Whirling around, he stomped down the ramp.

As soon as he vanished around the corner I scampered after him.

I was only halfway down the ramp when I spotted the bar in question. If there was anything left to question, that is. Even from twenty-something yards away I could make out the shattered windows, yelling, and flaring police lights surrounding the Sloshed Josh Bar and Lounge.

Great.

Tapping into my skeletal structure, I glided weightless across the grass. I clung to the shadows on the off chance that Fantom turned around, although this was the least of my worries.

"Fantom!" exclaimed a police officer as he approached the perimeter. "He's here!"

"Thank goodness."

The officer who was seemingly in charge swept up to Fantom's side. "We've tried communicating with this guy, but he's plastered out of his mind. I was thinking—"

"I've got it under control, lieutenant," said Fantom. "If we can't communicate with words, then we'll just have to communicate with force, won't we?"

Fantom brushed past the lieutenant and stepped through the broken door, hanging by one hinge.

The time for sneaking was over. I rushed out of the shadows. I slowed only slightly as I drew the gazes of several surprised officers.

"I'm with him," I announced in a hasty, uncertain tone.

The lieutenant lifted an unconvinced eyebrow. He raised his hand halfway and opened his mouth, but stopped himself. I took that as my cue to keep going. Glass crunched beneath my boots as I entered the shattered building.

I immediately took cover behind a fake plastic tree.

The bar might have looked fancy with its artsy postmodern furniture and ambient, neon blue lights if it weren't for all the bodies strewn everywhere. Black eyes and bloody noses all over the place. Not all of the people were out cold. Quite a few were still groaning or fumbling on the floor. One guy with his head resting on a table was even singing a Bon Jovi song, although I was pretty sure he hadn't been a part of the fight and was so smashed that he probably didn't even know what was going on.

And then there was Flex—doubled over on the bar top, barely balanced on his stool. His dreadlocks were matted over the left side of his scraggly face. He raised a glass unsteadily and puckered his lips to find it but ended up pouring the drink all over the bar top. Flex scowled at the empty glass and dropped his face in the puddle.

"Look at you," said Fantom, his face pinched in revulsion. "Disgusting. And you call yourself a Superhero?"

"*Ohhhhhhh*," said Flex, lifting his head disjointedly, his mouth and eyes both wide. His sopping wet dreadlocks dripped in front of his face. "You wanna start with me, hotshot? I'll show you . . . I'll show you what . . . I'll beat you so hard you'll . . . you . . . you're stupid! Where are you, anyway? You wanna start with me?"

"I'll be honest," said Fantom. "I don't want to be anywhere near you. It's two in the morning. I want to be in bed. Unfortunately, you're such a *joke* that you need a *real* Superhero to show you your place."

Flex's unsteady, wavering gaze finally narrowed on Fantom. He squinted between his soaked dreadlocks.

"Fantom?" He blinked his glazed eyes which were instantly swallowed in a dirty glare. "What do you want?"

"What do I want? I *want* to not have to babysit an idiot who thinks he's a superhero. What do you think you're doing, anyway?"

"Uh . . . getting drunk. Duh. What does it look like?"

"It *looks* like you started a fight and caused several hundred dollars' worth of property damage."

"He started it," Flex grumbled, raising his arm to point at no one in particular.

"He?" Fantom repeated incredulously. "Who's 'he'? You've incapacitated the entire bar!"

"No I didn't," said Flex, shaking his head in a woozy sway.

"Flex . . . they're all unconscious."

"Psh! No they're not." Flex steadied his head and attempted to absorb his surroundings. "See? He's just fine."

Flex pointed to the guy who was still singing with his head propped on the table. The Bon Jovi lyrics had been replaced by a Journey song, and every word was slurred into an unintelligible slush.

"Flex, I'm going to escort you out of here," said Fantom. "And then the police are going to talk to you. Okay?"

"Oh, I see," said Flex. "First you take my sidekick, and now you want to take my freedom. Okay, whatever you say, boss."

My insides tightened. He just had to go there, didn't he?

Flex extended his wobbly arms, wrists together. "Cuff me, Captain America. I'm ready."

Fantom's jaw clenched, drilling Flex with his gaze. He seemed to be deliberating whether it was worth it to argue with someone this drunk.

"I didn't *take* Marrow. I gave him an offer, and he chose to accept it."

"You're just a glory-seeking psychopath who gets whatever he wants," Flex spat.

"You want to play that game?" Fantom challenged. "Fine. Marrow, come join us."

Both Flex and I went rigid almost simultaneously.

"Yes, I know you followed me in here, Marrow," said Fantom. "Come on out."

Shuffling out from behind that stupid plastic tree, I felt like all the eyes in the world were suddenly focused on me. Flex's ashamed gaze was almost more than I could handle. He looked at me for only a brief moment before averting his gaze to the floor.

"Flex thinks I took you unfairly, Marrow," said Fantom. "So I'm giving you a second chance to make your decision. If you want *this* to be your mentor," he gestured as though Flex were a ripped open sack of garbage, which honestly didn't look that far from the truth at the moment, "so be it."

My gaze shifted from Fantom, whose arms were folded patiently, to Flex, who was glaring holes into the floor like his life depended on it.

"Flex . . . what's going on?" I asked, unsure what else to say.

Silence. Flex was winning his staring contest with the floor.

"Flex, talk to me. Please!"

Flex pulled his wet dreadlocks away from his face. His mouth opened only slightly, but he seemed to immediately reconsider the thought. Sliding off of his stool, he staggered past Fantom. He passed without even looking at me, cutting straight for the door.

"Flex!" I said. "What are you doing?"

"Turning myself in to the police," said Flex. "They're going to arrest me either way."

I opened my mouth, but the words didn't come, and Flex certainly wasn't going to wait. He stepped outside with his hands up. The silhouettes of several officers emerged from the blinding lights. One was already removing a pair of handcuffs from his belt.

"Wait!" I said, desperate to say something—anything—that would make a difference. "We . . . we can bail you out. Right, Fantom? We can bail him out, right?"

Fantom smiled, or at least he pretended to. "Of course we can, Marrow."

"NO!" Flex roared, whipping around. This sent all of the police into a frenzy, several reaching for their guns. "I don't want his filthy money!"

Two officers took Flex from behind, and not so gently either. One pushed him to his knees, and the other cuffed him.

"Flex!" I cried. I literally cried. Tears were seeping across my mask and down to my chin. I was crying in front of the only male role models I had ever had as well as half of the Cosmo City police department, and I didn't even care. I didn't care how weak it made me look. I didn't care what anyone thought. All I cared about was that my best friend was abandoning me, and yet, in a twisted sort of way, it felt like I was the one who had abandoned him.

"I don't need your pity, Marrow," said Flex.

Even as he spoke, however, something glistened in his eyes, betraying his words. But that didn't stop the police from jerking him up by his biceps and throwing him in the back of a patrol car.

CHAPTER 33

"I'm going to be coordinating things with the police today about making preparations for the Cronus Cannon," said Fantom. "I've asked Gustav to forward all emergencies to Nova, Apex, and Specter. This will give you a chance to relax. I figure you need it with everything that's transpired lately."

I nodded my heavy head—more out of instinct than acknowledgment.

The dining table was huge, easily twenty feet long. Fantom and I sat at opposite ends, and the distance between us was thick with awkward tension. I reckon that was mostly my fault.

"You haven't touched your food," said Fantom.

That wasn't entirely true. I had succeeded in stabbing the yolks of my fried eggs and shoving their bloody yellow corpses into my hash browns and then mixing it all together with my every-kind-of-berry crepes. The end result looked like something had died a gruesome death on my plate.

I took a forkful of the breakfast slop and quietly shoved it in my mouth, forcing myself to chew. I had to give Gustav props. Even after desecrating his breakfast masterpiece, the food still tasted pretty dang good.

It was unfortunate that my stomach instinctively wanted to throw it all up.

"Is everything okay?" he asked.

"Yeah," I lied. "Everything's fine."

I strained my face into a fake smile. I knew I wasn't fooling anyone, though, so I don't know why I even bothered.

Fantom set his fork gently on his plate. "Is this Flex thing going to be a problem?"

The guy sure had a knack for subtlety, didn't he?

I didn't know what to say to that, so I took the subtle approach as well.

"May I be excused?" I asked.

Without waiting for permission, I stood up and left.

I started for my room knowing full well that I would probably get lost. Despite the grand tour, the Tartarus was still a maze to me—a big, underwater, glass maze with mutated sea monsters trapped inside.

Can a kid get so lucky?

I was so lost in my own thoughts that I almost didn't notice it as I passed—a glass door with yellow caution stripes and a numbered security pad. In bold black letters were painted the words:

L-01/SE-27
Restricted Area
Authorized Personnel Only

It obviously wasn't the door from my dream, but heck if it didn't ring some serious bells. What were those letters and numbers at the top anyway? Was it some sort of code?

You know those moments when you remember something you shouldn't remember? When it comes to you as easy as your own name? Well . . . maybe you don't. But if moments like that existed, this was suddenly one of them.

L-00/NE-00 . . .
2-3-5-8-13-21 . . .

It was like they were carved into my subconscious. But how? Normally, I would forget my dreams as soon as I woke up. How was this dream so different?

When you had something you really didn't want to think about—and I had plenty—it was easy to run with a ridiculous idea like this. What was this dream door? Did it really exist? If so, where was it?

I glanced down at my wrist communicator.

It was time to see just how useful Gustav could be.

* * *

"Well, I'm glad you called me," said Dr. Jarvis, flattening his comb-over across his shiny, balding head. "It's refreshing to see an inquiring young mind seeking after knowledge. These days it's always about video games and break dancing."

"Break dancing?" I said.

"It's a little suspicious if you ask me," said Gustav. "Vhen I vas a young boy in Nizhny Novgorod, life vas much more simple. Ve entertained ourselves by getting into fights and pulling girls' pigtails and biting vild animals."

"Wow that's . . . uh . . . that's something," I said.

"Biting wild animals?" asked Jarvis in mild alarm. "Is that even sanitary?"

"My family vas not superstitious," said Gustav. "Ve did not believe in such things as germs and ghosts and stuff."

"Ah," said Jarvis, pressing his glasses further up the bridge of his nose. "That's . . . interesting."

"Vhy do you vant to see a map, anyvay?" asked Gustav.

"Just . . . curious," I said.

"Suspicious indeed."

"Don't listen to him," said Jarvis. "I was curious when I was your age too. Tried to build my own nuclear reactor once. Plutonium's a little hard to come across when you're in the seventh grade though."

"And people think Russians are scary," Gustav muttered under his breath.

Jarvis continued to lead the way while Gustav and I followed. We entered a sphere chamber that Jarvis called the Command Center.

Personally, I thought it looked just like all the other sphere chambers, but I wasn't about to tell Jarvis that. The one distinguishing feature was a round central table with a computer interface built into it. The entire surface was like a gigantic touch screen. Jarvis navigated through several options with the flick of his finger. At last he selected one final icon and the entire table lit up. Glowing blue projector streams joined together, creating a three-dimensional image of the entire Tartarus.

"Welcome to the Tartarus," Jarvis announced gleefully. "This is the best map of the facility you'll ever see."

Jarvis guided the hologram with his fingers on the interface, rotating it for a three hundred and sixty degree view and slowly zoomed in. As he did, I noticed little white words pinpointing various rooms and corridors, labeling them like blueprints—from gigantic features like the Cronus Cannon and the Gaia Comet to the loading docks and the various functions of each sphere chamber. As Jarvis zoomed in further, I finally found what I wanted. There were dozens of them—tiny doors labeled with similar combinations of numbers scattered on every level of the Tartarus: L-03/NW-12, L-05/W-09, L-02/SW-17 . . .

As I looked at the Tartarus from this eagle-eye view, the letters and numbers suddenly made sense and came together to form a bigger picture: L-01, L-02, L-03 . . . Those were levels on the Tartarus. And the second set of letters were also grouped together in vertical waves: S, SE, E, NE . . . Those were directions: south, southeast, east, northeast. The numbers associated to these were more sporadic, but it didn't take a genius to figure them out. They were the individual room numbers, repeating on each level.

But what were they?

"What are these rooms?" I asked, struggling to point to all of them at once. "The ones with the letters and numbers."

"Those?" said Jarvis. "Those are the control rooms. They access various functions of the Tartarus and the Cronus Cannon."

"Control rooms?"

"In general, the Tartarus is its own super computer system," Jarvis explained. "It operates and sustains itself on its own. We, the scientists on board, merely study its operations and findings in regards to the Gaia Comet. But if something were to go wrong and some part of the system needed to be overridden, the control rooms would be where we would do that."

I listened to his words, but my gaze still hadn't left the hologram. I leaned closer over the table, cocking my head to view the bottom of the Tartarus. The most crucial piece of the puzzle was missing.

There was no L-00/NE-00.

I bit my lip, struggling for the best way to ask about a room that didn't seem to exist.

"So level one is the lowest level?" I asked. "There isn't like . . . a level zero or anything?"

Jarvis's lighthearted expression faded, scrunched into a scrutinizing look. "Level zero? Well that wouldn't make much sense, would it? Might as well have a room number zero. I mean, that's like saying it doesn't exist."

I forced a weak laugh that fell dead in my throat. "Yeah . . . I guess so."

* * *

Specter's house was part Professor Xavier's mansion, part military training facility, and 99.9 percent pee-your-pants awesome—emphasis on the "peeing-your pants" part. Fortunately, my bladder and I narrowly fell into the lucky 0.1 percentile.

Narrowly.

We pulled onto the longest driveway I had ever seen. At the end was a gate with a camera—and a turret gun—pointed at our faces.

"Hallo, Specter, my dear," said Gustav to the camera. "Hurry, you must open the gate for us. Young love awaits. Little Marrow's heart yearns for his *golubushka*."

"Wait, what?!" I said. "Gustav, I'm gonna kill you!"

The turret gun retracted and the gate opened. We proceeded to drive through the Specter Estate which was shaped like a horseshoe.

Building after building—sleek, savvy sandstone structures—passed us on either side, loosely connected by stone pathways. Eventually they came together into the main part of the estate, this artsy manor of slanted sandstone surfaces and sharp edges. Gustav hadn't even parked the limo before Sapphire came running out. Her blue hair was an ocean crashing against the pale shore of her face.

As soon as I exited, her body crashed into me, and I crashed into the door of the limo.

"Hey, hey, hey, vatch the paint job, you treacherous little heathens," said Gustav.

Sapphire ignored him, continuing to hug me to death and crush me into the side of the vehicle. When she finally pulled away, she sighed.

"I miss human beings that aren't Specter," she said.

"Really?" I said. "I couldn't tell."

Specter exited the manor in long strides, still wearing her skintight Super suit. Each step seemed to emphasize her curves. And oh boy, did she have curves. Like, the curves of Lombard Street in San Francisco had nothing on her. Nothing!

Gustav seemed to appreciate where I was coming from because he immediately stood up straight and ran his beefy hand through his hair.

"Hello, Marrow," she said. "Hello, Gustav."

"Miss Specter," said Gustav. "You look as radiant as the electromagnetic glow of Cherenkov radiation in an undervater nuclear reactor."

"Oh, Gustav," said Specter, smiling this smile that turned my insides into microwaved butter. "You're too much."

"So," said Sapphire. She seemed to say this extra loud, as if to remind me that she was still there. "What do you need a VCR for, anyway?"

I lifted the videotape, still in its manila envelope packaging. "This."

"And what, pray tell, is that?"

As Sapphire led me to the surveillance room, I explained everything. The surveillance room wasn't far, but it *was* located at the very top of the three-story Control Tower—the keystone of the Specter Estate's technological infrastructure. There was a stairwell, but we took the elevator. The surveillance room wasn't especially elaborate—just a single chair perched in front of a whole lot of TVs, packed together like ice cubes in an ice cube tray. They displayed every angle of the Specter Estate. In one particular corner was a various assortment of recording equipment.

And a VCR.

"So we're watching a home movie," said Sapphire. I didn't think she could look or sound less enthusiastic if I brought a documentary on the history of grass.

"At least that's what Flex thinks it is," I said.

"Yay." Her tone was flat and anything but yay-ful.

"This is the thing Oracle sent Flex right before she betrayed us. Doesn't that make you just a little bit curious?"

"Personally, I'd rather watch cat videos on YouTube. But whatever."

I ripped the manila envelope off, revealing a plain black video-tape—no label or anything. I inserted it in the VCR and hit play.

The plain blue TV screen flickered to a darkened kitchen illuminated almost exclusively by seven candles on a birthday cake. The young, sandy-haired boy sitting behind the tower of chocolate was grinning wildly, exposing his two missing front teeth. He was surrounded by friends and looked like this was the happiest day of his life. The camera was horribly off-center, cutting off the top of the boy's head and making it obvious who was behind the camera.

"Okay, Flex, make a wish," said a younger-sounding Oracle behind the camera.

Seven-year-old Flex let his big eyes drift up as he pondered.

"I wish I was the stwongest Supewhewo in the wowld," said Flex in his most serious tone. "So if you wewe evew in twouble, Auntie Owacle, I could save you."

"Aw," said Oracle, chuckling softly. "That's very sweet of you. But you're not supposed to tell us what you wished for."

Flex's eyes went wide with alarm.

"It's okay though," said Oracle. "Go ahead and blow out your candles, sweetie."

Flex's scrawny chest puffed as he inhaled and then threw his body forward as he blew.

The picture flickered with sudden static.

The birthday party was gone, replaced by a new image—a dark hallway. The camera wasn't moving.

Sapphire leaned forward. "The heck? What just happened?"

I mirrored her, leaning closer to the still, dark image. "It looks like somebody taped over the video."

The camera moved, inching forward slowly.

"Hello?" said Oracle's voice. "Is someone there?"

Oracle guided the camera down the hall, descending hesitantly down stairs that creaked with each step. The stairs ended in her familiar living room. Well . . . what *used* to be her living room. Every vase and laced doily was exactly as I remembered it. Whenever Oracle filmed this, it wasn't long ago.

"Spine?" she asked. "Is that you?"

I went rigid at his name.

"If that's you, Spine . . . I've been seeing you," said Oracle. "You keep appearing in my foresight."

For some reason, there was doubt in her wavering tone.

"But you're not Spine . . . are you?" she said. "Are you a friend of his?"

No response. Nothing.

"Are you a Telepath?" she asked. "I can feel *something*. Something trying to reach into my mind."

There was a slight, indiscernible sound, like scratching. I would have missed it if I wasn't sitting right in front of the TV. But whatever the case, it caused Oracle to whip her camera to the side. She plunged through her living room and past the kitchen. She stopped at the sliding door to her tiny excuse for a backyard, which was enclosed within a claustrophobic chain-link fence. The lights were shining on her porch. I didn't know if the lights were motion sensors, but Oracle's breath was heavy and frantic. Everything was glistening and wet as if it had just rained. The light reflected bright on the puddles.

The camera crept closer. A withered hand extended into the view of the camera, pulling the sliding door open.

"Who are you?" asked Oracle.

Whoever was out there—if anyone even was out there—didn't respond.

"Why are you trying to get inside my head?"

Again, no response. Oracle waited several long seconds before lowering the camera. The video ended in a flurry of snowy static. When the image returned, we were staring at the very same birthday the video had started with.

"Well," said Sapphire. "That was thoroughly weird."

I just kept staring at the screen—at the birthday party—but really, I was staring *through* everything. Lost in my own jumble of thoughts.

"Marrow?" said Sapphire. "Hello, Marrow. Earth to Marrow. Ground Control to Major Tom. Is anyone aboard the U.S.S. Marrow?" She waved her hand in front of me, finally eliciting a blink.

"Why would Oracle send this?" I asked.

"Um, you said it yourself. She was just trying to lure you and Flex to her place. All she needed was something to get your attention." Sapphire gestured elaborately to the TV screen. "Mission accomplished."

"You think she staged that whole scene?"

"Yes. Yes, I do."

"What about the part where Oracle thinks it *isn't* Spine who's lurking around her house?"

"What about the part where WHO CARES? She used you and Flex as Spine bait! She threatened to kill you guys! She's obviously a twisted old psycho-grandma who has way too many cats and not enough CAT scans."

I pressed my lips into a straight line. Sapphire was right. It was ridiculous to try and make sense of a woman who was possibly mentally unstable.

"Can we just like . . . I dunno," said Sapphire. "Play Mario Kart or something? I really need to do something fun before Specter sentences me to death on that stupid obstacle course."

"You have Mario Kart?" I said. My mouth slipped into a grin.

"Heck yes, I do. And you better believe I'm gonna shoot one of those blue turtle shells at your head."

"Bring. It. On."

* * *

Marrow . . .

Nero was standing in front of the door with yellow stripes bleeding across it—L-00/NE-00. The door stood out from the shadows like a monolith floating in space. He clenched his trembling hands into fists, but there was no masking his fear. He reached for the security pad and punched in the numbers slowly, almost reluctantly.

2 . . . 3 . . . 5 . . . 8 . . . 13 . . . 21.

Marrow . . .

The door sliced open.

Nero's eyes went wide, his pupils swallowing his irises. He did not see the thing that emerged from the shadows behind him until it was too late.

His scream became my scream.

I flew up in my bed, thrashing against my covers and drenched in my own sweat. My heart throbbed and my breathing was rapid. My eyes darted around the room until reality caught up with me.

A dream. It was that same dream.

I glanced at my bedside alarm clock—3:07 a.m. From there, my gaze slowly shifted to the door.

You know those moments when you're about to do something really stupid, but you know there's no talking yourself out of it?

Yeah. It was time to go exploring.

I jumped out of bed and got dressed, putting on my entire crime-fighting shebang—except my communicator. If I was going to snoop around, it was kind of a good idea that I *not* wear a tracking device.

I retracted my bone density and drifted out of my room like a shadow.

The Tartarus was dark and dead. Even with all the machinery, the facility was an empty shell without the scientists moving about. Several of the computers were in sleep mode. Those that weren't continued to purr and blip and blink like stirring creatures. Misty green light continued to emanate and swirl from the jagged surface of the Gaia Comet. It seemed more prominent than ever, casting the entire facility in an ethereal glow.

I stood slightly dumbfounded when I reached the glass door labeled L-01/NE-01. Beside it was a glass tube elevator. If such a door as L-00/NE-00 existed, I had to be practically standing on it.

I turned away from the door and went for the elevator. The control panel labeled levels one through six. That was it. I ran my hand across the control panel as if it might be hiding one last button that would allow me to go down. No such luck.

I don't know what I had expected to find, but I had deduced this much—my detective skills made Scooby-Doo and Shaggy look like Sherlock Holmes.

This was a dumb idea. I was going back to bed.

Stepping off the elevator, I started back the way I came. My sense of adventure had been completely devoured by the groggy crankiness that was typical of anything being done at three o'clock in the morning. I was so groggy it was a miracle I even noticed it—an empty *clank* beneath my step.

I stopped.

The floor consisted of light metal paneling. Such a sound would not have bothered me if it wasn't for one glaring detail—I hadn't normalized my bone density yet. At the moment, I hardly weighed anything.

I tapped the panel again with my toe. The metallic emptiness resonated deep below.

It was hollow.

Stooping down to my hands and knees, I dug my fingernails around the sides of the panel. It was difficult to get a firm grip, but once I did, the panel lifted easily enough. I slid it aside.

In the panel's place was a concrete hole with a steel rung ladder. The bottom was too dark to see. Assuming it did have a bottom, that is. I suppose it was always a possibility that the Tartarus had a secret passage to China.

Now that I had finally found what I was looking for, I suddenly wasn't too keen on exploring.

I went down anyway.

The ladder didn't go down far, eliminating the China possibility. I turned around, surprised to find light in the distance. Dim light, but it was light nonetheless. The corridor only traveled one way. I proceeded forward with cautious steps.

Everything was beginning to look way too familiar. The dark, dank, metal walls, the running pipes, the occasional light bulb leading the way. One particular light bulb flickered and buzzed, causing my insides to flutter. It seemed like exactly the sort of thing to happen in a horror film before the unsuspecting victim was eaten by a ghost. Or whatever the heck it is that all those angry Hollywood ghosts do to people.

I got so distracted by this ridiculous train of thought that I almost didn't see it appear. Those haunting yellow stripes sliced through the shadows.

The door.

I approached it like a hunter approaching a large, dangerous predator—except I imagine a hunter would probably have a clue what the heck he was getting himself into. When, at last, I found myself standing at the door, I could barely move.

"I'm a Superhero," I breathed to myself. "I laugh in the face of danger."

I forced a pathetic excuse for a laugh to reassure myself.

Taking a deep breath, I punched the numbers into the security pad. The door zipped open, releasing a hum of channeling energy.

The room was not what I expected. In fact, it was a stretch to even call it a room. It was more like a cave. The floor, the walls . . . everything was rocky, except for the ceiling which consisted entirely of metal grating, bathing the stone chamber in slits of green light. It was also empty, except for a single titanium pod that was built into the rock with a black-tinted hatch. Wires and coils sprouted from the roof of the pod, snaking up through the ceiling grating. As my gaze drifted upward, I realized where I was at.

I was literally *inside* the Gaia Comet.

Or at least halfway inside. The grating was merely the floor for the lowest part of the scaffolding infrastructure built around the comet. From this vantage point I could see the Cronus Cannon from its colossal base.

My gaze narrowed back on the pod. What was this thing?

Fear was replaced by gnawing curiosity. I approached the tinted hatch door which had no handle. This dilemma solved itself as I merely touched the surface. The hatch reacted instantly, shifting outward slightly with a hiss of released pressure, then slid upward.

The inside of the pod was all wires and tubes feeding into a single chair. A dome-shaped helmet was perched at the top of the chair, clearly positioned for someone's head to fit comfortably inside.

"Hello, Fantom," said a voice—a computerized female voice that caused me to jump and nearly have a heart attack. "Are you ready to initiate Project Cronus?"

A holographic image had appeared on the back of the hatch—the outline of a handprint.

"Place hand on hologram for security identification," said the voice.

Crap. This was my cue to leave.

I backtracked my way the heck outta there. I made my way out of the hidden, level-zero control room, through the glassy corridors, and back to my room. I hadn't even opened my door when I heard the buzzing/ringing sound.

Huh?

I swiped my keycard, and the door's control panel blinked green. The door slid open. That's when I saw the culprit, flashing and vibrating on my nightstand.

My communicator—it was going off.

Crap crap crap crap crap.

It stopped ringing and vibrating the moment I reached it, but the display was still lit up. It read: *9 missed calls.*

FREAKING CRAP SANDWICH.

I exited out of the screen to view my missed calls. They were all from Specter. Which meant they were *really* all from Sapphire. This calmed me down a little—at least Fantom or someone wasn't trying to contact me for an emergency—but it made me panic for an entirely different reason. Why would Sapphire try to call me a gazillion times in the middle of the night?

I selected Specter's name and hit "Call."

Sapphire's face appeared almost instantly—but a completely different Sapphire than the one I knew. This one had puffy, bloodshot eyes, and her face was glistening from what had clearly been a good, hard cry.

"Sapphire?" I said. "Are you okay?"

Her trembling lips hovered open. And then her face collapsed into a choking, sobbing mess.

"Sapphire, what happened?"

"H-h-he's gone," she said. "They . . . they took him."

"Who? Who's gone?"

"Whisp," she said, weeping. "They took Whisp."

CHAPTER 34

The communicator practically slipped out of my fingers. I snapped out of my daze, struggling to form words into coherent sentences.

"Wha—? Who took him?"

"Th-th-th-the police," said Sapphire. She sniffed again, seeming desperate to compose herself. "They just arrested him. Nova tried to stop them, b-b-but they took him anyway."

"I don't get it. Why would they arrest Whisp?"

"Haven't you been watching TV? It's the Cronus Order. They arrested him because of the Cronus Order."

"But he's not a Telepath!"

"According to the police, he is. They called him an animal-Telepath. I mean, technically that's what he is. He communicates with animals telepathically."

"That's ridiculous! How can they even consider that the same thing?"

"I think it's because Oracle used him to control her cats. Once it got all over the news that she was controlling cats too and they realized she used his power, they linked him as a threat."

I was speechless. Whisp—shy, innocent, inhaler-huffing little Whisp . . .

Flex was right. This wasn't justice. There wasn't anything even remotely just about it. It was just wrong.

"So what?" I said. "They're just going to take his power?"

"At eight a.m." said Sapphire, sniffling. "The police said he's going in with the first batch of Telepaths. It's sick, Marrow. They're televising it live and everything."

My grip tightened on the communicator while my free hand balled into a fist.

"We can't let them do this," I said. My brain was spinning too fast. "We have to stop them."

"Marrow . . ."

"There's still time. We can save him!"

"Marrow."

"We're stronger than the police, Sapphire! We can—"

"MARROW."

Even over the communicator, Sapphire's voice was piercing and irrefutable. My gaping mouth closed.

"Marrow, there's nothing we can do," she said. "We can't take on the whole world."

She was right. Even though we were strong—Superheroes-in-training, even—there was nothing we could do to save Whisp. He was beyond saving.

"So we just sit here while they take his power away?" I asked. My voice was cracked and defeated.

Sapphire pulled the communicator away from her face. Even with silence on the other end, I could tell that she was crying again.

"I just . . . I just want to be with someone," she whimpered. "I can't do this alone. Can you come over?"

I glanced at the time display; it was four in the morning.

Four in the morning in a research facility at the bottom of the ocean.

"Yeah," I said. "I'll be there."

I ended the call, only to call Gustav a few short seconds later. It only rang once.

"Yeah, yeah, yeah," said Gustav. He was rubbing the sleep out of his eyes. "Specter already called me."

Welp. That stole my thunder. So instead, probably sounding a little too surprised, I said "She called *you*?"

"Fantom had to take an emergency call. So yeah, she called me."

"Wait, what? He got an emergency call? Like, a crime-fighting, justice-fulfilling, save-the-day sort of emergency call?"

"Yes. That kind of emergency call."

"And he left WITHOUT ME?"

"Oh, believe me. This is not the sort of emergency call that Fantom takes sidekicks on, nor is it *vone* that you vant to be involved in."

"Oh," I said, sounding thoroughly hurt. Because, like, what else was I supposed to say?

"Trust me, Fantom's doing you a favor. Besides, you do vant me to take you to Specter's place, yes?"

That snapped me out of my elevated moment of self-pity. I'd already made a promise to Sapphire. Right now, *she* needed me.

"Meet me at the loading dock in ten minutes," said Gustav.

* * *

It was still dark when we arrived at Specter's place. Nevertheless, Sapphire was sitting on the front porch, hugging her knees. Her blue eyes were still framed in red bloodshot lines. The moment I stepped out of the limo, she tackled me in a hug. Not the playful tackling hug from before though. She squeezed me tight, like I might disappear if she gave anything less. And then she glanced down at the thing in my hand—Oracle's videotape, stuffed back in its manila envelope.

"You would," she said. Her tone wasn't accusing or even irritated. Simply matter-of-fact.

"You know," I said, "in case we get bored."

Sapphire rolled her bloodshot eyes. "I'll never get bored of kicking your butt at Mario Kart."

We entered the front door of the manor, following behind Gustav. Specter's interior decorating maintained an awkward balance between rustic countryside cabin and modern art. Polished wood surfaces. Space-age furniture designs. Classic Victorian fabric patterns. Sharp modern edges and angles. Wildlife decorations intermixed with indecipherable, avant-garde art. It was weird and arguably kitschy and awesome.

Specter was curled up on the loveseat with a coffee mug in her hands, wearing a silky bathrobe. This *might* have been the hottest thing in the universe . . . if I didn't feel so craptacular inside. Gustav sat down on the adjacent recliner and the two of them quietly discussed stuff that I didn't even care to eavesdrop on.

Instead, I offered to make Sapphire something to eat. She wasn't hungry. I asked her if she wanted to watch the news—you know, just to stay current on everything that was happening. She said she'd rather stick her head in the microwave.

So we just sat there. Or rather—I sat there. Sapphire curled up into a ball and cuddled against me, squeezing my arm tight and nestling her head into my chest. We stayed like this for a long time. We stayed until the sun peeked its reluctantly bright head over the horizon. I expected cuddling like this to feel a little more romantic. Instead, I felt empty helplessness expanding inside of me. Occasionally Sapphire would start quivering like she was on the verge of falling apart again. Just when it seemed like she was doing really good, she asked what time it was. I glanced at the kitchen clock and winced.

"Seven fifty-two," I said.

Eight more minutes until Whisp had his powers taken away forever. The knot in my chest was suffocating.

Sapphire fell apart in my lap—shaking . . . sobbing.

I held her as the minutes ticked closer. The worst part was that I remembered that power-extracting chamber so vividly. The way that the Cronus Cannon pointed directly into it—like a gun to someone's head. The shocking size of the spherical glass chamber. Dr. Jarvis's words echoed in my skull:

We actually designed it to contain more than one subject if the need ever arose.

I couldn't stand it. It was like they had *planned* for this! Everything about the Tartarus and the Cronus Order made me sick. And don't even get me started on that hidden chamber beneath the Tartarus, located on a level zero that, according to Dr. Jarvis, shouldn't even exist! What the heck was going on?

At last the time came—the minute hand lurched like a swinging axe, slicing into the twelve.

The silence was chilling. I glanced down at Sapphire whose downcast gaze was entranced on the floor.

Whisp . . .

* * *

Sometime during the deathly silence that followed, Sapphire fell asleep. I was glad. She needed it.

I wasn't even close to sleepy. Instead, my alert gaze was riveted on the manila envelope that I had left on the kitchen counter.

I carefully slid my fingers into Sapphire's blue hair and lifted her head off of my lap. Sliding as stealthily as I could across the cushion, I wiggled myself free of her arms and gently set her head back down.

I left the house and made a straight line for the Control Tower. A brisk walk and two flights of stairs later, I was in the surveillance room. I popped the videotape in the VCR and pressed play. I was once again introduced to a seven-year-old's birthday party.

"Okay, Flex, make a wish," said Oracle.

I pressed fast-forward. I hit play as soon as the birthday part was cut short by a dark hallway.

"Hello?" said Oracle's voice. "Is someone there?"

I watched closely—intently—as Oracle crossed the hall, descended the stairs, and entered her familiar living room. I don't know *what* I was looking for, but whatever it was, I was looking hard for it. A clue. *Anything* to make sense of this bizarre video.

"Spine?" said Oracle. "Is that you?"

Spine was the obvious culprit. If Spine broke into her place, sending us this video to lure us there made perfect sense.

"If that's you, Spine . . . I've been seeing you. You keep appearing in my foresight."

And then her voice wavered.

"But you're not Spine . . . are you?" It wasn't a question—not really. "Are you a friend of his?"

She wasn't just asking. The way she said it, it was like she *knew* it wasn't Spine. But who could it possibly be?

Yeah, Sapphire thought the whole video was staged. But why? Why would Oracle make a fake video, hinting that there was anyone or anything to worry about other than Spine?

"Are you a Telepath?" she said. "I can feel *something*. Something trying to reach into my mind."

And then there was that slight scratching sound. Oracle plunged through her house, clear to the sliding back door. Her porch lights illuminated just how small her backyard was, confined within a chain-link fence. The lights glistened on dewy grass and reflective puddles after a fresh rain.

"Who are you?" said Oracle. "Why are you trying to get inside my head?"

Oracle lowered the camera, and the screen was lost in a blizzard of static. And then the video was back to seven-year-old Flex's birthday party which I had no interest in.

I hit rewind and watched Oracle backtrack her way through the whole house. When she was back in the dark, upstairs hallway where she started, I hit play.

And then I proceeded to watch the whole thing all over again. I focused even harder on the details—every word, every movement, every shadow. In the end, my obsession came down to a single line:

"But you're not Spine . . ."

If Oracle hated Spine so much, why would she lure us to her with a fake video that pointed the finger of blame at someone else? It didn't make sense. It was like she was trying to tell us something. But what? And better yet, why? If she just wanted to use us as bait, why would she be trying to tell us anything?

Maybe Sapphire was right. Maybe I was overthinking this.

The door to the surveillance room opened. I nearly fell backwards in my chair.

"You nerd. How did I know you'd be in here?"

It was Sapphire.

"Sweet Mother Teresa," I said. "You scared the crap out of me."

The good news was that she looked ten times better. Apparently sleeping it off did emotional/psychological wonders. The bad news was that she was drilling holes through me with her skeptical gaze.

"What?" I said.

"You do realize," said Sapphire, "that Einstein defined insanity as doing the same thing over and over again and expecting different results."

"You do realize," I said, "that I don't care."

"Yeah, I've realized that much."

"Good."

Sapphire's gaze drifted past me to the TV screen. "It *is* weird though. I'll give you that."

"Which part?"

"All of it. I mean, who plans out and choreographs something like this? Just to get you guys to come to her house? That's beyond psychopath weird. That's just . . . *weird* weird."

"Um, yeah. That's what I've been saying."

I followed Sapphire's gaze to the TV screen. Oracle was looking through the screen door, talking to herself or who-knows-what.

Oracle lowered the camera and everything became static.

Sapphire went rigid. "Wait. I saw something."

I shot Sapphire an incredulous stare. "What?"

"Go back. Rewind."

I wanted to press for details, but I pinched my mouth shut and hit the rewind button.

"There," she said.

I hit play.

"Why are you trying to get inside my head?" said Oracle.

She was staring out into her backyard once more. I squinted beyond her lit-up back porch, straining to see something in the shadows.

She lowered the camera and the screen erupted in electric snow once more.

"There!" Sapphire exclaimed, pointing. "Did you see it?"

"See what?" I asked in exasperation.

"The puddle! There was something in the puddle!"

"In the . . . puddle?"

"Like a reflection or something," she said, nudging me out of the way and claiming my seat in front of the VCR. "Here, I'll show you."

A blue fingernail tapped the rewind button, reversing out of the birthday party and the TV snow in between. She quickly hit play.

"Why are you trying to get inside my head?" said Oracle.

The camera was too far forward for me to make out the puddles on the porch. I inched closer to the TV in anticipation.

Oracle lowered the camera, and Sapphire hit pause.

The camera fell squarely on the largest puddle. The reflected image was the roof ledge . . . and a silhouette perched atop it. The silhouette was blurry, but I had seen this person too many times to not recognize him. Though most of his body was in shadow, his signature red cape was unmistakable.

"Fantom," I said.

Sca-REEEEEEEEEEEEEECH!

It came from outside—the sound of rubber screaming against asphalt. A car door opened and slammed shut, and then the most familiar, psychotic voice in the world started screaming, "Marrow! *Maaaaaar-rooooow!* Where the heck are you, Marrow? Dang it— MARROW!"

Sapphire raised a blue eyebrow. "Is that Flex?"

I couldn't even register life at the moment. I couldn't process what I had just seen on the video. *Fantom* was spying on Oracle? And now Flex, who was supposed to be in jail, had tracked me down to Specter's house and was screaming my name like a maniac?

I rushed to the window of the of the surveillance room and slid it open. From this third-story perspective, I had a perfect view of the Specter Estate.

"Flex?" I said—loud enough that he could hear me. Flex was already storming towards the front doors of the manor, seconds away from barging in like he owned the place.

Flex halted, whipping around in every direction until his eyes locked on me. "Marrow!"

"What are you doing? I thought you were in jail."

"I was. I broke out."

"You what?" I said, blankly.

"Long story. Listen, we need to get out of here, like, five minutes ago, okay? We gotta go."

I glanced from the crazed, wild-eyed look on Flex's face to the retro Chevy Impala parked crookedly in front of Specter's house. "Whose car is that?"

"I dunno. The prison guard's, maybe? I broke in and hotwired it."

"You WHAT?"

"*Guuuuuuuhhhhh!*" said Flex, pretending to strangle some invisible thing in each of his hands. He then whipped his elastic arm and flung it at me. I backed away because I knew where this was going, and it was a health hazard on multiple levels. Flex's hand latched onto the open window frame, and then the tension in his rubber limb ripped him off his feet. He slingshotted towards the window and *whooooooshed* inside.

And splatted against the wall—squished flat like a cartoon character.

His right hand was the first thing to peel away, and he proceeded to peel his face off the wall. He puffed out into his normal three dimensions and staggered away from wall, slightly disoriented.

"Listen, we need to go," said Flex. "NOW."

I was still blinking, trying to register everything, and Flex's irrational urgency was only making it worse. It was only when my gaze drifted back to the TV screen—to Fantom's blurry reflection—that my bearings realigned.

"It was Fantom," I said. "Fantom was spying on Oracle. Not Spine."

"Yeah, I know," said Flex.

"You *know*?"

"Look, there's no time to explain. We need to get the heck outta here right now or we're—"

Sapphire laughed.

Flex's sentence derailed. Both of us turned as her head tilted back. Her laugh was low and drawn-out in an unstable, maniacal sort of way. When she lowered her head, her eyes narrowed on me.

Except they weren't her eyes. They were pure white.

"You kids just don't stop meddling," said Sapphire. "I mean . . . I feel like I'm dealing with Scooby-Doo and the Gang. Like . . . can we just go five minutes without you brats trying to solve mysteries?"

"Crud," said Flex.

I tripped and fell backwards. Then I backed the heck away from Sapphire in a frantic crab walk.

As I did, the surveillance room door opened behind me.

I spun around on the floor. There, standing in the doorway, was the greatest Superhero of all time, framed in his red cape—Fantom.

His eyes were tainted by something purely evil.

"And it's a real shame too," said Fantom and Sapphire's combined voices. "Because I was really looking forward to you being my sidekick. It would have made for some great publicity."

Fantom stepped forward and shut the door behind him.

"Now I have to kill both of you."

"You . . ." I said, breathless. "How are you . . . ? What are you . . . ?"

That was about as far as my coherence seemed to go.

"What am I?" said Fantom, cracking a smirk. "That's the real question, isn't it?"

Slowly climbing to my feet, Flex and I backed away in a direction where he and Sapphire were both in sight. My gaze hesitated on Sapphire.

"You're a Telepath?"

"*UHRRRRR!*" said Fantom, imitating an obnoxious buzzer sound. "Close, though. Try again."

My brain was spinning and the word came before I could even process it.

"You're an . . . Omnipotent?"

"*Ding, ding, ding,*" said Fantom, smiling wider and clapping his hands. "We have a winner."

Even though I'd guessed it, I couldn't believe it. It was impossible. Unheard of. "So you're an Omnipotent *and* you have super speed, super strength, *and* you can fly?" I asked. My voice came out as practically a squeak on "fly."

What kind of Super had that much power?

"Ah, now that's where things get a little complicated," said Fantom. "You see, I actually *don't* have super speed or super strength, and I *can't* fly."

My jaw fell open. "What?"

"I know, right?" said Fantom, laughing at my reaction. "Who saw that coming? Let's put it this way: I'm not just *any* Omnipotent. I am *the* Omnipotent. I mean . . . I'm practically God in spandex."

"I don't get it," I said, shaking my head absently. "I've *seen* you use those other powers! What do you mean you don't have them?"

"No, Marrow," said Flex. "What you *saw* was good acting."

Fantom smiled at this. "Right up there with the great ones like Clark Gable and Humphrey Bogart," he said. "I've simply been practicing for a very long time. For example, if I need to pick up something to throw at an opponent . . ."

Fantom approached the couch and lifted it off the ground by grabbing one of its legs.

". . . I let my mind do all the heavy lifting."

He released the couch and it remained suspended in the air. As he walked away, the couch floated down like a balloon. He began pacing slowly around me.

"It's the same for anything else," he said. "If I want to punch somebody, my mind does the punching. If I *get* punched, my mind creates a protective telekinetic barrier around me. If I need super speed or if I need to fly, my mind carries me. It's not even mentally strenuous.

The only tricky part is making it look real. So naturally, I take that look on your face as the greatest compliment."

"But why pretend?" I asked. "Why not just let everyone know you're an Omnipotent?"

"Hmm," said Fantom, pressing a finger to his lips. "Let's think about how well that worked for all the other Omnipotents out there. Oh yeah. They're extinct. Well, how about the Telepaths? Oh yeah. Everyone hates them. But Superman? *Everyone* loves Superman. I simply did what every kid does: I decided what I wanted to be when I grew up. I wanted to be Superman. But that's only my telekinetic power. The *true* mastery of my art is in my telepathy."

Fantom ended his pacing at Sapphire's side and placed a brawny hand on her slender shoulder.

"Some people might call me a puppet master. But I don't like that title. It makes me sound like a villain. I prefer the title 'director.' I like to think of myself as a modern-day Hitchcock of sorts. Cosmo City is my set, and its citizens are my cast and crew."

It was both obvious and inconceivable as I realized what he meant.

"By the way," he continued, "you don't have to worry about Specter or Gustav interrupting our little heart-to-heart. They're in the same state as our dear friend, Sapphire, here."

"You were controlling Oracle," I said. "You were controlling all of those people."

Flex tensed as I said this. Even if he didn't seem surprised at all.

Fantom's grin grew sinister. "More than that."

"Huh?"

"'All the world's a stage,'" said Fantom, gesturing his arms outward "'And all the men and women merely players: They have their exits and their entrances.' Shakespeare, in case you care to know."

I had no idea what he was talking about, and I certainly didn't know what Shakespeare had to do with anything.

"This is my story," he said. "I've been in control of everything every step of the way. Every chapter of my success has been carefully scripted. Every fight choreographed."

His head lowered, eyes narrowed on me.

"Every villain has been my carefully selected actor—my puppet."

My defensive stance went limp. My mouth was dry. I couldn't breathe or even blink. But not because of the *hundreds* of so-called "Supervillains" who were suddenly proven innocent by this single confession.

My mind was frozen on a single one—my father.

"It's not easy making a Supervillain, you know," said Fantom. "You can't just take control of someone's brain and make them go evil. No one's going to buy that. But say you have a Super with the ability to manipulate fire, and that Super has a brother who means the world to him. If that brother were to be . . . *ahem* . . . mugged and killed, suddenly we have a drive for vengeance. Now you can take control. A few arson-based crimes later and bada bing bada boom, the Supervillain Torcher is born. I mean, with a name like that, the kid was born to be evil! But if you *really* want to create a Supervillain with reputation, you have him—or her—kill other notable Supers. Like your dear friend from the Final Challenge, Arachnis. A mutated spider lady is scary all by herself—a mutation that I helped to stimulate once I was inside her head, I might add. But a mutated spider lady that can kill an Omnipotent like Cortex? Now that's something truly terrifying."

Fantom mockingly widened his eyes and covered his mouth. "*Whoops!* I suppose that means I'm partly responsible for the extinction of the Omnipotents. Oh well. Survival of the fittest, right?"

I was hardly paying attention to a word he said. My mind had only one focus and it was eroding my brain away.

"My father," I breathed. "He's . . . innocent?"

"Ah, your father," said Fantom. "My greatest creation and also the greatest thorn in my side. I spent so much time and energy building him up to be the perfect villain—arranging your mother's death, letting him spiral into madness. And when I finally seized control of his brain . . . it was poetic. A thing of beauty. He was the arch nemesis I had always dreamed of. People were *terrified* of him. When it finally came time to kill him . . . I couldn't do it. Not with the reaction I was getting from Cosmo City. Spine was just too good to let go of. So I kept him. Whenever Cosmo City seemed to become complacent about my presence and other villains simply weren't cutting it, I knew it was time for Spine to strike back. This, of course, went on for years. Things were going so well . . ."

Fantom shook his head with a look of distaste.

"But alas, all good things must come to an end," he said with a sigh. "The bone matter in Spine's skull adapted until it created a brain barrier immune to my telepathy. He simply slipped through the cracks. He vanished before I could do anything. I haven't had a decent night's sleep since, you know. Spine had the potential to ruin this utopia I've been striving so hard to create. Until now, that is. I actually suspected that he was keeping an eye on you a while ago. That's part of the reason why *I* intervened in your Final Challenge, letting Nero win instead of you. I wanted your father to see his son's future crumble right in front of him. Any doubt I had about your father watching over you was erased when you were kidnapped by that Nightmare fellow. Your father *used* Nightmare's power so the bone matter in your skull could adapt the very same immunity. He obviously didn't want me using you like I did him—which, I'll admit, is an extremely tempting notion.

"Once I knew Spine was watching, I took control of Nero and threatened your life. It helped that Nero was snooping around in places that he shouldn't have been. Alas, that plan nearly backfired on me when that pathetic little parasite tried communicating to you using his telekinesis as Morse code. I only barely caught him before he could rat me out. Fortunately, I had been planning to frame Oracle for quite some time. All that spying, working endlessly to get inside her head . . . It was totally on the fly when I had Nero say her name instead of mine. It was rushing ahead of my intended schedule, but I have to say, it couldn't have worked better. Oracle was the perfect scapegoat, using you and Flex as bait to lure Spine out directly. I'll be honest. Beating your dad's head into the ground was the happiest moment of my life."

Fantom rolled his eyes up, his mouth splitting into a sadistic grin of euphoric bliss. "I've been waiting to do that for years."

I had been completely numb until this point. A tear burned down my cheek like acid. I glanced down to find my hands squeezed into fists and shaking. Electricity surged through my veins. Making my bones light, I screamed and flew forward. My fist exploded with the force and precision of a missile.

My momentum came to a jarring halt. A dozen invisible hands gripped me, inside and out. I hung hopelessly in the air, gasping, barely able to breathe.

I wasn't done yet. I extended my fingers out and pushed the density hard into my fingertips. Twelve-inch bone spikes ripped beneath my fingernails, glistening in a thin layer of mucus. The tip of my middle finger spike barely grazed Fantom's throat, drawing blood.

"Son of a bean-dipped mother Frito!" said Fantom. He staggered back and grabbed his neck. He pulled his hand away, revealing a small dab of crimson. "Picking a fight with the most powerful Omnipotent in the world, eh? You've got guts, Marrow. I'll give you that. Unfortunately, guts can be spilled."

Fantom reached his arm forward, twisting his curled fingers.

My insides were suddenly gripped in a vice—twisting, crushing. I gagged and coughed, spitting blood.

"Marrow!" said Flex. The moment he moved towards me, Fantom raised a hand. Flex went rigid. He contorted like a dying insect. His face pinched, and he screamed through his teeth. "*Urrrrrgh!*"

Fantom quickly flicked his fingers open, thrusting both palms forward. Flex and I flew backward, crashing into the drywall which cracked and caved around us. The tension on my insides was released, however, which was all I cared about at the moment. We remained telekinetically glued to the wall as Fantom approached.

"You certainly have your father's fighting spirit, Marrow," he said. "Still throwing punches, even when the fight's already over. I like that."

"How can you even pretend to be a hero?" I said. "You're more evil than the fake villains you're defeating!"

"Ah, you see, that's where you and I would have to disagree. Do you remember what I told you the other day? About standing as a symbol for goodness and justice? I actually believe that. I believe that I *am* that symbol."

"You've got to be kidding me."

"No, I really do," said Fantom. His expression was disturbingly sincere. "You don't know the numbers like I do. When you eliminate all the staged crimes that I'm responsible for, Cosmo City actually has the lowest crime rate of any major city in the world. Criminals in Cosmo City are *afraid* to commit crimes because of me. And hey, who can blame 'em? I've created a utopia where evil is always defeated and good always prevails."

"Yeah, except that makes you the biggest criminal in Cosmo City," said Flex. "You're no better than some lousy, mafia warlord. Just because you control the crime doesn't mean it isn't there."

"Flex, Flex . . ." said Fantom, shaking his head. "You understand so little. Comparing me to a syndicate leader is like comparing God to an annoying televangelist. I don't need men or guns to get what I want. I don't need the law to tell me what to do. I *am* the law. I was chosen for this."

"Chosen," I said. "Wow. Have delusions of grandeur much?"

"You don't believe me?" asked Fantom, raising a challenging eyebrow. "You know, I'm surprised, Marrow. You haven't even asked how I became so powerful to begin with."

Honestly, I hadn't even thought about that. But the way he was bringing it up now, he made it sound like there was some big secret to it.

"What does that matter?" I asked.

"Oh, it matters," said Fantom, his countenance darkening. "In fact, everything centers on it."

"Oh really?" I said skeptically.

"What if I told you that there's something living inside of me?"

"Inside of you?" My skepticism upped a notch.

"Would you like to meet it?"

This conversation had just gone from crazy to cuckoo for Cocoa Puffs.

"It normally speaks directly to my mind," said Fantom. "But it loves when I let it out every once in a while."

Fantom closed his eyes.

This was ridiculous. I didn't know what kind of joke this was supposed to be, but I didn't want to stick around for it. I struggled against the invisible force securing me to the wall. Even without Fantom paying any attention to me, I couldn't budge.

Not that it mattered. The moment Fantom opened his eyes, I went rigid.

His eyes were glowing neon green. Not just his irises. Everything. His pupils, the whites of his eyes—gone. Swallowed in green energy and pulsating with concentrated power.

I had seen those eyes before—the same eyes from my brief mental breakdown on the Tartarus elevator. The same ones that were now haunting me in my dreams.

"Hello, Marrow," said a new voice—a conglomeration of synchronized voices of various pitches and tones. Emotionless. Soulless. Like a choir of the undead. "I told you Brother wanted to kill you."

Fantom blinked and his eyes were human again.

"Now, now," said Fantom. "What have I told you about revealing my evil plots to strangers, Gaia?"

Gaia? No. That was impossible.

"Sweet, merciful mother of crap," said Flex. "I did *not* see that coming."

Fantom blinked again, flooding his eyes with neon green energy once more. "Their minds are shielded, Brother. Why can't we see inside of them?"

He blinked again.

"Just be patient, Gaia," said Fantom. "We'll be able to get in soon enough. If we got inside Oracle, we can hack our way into any brain. You were able to communicate to his mind on the Tartarus after all."

"Gaia . . ." I said in shock. "You . . . you can talk to the comet?"

"Not the comet itself," said Fantom. "The mind of the comet. The spirit of the comet, I suppose you could say. Gaia is a bodiless symbiotic alien life form whose life's essence is connected to the comet. It is the energy of Gaia's life force that continually gives birth to Supers."

"And you can talk to it?" I repeated.

"In a manner of speaking. Gaia's mind is attached to my mind."

"H-h-h-how?" Flex sputtered. "How is that even possible?"

"Ah, Flex," said Fantom, shaking his head. "Don't you know my legend? A young child is sailing on a boat in the ocean with his parents. The Gaia Comet strikes, killing his mother and father instantly, but the boy survives— and emerges as the most powerful Super of all time."

Fantom paused, chuckling to himself, as if he were about to let me in on the greatest joke of the century.

"What if I told you that I *did* die?"

Worst joke ever.

"I died, but Gaia brought me back to life," said Fantom. "Melded together with my mind. But this isn't your average Invasion of the Body Snatchers. Gaia agrees with everything I think. Feels everything that I feel. And supplies me with a considerable amount of power to do what I need to do. You could almost say that we are one in the same being."

Fantom blinked, and his eyes were glowing neon green again.

"Do they know our plans?" said Gaia in his haunting symphony of voices. "Do they know how we get our powers, Brother?"

"How you *get* your powers?" said Flex. "But I thought—"

Fantom blinked again, taking control. "—that my power comes from Gaia," he said, finishing my thought. "And it does. When Gaia melded with my mind, my telepathic and telekinetic powers increased exponentially. But that only scratches the surface of our capabilities. You see, with Gaia and I combined . . . we can *absorb* the power of other Telepaths and Telekinetics."

"What?" I said. "But how?"

"Well, I can't explain the science of it to you," said Fantom. "What I *can* tell you is that we can telepathically delve into such a Super's mind and rip the power right out of his or her brain. When that happens, the power naturally fuses with Gaia and me. That's the other reason that I was so keen on interfering with your Final Challenge and letting Nero win. Taunting Spine with your loss was appealing in theory, but I also *really* wanted Nero's power. It's not every day that you come across such strong, fresh telekinetic energy."

"You stole Nero's power?"

"Ripped it right out of his smug little brain right after he tried to rat me out to you and your friends."

I couldn't believe it. Nero was not only comatose, but he was powerless. Everything he had worked for—gone. I couldn't feel any of the resentment I used to have for him. I only felt sick.

"But that was just a little something to tide me over," said Fantom. "Even collecting Oracle's power—which is immense, I might add—is small in comparison to the true fruit of my reckoning."

I didn't want to ask. So naturally, I did. "What's that?"

"The Cronus Order," said Fantom. "The largest gathering of Telepaths the world has ever known. Like Nero, my reason for using Oracle had dual purposes. Can you imagine? All that power in one location."

"But . . . their powers were just taken by the Cronus," I protested.

"The first batch, yes," said Fantom. The corners of his lips twitched, fighting another sadistic smile. "Well . . . supposing that the Cronus works like I said it does."

Oh no. This was bad. This was really bad. As if the Cronus Order wasn't horrible enough on its own . . .

"What do you mean? What does the Cronus really do?"

"Oh, it takes their powers alright," said Fantom. "However, it's not so much a machine as it is . . . oh, what's the word? An *amplifier*? You see, below the Cronus, there is a centralized compartment cell designed specifically for me. The Cronus only works if Gaia and I are powering it with our cerebral energy. And when that happens . . ."

The chamber beneath the Tartarus! Oh crap. Oh crap crap crap crap crap.

"You steal their power," said Flex.

"Like candy from a baby," said Fantom. "And baby, it's Halloween. Nero actually found the compartment cell, the little snoop. That's when I decided to revoke his brain privileges permanently."

"And Whisp," I said. "You stole his power too?"

"The animal whisperer? Funny you should mention him. I actually made a *special* effort to target him and secure his power. Oh boy, do I have plans for that power!"

I didn't even want to know. I was slightly more terrified about the rest of the power he was absorbing.

"Top that off with Oracle's vast power and the telepathic energy of over a hundred other Telepaths . . ." Fantom breathed in and sighed blissfully. "Have you ever tried on glasses or contact lenses for the first time? Well . . . I haven't. But I'd imagine it'd feel similar to this—on steroids and multiplied by a billion. And hey, that's just the appetizer. While the Cronus Order is still in effect, there are still thousands of more minds to come. And believe me, I intend to absorb every telepathic mind in existence."

Fantom yawned, interlocking his fingers and stretching them behind his head. He turned to glance at a clock hanging on the wall and shook his head.

"Oh, would you look at me," he said. "Monologuing again. I apologize about that. You have no idea how maddening it is to have a perfect plan like this and not be able to share it with anyone. And here we are now. You two know everything, and now I have to kill you. I was really hoping to somehow break past these mental barriers of yours, but the more I think about it, the more impractical it seems. Even with all my new power, it could take weeks for me to penetrate them. Maybe longer. And I obviously can't keep you quiet for that long without arousing suspicions. Such a shame too. Marrow, you would have made the perfect follow-up villain to Spine. You have the motive, the power, the tainted reputation . . . everything. It would have been beautiful. Poetic, even."

Fantom pulled his gaze from me, focusing instead on white-eyed Sapphire who hadn't budged.

"But alas . . . I'll just have to settle for your girlfriend, you, and Flex killing each other in a Mexican standoff. I'm sure the police will concoct their own viable motive. They always do."

Even telepathically pinned to the wall, my body tensed.

Fantom turned to the water fountain. The knob pressed down and water sprayed from the faucet. But instead of arcing back down into the fountain, the water redirected horizontally in a concentrated stream, slithering toward us like a liquid snake. The knob popped up again, shutting the water off, but the levitating stream was already several feet long. Sapphire raised her hand. As the water reached her palm, it reformed and solidified into an icy javelin, pointing at Flex.

My own hand raised as well—the one with inch-long bone spikes still protruding from my fingertips—pointing at Sapphire. Flex's arm raised, stretching towards me.

A force wrapped around my throat. My windpipe closed off.

"Flex was so upset that Marrow left him for me, he decided to kill his former sidekick," said Fantom. "Sapphire reacted instantly, attacking Flex. And Marrow, who still cared for Flex, tried to stop his girlfriend at any cost. All three died instantly. Oh, this is good."

My suffocating gaze darted between all the sharp edges that were aimed to collide. I desperately tapped into my skeletal structure, struggling to retract my claws, to break free of Fantom—to break free of Flex's chokehold—but Fantom's telekinesis was impenetrable.

"It's been a pleasure, fellas," said Fantom. And then he winked. He actually winked. "Oh, and Marrow, tell your mom I said hi. She was a babe."

The room was blurry. Fading. I gasped, choked, and wheezed as my starving lungs crumpled. Sapphire reared her icy javelin back, aiming at Flex. I flew at her—dangling from Fantom's telekinetic strings—my claws aimed at her heart. They would both be stabbed simultaneously.

And me? I had already breathed my last breath.

CHAPTER 35

This was it. We were dead. My whole life became an instantaneous slideshow of flashing images. Unfortunately, it was very short and slightly depressing. I squeezed my eyes shut, hoping that it would all be over quick.

Fantom screamed.

I opened my eyes and several things happened at once. Sapphire veered off course, stabbing her icy javelin into the wall beside Flex. Flex and I dropped to the floor, barely managing to land on our feet. Fantom backed against the far corner, staring at his hands in horror.

Or what was left of his hands.

They were melting. His hands were like wax, bending and dissolving—dripping onto the floor.

That lasted for only a brief moment. An instant later, his hands were whole again. Fantom blinked, looking at his hands, front and back.

Nightmare materialized out of nowhere. Swinging a massive gorilla arm, he nailed Fantom in the face. Fantom spun a full three hundred and sixty degrees before hitting the floor.

Nightmare was still wearing the same weathered trench coat and ugly face I remembered. But he also had a strange but familiar metal helmet clutched in his massive grip.

A mind cuff.

"You ugly-as-butt, monkey-faced Neanderthal!" said Flex. His gaze was still riveted on the icy spear in the wall. "What took you so long?"

"A thank you will suffice, you greasy hippie-troll," said Nightmare.

"Whoa, what?" I said. "You two *know* each other?"

"Long story," said Flex. "CliffsNotes version: I was in jail when he did his weird hallucination thing in my head, except mostly he just showed me that he and Spine were the good guys, and Fantom was a power-sucking, villain-creating, Omnipotent psychopath. So I broke out of jail."

He made it sound like he shoplifted candy out of Wal-Mart.

"You just broke out," I said, somewhat mockingly. "Just like that."

"Dude," he said. "I'm made of rubber. I squeezed through the bars."

Sapphire blinked several times, snapping out of her mind-controlled daze with confused blue eyes. She glanced down at the icy spear her hands were still gripping, jutting from the wall. "What? What just happened?"

Then she turned to find Nightmare standing over Fantom who was sprawled on the floor.

And then she screamed.

Nightmare didn't waste a moment. Approaching her undeterred, he shoved the helmet on her head and latched it shut. He then whisked her off of her feet and tucked her effortlessly under his arm.

"Hey!" said Sapphire, kicking and flailing. "Put me down!"

Nightmare ignored her, redirecting his determined gaze to me. "We need to get out of here. Now."

My brain seemed to be frozen as a gazillion questions battled through my mind at once. All of those questions seemed to diminish as Fantom rolled on the floor and groaned.

"Yeah," I said, nodding anxiously.

Nightmare, Flex, and I bolted out the door, racing down the long, bleak hallway of the Control Tower while Sapphire continued to scream.

"Why didn't you put the mind cuff on Fantom?" I asked.

"He's too strong," said Nightmare. "His mind would break through and he'd just rip the mind cuff off telekinetically."

"Well why am *I* wearing this stupid thing?" said Sapphire, fumbling with the strap. "I don't have mind powers!"

"Mind cuffs work both ways. They don't just keep mind powers in. They keep mind powers out as well. From a distance, this should keep Fantom out of your head . . . mostly. I hope. We have to protect ourselves from him."

"What about you?" I said. "Don't you need one?"

"I have my own mental defenses. He can enter my head, but he'd be crazy to try. There's some scary stuff in there. Other Telepaths have tried and ended up needing serious therapy afterward."

I believed it.

"That was a pretty good hallucination," I said. "Melting hands. Glad you never used that one on me."

Even as we ran, Nightmare shot me a wide-eyed stare. "You saw that?"

"Of course I saw it. Why wouldn't—"

I didn't even finish. The words fell dead in my throat.

"Your mental barrier is collapsing," said Nightmare. "Fantom's more powerful than I thought. I'm surprised he didn't realize how close he was. One more nudge and he would have been inside your head. If he finds out . . ."

Nightmare didn't finish his thought. He didn't need to.

I was one step away from being Fantom's next headline Supervillain.

I swallowed hard. Nightmare still had no idea just how powerful Fantom really was now. He didn't know how powerful he would become if we didn't stop him.

"So what's the plan?" I asked.

"For the most part, it consists of running really fast. And maybe, if we don't die, we'll rescue your father."

"Fast," I said, nodding vacantly. "I can do fast."

We were just rounding the corner to the stairwell when the entire wall around the surveillance room door exploded. Shards of wood and broken debris sprayed the opposite wall, swallowed in billowing dust. A red cape flared amid the smoke.

"Faster," said Flex, hurtling down the stairs. "Gotta go faster."

"Let me go!" Sapphire insisted, pounding Nightmare's thigh with her fists. "I have legs, you know!"

"Sure you do," said Nightmare. Flying down the stairs two steps at a time, he clearly had no intention of putting her down.

"Fine," said Sapphire. "You want fast? I'll give you fast."

She reached her hands up, pointing her blue fingernails to the top of the stairwell. A water fountain rattled on the wall. Fantom stepped directly in front of it.

"You!" he growled. "I'm going to kill—!"

Whether it was intentional or not, the water fountain exploded, erupting in a concentrated blast that threw Fantom down the stairs as water flooded down the steps. Just as it was gushing past our feet, threatening to throw off our balance, it froze. The stairwell became an icy slide, rounded up on the tight curves. Nightmare lost his grip on Sapphire and all four of us spiraled downward. Fantom's body was lost behind us, frozen in the ice.

"*Seeeeeeeeee?*" said Sapphire as we slid. "This is *waaaaaaaaaay faaaaaaaaaasterrrrrrrrrrr!*"

"You're *insaaaaaaaaaane!*" said Nightmare.

"*Heeeeey*, at least I took care of *Faaaaaantom, riiiiight?*"

Even though Fantom was far out of sight, frozen somewhere between the third and second floor, a reverberating crack resounded from above, followed by the sound of shattering. We hit the bottom floor running.

"Not so much," Nightmare muttered under his breath.

Sunlight splashed across us as we dashed outside, cutting across the long Specter Estate driveway.

"Can't you use your hallucinations on him again?" I asked.

"Not like that," said Nightmare. "He'll be expecting it now. The only way I'll trick his mind now is if I take a more subtle approach."

"Subtle?" said Flex. "What's *that* supposed to mean?"

"Don't worry. I have a plan."

"Screw that," said Sapphire. She glanced anxiously back at the Control Tower. "Where do we *run?*"

"Good question," said Nightmare. "I don't know."

"WHAT?"

"Nightmare," said Flex. "I just want to take this moment to let you know that I hate you."

Nightmare ignored him. "We're supposed to be rendezvousing with someone here," he said.

"Who?"

A subtle *whoosh* drew all of our attentions. We all turned to find an all-too-familiar black man who easily matched Nightmare in size standing near the base of the Control Tower. Like Sapphire, he was also wearing a mind cuff and seemed especially glad to have it

"Havoc!" Sapphire and I exclaimed simultaneously.

Just as Havoc was turning around, the bottom of the ice-covered Control Tower stairwell exploded in chunks of wood, sandstone, and ice-turned-slush. Fantom emerged from the smoldering rubble, wafting the smoke from his face.

Havoc—our ticket out of here—was now sprawled on the stretch of parking lot between us and Fantom, scraping himself off the asphalt.

We flew toward him.

I resisted tapping into my skeletal power, keeping pace with Flex, Sapphire, and Nightmare's desperate sprinting. At this point, Fantom had regained his bearings and narrowed his furious gaze on us—only a few yards from Havoc who was now staggering to his feet.

Fantom blasted towards us, cape flaring behind him like a trail of fire.

Havoc only now realized his precarious position and extended his arms out to us. Nightmare, Flex, Sapphire, and I all lunged, arms reaching to grab any part of his body.

We collided in a tangle of flesh. I was only focused on Havoc's leg, which I clung to desperately as gravity became a vacuum through space and my insides flattened against my ribcage. I closed my eyes before they could get sucked out of their sockets.

I never hit the asphalt of the parking lot, but our final destination made up for that. When gravity was back in force, I landed stomach-first on a solid tile floor. I dared to open my eyes. The first things I saw past Havoc's heavy boot were the wheeled legs of a hospital bed. A broad, hanging arm was handcuffed to the bedframe. The thick, calloused fingers with chipped, claw-like nails were unmistakable.

Dad . . .

My thoughts didn't make it far past that point. There was a sickening *smack* of flesh, and Havoc's leg whipped out of my grip, kicking me in the face. I didn't even have a moment to register the pain. An invisible force seized me from the inside, placing special pressure on my throat, Darth Vader-style. I lifted off of the ground, kicking and grasping at my neck in a futile effort to stop the choking. It wasn't until now that I noticed Flex, Sapphire, Nightmare, and Havoc levitating with me in the same dismal predicament. Everyone was gasping for air except for Havoc who was completely unconscious, dangling like a puppet on strings. Together, we formed a swaying circle around Fantom. Behind his mask, his manic gaze was concentrated on Nightmare.

With so many of us crowded together, the hospital room was a claustrophobic, stale little cave of white surfaces and sharp edges. My gaze shifted past it all, settling on my father. His scraggly hair was a tangled mess over his beaten face—cut, bruised, and swollen. And yet, despite the damage, his unconscious expression was so peaceful. Serene.

"You fools," said Fantom. "Did you really think you could stop me?"

Nightmare gritted his teeth, fighting to breathe. "There's no way . . . you'll get away . . . with this . . ."

"Get away with it? I've *already* gotten away with it. I've been getting away with it for decades! All of you are just pawns. My puppets. Spine, Oracle, every villain who's ever been worth front page news. Heck, I'm even inside the head of the President of the United States! I control whatever I want. I *kill* whoever I want! And do you know why? Because this is *my* city. Cosmo City belongs to me! I'm not just an Omnipotent, Nightmare. I. AM. GOD."

Nightmare didn't respond. In fact, it looked like he was crying. His face was so red—practically purple—that it wasn't until several seconds later that I realized he wasn't crying at all.

He was laughing.

"Oh great," gasped Flex. "Nightmare's lost it."

"What's so funny?" said Fantom. "Do you think it's funny that you're about to die?"

"I'm sorry," said Nightmare, wheezing. "That was just . . . too perfect. I couldn't have . . . scripted it better."

"Huh? Scripted . . . what?"

The entire room around us crackled and distorted. The walls shifted and expanded, growing transparent. Everything around us dissolved. Even my father on the hospital bed. Several sleek machines with blinking lights and computer display screens materialized in the open space. We were soon swallowed in a vast blue glow. A school of orange and white fish swished in unison overhead. We were underwater, encompassed in a spacious chamber of honeycomb glass panes forming a sphere—merely one in a visibly circular infrastructure of spheres. At their center was a rock formation emanating a glowing green mist.

We were on the Tartarus.

That was only half the shock. Where Spine's bed had been, there was now a crowd of people. Not just scientists. News reporters. Camera men. An army of police officers who were in the process of escorting men, women, and children clothed in hospital robes and mind cuffs. All of them were frozen in place.

All eyes were on Fantom. More importantly, all cameras were on him.

We were on live television.

Amid the news reporters standing on the front line was Donnie Danson with his gravity-defying hair. His toothy smile was replaced by a slack-jawed look of astonishment.

"Sweet mother of Mike Wallace," said Donnie.

Nightmare, Flex, Sapphire, Havoc, and I all dropped to the floor. I was so disoriented that I landed on my face, but that was okay. Oxygen had never tasted so wonderful.

The look on Fantom's face tasted even better.

Havoc and Nightmare had planned this. Havoc had actually teleported us to the Tartarus, and Nightmare had masked it as Spine's hospital room with his power.

This is what Nightmare meant by taking "a more subtle approach." I would have stood up and started applauding right then and there if I wasn't so dizzy.

"*Awkward!*" said Flex under his breath. He was covering his mouth, attempting to hide an irrepressible grin

"I . . . uh . . . I can explain," said Fantom. "It's . . . you see . . . um . . . him!" Fantom pointed a wildly accusing finger at Nightmare. "He's a Telepath! He was controlling me. He's trying to frame me! He . . . has telekinetic powers too. I mean . . . he's an Omnipotent! He's trying to make it look like I'm an Omnipotent, and I'm not!"

Nightmare merely folded his gorilla arms and snickered. He made no attempt to defend himself.

A higher ranking police official with a Tom Selleck mustache gestured to two of the officers beside him and emerged from the crowd. The Tartarus chamber was in complete silence as they approached Fantom. I recognized one of the officers at his side as Jenkins, who had interrogated me after the blowout at Oracle's house.

"Hello Fantom," he said, forcing a smile. "My name's Lieutenant Reese. Would you mind if some of my men escorted you back to the station? I just want to ask you a few questions."

"Why do you want to ask me questions?" said Fantom. His eyes were wild, darting around the silently observing crowd. "I'm innocent. Nightmare's the one trying to frame me! Why don't you escort him to the station?"

"We're going to bring everyone back to the station for questioning and get this all sorted out. But I would appreciate it if you would let Parker and Jenkins escort you to the submarine."

"How come you don't have any officers grabbing them? I'm a victim here! I demand to be treated with respect!"

Jenkins's hand twitched at his holster.

Fantom apparently noticed this because his hand lunged out, grabbing Jenkins in a telekinetic grip. Jenkins choked and gagged, grabbing at the invisible force around his throat.

"You think you can pull a gun on ME?" Fantom roared.

Reese and Parker both reached for their guns. Fantom swung his other arm, and the two of them flew back, crashing into the obstacle course of computers and machines.

At least fifty other officers reached for their holsters and whipped out their guns.

"Put your hands up!" said one.

"Oh," said Fantom. His eyes were distant, with a slightly crazed lack of focus. "Okay. If that's what you want."

Fantom thrust his hands in the air. As he did, nearly everyone in the crowd flew up in unison. But no attempt was made to hold them up, the disarray of flailing limbs and screams came crashing down, tumbling on top of each other.

"How dare you," Fantom snarled. "I was your hero. And this is how you treat me?"

It wasn't until now that I noticed Nightmare crawling to his knees. He crept over to Havoc who was still lying in an unconscious heap, shaking him gently.

"Havoc," he whispered with an unsettling sense of urgency. "Wake up. We need you."

"Fine," said Fantom. "You want to make me the villain? Then I'll be the villain."

Fantom's eyes erupted into blazing green fiery orbs—Gaia's eyes. But something was different. There was too much twisted, maniacal passion in his expression for it to be just Gaia.

"I'll be the greatest and most terrifying villain that Cosmo City has ever seen!" Gaia's eerie chorus of voices was joined by Fantom's distinguished voice at the forefront.

I didn't know how, but Fantom and Gaia had somehow merged together—more than they already were, at least. The end result was horrific.

He threw his arms in the air, fingers contorted. The floor jolted with a sudden tremor that knocked several screaming people off their feet. I barely kept my balance with my arms extended. The entire Tartarus began to tremble—like an earthquake, minus the minor detail that we were nowhere near solid earth. Metal groaned with the lurching movement. Machines rattled. Loose objects shifted with the vibrations. My gaze then wandered to our outside surroundings. The flowering colors of the surrounding coral reef descended into shadow. The ocean floor slipped out of view.

"What's happening?" said Sapphire. She clung to my arm for balance.

Something was moving. But it wasn't the ocean floor. Bubbles fizzled around the network of spheres, flooding past the glass surfaces. Water was rushing past us.

The Tartarus was being *lifted*.

Not just the Tartarus—the entire Gaia Comet was being elevated as well. Its swirling green mist trailed downward as the rising Tartarus gained momentum. The spider web of dancing light on the ocean's surface reflected brighter and brighter.

"Oh crap," I said. "Hold on."

Sapphire didn't need to be told twice. She squeezed my arm even tighter, cutting off my circulation. I tapped into my bone structure, weighing my feet down, and wrapped my arms around Sapphire.

"I am *so* not drunk enough for this!" said Flex.

The Tartarus heaved and lurched, metal groaning against the changing water pressure. And then it burst free of the ocean surface. Water gushed down the rounded glass surfaces, raining down on the fizzing sea below. The airborne research facility jettisoned upward even faster now that there was no water to restrain it. A hundred feet. Two hundred. Three. The ocean became a distant blue slate.

The Tartarus slowed to a jarring halt. We were hardly floating in midair though. The Tartarus changed direction, and the distant ocean drifted beneath us as we soared parallel to it. The horizon was separated by a silver line of spires. Even from miles away, I could make out the sharp, defined edges of the looming CTN Tower, stabbing into the heavens.

We were flying to Cosmo City.

Fantom's eyes—Gaia's eyes—shifted to Sapphire and me. "Would you two like to see what I can do with your friend's power?"

Fantom raised his palm and then balled it into a fist.

Clink—clank—sheenk! Sharp, metallic sounds echoed from deep below in eerie percussion. As soon as those sounds ended, the silence was swallowed in something new. Scratching. Screeching. Howling. Roaring.

Boom, boom, boom . . .

Although Fantom could easily take control of every human in the room, he clearly had something worse planned for them. With Whisp's power, Fantom had an entire army at his disposal.

An army of mutated sea creatures. And we were trapped inside the suspended Tartarus with them.

I silently approached the rounded glass wall, eyeing the spherical chambers below. Though the glass hallways were distant and obscured by the glare of sunlight, I could make out something—hundreds of somethings—scurrying through the glass passageways and into the elevators.

"I hope you people like sea food," said Fantom. "Because that's what's having you for dinner."

CHAPTER 36

The entire room erupted into pandemonium.

People were running and screaming, cops were yelling and carelessly waving their guns, and Fantom was hovering over the whole scene, gleefully watching the chaos like a kid who had just stepped on an ant pile.

Several of the elevators—packed like monster sardine cans—were beginning the long ascent to our level.

"I hate seafood," said Flex.

"Marrow! Sapphire!"

Sapphire and I both whipped our heads simultaneously. Whisp emerged from the commotion in a hospital gown and handcuffs, fighting his way through the crowds.

"Whisp!" I said.

Sapphire shrieked, covering her mouth. Racing forward, she attacked him in a fierce hug. When she finally released him, she was in tears.

I jogged forward, catching up with them. "Hey, buddy," I said, forcing a bleak smile. "How're you doing?"

"On a scale of one to ten?" said Whisp, mimicking my sad attempt at a smile. "Probably negative infinity."

I grimaced. "That bad, huh?"

"Well, it's a little depressing that my power was not only stolen from me but is *also* the thing that's going to get us all killed."

"Yeah. Doesn't get much more depressing than that." I glanced down at his swollen, handcuffed wrists. "Here, let's get you out of these things. Sapphire, can you ice up the chain?"

Sapphire sniffed, wiping her eyes, and grabbed the chain. Frost hissed, creeping and spreading across the chain links. She let go.

"Hold it steady," I said.

Whisp pulled the chain taut. I swung my hand down in a karate chop, going from light to heavy in an instant. The chain snapped in a clean break, barely tugging Whisp's arms in the process.

"What are we going to do?" said Sapphire. Her tear-stained gaze was now riveted through the glass walls. The first wave of monster-filled elevators had nearly reached our level.

I had no answer. Instead, my gaze wandered to Nightmare who was shaking Havoc's limp form more furiously. "Wake up, Havoc. Wake up, wake up, wake up."

Havoc's eyes fluttered open.

"Havoc!"

Havoc blinked as his gaze shifted from Nightmare to Sapphire to Whisp to me and then drifted to the mass hysteria around us.

"Wha—what the—?" said Havoc.

"Fantom just lifted the entire Tartarus out of the ocean," said Nightmare. "He's controlling all of the mutated sea creatures on board. Do you think you can get it to work?"

Get it to work? What the heck was "it"?

Havoc continued to blink, adjusting his jaw from left to right. "Uh . . . yeah," he said. "Piece of . . . cake. I'm sure I've only got a minor concussion."

I couldn't tell if he was being sarcastic or serious.

Havoc's gaze shifted to Whisp. "I'll need you to come with me."

"M-m-m-me?" said Whisp. "Why?"

"You know computers, right?"

"Uh . . . yeah."

"Then I need you." Havoc turned to Nightmare. "Give me fifteen minutes, okay?"

"Fifteen minutes," said Nightmare. "Be watching for your cue from the surveillance cameras."

Havoc nodded. Grabbing Whisp's hand, the two of them vanished in a subtle ripple of air.

"Okay, what's going on?" I asked. "What cue?"

"I've got a plan," said Nightmare. "Flex, I need you to distract Fantom."

"Distract Fantom?" said Flex. "How in the holy name of Bob Marley do you propose I do that?"

"I dunno. Insult his masculinity. Tell him fart jokes. Say morally questionable things about his mother. Be your usual derogatory self. The world is your oyster, Flex. Just, whatever you do, keep him on this side of the Tartarus!"

"I am *sooooooo* not drunk enough for this."

And with that, he turned to Fantom who was still levitating over the chaos, cupped his hands over his mouth, and said, "HEY, FANTOM! HAS YOUR MOM BEEN SAVED?"

Fantom turned. Gaia's electric green eyes blazed in his eye sockets.

"BECAUSE SHE'S SO FAT, SHE'D HAVE TO GET BAP-TIZED AT SEA WORLD."

Fantom's nostrils flared, and I swear, he was breathing a hurricane out of each one.

"Welp," said Flex. "I'm screwed. See you, losers."

Flex whipped his stretchy arm at the nearest doorframe, latched on, and slingshotted himself out. Fantom swooped after him.

"Is he going to be okay?" I asked.

"He'll be fine," said Nightmare. "Listen, I need you and Sapphire to hold off the creatures. Get all the police you can to help you. Have them organize the others and form a perimeter. We have two entrances we need to secure."

A sudden burst of screeches, wails, and hungry snarls erupted louder than ever. My gaze darted past Nightmare to an adjacent sphere. A glass elevator door slid open and a mass of slimy bodies, appendages, tentacles, and claws spilled out into the neighboring chamber.

"We don't have time!" said Sapphire. "They're already here!"

I want to say something snapped inside of me. It probably would have been cooler. But it wasn't like that. I felt calm. And at the same time, something was wrenching my heart—twisting it inside my chest, folding it inside out.

The emptiness in Whisp's face.

The tears in Sapphire's perfect blue eyes.

I knew what I had to do.

"It's okay," I said. I rested my hand on Sapphire's shoulder. "I'll secure that entrance. You go talk to the police and secure the other entrance."

Sapphire's eyes grew big. "What? No! You can't do that by yourself. You'll get killed!"

"You kidding?" I said, forcing my cockiest grin. "Don't you know who I am? I'm Marrow—son of the greatest fake villain of all time. I've got this."

I planned to say something cocky like that. I didn't want her to worry. I wanted her to know that everything was all right. Even if it wasn't.

What I didn't plan on doing was what I did next.

Grabbing Sapphire by the waist, I pulled her close. Her big blue eyes went even wider. Our faces hesitated only inches away from each other.

Then I kissed her.

This was no wimpy Disney kiss either. This was like Han Solo kissing Leia before he was about to be frozen in carbonite. Like Mr. Smith kissing Mrs. Smith. Like Spider-man kissing Mary Jane. All those rolled into one.

As our lips parted, our eyes opened. We stared at each other for several long seconds—mouths open and eyes large like two scared animals.

Okay, now it was weird.

Blushing, I whipped around and bolted to my entrance.

"Marrow!" said Sapphire.

I didn't turn back. There was no turning back now.

The sliding glass door zipped open as I approached. It whizzed shut again as I entered the long hallway—a rounded metal framework with long, curving glass panes. The only additional features to the otherwise empty passageway were intermittent surveillance cameras and even an occasional display screen, the kind that I assumed played annoying informative videos for tourists. Thankfully, they were all turned off.

The sliding glass door at the far end of the hallway zipped open. A menagerie of slimy and scaly mutated monstrosities poured in.

I tapped into my bone structure, taking a defensive stance.

Bounding forward at the front of the pack was a top-heavy, mucus-covered sea gorilla. At least that's what it looked, with forearms three times the size of its legs. Except where a face should have been, there was a gaping mouth with teeth spiraling all the way down its throat. Tendrils writhed and squirmed from the top of its head and down its hunched back.

Defense? Psh! Offense is the best defense.

My body became light and I dashed—practically glided—across the floor. I pulled my arm back and swung, packing as much density as possible into my uppercut. The sea gorilla lunged, mouth open to swallow me whole, but my fist connected with its jaw. *Snap!* I felt the shift of its jawbone breaking. The sea gorilla toppled backwards, crushing an agile, six-limbed mutant under its massive frame with a sickening crunch. Green blood seeped out from underneath.

The hulking sea gorilla's corpse was almost a blockade in and of itself.

The second wave didn't find this a problem, however—a swarm of gangly humanoid creatures with lanky, clawed limbs and saucer-eyed, jagged-toothed piranha faces scurried and sprung over the corpse with nimble grace, screeching and howling. The creature at the head of the pack lunged at me. I swung my heavy fist like a wrecking ball into its abdomen. The creature doubled over as its rib cage caved in. Another clawed limb lashed out at me. I snatched it by the wrist with my light hand, solidified the bones in my arm, and swung it three hundred and sixty degrees. The violent patter of smacking flesh reverberated through the glass hallway. I released the creature, flinging it at the last creature bounding over the corpse. I nailed it in the face with its cousin, causing it to buckle midair. One of the creatures I had just knocked over staggered upright. I brought my solidified elbow down on its skull. The creature collapsed.

A writhing mass of tentacles erupted over the thick corpse. Clinging their suction cups to the glass, they heaved a snapping, rotten-toothed mouth that could easily swallow me whole. The mutated octopus filled the entire hallway. With so many tentacles wriggling and twisting, there was no way of getting past it.

Well . . . no conventional way.

Retracting the density in my fist, I took several steps back. The real-life kraken squeezed its way around the corpse. The moment it burst free, I sprinted. My lightened frame flew. My feet barely touched the floor. The kraken opened its mouth wide as I approached, like I was a piece of candy being tossed into its mouth.

Unfortunately, the mouth was what I was aiming for.

I lunged, thrusting my fist forward, pumping in as much density as possible. Four foot-long bone spikes sliced directly out of my knuckles. I gritted my teeth through the pain.

My plunge through the kraken's throat lasted only a second, immersed in its putrid, steamy breath. I sliced through its gooey innards like gelatin, only to blast out the back of its bulbous head. Green guts splattered around me. I landed in a mucus-slickened roll. The kraken remained stationary for only a brief moment before crumpling to the floor.

Something slithered around my legs. The moment I glanced down, my feet were ripped out from under me. Thick turquoise coils wrapped around me with crushing force. They pinned my arms to my side. I hastily solidified my skeletal structure before I could be crumpled like an aluminum can. An elongated body weaved over me, attached to a bulky, serpentine head the size of small wheelbarrow.

A snake—a mutated sea snake. Of course it had to be a snake.

Pinned like I was, I had no momentum. Without momentum, my power was useless. Think, Marrow. Think!

The snake's coils spiraled further around me, swallowing my shoulders and ankles.

No. My power wasn't useless.

Because my dad's power wouldn't be useless in this situation.

I desperately tapped into my skeletal structure. Although my density was already maxed out, I clenched my teeth, pushing that density into every joint in my body. I could feel the sweat beading on my face from the pressure.

"I."

A forked tongue hissed out of the snake's scaly mouth, grazing my face.

"Hate."

Rearing its head back, the snake pierced me with its hungry, beady eyes.

"SNAKES!"

The snake struck. So did a dozen impaling spikes from my body—shoulders, elbows, kneecaps—the whole enchilada. Some spikes stabbed out of me from places that weren't even joints. I cringed as fiery pain stabbed through every inch of my body.

I was a human pincushion. And the snake was a shish kabob. Its bulky head dropped beside mine. Its mouth lolled open at me.

I winced again, retracting my spikes, and fought my way out of the lifeless coils binding me. I staggered to my feet, fists up, ready to punch the head off the next thing that snarled its ugly face at me.

There was no snarling. There was nothing.

I turned back around. I had left a pathway of death and destruction behind me. Mutant corpses littered the hallway and the glass was splattered and glazed in green. I glanced down at myself. It looked like I was covered in snot.

Good thing I kissed Sapphire earlier because I *definitely* wasn't getting anything now.

A sharp *crack* sounded from the adjacent chamber—the elevator. I couldn't even make out what was behind the glass door. It was simply a compacted mass of tense, gray flesh.

The elevator door struggled to slide open. As it did, a muscular gray arm the size of a tree slumped out. Claws jutted from its stumpy, webbed fingers.

Crap. I knew exactly what this thing was.

Grating its claws into the metal floor, it heaved itself out of the elevator. Its head was a thick slab of meat with beady eyes, ending in a pointed snout and exposing serrated razors for teeth from its exposed gums.

Specimen 751—Thresher.

The metamorphosed great white shark snarled as it hauled itself onto the floor. Its curved dorsal fin popped back up; the rippling muscles of its upper back emerged. Forget riding the elevator. Thresher had squeezed and wiggled his way up the entire elevator shaft! Hoisting itself upright, Thresher towered over the network of supercomputers. Its head practically scraped the top of the sphere.

My gaze shifted from Thresher to the hallway entrance. There was no way that thing could fit.

Just like there was "no way" it could fit in the elevator shaft. Crap.

Boom, boom, boom!

Thresher stomped to the hallway. It lowered itself onto its white underbelly, propped up on vein-bulging forearms. A glass door half its size zipped open. Scraping its claws into the metal floor once more, Thresher shoved its colossal body into the cramped space. Even with its thick shoulders bunched together, it filled the entire passageway. Squirming back and forth, Thresher wriggled forward. A spider web of cracks snaked across the glass. It heaved closer. With every writhing movement, the glass splintered wider and finer, filling the entire rounded surface. I felt the brush of air with every snap of Thresher's jaws.

The kraken wannabe was one thing. But there was no way I was jumping inside this thing's mouth.

I didn't have to. The metal framework groaned beneath Thresher's weight. The sound drowned out its snarls. The shark's head perked up. The floor beneath it lurched, bending down an inch. The metal wailed louder than ever under its last string of resilience—*KIREEEEEEEEEEK!*

The passageway collapsed.

The floor caved in from both sides of the hallway—two slanted slabs of metal meeting together in a gaping fissure. The wind howled from below. Thresher clawed desperately for something to hold on to, but its massive gray form slipped through the opening. It plummeted to the distant shoreline below. The metal framework above crumpled down as well. Shattered glass rained down in a storm of glistening shards

The floor buckled beneath me.

I fell, sliding down the slanted surface. My hands grasped aimlessly. A shaft of metal framework swung down, scraping the floor beside me. I frantically latched onto it. I skidded to a halt, hanging with my stomach against the slanted ledge—only inches away from a lethal plunge. My legs dangled and swayed in the open wind. Struggling to pull myself back onto the slanted surface, I tapped into my bone structure, reversing my density.

The top of the slant groaned. Not good.

I released the shaft of metal and flew up the ramp. The slanted ledge dipped slightly lower. My foot slipped.

KIREEEEEEEEEE—

I lunged, gripping the top of the broken, slanted slab—only inches away from the solid ledge. My arms quivered under the pressure and nerves. My teeth gritted.

The slanted slab broke. Thrusting every ounce of strength I had in my arms, I hoisted myself over the edge of the freefalling slab. Time seemed to slip into slow motion. My feet touched the other side of the slab as it flipped entirely. I dashed across the falling surface as if I was running on water, braced my foot on the opposite ledge and launched myself. My right arm flailed out. So close.

My momentum ended. My hand missed by inches.

Before I could fall, a body hit the ledge and a hand snatched mine. A hand with blue nail polish.

"There's no way my first kiss is dying right after he kisses me!" said Sapphire through gritted teeth. "NO. FREAKING. WAY."

Strands of loose blue hair strayed across her determined face. Apparently she had lost her mind cuff helmet somewhere in the chaos. Frost formed over our hands, freezing them together. I wasn't going to fall without taking Sapphire with me. Fortunately, I only weighed about half my normal weight. Sapphire hoisted me up. I flung my free hand onto the ledge, pulling myself up the rest of the way. The frost instantly melted off of our frozen hands. Together, we collapsed on the edge of the severed passageway.

"Thanks for saving me," I said, breathless.

Sapphire was breathing heavily as well. She attempted a casual shrug. "Hey, I'm a Superhero. That's how I roll."

She shifted over onto her side. When she looked at me, she had that look that girls always have when they want you to kiss them. You know—when their eyes get big, and their lips are all soft and slightly parted. I've seen enough James Bond movies. I know that look.

The TV screen hanging over us flickered with static, drawing Sapphire's big kissy eyes away from me. The screen crackled and distorted before focusing on a single figure—a figure that caused me to bolt upright.

My dad.

The bruises on Spine's face were gone. He didn't even have a scratch. I remembered Flex saying something about our power giving us accelerated healing, but holy cow!

Just as alarming was the backdrop. Though the camera was trained on him, the rounded glass in the background was obviously from a sphere chamber of the Tartarus. A section of the glass was cut out, however, replaced by a shimmering metal rim, the inside of which extended into a sprawling tunnel with a soft green glow at the end.

No . . . It wasn't a tunnel at all. It was the barrel of the Cronus Cannon.

"Hey, Fantom," said my father, sporting a cocky grin behind his beard. "Heard you were having a party without me. Thought I'd drop in."

His voice echoed throughout the Tartarus. However Spine was transmitting this video, it was clearly being played on every screen in the research facility.

"So here's the thing," he said. His grin vanished. "We have a debt to settle. And we're going to settle it right here and now. Sure, you can beat me when you're controlling me as your little puppet. But I dare you to face me like a man. Because I promise you, Fantom—I'm going to kill you."

CHAPTER 37

If this was Nightmare and Havoc's brilliant plan to stop Fantom, I was going to throw up.

Yeah, I knew my dad was strong. But Fantom, even without his telepathy, was an unstoppable force. He had been stealing telekinetic power from Supers like Nero for decades.

He was going to squash my dad like a bug.

Scrambling to my feet, I took off down the broken passageway to the chamber I had come from. Sapphire trailed close behind me.

As the door to our original chamber zipped open, the sound of rapid gunfire was accompanied by a chorus of ghastly screeches. Both seemed to simmer down almost instantly. We rushed past a considerably calm group of news crew members and Telepaths in hospital gowns, encompassed by half a dozen armed police officers.

Fantom was gone.

"Is everything okay on that end?" said an officer.

"Yeah," I said. "You don't have to worry about anything coming from that side, I promise."

We continued past them to the far entrance. The sliding door remained open, held by a small mountain of broken furniture and expensive shattered computers. Dozens of police officers had taken cover behind it, armed and sweaty. All of them had ceased fire.

"Don't forget to reload," said Lieutenant Reese. He was perched behind a desk at the very top of the mound. He proceeded to remove and inspect the clip from his own weapon.

"Lieutenant Reese," said Sapphire. She rushed ahead of me. "Is everything going alright?"

"We've held 'em back so far," said Reese. "We're running low on ammo though. Don't think we can hold 'em back for too much longer."

"Fantom went through here?" I asked.

"Yeah," said Reese. "Flew right over the top of our blockade. And boy, he looked ticked. I don't think he likes being called out in public."

I swallowed hard. "I need to get through."

Reese raised an incredulous eyebrow at me. "You what? You do realize that's the side the monsters are on, right?"

"That's the side my dad's on." My hardened expression didn't flinch. I wanted everyone to know just how serious I was. They had the same mounted display screens in here. They knew what was happening. I wasn't about to let a bunch of cops stand between me and my father.

Reese stared me down for several long seconds. Then he nodded. "Men, back away for a sec. Let the kid through."

"What?" said Sapphire. As I started for the mound, she latched onto my arm. "Marrow, no! What do you think you're doing?"

"My dad can't fight Fantom," I said. "Not by himself."

"So what?" she said. "You're just going to barge in there and die with him?"

"Well I'm not going to let him die all alone!" I snapped.

Sapphire recoiled slightly with a hurt look.

I bit my lip in response, my face softening. "I . . . I'm sorry," I said. "I'm just . . ."

"No, I understand," said Sapphire quietly, staring at the floor. "He's your dad."

"I just want to see what's going on. I know this is part of Nightmare and Havoc's plan somehow. I just . . . I want to know what the heck their plan *is*."

Sapphire glanced up timidly from the ground. "You promise you won't go in there with them? You'll just look through the glass?"

I hesitated. Sapphire's big blue eyes stared up at me pleadingly.

"Promise," I said, extending my pinky.

Sapphire shoved my pinky aside, pulling me into a fierce hug. When she finally let go, she was teary-eyed all over again. I couldn't stand to see her cry.

So I turned and quickly scaled the mountain of broken furniture and electronics.

Hopefully I wouldn't have to break my promise.

I rushed with light feet down the corridor. The last thing I needed was to not make it around the corner in time and be in the line of fire when the next wave of mutants came crashing in. As I distanced myself from the solemn voices of the police, I found myself immersed in eerie silence.

I barreled into the next sphere chamber. My eyes went straight to the elevator. None of the buttons were lit up. Through the glass, I could see it was still stationary on our floor.

What was going on? Where was the next wave of creatures? I knew for a fact that there was still a butt-load more of them.

The thought occurred to me that maybe they just weren't coming. If they were under Fantom's control and he was off to fight my dad, then maybe he was too preoccupied to keep them coming. Or maybe he just wanted to kick back and enjoy the carnage rather than let it happen while he had his attention focused elsewhere.

I pulled my gaze from the elevator, shifting it down the long glass passageway to the next chamber. It was this chamber that the vast barrel of the Cronus Cannon was pointed into.

Even from the great distance, I could make out the red of Fantom's flapping cape. The sliding glass door whizzed shut behind him.

Then a large hand clasped my shoulder.

I screamed—probably like a girl. Whipping around, I nearly tripped on my own feet. Nightmare towered over me. Not only that, but his big primate lips were curled into an amused grin.

"Yeah, yeah, laugh it up," I said.

"Oh no, I'm not smiling about that," said Nightmare. "Well . . . okay, maybe I am a little. I was actually smiling about what's about to happen to our friend, Fantom."

My eyebrows lifted. "You mean this is part of your plan?"

Nightmare's grin grew wider. "Let's go get a closer look, shall we?"

Nightmare led the way at a brisk pace, and I trailed close behind. Though we were still a ways from the Cronus chamber, the mounted display screens showed Spine and Fantom staring each other down in a cold, silent standoff.

Fantom's eyes were still glowing green behind his mask.

"Do you really think you stand a chance against me?" said Fantom in Gaia's multitude of voices. His voice still stood out loudest and most distinct among them.

"I don't *think* I stand a chance," said Spine. "I said I'm going to kill you. And I'm a man of my word."

Fantom snorted. "And how exactly do you plan on doing that?"

"I know something that you don't."

"You're lying."

Nightmare and I finally reached the Cronus chamber, cautiously approaching the glass barrier. Because Fantom was still somehow in control of his face, his expression was tense. I even detected a hint of nervousness. Even though the odds were clearly in his favor, it was obvious that no one had ever challenged him like this before. He had probably never fought a real, honest fight in his entire life.

"How did you even get here?" said Fantom.

"Ah, now that's a good question," said Spine. "The obvious answer would be that I got here the same way you, Nightmare, Flex, and the kids got here—Havoc's teleportation. However . . ."

A gentle hum sounded behind him. It revved up to an escalating roar. The long tunnel behind him lit up in an intensifying green glow.

". . . the truth is that I'm actually *not* here," said Spine. His very being seemed to flicker and distort like an illusion. "Havoc, NOW!"

Spine vanished. A hallucination! I glanced up at Nightmare who was now laughing. Fantom turned to face us, and Nightmare simply waved back.

And that's when the hallway door zipped open and shut behind us. I don't know *where* he came from or *how* he got here. He just was.

Spine. The *real* Spine. My dad. Had he been hiding on the Tartarus this whole time?

Then again, he'd been hiding for most of my life, so I don't know why his lifetime game of hide and seek should be so shocking.

"Pulling the wool over Fantom's eyes three times in one day," said Nightmare. "I think I'm on a roll!"

Spine didn't laugh. He didn't even smile. He *did* offer a brief glance my way. He glanced away just as quickly when he realized I was staring at him.

His gaze focused instead on the man who ruined his life because he was sure as *heck* gonna enjoy this.

But he didn't know what I knew. I didn't laugh either. I couldn't even breathe.

If using the Cronus Cannon on Fantom was Nightmare and Havoc's big plan, then we were dead meat.

Reaffirming my dread, Fantom smiled. A blast of raging green energy swallowed him whole, filling the entire chamber.

"Marrow, are you alright?" said Nightmare. "It's okay. We beat him!"

"No . . ." I said, shaking my head. "It's not going to work."

"What are you talking about? Of course it's going to work."

"The Cronus doesn't absorb powers. All it does is amplify Fantom's power. There's a compartment built under the Cronus where it channels his energy. He has the ability to steal the mind powers of other Telepaths and Telekinetics. That was the whole point of the Cronus device—so he could steal everyone's telepathic power when the Cronus Order was given."

Spine's cold eyes shifted from me to the glowing chamber. "You mean . . . ?"

"I mean that machine is just a flashy show. It doesn't do anything unless Fantom's controlling it!"

His jaw slackened. Slowly, he turned to the glass surface and the pulsating green energy flowing behind it. A red cape flapped closer, slowly approaching the entrance.

"Marrow . . . get out of here." Though Spine's voice was firm, his quivering eyes betrayed him. Bone spikes splintered from his fingers and joints while thick bone plating quickly covered the rest of his body. He looked like a kick-butt combination of Wolverine and Iron Man.

"What?" I said. "What about you?"

"I said get out of here!" Spine snapped. When I didn't move, he grabbed me by the shoulders and shook me. "I didn't come here today to watch my only son die, Marrow." He shoved me down the hall, and I staggered. But stubbornness is hereditary. I tapped into my skeleton and spiked my bone density outward. By the time I regained my balance, I had my own painful set of bone armor and spikes. I almost cried from the pain; how did my dad make it look so easy? He pointed a fierce finger at me. "Go. NOW."

I didn't budge. I stared my father down like he was the real enemy—an enemy who I loved and hated all at the same time.

"Dammit, Marrow!" he screamed. "Did you hear me?"

"Screw you," I said.

That shut my dad up. He didn't seem to know how to respond to this.

"You think you can just waltz into my life and tell me what to do?" I said. "You may be my dad, but you don't get that privilege until you've *earned* it. You don't get to *die* for me until you've *lived* for me, okay? If you're going to fight Fantom, I'm going to fight him with you, and that's that. Got it?"

Spine glared at me. His hard, heavy gaze was this furious thing, breathing fire out of his irises. And then it calmed. Just like that—like the eye of a storm. He walked toward me and placed a firm hand on my shoulder. "Marrow, I've lived every day of your life for you, even if you couldn't see it. If I'm not willing to lose my life for you, how can I protect you?"

His gaze shifted to Nightmare who was still observing quietly.

"Nightmare," he said, "if you've ever been my friend, you will get my son out of here right now."

Nightmare's face was as grim as it was ugly—maybe even grimmer—which seemed like a universal anomaly considering the unparalleled level of catastrophic ugliness that was his face.

He nodded and stepped forward.

"Wait, what?" I said. "No. Nightmare, NO! I swear, if you—!"

But it was too late. Suddenly, I was sinking in a tar pit—an honest-to-freaking-goodness *tar pit!*—except not really because I already knew this was yet another one of Nightmare's hallucinations rendering me defenseless. A lake, thick and black and bubbling—hot but not scalding—like an immense molasses Jacuzzi. The sky was a bleak, gray slate, encompassed by a swampy horizon. Endless, rotting marsh.

But I wasn't defenseless.

"No," I said. I tapped into the intricate bone density of my skull, fluctuating it to any and every degree. I felt like I was playing with the sound functions on a car stereo. "No no no no no no no no no no no no no no!"

I could shut it off. I *had* to shut it off. Because if I didn't, my dad would die. He didn't stand a chance against Fantom all by himself.

"DAD!" I screamed.

The swamp shattered—like I had taken a baseball bat to the infinite TV screen of life. The illusion fell away in broken shards. Suddenly, I was bouncing up and down, slung over someone's shoulder—Nightmare's, obviously.

A short distance behind us, Spine was levitating in the air, his wrists and ankles pinned by an invisible force. He was left to squirm fruitlessly against a power that could not be overcome or defied by physical strength.

Fantom loomed over him.

"I've invested way too much time and energy in you," said Fantom. "I'm going to save your death for later. I'm going to *savor* it. But, in the meantime, we need to make you fit in a to-go box."

One by one, Spine's arms and legs snapped and cracked, breaking at awkward angles. He screamed. Howled. An animalistic sound that defied humanity.

"Dad!"

Fantom's glowing green eyes homed in on Nightmare and me. He tossed Spine aside like a crumpled piece of trash.

A sliding glass door zipped shut between us—but only for a second.

The door shattered before it could even detect Fantom's presence. He blasted through it, and broken shards rained down. Nightmare and I toppled across the floor. I hit the glass wall to the side, my armor absorbing some of the impact. Before Nightmare even stopped rolling, Fantom lifted a hand. Nightmare rose off the ground, hopelessly suspended.

"You, on the other hand . . ." said Fantom. His luminescent eyes shifted past Nightmare to me. "Marrow, would you like to see what happens to people who think they can make a fool of me?"

Fantom raised both of his hands, palms close together.

"Marrow . . ." Nightmare gasped. "Run—"

Fantom jerked his hands in a circular motion.

Nightmare's head snapped sideways. His eyes rolled back, and his body collapsed to the ground in a lifeless heap.

"NIGHTMARE!" I screamed.

Before I could even move, Fantom flicked his arm to the side. There was no time to change my density and brace for the impact. My entire body swung sideways, gliding across the ground and smashing into the glass. Shards of bone and glass flew everywhere. My armor was gone. Fantom swooped down behind me. Closing his fist and pulling his arm close, my legs were whipped out from under me. My body hit the floor facedown, almost breaking my nose against the glass. Fantom lifted his heavy boot and pressed it hard against the base of my skull.

Was it even worth trying to fight back? Just by looking at them, Fantom had broken my dad's arms and legs and *killed* Nightmare. He was like a cat toying with an insect. As soon as he was bored torturing me, I was dead.

My head was too numb to think. My gaze shifted through the glass to a distant sphere on the opposite side of the Tartarus. I blinked when

I noticed several police officers congregated on the exact opposite side of the Tartarus. They were pulling something—something *humanish*, with arms stretching from doorway to doorway.

"Any last words?" said Fantom. "That's what villains are supposed to say at a time like this, aren't they?"

"Flex . . ." I said.

"I beg your pardon?"

Time. I needed just a few more seconds.

I gritted my teeth, tapping into the bones in my spine and neck. I pushed the density out as hard as I could.

This was going to hurt.

Spikes erupted all the way up my back and neck in a centered line. It felt like someone had just sliced a knife all the way down my spinal cord. I felt just enough friction from one particular spike to know it had sliced through Fantom's foot.

Fantom and all of Gaia's voices screamed in a blood-curdling choir of bloody murder. That alone was worth the pain.

On the opposite end of the Tartarus, the group of police officers flattened against the furthest wall of the chamber, pulling as far as they could go.

And then they let go.

Flex flew, feet first, breaking through the glass of the opposite sphere at a near-impossible velocity. He was on a straight path, shooting right at us.

"I'll kill you!" said Fantom, limping on one foot. "I'll tear you into bloody little—"

Flex crashed through the glass, kicking Fantom right in his snarling face. Fantom flew backwards, smashing out the opposite side of the glass hallway. He plunged down.

Flex's impact with Fantom had slowed him considerably, but he teetered on the edge of the jagged glass opening, flailing desperately for balance. I jumped up from the floor, pulling him back.

"*Hoooooooooooly* crap," said Flex. His eyes were bulging like golf balls from their sockets. "Remind me never to do that again."

272

I had never been so glad to see Flex. I wanted to hug him and cry a whole bunch, but instead I decided to play it cool and said, "Nice aim."

Flex nodded, resting his hands on his knees, breathless. "Yeah, well his face is lit up like a Christmas tree. It's kind of hard to miss."

Flex's gaze shifted past me. "Nice spikes," he said, observing the newest additions to my body. "You look like a stegosaurus."

I laughed. I never thought I would laugh again, but here I was laughing. It felt weird and wrong and amazing all at the same time. I took a deep breath and braced myself as I retracted the spikes. Fortunately it didn't hurt nearly as much going back in.

"YOU," Fantom roared. "I'LL KILL YOU."

His tense form hovered beside the gaping hole in the shattered glass passageway. I jumped back. His and all of Gaia's voices were seething with fury, green eyes blazing with equal intensity.

"The next time you try to push someone over the edge," said Fantom, "you should probably make sure they can't fly."

The air behind him rippled as he blasted towards us.

In that very instant, something new materialized, intercepting Fantom's path. A solid fist connected with his face, throwing him off course. No sooner did the figure appear, he was gone in an instant.

Havoc.

Havoc materialized again directly in front of us. Unlike Sapphire, he was still wearing his mind cuff and didn't look like he'd be giving it up anytime soon. His face was an uneasy grimace that I had never seen before. I assumed he already knew about Nightmare.

"You two make a run for it," he said. "I can hold Fantom back."

He didn't even wait for a response, vanishing an instant later.

"*HAVOOOOOOOOOOC!*" Fantom howled. "I'm going to—!"

Havoc flashed beside him in midair once more, stringing in another swift blow to the face. Fantom spun backwards as Havoc disappeared again.

"Come on," said Flex. He grabbed my arm, pulling me beside him in a brisk pace.

Wearing the mind cuff, Havoc was a formidable obstacle for Fantom. But he was hardly a match. It was only a matter of how long Havoc could keep it up, dancing with the most powerful being on earth.

The most powerful *beings* merged together.

My apprehensive gaze shifted to Nightmare's lifeless form.

"No," I said. I tugged my arm out of his grasp.

Flex turned and shot me a disbelieving stare. "What do you think you're doing, Marrow? We have to get out of here or we're going to *die*!"

"What about Havoc?"

"Are you kidding me? He's a Teleporter. He can teleport out of here whenever he wants." Flex grabbed my arm again and started to run, holding even tighter when I struggled again.

"What about Sapphire and Whisp? What about everyone else on the Tartarus? There's like a hundred people on here. How are we supposed to get them off?"

Flex grabbed a handful of his dreadlocks with his free hand and groaned. "I don't know, Marrow. What do you want me to tell you? Do you want to stay here and fight Fantom? Is that what you want? Even if we both fought him *with* Havoc, there's no way we can beat him. He'll slaughter us."

"There has to be *something* we can do to stop him."

"Like what? Go back to this alien's home planet and find some radioactive space rock that we can use against it? This *thing* isn't Superman. There *is* no kryptonite. This isn't some comic book, Marrow, this is real life."

As Flex spoke, my gaze shifted past him and through the glass passageway. My focus became intent on the Gaia Comet, emanating its green glow—somehow still miraculously attached to the Tartarus.

"The comet . . ." I said.

"What?" said Flex. He turned around, following my gaze to the Gaia Comet. He shook his head furiously. "No, Marrow. That rock isn't kryptonite. Didn't you hear Fantom when he said that the comet is what gives him his—?"

"I'm not talking about using the comet as kryptonite, dummy. I'm talking about destroying it."

"Huh?"

"You said it yourself. The comet gives Fantom his powers. He lives on the Tartarus so he can be near it. And then, when he does something crazy like lifting the Tartarus out of the ocean, he lifts the *comet* up with it! I mean, it even has the same green glow as his eyes right now. This alien, Gaia, is connected to the comet. If we destroy it . . ."

"We destroy Fantom," said Flex. breathless. "But . . . what could we possibly hit it with that would destroy it?"

I had wondered the exact same thing. We were inside a research facility floating a thousand feet or more in the air. Havoc was our only way off of here, and he was preoccupied in a death match with the root of the problem. We had no missiles. No bombs or bazookas.

But we did have something.

"Me," I said. The single word seemed to weigh a million pounds dropping out of my mouth.

"What?"

"We have to do the slingshot."

"WHAT?"

"It's the only weapon we have," I said. "If we can break the glass at the back of the sphere and I hit you full force in the opposite direction, you should be able to slingshot me back through the barrel of the Cronus Cannon fast enough to—"

"Are you insane?"

"I think I can cover myself in bone for protection," I said. "I've been getting better at it and—"

"Marrow, you'll die!"

"You don't know that."

"Shooting you a couple hundred miles an hour into a radioactive comet? Yes, I do. It's suicide."

"So is bungee jumping across the Tartarus to kick Fantom in the face."

Flex snorted. "That's different."

"No, it's not," I said. "We either do this or we let Fantom kill everyone else on the Tartarus. Besides . . . if you aren't willing to lose your life, how can you save anyone?"

Flex's jaw went rigid. He stared me down for several long seconds. At first I thought he was going to get mad at me—yell at me for using my father's words against him.

Instead, he simply nodded. "Yeah . . . okay."

Neither of us needed any further discussion. We'd already wasted enough time. We rushed down the passageway and into the Cronus Chamber. Flex darted straight for the opening on the Cronus cannon while I dashed to the rounded glass at the back of the sphere. Spinning on one foot, my other leg flew up. I tapped into the bone structure of my foot, blasting density into my swinging kick. The entire honeycomb-shaped glass pane went white in a mosaic of tiny spider-webbing cracks. I kicked again, and the pane shattered.

When I started back to the opening of the Cronus cannon, Flex was already gripping both sides of the rim, his arms stretched nearly twenty feet. I ducked under his thin, taut arm and continued down the barrel—a seemingly endless stretch of silver masked in a distant green glow. I continued down the stretch for a ways. I'd need all the running start I could get.

This was it.

"Marrow?" said Flex. His voice echoed down the barrel.

"Yeah?"

His voice hesitated. "I love you, bro."

I blinked back the acid moisture that wanted to burn through my eyelids again. "Love you too, bro."

Something heavy hit the floor beside Flex—a body. Twitching. Barely alive.

Havoc.

There went our distraction.

"What are you doing?" said Fantom and Gaia's multitude of voices.

"Now, Marrow!" Flex screamed. "Now!"

My bones became light. My feet were clouds on the ground. I was a bullet.

I shot forward.

I hit Flex so fast, his entire body folded around me like a ridiculous rubber tarp. We *whooshed* across the Cronus chamber. As my foot landed on the very edge of the chamber where I had broken the glass barrier, I launched myself forward still. I could feel the tension in Flex's elasticity as we slowed to a halt in midair.

"What the devil?" said Fantom.

SNAP!

I zipped through the Cronus Chamber and into the barrel of the Cronus cannon faster than I could blink. The tunnel whizzed past me in a shadowy silver blur, tinted in the ever-increasing green glow. The racing wind threatened to rip my face off. My senses were numb. I couldn't even breathe.

The tunnel exploded behind me. I felt the air ripple and burst. I made the mistake of tilting my head back.

A red cape flared, gaining on me. The green glow of Fantom's eyes was gone. Even hidden behind his black mask, the fear was evident in the way his real eyes glistened. In the sick, twisted shape of his mouth . . .

I whipped my head forward again. The blazing green of the Gaia Comet was blinding now—like an alien sun. I was only seconds away from impact. Tapping into my skeletal structure, I exploded my density outward, pushing harder than I'd ever pushed before. *I* was the comet. Spikes erupted—not just from my joints. I felt like I was being stabbed in every pore of my body. Jagged bones splintered out from every inch of my frame.

I was swallowed in spikes just as I was swallowed in green infinity.

Everything went black.

CHAPTER 38

I woke up in a world of white.

Literally.

There was no floor. There was no ceiling. There was no anything. Just an endless white stretch reaching into infinity. Blinking desperately, I struggled to adjust my eyes to the whiteness. I sat upright on an invisible surface that felt both solid and like nothing at all.

No. There was something. A gradual golden glow that intensified around me. I was being swallowed in it. I turned both ways, thinking maybe it was coming from behind me. Then I looked down.

I didn't have a body.

At least . . . not really. Where my body should have been, the whiteness seemed to distort around an invisible shape. I climbed to my feet and glanced at my hands, turning them back and forth. I could make out my outline, but other than that, I was just a transparent distortion. Except for one significant detail . . .

The golden glow was coming from me.

Or from my chest, at least. Floating at my core was a soft, simmering ball of effervescent energy. My invisible outline hardly contained it. The golden rays seared through my transparent form, flooding the whiteness around me. I felt like a miniaturized humanoid version of the sun.

"Marrow . . . ?"

The voice was a raspy wheeze, but I somehow recognized it enough to make me cringe. I reluctantly turned around.

It was Fantom.

Or . . . it used to be. Fantom was the same invisible shape as me, but much smaller. His transparent face was gaunt with the subtle hint of sunken eyes and emaciated cheekbones—a barely recognizable shadow. He was bent over on sticks for arms and legs and seemed to be having trouble doing even that. Like me, he also had something floating in his chest . . . but it was black and about the size of a walnut. A subtle flicker of purple energy glazed the edges, but otherwise, the thing looked pretty shriveled and dead.

"I can't move . . ." Fantom wheezed. "Why can't I move . . . ?"

His clear, sunken eyes shifted past me. "Gaia . . ."

I turned back around.

The creature standing only feet away from me was nearly twice my height and about half my width. Its limbs were like young tree branches with three gangly fingers or toes sprouting from each. Its neck was nearly as long as its slender abdomen, towering erect to a perfectly circular head—no eyes, no mouth, or any distinguishing features at all. The only exception was a core like the one in my chest, except it was glowing neon green.

Though it had no eyes, I could tell that it was ignoring Fantom and focused solely on me.

Hello, Marrow, said Gaia's conglomeration of voices directly into my mind. *I am sorry for trying to kill you. That is normally not in my nature.*

What was going on here? Where were we? Why was this psychotic alien suddenly apologizing? Especially after I had just tried to destroy its comet.

"Are we dead?" I asked. I glanced around at the endless whiteness around me. "Is this . . . heaven?"

Your subconscious energies have somehow become temporarily submerged within my subconscious.

"Our *whats* have done *what* inside your *what*?"

You're inside my head, said Gaia. *Similar to the way I was submerged within Fantom's subconscious, only reversed. And allow me to be the first to* say that this is highly unusual. You are the first carbon-based lifeforms of your kind to perform such a feat. Such a surprising side-effect.

"But the comet is destroyed, right?"

No, fortunately. Your hypothesis to destroy the Gaia Comet by collision with yourself at a very high speed was incorrect. In human terms, you were like a very fast insect hitting a stationary train at a high speed. The train is not damaged, but the insect is. If your hypothesis had been correct, the explosion of the Gaia Comet would have been catastrophic. The comet's energy is composed of stable antimatter—the destabilization of which would have produced an explosion comparable to the Big Bang. I don't know about the rest of the universe, but the Earth would surely be destroyed, and your galaxy would likely be thrown severely off its gravitational orbit.

My metaphysical jaw unhinged. "Wait, what? But . . . how? How can that blow up the Earth? I mean, the Comet hit the Earth from outer space, right? How come the freaking galaxy didn't explode?"

I apologize. This must all be very confusing for a non-collective-mind being. Let me explain: Your Earth did not explode when the comet first landed because the ocean provided a cushion that reduced the chances of destabilization. Our landing calculations were almost perfect. Does that make sense?

"Yeah." My metaphysical heart stopped. "Wait, you said I was like a bug hitting a train . . . am I dead?"

Almost certainly. It is unfathomable that your body even survived the impact.

"But . . . the Tartarus! What happened to the Tartarus?"

Nothing has happened to the Tartarus. Yet.

"Yet?" I said. My tone was one notch past hysterical and I was an eye twitch short of a mental breakdown. "What do you mean, 'yet'? What the heck's that supposed to mean?"

According to my calculations, the comet and the Tartarus will hit the earth in exactly three minutes and forty-seven seconds. You see, the Tartarus runs on nuclear energy. The nuclear explosion will destabilize the antimatter of the comet and destroy the planet.

I collapsed onto my hands and knees. My arms started shaking and then I just dropped my face on the invisible floor. My eyes burned and I starting crying tears that my soul body couldn't produce, sobbing uncontrollably. All of my insides felt like they were imploding—even though I didn't technically have insides.

Meanwhile, Fantom started laughing in his wheezy excuse for a voice. It almost sounded more like coughing.

"We showed those pathetic insects, Gaia . . ." he rasped. "And they thought they could stop us."

I didn't even care about Fantom anymore. I just wanted to die. Except, in a sense, I was already dead. This was worse than being dead. I was in Hell. I wanted to just rip that golden orb out of my chest and crush it in my transparent hands.

To my surprise, as I opened my burning eyes, the orb was shining even brighter than before. It hurt just looking at it. As I stared up into the white expanse, it was obvious that my luminescent golden glow could have filled a football stadium.

Why did you do it? said Gaia.

"Do what?" I asked.

Try to destroy the comet. Surely you knew that the probability of you surviving was less than 3.5 percent?

"My friends were on the Tartarus. Flex, Sapphire, Whisp, Havoc . . . and all those people. *And* my dad. Him too. I couldn't just let them all die."

And then I felt sick all over again.

"A lot of good it did," I said. "Everyone I've ever loved . . . they're all going to die because of me."

Marrow, said Gaia. *May I request something of you?*

I pulled my heavy head up, straining to meet his nonexistent gaze. I couldn't talk though. Breathing was painful enough—if I was really breathing, that is.

I can see to it that you survive this, said Gaia. *And then I would like to become a part of your mind.*

"What?" I said.

"No . . . !" Fantom gasped. "Gaia! What are you doing? You're a part of *my* mind!"

I know that must sound like an unusual request, said Gaia. *That is the sort of research my kind does. As we select a world to study, we do it through the eyes of a host. Though it's a gradual process, we eventually begin to think as the host thinks. It's all a part of our research, getting to understand the world better and knowing how to interact with it.*

"Gaia!" Fantom screeched. "No, Gaia! I need you!"

Gaia tilted its head slightly, and I could tell that it was finally paying heed to Fantom

Personally, I don't enjoy being inside Fantom's mind. He was a pleasant enough specimen when he was young, but now . . . I don't like the effect his thinking has on my mind. His greed and hatred is consuming. And as you can see from his current state, his subconscious has become extremely dependent on my energy. Without me, he would be a human vegetable. You could almost say that our symbiotic relationship digressed to a more parasitic nature. It will be a very long time before his subconscious recovers.

"Gaia . . ." said Fantom. He had exerted the last of his strength, and his head was now cocked at an awkward angle on the invisible floor.

Gaia returned its indiscernible focus to me. *Will you do it, Marrow? Will you let me study you? I can assure you that it is for the sake of a better universe.*

"A better universe?" I said. Now that I could finally speak, my devastation was replaced by something new. I was still shaking, but my fists were trembling most of all. I wished I could feel my fingernails digging into my palms—any physical pain at all. "My planet is dying because of you."

Gaia didn't respond. Instead, it tilted its head to the other side.

"My father has been a fugitive for as long as I can remember because of you," I continued. "Every bad thing that's happened is because of *you*! Because you gave power to that . . . that *thing*!"

I stabbed an accusing finger at Fantom. He merely glanced at me from his awkward angle on the floor and laughed—a slow, disturbed laugh that wrenched my insides. Whatever Fantom was, he sure as heck wasn't human.

It's true that my research through Fantom has wrought destructive results, said Gaia. *To be fair, his mind was much different as a child. His motives were much more pure. It's possible that the power he accumulated through me is what led to his corruption. I never could have calculated that he would become what he is now.*

"And you want to give that power to me," I said.

That is correct. I am intrigued by the wavelengths of your subconscious. The fact that your subconscious has become temporarily lodged in mine speaks for itself. Judging from what I see, I believe my power would be used to much different effects in your hands.

"Forget it," I said. "I don't want your power. I don't want you inside my head. I don't want to live *anywhere* without my friends, thinking about all the funerals I can't go to because THE PLANET IS ABOUT TO BLOW UP! Screw you, Gaia. Screw you *and* your power *and* your stupid research. I don't want any part in it."

I figured that would be your response, said Gaia. *I must admit that it only makes me want to study you that much more.*

"Yeah, well, it's not happening."

Gaia pressed six of its spindly fingertips together, as if in contemplation. Its green orb flickered in thought.

I don't think you realize what you can do with my power.

"I don't want to hear it."

With my power, you will have all the omnipotent power that Fantom had—

"Did you not hear me? I DON'T WANT—"

—and you can possibly stop the Tartarus from crashing.

"—IT! Wait, what?"

That shut me up. There was no way I heard right. I was silent for several long seconds before saying, "What do you mean?"

Fantom only had his telepathic and telekinetic power because of me. I am offering you the telekinetic power that could stop the Tartarus and the comet from hitting the Earth and exploding.

Fantom contorted his transparent body at an even more awkward angle from the invisible floor. "Huh?"

I couldn't believe what I was hearing. My heart leapt inside of me—except I didn't have a heart. Maybe it was that golden orb thingy inside me. It did seem to be glowing and pulsating brighter than ever now.

There are a few conditions, however, said Gaia. *Once I am a part of your mind, you'll have access to my power, but only you will be responsible for stopping the Tartarus and the Comet from impacting the earth. If you can't stop it, then I will be forced to open a wormhole in the fabric of space and time so we can escape, and we will continue my research elsewhere. My kind uses wormholes as sparingly as possible. The ripples in the space-time continuum can distort our research. And before you ask if I can use the wormhole to go back in time to stop earlier events on Earth, the answer is no. If you were to encounter your past self, it's possible that the space-time continuum would implode into a black hole and devour your planet. That would be detrimental to our research.*

"So we're traveling back in time to stop the Tartarus?"

No, why would you think that?

"But you just said that the Tartarus only had three and a half minutes before the crash! We've been talking for at least that long."

Ah. I don't think you understand. The transfer of information between our connected minds is almost instantaneous. We have been communicating for no more than twenty earth seconds.

"Oh . . ." I nodded slowly. "Okay . . ."

If you agree to this, I will be inside your mind until you die, said Gaia. *This will be non-negotiable. As this is a lifetime commitment, I understand if you need more time to think it over—*

"I'll do it," I said. As Gaia's words finally sank in, I found myself trembling again. Flex. Sapphire. Whisp.

My dad.

I could save all of them.

Gaia interlocked its gangly fingers. *You are sure of this?*

I nodded, biting my lip. "Yes, but . . . I do have a question."

What is that?

"What happened to all of the powers that you and Fantom absorbed?"

Those powers were released the moment my vessel was fractured and my mind was separated from Fantom's, said Gaia. *Those powers will have undoubtedly returned to the humans they once belonged to. Such powers have a strange sense of familiarity like that. They always drift back to what they consider home.*

That was good to know. I couldn't have handled having all those stolen powers inside of me. But still . . . that wasn't enough.

"Do I have to accept your power?" I asked.

Gaia cocked its perfectly round head. *I'm afraid I don't understand your question.*

"Like . . . I know I need your power to save my friends and all," I said. "But after I save them . . . can you take the power away from me? I don't want it."

The power is a part of me, said Gaia. *I can hide it in a dormant part of your brain where it will be extremely difficult to reach, but it will still be a part of you. If you dig hard enough, there will be nothing I can do to keep you from accessing it.*

"Okay . . ." I said, nodding solemnly. "Do that. As soon as I save my friends, hide your power from me."

As you wish. Are you ready then?

"Yeah. I'm ready."

Gaia extended an elongated arm, pressing a thin finger against an invisible wall. A pool of swirling blackness opened, accompanied by an intense howling wind. An array of neon colors seared into the nothingness as the vortex expanded. In mere seconds, the shadowy neon maelstrom was as tall as Gaia.

"No . . ." said Fantom, scraping the invisible floor with his emaciated fingers. "Don't . . . leave . . . me . . ."

I struggled to pull my gaze from Fantom. "What will happen to him?"

Unfortunately, due to Fantom's dependency on me, I have become the most integral part of his brain. Once my subconscious detaches from his, he will die.

I finally ripped my eyes away. Staring into the swirling abyss, I nodded. "Let's go."

Gaia took my hand, its seemingly jointless fingers wrapping around mine. Together we stepped into the darkness.

CHAPTER 39

Marrow . . .

I was flying—soaring through a vast nothingness. Slicing through the shadows . . .

"Marrow . . ."

The wind was attacking me from all sides—a fierce, biting wind. Cold . . . merciless . . .

"Marrow!"

The darkness vanished as I opened my eyelids. Flex was hunched over me, his dreadlocks whipping aimlessly around his face. His eyes were huge, swallowed in panic.

"Flex?"

We were back in the broken Cronus Chamber which was hardly a safe place with the gaping hole I had kicked in the glass. The shattered section was a raging vacuum, violently trying to suck us out into the open atmosphere. I realized that the only thing holding me down was Flex, clutching my collar while he continued to grip the rim of the Cronus cannon.

But something was different. Even though the Tartarus was hurtling downward, I felt remarkably aware of every detail around me. Every jagged edge of the shattered hole. Every loose object floating in our descent. Everything was sharper. Crisper. Clearer. I felt a throb of life from every human and creature aboard the Tartarus.

I had never felt so alive in my entire life.

"You're alive!" said Flex. "How the heck are you alive?"

"Long story," I said. "There's no time to explain."

Flex lifted an eyebrow. "Huh? Explain what?"

I opened my mouth but hesitated.

Flex hadn't said that at all. His mouth hadn't moved. He *thought* it. I was reading his mind.

But seriously, though. There was no time to explain. My gaze darted past Flex to the bleeding evening sky rushing past us. Who knew how close we were to hitting the ground?

I pulled myself free of Flex's grip, staggering upright. The wind immediately threatened to rip me off my feet, but I could already feel the new power emanating from my being. With just a simple thought, I pinned my feet to the ground.

"Are you insane?" asked Flex. "What are you doing?"

At a time like this, I figured that the best explanations were the unspoken ones. Concentrating on the invisible force holding my feet down, I redirected it to my soles. Taking a deep breath, I steadily lifted myself off the ground.

Flex's jaw dropped.

"I'm gonna save our butts," I said.

With that, I let myself get sucked out of the Cronus Chamber, telekinetically pushing myself from the broken glass edges.

If I thought the wind was intense before, nothing could have prepared me for this. The air was sucked right out of my lungs. The wind ripped and clawed at my skin. I toppled and flailed through the air like a broken kite.

Don't focus on your surroundings, a familiar chorus of voices entered my head. *Focus on within.*

"Gaia?" I said. "Is that you?"

Of course it's me, said Gaia. *How many other extraterrestrial life forms do you have living inside your head?*

"I thought you weren't going to help me."

Yes, well, I would be disappointed to see you die again before I even began my research.

"Yeah, I wouldn't like that either."

I closed my eyes and struggled to tune out the thrashing wind. Inhaling through my nose, I scraped within myself for power.

Somehow, I sensed a golden flicker inside of me. A spark. Then it exploded.

The wind halted.

No. Not the wind. I opened my eyes.

I had halted. I was floating perfectly still in midair. My gaze lowered to the Tartarus and the Gaia Comet, spiraling as it plummeted. From a distance, it looked like a funky rock baked inside a donut made out of glass bubbles. Which doesn't really make any sense, but whatever, that's what it looked like.

The jagged silver edges of Cosmo City were not far below.

All it took was a thought. Suddenly, I was zipping downward, body straight and arms tucked to my side. All of the intricate details of the Tartarus infrastructure became clear. I pushed my arms forward as I plunged, but not for the sake of looking like Superman. My fingers extended and I reached to the Tartarus, struggling to make some telekinetic connection.

I felt it.

The sudden jarring force seemed to rip at my veins. My fingers contorted, and my back arched, as I fought to pull back. I screamed through gritted teeth. My momentum slowed but only slightly. The Tartarus groaned as I pulled but showed no sign of stopping, pulling me down with it instead.

Dangit. How did Fantom make this look so easy?

I needed a different angle. Maybe that would help. Rocketing back down, I closed in on the Tartarus again. But instead of maintaining the same speed, I whizzed faster. There was no time to go around. I weaved through the tight infrastructure of the Tartarus, dodging a labyrinth of sphere chambers and glass passageways.

The city was only a couple hundred feet below us. I could see the cars moving below. Several of them had stopped in the middle of the street—no doubt, to watch the comet with a built-on research facility falling from the sky. Fortunately, we had missed the spires of the tallest skyscrapers. But at the angle we were falling, we could easily wipe out a chunk of the city and smash down several skyscrapers from the base. There was no way I could stop this thing in midair. Not this close to the ground. But if I could redirect it . . .

My gaze averted to the not-so-distant coastline. I could barely make out the sandy line of beaches.

I pushed. The metal infrastructure wailed under the sudden pressure, slowing ever so slightly. The force drove me downward. I clenched my teeth, bracing myself against an invisible force beneath my feet and pushed harder. Even though I was pushing with my mind, the exertion somehow felt every bit as physical as pushing with my body. Fingernails clawed through my veins. The Tartarus lurched. The metal surface crumpled beneath it. The glass below cracked and shattered. I angled my trajectory slightly, redirecting my focus to the coast. Metal screeched as the Tartarus tilted. Its descent swayed and curved.

My feet hit the ground.

Surprisingly, my body didn't buckle on impact. Instead, the street was demolished beneath me. Rock and asphalt spewed upward as I slid down the street at a harsh angle, digging myself into a deeper hole. My feet burned. The Tartarus was screaming at this point, its gigantic form casting a foreboding shadow.

The shadow swept past me as the Tartarus angled down on the coast. It disappeared behind the building-laden horizon. A volcano of sand and water erupted into the air. The splash sounded like a tidal wave and the earth shook, rattling me especially since I was buried halfway in it.

And then silence. Pure, beautiful, terrifying silence.

The asphalt crater was scalding as I tried to climb out of it. I could feel the heat wafting up and distorting the air around me. Fortunately, my jumpsuit handled the burning surfaces extraordinarily well. I staggered out of the hole. A perimeter of cars surrounded me. People slowly exited their vehicles, hundreds of eyes pinned on me. And then the voices swarmed, echoing through my skull.

—look at that—Oh my gosh!—in the name of—who is that kid?—the Tartarus—Holy crap!—was that thing?—sweet mother of—is anyone hurt?— hit the beach—what happened—the size of that hole—!

I thought my brain was going to burst out of my ears. I bent over, my head in my hands, pressing my fingers against my temples.

"Stop it!" I screamed

The voices were cut short, as if a door had been slammed shut in my head.

I didn't pay attention to the startled looks I was receiving now. I had only one focus. Running to the end of the street, I was greeted by a long mound of dirt and wild brush. A sign with chipped, peeling paint was perched at the very top.

Welcome to Cosmo Beach

I was too impatient to use the flight of wooden stairs ascending the mound a short distance away. Instead I scurried up the mound in front of me, scraping past the dry dirt that crumbled beneath my feet. As I stumbled to the top, the setting sun melted across the Tartarus, jutting out of a sprawling sand crater at a slant. The spheres glowed orange, casting white distortions of light in the sand. Several hatches were open and people were reeling and wobbling out. One police officer crawled onto his hands and knees and kissed the sand as he made contact with solid ground.

You did it, said Gaia. *I am not sensing a single casualty from the impact.*

I couldn't even form words, giving a sigh of exasperated relief instead.

Would you like me to hide my power from your mind now? I should warn you that it will be a physical shock to your body having so much power withdrawn like that.

"Do it," I said.

As you wish. You may want to brace yourself—

Everything went black.

CHAPTER 40

It all started when I woke up in Cosmo City General Hospital, surrounded by friends—Flex, Whisp, and Sapphire who kissed me right on the lips before I could even mentally process that kissing was a thing we did now. That, in and of itself, might have been enough to send my poor, fragile heart into cardiac arrest. Sapphire finally parted her lips from mine, and I was sure I was redder than the average Corvette.

"Wow," I said. "I need to wake up in the hospital more often."

"Please don't," said Sapphire.

"I second the 'please don't' request," said Whisp.

"Yeah, hotshot," said Flex smiling. "Make this a regular occurrence and I'll give you a *real* reason to wake up in the hospital, you narcissistic little glory-turd."

"Lick my pits, you feet-smelling butt-monkey," I said.

Flex playfully punched my shoulder and shook his head. "Man, I missed your ugly face."

Sapphire just rolled her eyes. "Boys."

And that's when I noticed a fourth head in my cramped hospital room, and I wondered how I hadn't noticed him there before. I mean, aside from the fact that he's a skinny little weasel who would disappear if he turned sideways.

He still had a swollen black eye from our last fight.

"Marrow," he said.

"Nero," I said. "You're alive."

"Yeah, well, you punch like a girl." And then Nero winced. "I mean . . . what I meant to say was . . . what you did—Fantom and the Tartarus and everything—was pretty cool."

"Thanks."

Nero scratched his head and glanced at the floor and shuffled his feet awkwardly. He appeared to have reached his one-vague-compliment quota for the day.

"You were communicating to us through Morse code while you were in a coma," I said. "That's pretty cool too."

Nero smiled—like a *real* smile, not his stupid trademarked smirk. "Thanks."

I glanced past Nero, scouring the corners of my cramped hospital room. Nero had popped out of nowhere, and I kind of hoped that someone else would pop out of nowhere as well, even though he was roughly the size of seven Neros.

But my dad wasn't there. I don't know why I hoped he would be.

* * *

When your life is perpetually weird, things feel infinitely weirder when your life achieves a state of normality. For an aspiring teenage Superhero with an alien living inside his brain, my life felt astronomically normal and non-life-threatening, and it was freaking me out.

Like the fact that I was not only living like a slob at Flex's apartment, but I was playing video games with him, and it was awesome.

"Falcon Punch!" Flex exclaimed as Captain Falcon punched me in my cute, pink jiggly-puffy face.

"C'mon, Jiggly Puff!" I said. "Get your Pokémon butt off the floor and—yes! YES! Eat my magic star wand, you fiend!"

I whacked Captain Falcon in the face, and he plunged over the edge of Yoshi's Island.

"*Noooooooooo!*" said Flex—a long, awkward wail like Darth Vader's infamous "*Noooooooooooo!*" but several octaves higher. "Dang it. How do you always beat me?"

"Beginner's luck?" I said.

"Whatever. Rematch. You're going down this time. And to make it especially embarrassing, I'm playing as Princess Peach. Victory *and* the distribution of public humiliation will be mine."

"Bring it. I'm playing as Kirby."

"What is it with you and all these cute, fat, little pink blob people?"

"C'mon, you know Kirby's the best."

"I know that you have an obsession with cute, fat, little pink blob people. That's all."

The next arena opened and we proceeded to beat the snot out of each other to absurdly peppy battle music.

"Heard from your dad?" asked Flex, trying to sound casual, but failing miserably.

"No." I tried to play it cool, like I didn't care, but it had been two weeks since I got out of the hospital and my dad was just as much an absentee parent as he had been for the last fourteen years.

"Oracle invited us over for dinner," said Flex, quickly changing the subject.

"Sweet," I said.

"You say that now. But little do you know, she's can't cook. Heck, she's a worse cook than me. And I'm a terrible cook."

"You *are* a terrible cook," I said. "Like that time you tried to make mac n' cheese by cooking Kraft singles on top of noodles?"

Flex laughed, even as Kirby roundhouse kicked Princess Peach in the face. "Okay, maybe Oracle isn't *that* bad."

* * *

Everyone was dressed in black. It was a harsh contrast to the rich green surrounding us. Soaked from a fresh night's rain, the willow trees all appeared to bow over Nightmare's grave. His mahogany casket glowed under the warmth of the rising sun.

Sapphire gripped my hand tighter. It surprised me how emotional she was over the death of someone she never knew. Then again, I didn't really know him either. Yeah, we'd spent a few days of torture interrogation together. Yeah, he was the only friend my dad had had in years. Yeah, he had died saving my life. But I didn't know the guy. Then again, you didn't need to really know somebody like Nightmare to know what he stood for.

Havoc—with an arm in a sling—stood at the foot of Nightmare's grave, separate from the people on either side. Crowds of people who never knew Nightmare. But they knew exactly what he had done for us. What he had done for all of Cosmo City.

"What is a hero?" said Havoc. "I think a lot of us forget the answer to that question, what with a society that makes fancy celebrities of Superheroes, lifting them up on pedestals—Superheroes who get million-dollar endorsement deals and their faces plastered all over commercials. We start to think, 'Oh, well the face that's on TV the most must be the greatest hero.' He becomes the hero that we worship. But then a man like Nightmare comes along. We don't know who he is. We don't know what he's done. But he's saved hundreds of lives. Maybe thousands of lives if you consider the impact of what he's done. And he does it without recognition. He selflessly seals that heroic act with his own blood.

"Honestly, I shouldn't even be the one telling y'all this. Spine knew Nightmare way better than I ever did, but he wasn't exactly keen on the idea of public speaking. Everyone keeps asking me if I was friends with Nightmare. I mean, why else would I join him in his fight against Fantom? To tell you the truth, I had never met the guy. He knew who I was, though. He knew my power. He actually came to me asking for help. And he did it by telling me the truth about what was really happening. And you know what? A part of me nearly called the cops on him. But I didn't. There was something about him—an earnestness in his eyes—that I couldn't ignore. That, and I wanted to believe. I *wanted* to believe that decades of Superheroes weren't falling into corruption. I *wanted* to believe that a FIST sidekick intern wouldn't turn on his own classmate. I *wanted* to believe that a woman who we look to for leadership and guidance wouldn't turn her back on peace and rationality."

Oracle, in a black dress and shawl, smiled from across the grave. A tear slipped from her milky white eye.

"And so I fought with him," said Havoc. "And now here I am, speaking at the funeral of a man whose heroism I am unworthy to express. Nightmare isn't just a hero. He is a symbol. He is proof that there will always be good out there to outweigh the evil. As much as evil tries to make itself known to the world, the good is always there, silently fighting back."

Havoc cast a knowing glance my way and smirked.

"And if some of that good just happens to be loud and makes a scene in the process, the world will be all the better because of it."

As the funeral ceremony ended, I found myself detached, wandering away from the crowds. Even though Fantom was defeated, it didn't change the fact that Nightmare was still dead. It was like a lasting reminder that our victory wasn't whole. Maybe every victory was tainted like that.

"Whatcha doing out here?"

I turned to find Flex behind me. Like the rest of us, he was decked out in a black suit and tie, and he had even shaved off his scruff. It would have seemed horribly out of place, but his tie was extremely loose, and his top button was undone, adding a healthy dose of casualness.

"Avoiding human contact," I said with a weak smile. "You?"

Flex reached into his suit jacket pocket and removed a letter. "This is for you."

Grabbing the letter, I turned it over in my hands. It had the official FIST seal stamped on it. "What is this?"

"This is the official document stating that you are no longer my sidekick," said Flex.

"What?" I said, snapping my gaze up from the letter. "Why?"

"Well that's what you wanted, isn't it?"

"Before I knew that Fantom was a homicidal maniac. Is this for real, Flex? This isn't funny."

Flex chuckled, unable to hide his grin anymore. "Unfortunately, it is for real. But not because of that. I had a better reason for filing for a sidekick change."

Flex raised his arm and pointed past me.

"I know he'd never ask for it, but I think that guy needs a good sidekick like you more than I do."

I turned, following his index finger to Nightmare's grave . . . and the figure now kneeling over his casket.

My father.

Seeing him in a suit and tie was even more shocking with his beard neatly trimmed and his wild black mane of hair forced into a part. His big hands were clasped together, his eyes lowered in solemn reverie.

"So wait," I said. "If you filed for a replacement, who's your new—?"

Nero stepped from behind the nearest tree, grinning.

"Sorry for stealing your trainer, Bonehead," said Nero. "No hard feelings?"

As my initial shock faded, I smiled. "No hard feelings."

"Okay, okay, girls," said Flex. "This is touching and all, but Marrow needs to go talk to his new trainer now."

"Wait," I said. "What am I supposed to say?"

"I always prefer 'hello,'" said Nero.

"Ooh, hello," said Flex, nodding enthusiastically. "Hello's good."

Together, Flex and Nero shoved me forward. I staggered out into the open, stumbling to an awkward halt. As I glanced back, Nero shooed me forward while Flex mouthed the word "hello," winked, and gave me two thumbs up. I swallowed hard against the knot in my esophagus and shuffled towards the grave.

What do I say what do I say what do I say? Sure, hello was a good start, but I was going to need a whole lot more than one lousy word to take back all the horrible things I'd said to him at Oracle's house and on the Tartarus. I still remembered the hurt look on his face. That horrible, heartbreaking image was permanently etched in my memory. It made me sick just thinking about it. What if he hated me now?

I stopped several feet behind him. I was afraid to come any closer. I didn't have try to get his attention. My soft footsteps on the grass were enough. He glanced up, meeting my eyes for only a brief moment before averting his gaze.

The hurt was still there. I could see it carved in the hard edges of his face.

I lowered my head, focusing on my feet instead. I was too ashamed to look at his face.

"I know you probably don't want to see me," I said. My voice cracked and I struggled to clear my throat. "I am so sorry. I'm sorry about all the horrible things I said to you."

A teardrop fell from my stinging eyes, landing on my shoe.

"And I'm sorry about Nightmare," I said. "He died trying to save me. It's my fault that he's dead. I'm so sorry about everything—"

Two huge arms wrapped around me, pulling me close. I glanced up. My father's shoulders heaved as he wept into my hair.

"You . . . you're not mad at me?" I said, my voice trembling.

My father shook his head, tears streaming down the ridges of his face. "I'm not mad," he said. "This is all I've ever wanted."

"Dad . . . "

I didn't have to tap into my bone structure to hug him harder than I could ever hug any human being.

* * *

"You've got to be kidding me," said Whisp. "You've never played catch before?"

"I don't get the point of it," said Nero. "All you're doing is throwing a ball."

"That *is* the point! Here, I'm going to throw it to you. Are you ready?"

Whisp didn't even wait for a response. He chucked the ball in a smooth arch across the beach. Nero didn't move. He didn't even blink as it came to a gravity-defying halt only inches away from his face.

"There," said Nero. "You happy? I caught it."

"No," Whisp groaned, rolling his head back. "You're supposed to catch it with your mitt."

"Why would I catch it with a mitt when I can catch it with my mind? That's completely ineffective. I'd have to physically exert myself."

"Physically exert yourself? Are you kidding me? Oh my gosh, Nero, I'm the one with asthma here! Just throw me the ball already."

Nero blinked and the ball shot across the beach in a straight line.

"Ow! I meant throw it with your hand, Nero!"

Sapphire giggled as she nudged my shoulder. "Looks like they're getting along."

I snickered but didn't say anything. This moment was too perfect. Sitting atop the mound surrounding Cosmo Beach, the sunset was a blur of red and orange streaks glazed together on a painted horizon. The Gaia Comet and the glass spheres of the Tartarus wreckage glimmered below. The rising tide slapped against the slanted structure and then withdrew with a sigh. The scene looked just like the evening it had crashed here. Maybe that's why I was so insistent on coming back. It was that first moment, standing on top of this mound, that I knew everything was going to be alright.

"What are you thinking?" said Sapphire.

Yes, what are you thinking? said Gaia. *Your thought processes are very quiet lately. It's most unusual.*

"I'm thinking that I've got a talkative alien living inside my head," I said.

I'm merely inquisitive, said Gaia. *Remember, my kind is doing this research in behalf of the entire universe.*

"Gaia?" said Sapphire. "What's it saying?"

"Meh, just talking about the universe and stuff," I said.

Sapphire smiled and leaned into my shoulder. "You must feel pretty powerful having something like Gaia living inside your head. Has it told you any secrets about the universe lately?"

I turned my head, my lips hovering only an inch from hers. Then I kissed her.

"All I need to know about the universe is right here," I said.

What is power, really?

In a world of heroes and villains and clashing superpowers—a world where so much seems to end in blood and hate and tears—I can't claim to know all the answers. But I can tell you what I believe. I don't think true power has anything to do with these Super abilities we have as a result of Gaia. Even Gaia itself with all its energy and the secrets of the universe at its fingertips . . .

I don't believe that is power at all.

I believe true power is what drives someone who's been hurt to forgive his friend, helping him when he needs it the most. It's what drives a man to sacrifice his life for some kid he barely met. It's what drives a father to fight for the son he never knew.

This is the power that makes us heroes.

About The Author

Preston Norton has been reading superhero comics since he was old enough to look at pictures. And then he learned to actually read words, and they became a gazillion times better. Among Preston's impossible achievements, he once ate thirteen slices of French toast in one sitting, he read the entirety of *To Kill a Mockingbird* when he was twelve years old, assuming from the title that it would turn into a suspense/thriller murder mystery, and he somehow managed to receive an impressive scar from a pillow fight with his five-year-old little sister. He has a degree in English Education and has taught seventh and ninth grade English.

Want Preston to come to your school? Contact:
schools@futurehousepublishing.com

Connect with the Author!

Come LIKE Preston's Facebook page
to find out more about his books:

www.facebook.com/prestonnortonauthor

www.twitter.com/PrestonSNorton

Discover more remarkable books from Future House Publishing here:

www.futurehousepublishing.com

www.facebook.com/FutureHousePublishing